MW00856116

TALES OF THE BATMAN

EDITED BY
**MARTIN H.
GREENBERG**

MJF BOOKS

NEW YORK

Published by MJF Books
Fine Communications
Two Lincoln Square
60 West 66th Street
New York, NY 10023

Tales of The Batman

Library of Congress Catalog Card Number 95-76046
ISBN 1-56731-076-1

Cover Painting: Steve Stanley

Manufactured in the United States of America

MJF Books and the MJF colophon are trademarks of Fine Creative
Media, Inc.

10   9   8   7   6   5   4   3   2   1

Contents

TALES OF THE
BATMAN®

Neutral Ground

MIKE RESNICK

Kittlemeier's shop was in a poverty-stricken area of town. To say that it was unimpressive would be an understatement. Its windows were patched with plywood, and its door handle was so rusty it almost posed a physical threat.

The shop was not listed in any telephone book. Its door bore no street number. No sign proclaimed what it sold. Those who peered into it from the doorway saw only a dimly lit room with an ancient counter, an old-fashioned cash register, an out-of-date calendar from the local service station, and a curtained doorway leading to another room that opened onto the alley.

One would think, to look at it, that Kittlemeier's shop could not possibly attract any customers, and in truth it did not attract many. But those who needed Kittlemeier's particular services always seemed to know where to find him.

It was five o'clock in the afternoon when an elegant black limousine pulled up in front of Kittlemeier's shop and a tall, well-dressed man emerged from the backseat.

Neutral Ground

Lithe as a jungle panther—his custom-made suit barely concealing his heavily muscled frame—he walked the five steps to Kittlemeier's door, paused for just a moment, and then entered the shop.

A bell tinkled gently and old Kittlemeier, a measuring tape slung over his shoulder, a pencil tucked behind his ear, pushed past the curtain and greeted his customer.

"You are late," he said.

The tall man shrugged. "It was unavoidable," he said, and Kittlemeier noticed that the knuckles of his right hand were badly swollen.

"We must hurry," said Kittlemeier. "I have another appointment in fifteen minutes."

The tall man's interest was aroused, but he refrained from asking any questions. That was Kittlemeier's rule, and he honored it.

Kittlemeier reached below the counter and withdrew a yellow belt that was lined with exterior pouches.

"You see," he said, displaying it to the tall man, "I had to eliminate the container for the explosives in order to make room for the modified gas mask you will be using. You are quite sure of its dimensions?"

The tall man nodded.

"I took the liberty of making another slight change," continued Kittlemeier, showing him a different section of the belt. "The miniaturized winch for your silken cord was wearing against the leather here, and so I reversed the inset angle."

"I approve," said the tall man.

"A tungsten cord would be just as strong and take up less room," suggested Kittlemeier.

The tall man shook his head. "I prefer silk. It causes less damage to the hands."

Kittlemeier shrugged. "You might think about it in the future. You could add an extra twenty yards to its length, and I could always reinforce your gauntlets."

"Perhaps in the future, when the need for a longer cord arises," said the tall man. "You have something else for me?"

Old Kittlemeier nodded and reached beneath the counter again, this time withdrawing two long, dark blue gauntlets.

"Where is the power source?" asked the tall man.

"A lithium battery, sewn into the lining of each."

"And these will insulate against a temperature of a hundred degrees below zero Fahrenheit?"

"At least," said Kittlemeier.

"Good. I will be needing them to—"

"I don't want to know," interrupted Kittlemeier, holding up a hand. "What you do when you leave my premises is not my concern."

The tall man nodded, and for a moment he was aware of a clock ticking in the dusty stillness.

"I'll take these with me," he said at last, indicating the gauntlets.

"Have you considered the boots?"

"Yes. I very much like your suggestion."

"Good," said Kittlemeier. "Of course, I will need molds of your feet before I can equip them with springs enabling you to leap the required distance. Shall we make an appointment for, say, two o'clock on Thursday?"

"Why not now?" asked the tall man.

Kittlemeier shook his head. "I have another appointment. You must leave before my next client arrives. You know the rules."

"As you wish," said the tall man indifferently.

Neutral Ground

Kittlemeier set to work wrapping the belt and the gloves, then placed them into a nondescript shopping bag and handed them across the counter to the tall man.

"That will be..." He thought for a moment, then named a sum that did not seem too exorbitant to him. "In cash, as always."

The tall man grunted, withdraw his wallet, took out a number of large bills, and laid them on the counter.

"Until Thursday, then," said Kittlemeier.

"Until Thursday," said the tall man. He picked up his shopping bag, walked out the door, and entered the backseat of his limousine, which immediately pulled out from the curb and was soon lost from sight in the rush-hour traffic.

Kittlemeier put the money in his cash register, then checked his wristwatch. He badly wanted a cigarette, but his next client was never late, and so he remained behind the counter.

At precisely 5:15 p.m., a wiry man with thinning blond hair entered the shop, looking furtively into the shadows before he approached the counter.

"Well?" he demanded. "Are they ready?"

"Four of them are," answered Kittlemeier. "Two were completely beyond repair. I will have to make entirely new ones."

"Do it. And last time you gave me only eighty question marks. This time I want at least one hundred, and I want you to know I will count every last one."

Kittlemeier pulled out a pad of paper and began scribbling in his almost illegible scrawl. "One hundred question marks each," he muttered as he wrote.

"And the material must be strong, and the dyes waterproof."

"Waterproof dyes," said Kittlemeier. while scribbling furiously.

"Can you do it?"

"Of course," said Kittlemeier.

"I must have them by next Monday, because on Tuesday..." He threw back his head and giggled hysterically.

"Monday," said Kittlemeier, nodding. "Ten o'clock in the morning?"

"Ten o'clock," said the man.

Kittlemeier placed four neatly folded green costumes in a brown paper bag from the local grocery store. He then took a fresh sheet of scratch paper and scribbled a figure on it.

"This is more than we agreed upon."

"My original figure was for repairing six costumes. I did not plan on having to make two from scratch."

"You kept the old devices for the new costumes?" queried the man. "I would be very unhappy to find that I was paying for new weapons when the old ones were in perfect working order."

"I kept them," said Kittlemeier. "You can inspect them when you return next Monday."

The man stared at him distrustfully for a long moment, then pulled out a roll of bills and placed them on the counter.

Kittlemeier counted them carefully, then looked up. "Please bring another six hundred dollars with you on Monday, and then your account will be up to date."

The man nodded almost imperceptibly, then grabbed his bag, turned on his heels, and left.

It had been a long day, and old Kittlemeier was getting hungry. He sighed; it was satisfying to be known as the very best in your trade, but your time was so seldom your own.

He checked his watch again, and decided that he had just enough time to go out for a quick sandwich before Selina arrived for her fitting.

Command Performance

HOWARD GOLDSMITH

I

The Gotham City Department Store loomed before her. *What am I doing here?* she asked herself. Her brow wrinkled with the effort of recall. *Was it something The Man told me?* For a moment her eyes glazed. Then, suddenly remembering, Carol proceeded through the revolving door.

Her heart quickened as the security guard gave her the once over. Then he turned to answer a customer's question, and Carol relaxed. Dressed in a light blue sweater and designer jeans, she strode nimbly down the center aisle. She appeared about sixteen, with short dark hair and economical features.

What were my instructions? Carol halted momentarily, chewing her lower lip. A voice seemed to speak in her ear: *Walk to the back of the store.* Staring straight ahead, Carol glided past the cosmetics counter and maneuvered through a maze of dress racks. Not pausing to inspect the latest fashions, she proceeded with single-minded concentration.

As she approached the rear of the store, her step faltered. She glanced right and left, indecisive. The voice guided her again: *Turn right.* Carol turned mechanically. *The jewelry department is straight ahead.* Carol marched toward the counter.

Three customers clustered around the display cases. A middle-aged sales clerk approached them." May I help you?"

A woman asked to see a Longines watch. As the clerk brought it out, Carol sauntered over, her eyes seeking the diamond rings.

"I'll be with you in a minute," the clerk said, glancing at Carol.

"That's all right," Carol answered. "There's no hurry."

The customer standing next to Carol frowned at the watch's price tag. "I'll have to think it over," she said, drifting away.

Replacing the watch, the clerk turned her attention to Carol. Her eyes ran appraisingly over Carol, noting her age and dress. "Are you looking for anything in particular?" she asked.

Carol nodded. *Ask for the first ring on the bottom row,* the same inner voice instructed. Carol pointed to the ring. "I'd like to see that one, please."

The sales clerk made no attempt to conceal her surprise. How could a girl of Carol's age afford such an expensive diamond ring? She didn't appear wealthy. But looks are deceiving; some very wealthy families allowed their teenage children charge privileges. However, on a purchase of any magnitude, a parent's presence was required.

"I see you have a discerning eye," the clerk offered cheerfully, withdrawing the ring from the case. "This is a round one-carat diamond solitaire with a four-prong fourteen-carat yellow gold mounting. The list price is four thousand dollars. With a twenty percent discount, our price is three thousand two hundred."

Carol hesitated.

"Is it a gift for someone?"

"No, it's for me,"

The clerk's eyebrows rose. "Perhaps you'd like to see something else. The rings in this case are more moderately priced. They begin at two hundred dollars."

"All right. Could you show me that one?" Carol pointed to the tray in the middle of the case. "I'd like to compare the two rings side by side"

"Certainly. Of course this other one is a cocktail ring." As she bent over, Carol swiftly snatched the ring on the counter and replaced it with an imitation fished from her pocket. The facsimile was identical in all respects, except for the diamond which was paste—a cheap synthetic. The unsuspecting clerk brought out the cocktail ring and placed it beside the other. "This is a charming ring," she said. "A diamond cluster arranged in a sunburst pattern. Your friends will envy you."

"How much is it?" Carol asked.

"Only four hundred dollars."

"I like it," Carol said. "But I'll need my mother's permission. May I bring her in to look at it?"

"Of course," the clerk said, replacing the two rings.

"I'll see you soon," Carol said, turning on her heels. Her heart fluttered with the secret knowledge of the valuable ring concealed in her pocket. The saleslady hadn't suspected a thing. *Now just keep cool,* Carol told herself, feeling quivery. *You'll be out of this place in no time.*

She retraced her steps, trying to look as nonchalant as possible. But her heart pounded wildly as she saw the security guard eyeing her across the length of the store.

He couldn't have seen me at the jewelry counter. It was much too far and outside his field of vision.

The guard was stationed directly in front of the door with his arms folded sternly. He seemed to be following Carol's movements. *It must be my imagination,* she thought. *He's just staring straight ahead. Why should he single me out?* Had the saleslady detected the switch, after all, and tripped a silent alarm? An icy shudder ran through Carol's body. She searched for another exit. Spotting one at the right side of the store, she turned in that direction, her feet feeling heavy and numb. Her steps were leaden and agonizingly slow.

Approaching the side door, her heart fell. The door was bolted. A sign said, PLEASE USE FRONT ENTRANCE. Carol tugged furiously at the bolt, to no effect. *What am I doing?* she asked herself. *Even if I get the door open, an alarm will probably go off.* She realized that she had only succeeded in calling attention to herself. The guard was advancing rapidly toward her. *Just act natural,* she told herself. *Pretend you're a foreigner and can't read English. No, that won't work; my ID will give me away.*

Panicky, Carol searched for the ladies' room. *That's no good,* she realized. *I can't hide in there all day.* The guard was moving closer and closer. *Get rid of the ring!* But The Man would be furious if she returned without it. And the guard would see her reaching into her pocket. She was about to run, hoping to sidestep the guard and dash out the front door, when a man in plain clothes walked up to her. Seizing her arm in a firm grip, he identified himself as the chief security officer. "Please empty your pockets,"

A stab of terror cut through Carol like the point of a knife. Her body went limp and she began to reel.

"Get a hold of yourself," the officer said, steadying her.

Her pupils were glassy-looking, her face white.

Propping her up against the wall, the officer reached into the left pocket of her jeans. His hand emerged with the ring.

"Do you have a receipt for this, Miss?" he asked.

"N-no," Carol stammered. Her throat was so dry she could barely talk. She couldn't think straight. She felt confused and paralyzed with fear.

"You took this off the jewelry counter."

"No, it's mine! It belongs to me!"

The officer gave a sarcastic laugh. "Enough of that, young lady. I saw you pocket this ring and substitute the imitation."

Carol's shoulders collapsed helplessly. "How could you see me?"

"On closed-circuit TV. We have a hidden monitor mounted above the jewelry counter. I observed you from the moment you approached the counter until you left. Come with me."

He marched her back to the jewelry department, where the sales clerk stood glaring at her, holding the fake ring in her hand.

"Is this the girl?" he asked.

"Yes, that's her," the clerk answered tartly. "She looked suspicious from the moment I first saw her. You should be ashamed of yourself, young lady. A nice girl like you. You can tell she comes from a good family," she added, turning to the officer.

"That's a positive identification. What's your name?"

Carol hesitated.

"Let's see some ID."

Carol produced a card case from her back pocket. The officer thumbed through the cards. "Carol Logan. Is that your real name? We can easily verify it."

"That's my name."

"All right, let's go upstairs to my office."

"Please," Carol pleaded. "Can't you let me go? You have the ring."

"Let you go? This is a serious offense, Carol: a planned theft. Do you realize that constitutes grand larceny? People go to jail for stealing much less. Come this way."

"Such a pretty thing too," the clerk said, shaking her head. "It's a shame."

"Sixteen years old," the officer remarked, leading Carol away. The clerk clucked her tongue.

Carol sobbed as she entered the security office. "I didn't know what I was doing. I couldn't help myself."

"You helped yourself to a four-thousand-dollar ring," the officer cracked. "You knew exactly what you were doing." He motioned her to a chair. Seating himself opposite her, he emptied the contents of her card case on his desk. "Is this your residence, 112 Milford Street, Westbury, Connecticut?"

She nodded miserably.

"What brings you to Gotham City?"

"I attend school here."

"Do you live with your parents?"

"No."

"You're a runaway, aren't you?"

Carol nodded.

"How long ago did you leave home?"

"Two months ago."

"Have you been in touch with your folks?"

"No."

"I'll have to contact them, let them know what their daughter has been up to."

"Oh no! Please, Mister, don't tell them. I'm so ashamed."

You should have thought of that before. What made you take the ring?"

"I needed money."

"Where did you get the imitation?"

"I bought it in a secondhand store."

"Where you happened to find an exact duplicate of a diamond solitaire. Don't con me. You said you couldn't help yourself. What did you mean?"

"I meant I did it for the money."

"Someone put you up to it. A professional thief with a knowledge of fine jewelry. Who was it?"

"No one!" Carol cried. "I planned the whole job myself."

"Someone gave you the imitation. The same person who acts as your fence for stolen property."

"I told you I bought the imitation. I was going to pawn the diamond ring."

"Whom are you protecting? If you don't come clean, the police will get the information out of you. If you cooperate with me, maybe we can work something out. I want to know who the main man is. This isn't the first time someone pulled this scam. We were ripped off a week ago."

The mention of the words "main man" sent a warning shock through Carol. She mustn't give away the The Man's identity. If she did, she would pay with her life.

"I can't tell you anything else," she said flatly.

"You're scared, aren't you? Afraid of what he'll do to you. All right, have it your way. I'm turning you over to the police."

"No, don't!" Carol began to weep.

The officer softened. "Is this your first offense?"

Carol nodded.

Command Performance

"How can I believe you? If you're telling the truth, the judge may go easy on you, considering your age. But this is grand larceny, Carol, not a shoplifting offense. He won't let you off with a slap on the wrist. Unless you turn state's evidence—disclose your confederate—you'll end up in a girls' reformatory. Is your partner worth it?"

Carol remained silent, her lips tight.

"All right, before I call the police, this is the procedure. A female security officer is going to search you. Then we'll take your photograph for our files. We don't want to see your face in this store again. Ever. Understand?"

Carol's lips quivered. "Yes,"

He buzzed the female security officer. "Helen, will you please step in here?"

A tall uniformed woman entered. Her straight black hair was drawn into a tight bun. Surveying Carol with a frosty expression, she asked, "What's up, Ted?"

The officer gave her a quick rundown. "She may be under the influence of drugs."

"Let me see your arms," she snapped, rolling up Carol's sleeves with a rough tug. "There are puncture marks, all right. What are you on?"

Carol shook her head, "Nothing."

"Which do you prefer, coke or heroin?"

"Neither," Carol answered.

"Come on, who are you kidding? Your eyes are glassy. You show all the signs."

A wave of dizziness swept over Carol. She wished she could shut out their prying questions.

"All right, take her into the other room," said the officer. "Make sure she isn't carrying anything else from the store, and take her picture."

"This way," the woman directed, conducting Carol into another room. The officer picked up the phone and dialed the police.

Satisfied that Carol had concealed nothing, the woman led Carol back to the office. "Stand back against the wall," she ordered.

She snapped several Polaroid pictures, waited for them to develop, and gave them to the officer. He put them in a folder marked with Carol's name.

Carol sat and cried until the police came.

II

Dick Grayson sat gazing out the window of the Gotham High *Clarion* office, where he worked as a reporter. It was a sunny spring afternoon, and Dick was itching to go outdoors, but the bell wouldn't ring for another twenty minutes.

Maybe I can scare up some news at the police station, he thought. He conceived a new column he would call "The Police Beat." He wanted to do a story on teenagers and younger kids who got into trouble with the law. Maybe a series of articles would help promote understanding between adults and young offenders.

At last the bell rang. Dick jumped up, grabbed a note pad and pencil, and locked the office door. He drove to the police station, which was toward the center of town.

As he stepped inside, two policemen led Carol Logan into the station.

Carol! Dick thought, startled. She was in his class at school. He wondered what she'd done. He didn't know her well, but she seemed a nice girl—serious, quiet, hardworking.

Command Performance

Carol choked back a sob as the police booked her. A detective took her into the examination room for questioning.

Dick stepped over to Sergeant Brady, an old acquaintance,

"Hi, Dick. How are you?" Brady asked.

Dick explained that he was doing an article on juvenile crime for the *Clarion* and wondered if he could sit in on the questioning. "I know Carol," he added.

"That's against department policy," Brady said, "But if you want to wait here, I'll see what I can find out for you. I'm glad to assist a budding young journalist in his career."

"Thanks," Dick said, smiling.

"It will take a while."

"That's all right."

After a half-hour, Lieutenant Rose emerged from his cross-examination of Carol. Dick overheard his remarks to Sergeant Brady.

"She wouldn't finger the ringleader," Ross said. "She's terrified of him. We're stymied. I tried every argument on her. She says he'll kill her if she gives him away. Looks like she pulled the job under the influence of some hypnotic drug like sodium pentothal.

"That would explain her dreamy, mechanical behavior in the store—" Brady said.

"As if she were following someone's commands."

Dick stood up and approached them. Brady introduced him.

"This is Dick Grayson. He's OK. A talented reporter for the Gotham High *Clarion*."

Dick smiled. "Maybe Carol would open up for me," he said. "We know each other. I think she'd welcome speaking to a friend."

Howard Goldsmith

Ross said, "Carol is under eighteen and we're not allowed to release any information about the case to the press."

"I understand, Lieutenant. I was more interested in general about teenage crime and how to prevent it. I promise I won't report any specific details fo the case."

"It might be a good idea at that to have Dick talk to the girl," Brady said. "He's a good man. You can trust him." He winked at Dick. "Dick's her own age and talks her language. She feels intimidated by police questioning—but she might confide in him."

Ross rubbed his chin. "O.K. Nothing to lose. She won't open up to me. But don't push her, Dick. The girl's desperate and close to cracking. Let her turn to you for sympathy and understanding."

"I'll go easy," Dick said.

The lieutenant conducted him to Carol's cell. "There's someone to see you," he said.

Carol glanced up at Dick with a dazed look.

"I'll leave you two alone," Ross said, closing the heavily barred door.

"Hello, Carol, how are you?"

"Hello," Carol murmured in a hollow voice. She made a place for him on her narrow cot. Sitting down beside her, Dick touched Carol's hand. Tears started from her eyes.

"I'm sorry to find you in a place like this, Carol. I happened to be at the station. It must be a terrible ordeal."

"I thought leaving home was rough—going out on my own. But this is the worst experience of my life."

"Do you want to talk about it?"

Carol hesitated, biting her lip.

"It will make you feel better if you get it all out," Dick coaxed. "It hurts to keep all that emotion bottled up inside."

Command Performance

Carol began to speak in a barely audible voice. "It all started at home. Dad was very strict, especially about dating. I got yelled at all the time. I was flunking courses in school and was miserable at home. So I made up my mind to leave home. I went down to the railroad depot. I had enough money to take me as far as Gotham City and still have a few dollars left. I wasn't thinking straight. I didn't know anyone in Gotham.

"When I got here, it was late in the day. I got on a bus and just rode up and down till the driver made me get off. I was hungry and peeked through a luncheonette window. Then I saw this man sitting on a bench, looking straight at me. He was middle-aged and distinguished-looking, with thick gray hair and expensive clothes. He stood up and started toward me. I got scared. I thought he wanted to pick me up.

"'Excuse me,' he said. He had a very smooth voice, with a trace of a foreign accent. 'I couldn't help noticing your interest in the diner. Are you hungry, down on your luck?'

"I said, 'Please leave me alone,' and started to walk away, but he followed.

"'Don't be afraid,' he said. 'I'm not making advances. You look hungry and lost. I know how it feels. I've been in the same predicament.' His voice was very soothing. It kind of made you want to trust him. 'You're hungry, I know you are. Won't you join me for dinner?' he kept saying over and over. 'No,' I said. 'Leave me alone.' He just answered, 'You *will* join me. I know you will.'"

Dick interrupted. "He sounds almost like a hypnotist, repeating the same phrases over and over. That's how a hypnotist works, you know."

"I guess so. Anyway, I finally accepted his offer, almost against my will. I was so hungry, and like I said, he had this way of making you want to trust him. His eyes were strange. He could stare straight through you, as if he read your thoughts.

"After we ate, he asked me if I had a place to stay. I said I didn't—" Carol broke off abruptly, turning to Dick with a look of alarm. "You're not going to tell any of this to the police, are you?"

"Not if you don't want me to," Dick assured her. Dick wished he could persuade Carol to talk to the police but was afraid of interrupting her story.

"Promise?"

"Please don't make me promise, Carol—for your own good and for the sake of others, too."

"If you don't promise I won't say any more."

"All right, I promise."

"Because he'd kill me if he found out I told anyone about him."

"Who, Carol? Won't you tell me his name?"

Carol shook her head vigorously.

"All right, go ahead, Carol. He asked you if you had a place to stay."

"Yeah—well, I told him I didn't and he said he ran a shelter for homeless kids like me. When he said that, I started to see him in a different light. Before I'd thought he wanted to take advantage of me. But now I thought he was just being kind. I was so relieved to hear the word 'shelter,' and I wanted so much to think that someone cared about me and wanted to help. So I went along with him to the 'shelter.' Some shelter! It was a place for stray kids, all right. I was shocked—some of them were hung over, some were smoking pot. A few were high. I couldn't understand why they were allowed to use drugs. They used them openly right before The Man's eyes. They didn't try to hide anything.

Command Performance

"'You let them use dope?' I asked.

"'Each to his own,' he answered. 'Many of the kids are addicts. They don't tell me how to live, I don't tell them. I'm here to help them in any way they choose. If they are going to use drugs, I prefer they use drugs openly instead of sneaking them in under the pretence that they're clean. It's more honest that way. Don't you agree?'

"When I first walked into the place, it seemed like a crazy way to rehabilitate young people. But I went along with him, even though part of my mind still questioned.

"The Man introduced me to the gang. 'This is a new recruit: Carol Logan,' he announced. I wondered what he meant by 'recruit,' but let it pass. I got to know some of the other kids. When a guy came and asked me if I'd like a snort, I thought he meant a drink. He gave me some white powder he called 'H.' I didn't know what to do with it, so he showed me how to sniff it through my nostrils. It was the first time I ever tried heroin. I got sick to my stomach and had to throw up. The guy told me that's how most people react the first time. He tried to get me to take another snort, but I felt so sick, I said no. I wanted to leave the place, but I was tired and sick, and had no place to go. I asked The Man if I could lie down. He acted very concerned, and showed me to the girls' sleeping quarters. 'You *will* like it here. I'm sure you will,' he kept saying.

"It wasn't a shelter at all. It was a dope ring. They didn't use the word 'ring,' of course. Insiders called it 'The Circle.' The Man lures other kids in the same way he did me. He gets them hooked on drugs—if they aren't already. Then he sends them out to steal jewelry and things. He promises drugs to the kids who do, and threatens to cut off the supply if they don't obey.

"That first night he offered me some medicine to help me sleep better. It wasn't dope, he said, just something to make me relax. His voice was so soothing that even when I saw he was going to inject me with a needle, it didn't bother me that much. I said 'All right,' and he injected me with the stuff."

"Do you know what drug it was?" Dick asked.

Carol shook her head. "It wasn't dope. I'm sure of that. All it did was put me to sleep."

"He never mentioned its name?"

"I can't remember."

"Try."

Carol twisted her lips. "I'm trying, but it doesn't come."

"Was it sodium pentothal?"

Carol's eyes widened. "Sodium something. That might be it."

"Sodium pentothal is the so-called 'truth serum.' I did a report on it once. It's a drug that puts you to sleep and makes you more suggestible. It's used to brainwash people; it lowers your resistance."

"You mean he was hypnotizing me? Planting ideas in my mind? While I was asleep?"

"I think so, Carol, Start with this morning. Tell me everything that happened before you walked into the department store."

"That's just it. I can't. It's all a blank."

"The man gave you the imitation diamond ring. Didn't he?"

"I guess so. He must've. I don't remember."

"How else could you have gotten it?"

"I don't know. Nothing makes any sense. I found myself standing in front of the store. I had no idea why I was there or how I got there. I remember hearing The Man's voice. It was like he was speaking to me, telling me what to do."

Command Performance

"I think you heard his post-hypnotic suggestions. He must have used the drug and put you to sleep, and then gave you instructions. When you walked into the store, you heard his voice exactly as you heard it under hypnosis. Part of your brain acted like a sleepwalker's, obeying his commands."

"In other words, he programmed me to steal the diamond ring and leave the phony."

"Sure."

"You know what that story's going to sound like? 'I didn't steal that ring, Your Honor, I was hypnotized.' I'll never be able to prove that."

"Not unless you tell the police who The Man is and where to find him. Right now we can't even prove he exists, much less that he hypnotized you. You've got to tell the police everything—it's your only way out of this mess."

"I told you, I can't" Carol shouted. "Won't you leave me alone? I thought you understood. I thought you were my friend." She buried her face in her hands, sobbing convulsively.

Dick put an arm around her shoulders. "I am your friend, Carol. I'm sorry I upset you. Maybe you ought to rest a while—try to calm down." He stood up.

"Don't go, please! I'm sorry I yelled at you. I know you mean the best for me. If only I could make you understand."

"I have to go, Carol. They won't let me stay much longer. But I'll come back tomorrow." He stepped outside the cell and walked down the corridor. Behind him the cell door gave a resounding clang.

"Did you find out anything?" Lieutenant Ross asked eagerly.

Dick hesitated. "I promised Carol I wouldn't repeat it to the police."

"Oh no!" Ross exclaimed. "Are you going to clam up on me too? Why did you make that promise?"

"It was the only way I could get her to talk."

Dick made a quick departure from the station.

Ross shouted after him. "Don't come back here until you change your mind! Boy reporter!"

III

"I just got here myself," Batman said as Dick arrived at Wayne Manor. "Police Commissioner Gordon thinks the Joker and Catwoman have teamed up again. I'll have to leave soon. Want to come along?"

"I'm working on a case of my own," Dick said. "As investigative reporter for the *Clarion*."

"Sounds impressive."

"It involves a classmate of mine, Carol Logan."

"Fill me in."

Dick quickly summarized Carol's account of her meeting with The Man, his use of injections to make her docile, and her trancelike state at the department store.

When he was through, Batman asked, "Are you sure she didn't drop a hint as to The Man's identity?"

"Not a one. And not a clue to the location of the hideout."

"Well, we know this much. It's probably in Gotham City because that's where the guy met Carol. Not necessarily, but let's start with that working assumption. Now what do we know about him? He's involved with the dope market and uses hypnotic drugs with skill. He's middle-aged, smooth, persuasive, distinguished-looking, apparently well educated. His speech is polished, with a trace of a foreign accent. Where would you look for a man of that description?"

"It could fit a lot of men. There's a range of possibilities. We're looking for a strong authority figure with a knowledge of psychoactive drugs—and the skill to use them. Maybe a doctor."

"Possibly, but not necessarily," Batman said. "It could be someone like a medical aide or orderly with experience in a psychological setting."

"Or even a lab technician or chemist," Dick suggested.

"Now there's an idea," Batman said. "How about a biochemistry professor?"

"What better front for illicit dealings?" Dick said. "A teaching post would give him the trappings of respectability—and contacts with a pool of young people. Who would suspect someone in his position?"

"Right. But it's a long shot. How many professors know hypnosis? That narrows it down considerably. Maybe we're dealing with a professional hypnotist, or someone who once was."

"You mean a stage performer?"

"Yes. Unless we consider a psychologist who knows hypnosis. But that's farfetched. It's hard to picture a psychologist as the head of a dope ring!"

"I agree. So I'll look for a hypnotist."

"If he ever performed professionally, he should be in our theatrical file. Take a look."

"All right."

They went down to the Batcave. Batman got in the Batmobile. "Good luck," he said. "I hope you find him. But be careful."

"I will."

Batman left, and Dick punched into the computer. He found the names of five hypnotists. However, phone calls to their agents disclosed that three of them were on tour. Another had just returned from an appearance at the Hawaii Hilton. Dick ruled him out.

Down to the last one, he thought, dialing Alexander Kurtz's theatrical agent.

"I'd like to know if you still handle Alexander Kurtz," Dick asked.

"Not at the present time. He's inactive."

"You mean retired?"

"I'm not sure. He's only about fifty. He just went on to other things. To be frank, I haven't heard from him in years. I'm not sure what he's doing these days."

"The man I have in mind has a slight foreign accent."

"Kurtz is from Austria. Came here after World War II."

"It sounds like him." Dick gave Carol's description of The Man.

"That fits Kurtz to a T." The agent offered to contact Kurtz but Dick said he'd rather talk to him first himself. "If he's the one I'm looking for, I'll get back to you."

"All right." The agent looked up Kurtz's phone number and address. "I hope he still lives there."

Dick thanked him and hung up. He dialed Information. The operator informed him that Kurtz's number was unlisted. So he still lived in Gotham City. If he performed, he would surely list his number, Dick reasoned. Someone might want to call him for an engagement.

Before driving to the address Kurtz's agent gave him, Dick left a note for Batman.

The address was at the other end of town. Dick wore his regular clothes, in his role as investigative reporter. He took along a miniature camera to snap Kurtz's picture. If he was The Man, Carol wouldn't be able to hide her reaction to it. He hoped she would break down and identify him.

Command Performance

The house was located in a residential neighborhood. Dick parked near a phone booth and dialed the number the agent had given him. He waited expectantly as the phone rang...and rang. Finally he hung up. Chances are that it was still Kurtz's number, and he wasn't at home.

Dick walked up to the building. The name on the mailbox was faded, but Dick detected a faint K. While neighboring houses were almost indistinguishable, this one had an eccentric, forbidding character, with old-fashioned gables and turrets. Vines ran along the weathered siding like sinuous snakes. An enclosed porch creaked and swayed as winds twisted through its aged supports.

Dick grimaced. *A real eyesore. It's a good thing I'm not here to do a story for House Beautiful.* He pulled out his camera and snapped a picture. Could it be the Circle's hideout? Not likely. In a residential neighborhood, their comings and goings would be too conspicuous.

Dick knocked on the door. As he expected, there was no response. He tried the doorbell, but it was broken.

Walking briskly around the house, as if on official business, he came to the back door. Several hard raps brought no reply. Stiff and rusty, the doorknob refused to turn. Dick pressed it hard and, to his surprise, a hinge broke off and the door fell open. He took a tentative step inside, pushing the door back in place. The interior was dark and musty, with a stale, airless smell. The floorboards groaned and creaked at the least pressure. With the shades drawn there was barely enough light to see by. He made out the outline of a lumpy old sofa, then stubbed his toe against something hard. Bending over to inspect it, he recoiled with a stifled cry. A head stared up at him— the head of a ferocious tiger forming the front end of a tiger's rug.

Howard Goldsmith

This place must have been decorated by Jungle Jim, Dick thought.

He examined one of the walls. It was entirely covered with scimitars, sabers, broadswords, and rapiers. The opposite wall boasted a huge elk's head with wide, flowing antlers. Kurtz was undoubtedly a hunter who liked to flaunt his marksmanship.

Finding no evidence of dope downstairs, Dick mounted the staircase. The banister swayed and lurched under his hand. There were four rooms upstairs. The first he entered was entirely bare.

As he entered the next room, he rocked back on his heels in surprise. A pair of eyes bore through him with a look of such intensity that he felt transfixed and defenseless. For a moment he was unable to move. Then he realized he was staring at the two-dimensional face of a man on a life-size poster. Switching on a lamp, he read the legend underneath.

ALEXANDER KURTZ

MASTER HYPNOTIST

His Magnetic Presence Will Stupefy

and Mesmerize You

The poster showed a man with jet-black hair, thick eyebrows, a straight nose, and ample lips. His jaw was square, and it thrust out defiantly. This was a younger Alexander Kurtz, in his prime. Allowing for age, the picture was consistent with Carol's description.

The walls were studded with photographs of Kurtz's stage performances. In one photo he stood gazing at a young woman in a deep trance. For a moment, Dick saw Carol's face in the picture, and his stomach twisted.

Command Performance

Various mementos of Kurtz's stage career covered the dresser, in addition to artifacts collected from around the world. Kurtz had traveled extensively. While the house was rundown, the room itself was neat, with everything in its proper place.

He looked in the closet. There were two tuxedos, both shiny from too many dry cleanings. Kurtz must have worn them for his performances. Two safari jackets and a tropical pith helmet gave further evidence of his interest in hunting. An automatic rifle stood upright in a corner of the closet. Then Dick came across an unexpected find: a black-and-red cape, like the one worn by Bela Lugosi in *Dracula*. It probably indicated nothing more than Kurtz's flair for the theatrical, Dick thought. Or perhaps his interest in the bizarre and the violent? Rummaging at the bottom of the closet, Dick uncovered a werewolf mask with long canines and wiry tufts of hair. There were some drops of dried blood around the mouth.

Dick suddenly heard a noise on the pavement below. Dashing to the window, he pulled the shade aside. A man was approaching the house. He kept his head down, and Dick couldn't see his face. But he had little doubt that it was Kurtz. He carried a walking stick, tapping it along the street.

Dick bolted down the stairs and ran to the back of the house. As he reached for the knob, the door suddenly heaved inward. Dick had assumed that Kurtz would use the front entrance. Now Kurtz would notice that someone had tampered with the back door. Dick didn't want to confront him as a housebreaker. He raced into the living room, ducking behind the sofa. The light was too dim for Kurtz to have seen Dick's sprint up the corridor, but he probably heard his steps.

Howard Goldsmith

"Who's there?" The words rang out in a deep bari-tone—a voice accustomed to command. "Who is in my house?"

Dick remained crouched behind the sofa.

Kurtz stomped heavily through the hallway, tapping with his stick. "You might as well come out. It's only a matter of time before I catch you." Dick noticed a slight European accent.

Kurtz snatched up a heavy board leaning against the stairwell, balancing it with one hand as if it were a pool cue. For a man of medium build, he possessed unusual strength. Dick watched him take a few steps down into the basement and return with a hammer and nails. What was he up to? He proceeded to the back of the house. Turning the board diagonally, he began pounding nails into it.

He's boarding up the back entrance! Dick realized. *Trapping me inside.*

"I said it was only a matter of time." Kurtz called, with a robust laugh that echoed down the hall.

Pound, pound, pound.

"Come out and let me take a look at you."

A drop of perspiration rolled down Dick's back.

Pound, pound, pound.

"No one will ever break in here again. I'm making certain of that."

The job completed, Kurtz lay down the hammer and walked into the living room. He lit an old-fashioned hurri-cane lamp. Shadows leaped across the walls as he crossed the room and placed it on a table.

"Of course I could phone the police," he said, "but I prefer dealing with problems directly. You, Sir, whoever you are, are a problem. My problem."

Command Performance

He pulled a rapier off the wall and tested its point. Kurtz parried with an invisible opponent. "*En garde!* Hup-hup-hup." The blade whistled through the air with razor-sharp menace.

"Or do you prefer the broadsword?" He pulled it down from the wall and swung it back and forth with both hands. "Choose your weapon, Sir. Speak up!"

Dick swallowed hard, perspiration beading his forehead. He was no expert with blades, and certainly didn't want to stab Kurtz.

"You have violated the privacy of my home. You are a trespasser, an interloper. Yet I offer you a contest, a choice of weapons. I treat you like a gentleman, a worthy adversary. You spurn my invitation. Don't you have a tongue? Can't you speak?"

Dick remained silent, huddled into a tight ball.

"Are you dumb? Or dumbstruck? Ha, ha, ha. I am not an American by birth, but I savor the paronomastic possibilities of the English language. Have you ever reflected upon the ambiguities of the English phonic structure?"

He's toying with me, Dick thought. *The cat and the mouse. Does he know I'm behind the sofa?*

Kurtz took down a halberd, a long-handled weapon with a sharp point. "A marvelous medieval weapon. One of the prize possessions of my collection. The Middle Ages was an era when men settled differences privately in hand-to-hand combat. Simpler and more primitive than our complicated system of jurisprudence. But lethally effective in resolving conflicts." He balanced the halberd on the palm of his hand, then suddenly drew it back, and let it fly. The point drove through the center of the sofa, emerging an inch at the back.

Dick leaped up involuntarily, recoiling at the sight of Kurtz leering at him.

"So there you are," Kurtz said, his eyes dancing with excitement. He picked up a rifle and pointed it at Dick.

"I never miss," he said with deadly coolness. "At this distance I can peg you right between the eyes."

He's loony, Dick thought. *I'm the game and he's the hunter.*

With lightning reflexes, Dick shouldered past Kurtz into the hall and up the stairs, taking the steps two at a time. A shot whistled past his right ear, making it ring. Dick searched for stairs leading to the roof, but found none. He heard Kurtz's footsteps mounting the staircase. Dick fled into Kurtz's bedroom. That would be the last place Kurtz would expect him to hide. Under the bed? No, in the closet. Dick ducked inside, wedging himself into a corner behind the clothes. He felt something cold against his face. The muzzle of Kurtz's rifle. Dick wondered if it was loaded. He couldn't check without giving his position away.

A ridiculous predicament, he thought. *I'm right where Kurtz wants me. In his own room!*

Kurtz's heavy tread sounded in the hallway.

"Come out, young man. It will do you no good to hide. I know this house like the back of my hand. You are in my territory. On my turf. Ha, ha, ha."

Dick heard him open the empty room. His shoes shuffled along the bare wood floor. Then he heard the door click shut.

"One room eliminated, that leaves three," Kurtz called. "Before there was a twenty-five percent probability of guessing correctly. One out of four. Now the odds have increased to one out of three."

Dick heard his shoes clumping past the bedroom. He wondered if he had time to dash down the stairs to the front door. Dick had observed that the door was chained

Command Performance

and bolted. Kurtz could get off a shot before he managed to open all the locks.

"We're down to two rooms, young scholar. The guessing odds are fifty-fifty. Now which room is it? If I were a sportsman I would release you if I guess incorrectly. But I am not a sportsman. I'm a hunter. Now what were your thought processes when you selected your hiding place? You may have considered my bedroom the least likely place for me to look. So you ran straight into the lion's den. An audacious move on your part. I had better check the other room first, though, to make sure."

Dick heard him close the door and turn the key in the lock. He sprinted out of the closet and across the room. He tried to loosen the window lock. It was so old and rusty, he couldn't budge it.

Dick heard Kurtz unlock the door. He dove back into the closet, feeling like a trapped animal.

"So now we are down to one room," Kurtz said, entering the bedroom.I must thank you for affording me this unexpected sport. Now where are you? Under the bed or in the closet? I hope it's not the bed. That would reduce the entire exercise to slapstick. No, I won't even consider the possibility." He crossed to the closet. "Come out, come out wherever you are." He pushed aside the clothing, exposing the center of the closet. "Not there. You must be in one of the corners." He began poking into the closet with the barrel of his rifle.

"All right," Dick called. "I'll come out."

Kurtz slid the clothing to the other side. Dick sat curled up, eyes staring up at him.

"Now you want to come out," Kurtz taunted, poking his rifle at Dick. "Not so fast."

"Don't you think you've had enough fun?" Dick asked. "You have every right to be angry at finding me in your house. But I'm sure you did some dumb things when you were my age, too."

"You've found your tongue, have you?" Kurtz aimed his rifle at Dick's head. "Don't move a hair."

Dick flinched back. "Wait a minute! There's no need for a weapon."

"No need? For all I know, you may be a dangerous criminal. Breaking and entering is a crime, you know. I would be well within my rights to use this weapon against a burglar. I have to protect myself and my home. No jury would convict me."

"Mr. Kurtz, may I stand up and explain to you why I'm here? If you'll let me get my wallet, I'll show you my identification." He reached inside his pocket.

"Keep your hands out front where I can see them!"

Dick withdrew his hand from his pocket. "I'm an investigative reporter, Mr. Kurtz. Reporters often have to work outside official channels to get a story. You understand."

"A reporter! At your age? You can do better than that."

"I write for the Gotham High *Clarion*. My card's in my wallet. I'll show you if you don't believe me."

"All right, slowly reach into your pocket and remove the wallet. But remember, this rifle has a hair trigger. O.K., hand it to me. No, don't stand up!"

Dick gave him the wallet and fell back into his cramped position, knees pulled up to his chin. His muscles ached.

Kurtz flipped through Dick's ID cards."Dick Grayson, eh? So you *are* on the *Clarion* staff.Why are you hounding me?"

"I'm not hounding you, Sir."

"Why do you want to invistigate me?"

Command Performance

"I wanted to do a close-up story about a hypnotist. It's a fascinating occupation. When I didn't find you home, I began poking around the back of the house, and the door fell open. I could see some of the things on the wall, and I was curious. So I went inside."

Kurtz sighed. "I was hoping you'd be honest with me. Instead you insult my intelligence with this transparent fabrication."

"I wanted to see Alexander Kurtz, 'master hypnotist' in person. It's no lie. I've never seen you before. I've never witnessed a performance."

Kurtz eyes grew bright. "I haven't performed publicly in years. You want me to give a demonstration of my powers?"

"Yes, Sir. That's just what I need for my story. May I stand up now?"

"Remain where you are!" Kurtz's finger curled around the trigger.

"Whatever you say."

"You don't want to get up, Dick. You want to sit in the closet. You feel more comfortable where you are, don't you?"

"No, Sir."

"But it's getting more and more comfortable. Your muscles are relaxing. Actually, you're not sitting on a wooden floor, but on a velvet carpet. Feel how thick and soft it is."

He's trying to hypnotize me, Dick realized. *Don't look into his eyes.*

"Look at me Dick."

Dick averted his eyes.

Kurtz jammed the rifle under Dick's nose. "Look at me, Dick!"

From his position, Dick couldn't risk knocking the rifle aside. It would explode at the slightest touch. He obeyed Kurtz's command.

Howard Goldsmith

"That's better. It's restful sitting on a velvet carpet," Kurtz droned. "You feel relaxed. Your tension is draining away. You're getting sleepy."

Dick's eyelids felt heavy. He caught himself and sat up straight, shaking off his growing drowsiness. Struggling to break Kurtz's grip on him, he silently recited a poem. But Kurtz's velvet smooth voice seemed to invade Dick's thoughts.

"You cannot fight me. Do not try to resist. You want to sleep. You feel drowsier and drowsier. Your eyelids are heavy. You cannot keep them open. Let your eyes close, Dick. You'll feel much better."

Kurtz's face swam before him in a mist, his eyes two beacons of light. *No, don't go to sleep* part of his mind whispered insistently. *Don't listen to him. Get up! Stand up!* Dick began to rise on wobbly legs, swaying back and forth.

"Sit down!" Kurtz commanded. "You're still fighting me. Sit down, I say!"

Dick inched forward on his feet. His hand touched something smooth and metallic. The rifle! Suddenly alert, his thoughts raced. "Get back!" he shouted, brandishing the rifle. "I don't want to use this."

Kurtz burst into laughter. "What a sight you make standing there with an empty gun."

"What makes you think it's empty?"

"Young man, it was empty when I placed it there a week ago." He raised his own rifle level with Dick's eyes.

"How do you know I didn't load it? See those cartridge boxes at the back of the closet?"

Kurtz's eyes narrowed. "You're bluffing."

"I had plenty of time to load the rifle while you were inspecting the other rooms."

Command Performance

Kurtz glared balefully at Dick. "Even if it's loaded, the moment you touch the trigger, I'll blast you. You don't have a chance against a marksman."

"Don't underestimate me," Dick said. He had no desire to fire the gun if it could be avoided.

Kurtz laughed derisively.

"There's no need for violence," Dick said. "I'll just walk out of the house and we'll forget the entire incident."

"Let you go unpunished for your brazen invasion of my house?"

"I explained my presence here, Mr. Kurtz. What more can I say?"

"You can say your prayers before you meet your maker."

Dick lunged for Kurtz's rifle, but felt his own slipping from his grasp.

"Ha!" Kurtz laughed triumphantly. "I've got you now."

Grasping the clothing rod, Dick swung his legs out, kicking with both feet. Kurtz stumbled back, but managed to steady himself. As Dick's fingers curled around the rod, it began to turn. To his surprise, the back wall of the closet slid to one side, creating an opening a little more than a foot wide.

A secret panel! Dick leaped headlong through the opening, as Kurtz snatched at him. Dick discovered a catch at the side of the panel. As he pressed it, the panel slid closed with a *whoosh*. Thinking swiftly, he removed his belt and jammed it into the space where the panel slid, preventing Kurtz from opening it.

Kurtz pounded on the panel, frustrated and enraged. "You won't get away!" he cried. "I'll get you!"

IV

As Kurtz pounded insanely on the back of the closet, Dick proceeded down a narrow, dark passageway. He felt his

Howard Goldsmith

way carefully along the walls. Their texture had the coarseness of rough stones. Suddenly his right foot stepped out into space and he began to topple forward. With a gasp, he flung his hands outward, grasping at air. His arms struck an overhead arch that hurled him backward. He stood suspended on the brink of an unseen abyss, struggling to regain his footing. Clinging to the walls for support, he slowly recovered his balance. Then, cautiously, an inch at a time, he drew back into the safety of the passage.

Exhaling a long breath, Dick wiped sweat from his brow. It had been a close call. He felt as if he'd just stepped back from the brink of eternity. But he couldn't just stand there forever. He had the abyss in front of him, an armed Kurtz behind him.

Digging into his pocket for a coin, Dick tossed it into the void. It gave a *clunk*, and then a second *clunk*, as if rolling down a flight of stairs. The coin continued to echo down the abyss before it fell silent.

It must be a stairway. Dick pawed the ground with his shoe, feeling for the edge. He lowered one foot slowly and carefully. It came to rest on a step. He lowered the other foot and descended the stairs, haltingly, one at a time.

It seemed an hour before he reached the bottom. His shirt was soaked with perspiration. It felt good to plant his feet on solid ground again, but he still had no idea where he was. A dark labyrinth stretched before him, wrapped in silence and dust.

He continued forward, groping blindly through the passageway, his footsteps making a dull patter on the stone floor. As Dick turned a corner, he noticed a faint light flicker in the distance. The passage must lead to a secret chamber. Creeping catlike, on the balls of his feet, he drew steadily closer. The passage widened into a dimly

Command Performance

lit cavern. He found himself in a large, shadowy vault lit by an oil lamp. A heavy mixture of smoke and stagnant air filled the chamber.

Suddenly, with a creeping of his flesh, he saw something that made him reel backward with horror. It was a long coffinlike box with a round opening at one end. A women's head protruded through the opening, her hair hanging down in disarray. Dick drew a fist to his mouth. A heavy blade bisected the box in two. The woman's body had been severed in half.

Dick advanced closer—and drew a long sign of relief. He discovered that the woman was only a plaster dummy, lifelike in every detail. Dick realized that the "coffin" was a trick box used by magicians to saw a woman in two. He gazed about the chamber, his eyes lighting on other tools of the magician's trade. Caked with dust, they had laid unused for years. Yet Kurtz must come down occasionally, if only to replace the oil in the lamp.

As Dick crossed the chamber, it narrowed to a dark tunnel. He entered it with a sense of foreboding. He felt hemmed in, the walls closing around him. But he saw a light at the other end, and he inched his way forward. He was halfway through the tunnel when he heard a loud clang behind him. Whirling around, he saw a heavy steel grate slide down over the entrance, blocking his path of retreat. Kurtz was trying to trap him inside the tunnel. Dick raced toward the light at the other end and bounded through the opening. Gazing about, he found himself in another chamber. Behind him a grate slid down, closing the tunnel.

Kurtz let me escape from the tunnel, Dick reasoned. *He wants me inside this chamber. He knows exactly where I am.*

Howard Goldsmith

Dick walked around the chamber. It was completely empty. The walls were rough-hewn. Casting about for an exit, he found two ducts resembling ventilator shafts. They were identical in every respect. If he entered either one, it would mean crawling on hands and knees. The alternative was to remain buried in the chamber. But which duct?

He drew a coin from his pocket and tossed it in the air. *Heads it's left, tails right.* The coin came down heads. *Left it is then,* Dick decided, crawling into the narrow opening. It was a tight squeeze and slow going. Every foot of progress was an achievement. Dick thought of Alice falling through the hole in the ground, wondering where it would end. Of one thing he was certain; he would not end up in Wonderland—though Kurtz was as mad as the Mad Hatter. Kurtz could be toying with him, offering an avenue of escape, only to trap him alive in a narrow duct. Perhaps all his exertions were propelling him toward a dead end— a blank wall. Or he might be in a circular labyrinth without an exit. He would keep going around and around like a rat in a maze.

Dick came to two branches. Again he had to make a choice: left or right. A trickle of sweat rolled down his back. Without room to flip a coin, he decided to go right. After ten yards the tunnel widened and Dick had more room to maneuver. He heard a *swish*, and before he could react, an arm sprang out of the wall. It was long and hairy with an enormous fist. The fingers opened, clawlike, stretching toward him. Dick scurried back to safety. The fist continued opening and closing spasmodically. It couldn't be a human arm, Dick realized. It must belong to an ape. A gorilla. The arm groped back into the tunnel, reaching for Dick as he scampered away. Then, to his surprise, the arm suddenly went limp and fell to the ground, its fingers rigidly locked. Cautiously Dick inched toward it. It appeared stiff and lifeless, like the limb of a dead tree. Dick bent over it. He noticed coils where there should have been muscles and tendons. It was a mechanical arm whose coils had broken loose from its shoulder mounting.

"Nice stunt, Mr. Kurtz," Dick said out loud, wondering if Kurtz could hear him. "If you wanted to startle me, you succeeded. What next? King Kong?"

Dick took stock of his situation. Obviously, Kurtz had constructed a Chamber of Horrors, the kind seen at amusement parks. In fact, the whole building was a house of horror, consistent with Kurtz's bizarre personality. The hunter in Kurtz had constructed a giant trap, a maze to enmesh interlopers. He could toy with them like a spider playing with a fly.

Then again, perhaps he also had plans to revive his career as the morbid host of a creepy fun house—a kind of Vincent Price-type character. This would flatter his show biz ego. At the same time, it would bring a financial return from his investment in a Chamber of Horrors. Maybe Kurtz was giving the entire operation a trial run, with Dick as the subject.

Kurtz might be operating a panel of controls in the house above. The other possibility was that Dick had unwittingly triggered switches as he worked his way through the tunnels. If this was the case, Kurtz had no precise idea of Dick's location. The switches went off automatically in response to pressure. It was doubtful that Kurtz had installed photoelectric cells, his setup being too crude for sophisticated electronic equipment.

Dick continued inching forward through the duct. A strong breeze wafted toward him. It picked up in velocity, growing colder and colder as he advanced. The wind nipped at him with icy teeth, driving him back. But he saw a light at the end of the duct and pressed forward. He stepped out into a long, narrow room buffeted by polar gusts. *It must be a deep freeze,* Dick thought, his teeth chattering.

He started back toward the duct. He was within arm's length of it when a gate came down, barring his return. He rubbed his hands and hopped up and down, trying to maintain his circulation. He could see his breath in long frozen plumes. Dick began to jog, searching for an exit. Was there any way out of this room?

Without warning, he bumped into something unspeakably grotesque: a towering snow monster with icy tentacles and a cavernous mouth. Roaring and frothing, it shook up and down, tentacles whirling.

As Dick danced out of its way, it pivoted and lumbered after him with gargantuan, plodding steps. Dick ran in frantic circles, unable to find an exit. He spied a rectangular shape outlined against the farthest wall. It was no higher than his knees. As he moved toward it, the monster reared up before him, tentacles flailing. Dick ducked, sidestepped, and dove for the wall. The rectangle turned out to be a hinged door that swung open from the bottom. Scrambling through the opening, Dick plunged down a narrow chute.

He couldn't stifle a cry of "Help!" as he slid headfirst at dizzying speed. Unable to grab the smooth surface gliding past him, his efforts to check his rate of descent were futile.

He came to a sudden stop, his head colliding with something soft but solid like a pillow. He found himself in semidarkness, entangled with a cold sheetlike material. He thrashed about, unable to free himself. After tugging and wrestling for minutes, he managed to stand erect and

Command Performance

pull the clinging material off him. Then he realized he was standing in a laundry bin! He had been fighting with a bed sheet after sliding down an ordinary laundry chute!

A rustling movement made him start. He ducked down, peering over the edge of the bin. Something was moving along the wall. It was too dim to distinguish clearly—but its hazy silhouette appeared human. Was it Kurtz waiting to pounce? Or some other monstrosity of his?

The figure moved again, close to the floor, flitting like a shadow.

I might as well break the ice, Dick decided. "Who is it?" he called.

The figure halted momentarily, then disappeared behind a packing crate.

I'm a stationary target inside this laundry bin, Dick thought, *A sitting duck.* He hoisted himself over the edge and vaulted down to the floor.

"Dick?" a voice called out.

"Bruce! Is that you?"

Batman stood up behind the crate.

"Bruce!" Dick exhaled a long breath. "How did you get in here?"

Batman stepped forward. "I read your note and decided to see how your investigative reporting was coming along. Are you all right?"

"Sure. But how did you get in here?" Dick repeated. "And where are we anyway?"

"Don't you know? We're in the basement. I just arrived. Did you find out anything about Kurtz?"

"The guy's batty. He tried to hypnotize me. I escaped through a secret panel—straight into a Chamber of Horrors."

"Sounds like fun."

Howard Goldsmith

"Chilling fun."

"Is he The Man Carol spoke of?"

"I don't think so. His mind is too scattered to run an operation like that. How do we get out of here?"

"The same way I came in. Through the crawlspace. Didn't you make a surveillance of the place? It leads into the basement."

"I overlooked it," Dick said, embarrassed.

The crawlspace was a tight squeeze, but they managed to crawl through, emerging directly below Kurtz's bedroom.

"It's good to breathe fresh air again," Dick said, standing erect.

He looked up at the window. Kurtz stood gazing down at them. He pulled open the window. "Why did you come here?" he cried, shaking a fist. "What do you want from me?"

"Take his picture," Batman suggested. "You're probably right about him. But it won't hurt to get Carol's reactions."

Dick snapped a picture. As the flash went off, Kurtz sprang back as if shot. "How dare you!" he bellowed. "I didn't give you permission to take my picture."

"That's a right included under freedom of the press, Mr. Kurtz," Dick answered.

"You had no right to invade my house," Kurtz shot back, "on the pretext of writing a story about me. I'll press charges against you, Dick Grayson."

"I don't think you'll call the police, Mr. Kurtz. Unless you're willing to face a charge of reckless endangerment. And the police might be interested in seeing your Chamber of Horrors."

Kurtz coughed and sputtered. "I never invited you to come here. Can't you see, I'm a has-been, a washed-up showman. Just leave me in peace."

Command Performance

Dick felt sorry for the shell of a man that once was Alexander Kurtz.

"Why are you standing there?" Kurtz shouted. "Get out and stay out!"

"He seems far around the bend," Batman said. "But all showmen are good actors. Take another picture for insurance."

"He's not The Man, Bruce."

"You're not absolutely certain. He may have hypnotized you more than you think."

"He didn't!"

"Then take his picture."

"All right." Dick snapped another shot.

Kurtz raised an arm in front of his face. "Get out, I told you!"

"Mr. Kurtz," Dick called, "I'm really sorry to have intruded on your privacy. You must have been an ingenious artist in your day. I'd like to keep these pictures to remind me of our meeting."

Kurtz's face took on a radiant glow. He squared his shoulders, gathering himself into a dignified pose. Raising his eyes to the horizon, he gazed out loftly, like an actor giving a command performance. "Keep them if you like. You may take your leave now, young man. Both of you."

"Thank you," Dick called.

"Come on, Dick. Let's go," Batman said. "It's getting late."

Dick got into his car behind the Batmobile. As Batman started the motor, Dick reached outside impulsively and waved. If Kurtz noticed, he gave no indication.

As Dick's car pulled away, he glanced back again. Kurtz stood framed in the window, stiff and regal, gazing into space, as if reliving the glories of his past performances.

V

Dick radioed Batman from his car. "I'm just going to stop off at the *Clarion* office."

"Now? What for?"

"I want to write that piece on the Circle for tomorrow's paper."

"You won't mention Carol's name or her arrest, will you?"

"No."

"It could endanger her if you did."

"I know. I'll be careful not to refer to her."

Batman rode off, and Dick parked in front of the *Clarion* office. After he typed his column, he left it at the printer's. Then he went home, ate, and developed the two photographs of Kurtz. It was soon time to turn in for the night.

The following day, the *Clarion* featured Dick's column. It created a sensation around Gotham High, where school authorities were waging a campaign against drug peddlers. The column was picked up by a city newspaper and reprinted in the afternoon edition. Dick found himself a campus celebrity.

After school, he went over to see Carol. Lieutenant Ross pulled in the welcome mat. "I told you I don't want to see you here until you're ready to cooperate."

Dick explained that he had photographs of a man he wanted to check out with Carol.

"So who is it?" Ross asked impatiently. "Don't pull that Sphinx routine again."

"Alexander Kurtz," Dick answered, handing Ross the photos.

"Kurtz the hypnotist? He's aged considerably since I last saw him. It's worth a shot. But I'll be standing outside the cell. This time you won't hold out on me."

Command Performance

Ross conducted Dick to Carol's cell. "There's a visitor to see you."

"I'm glad you came back," Carol said to Dick.

"I can only stay a few minutes."

Carol's face fell.

"I have something I want to show you." He held out the two photographs.

Carol glanced at them, expressionless.

"Does he look familiar to you?"

"Why, should he?" Carol studied the photographs intently. "I don't recognize him. Am I supposed to? As far as I know. I've never seen him before."

"Forget it then," Dick said.

"But who is he? Aren't you going to tell me?"

"His name is Alexander Kurtz. He used to be a professional hypnotist."

"A hypnotist!" Carol's eyes filled with sudden understanding. "And you thought he was The Man?"

"It was just an idea."

Carol looked upset. "He's not the one, Dick. I told you, I'm not free to identify him. You played a cheap trick on me."

"It wasn't, Carol. I'm just trying to get you out of this mess. I'm on your side."

"It was underhanded and sneaky. You're trying to trick me into telling you his name." She moved to the end of the cot, her back to Dick.

"I'm sorry you feel that way, Carol." Dick turned to leave.

As Ross opened the door, Carol sobbed softly to herself. Dick made a move toward her, then shrugged, turned, and left the cell.

"You made a good try," Ross said. "You did all you could. I'll take the photographs now."

"You can have them, for all they're worth," Dick said. He left the station feeling he had let Carol down.

VI

Alan Spencer stood in front of the Curtis jewelry store, working up the courage to enter. The gold-plated bracelet The Man had given him seemed alive and hot to the touch. He fingered it gingerly in his pocket. Then he withdrew his hand and ran it nervously through his sandy hair. Glancing at the door, a chill swept over him, though the weather was balmy.

As he hesitated, he realized he might look suspicious loitering in front of the shop. Pretending interest, he inclined his head toward the window display. He wanted to turn and run, but how could he ever face the Circle again? The Man would be furious and boot him out, at least for the night. Where would he sleep? He had no income, no family to shelter him. *By sundown I'll need a fix real bad,* he thought. *It's too late to find another connection.*

Unable to postpone the moment any longer, he approached the door and pushed it open. Now there was no turning back. A bell tinkled over the entrance.

Mr. Curtis shot a sharp, appraising look in his direction. He was a tall, stylishly dressed man with close-cropped hair and a cool expression. Alan swallowed and advanced toward him. His feet sank into the plush velour carpet. It was like walking through an Arabian bazaar, with precious trinkets glittering on every side. Alan buttoned his sport jacket and straightened his tie.

"May I help you?"

"I'd like to see some bracelets. I'm looking for a birthday present for my ahnt." He assumed a wealthy, upper crust accent.

Command Performance

"This way, please."

Curtis crossed to the other side of the store, with Alan at his elbow.

"What price range are you interested in?"

Alan replied exactly as The Man had instructed. "I'd like to see that bracelet: second row, third from the left."

Curtis looked surprised. "That's two thousand dollars," he said, with an edge of doubt.

"I expected as much," Alan replied evenly. "May I examine it?"

"Certainly." Curtis brought out the bracelet. "This is from our Regal collection, a fourteen-carat classic gold Cleopatra bracelet."

Alan raised it to the light, studying it.

"It's a beautifully crafted piece," Curtis went on. "Your aunt will treasure it forever."

Alan placed it on the counter. "May I see that bracelet also? In the case behind you?"

Curtis turned around. "You mean this one?"

"Yes."

As Curtis unlocked the case, Alan snatched the bracelet and swiftly substituted the cheap imitation. The entire operation took a split second, just as he had rehearsed it.

Unsuspecting, Curtis turned and placed the second bracelet on the counter. "This is a fourteen-carat gold tubular slip-on with twisted wire. It sells for one hundred dollars. Obviously there's no comparison between the two."

"I see what you mean," Alan said. "I'd like time to think it over."

"Of course. This slip-on is really suitable for a younger person. Your girlfriend, for example?"

"I'll drop by again tomorrow."

Howard Goldsmith

I knew he couldn't afford the Cleopatra, Curtis thought. *Trying to impress me with his phony Ivy League accent.*

Curtis was about to put away the bracelets when his eyes snapped wide open. He scooped up the Cleopatra imitation, his jaw gaping. "Hey, wait a minute!" he cried. "Come back here!"

Alan was almost at the door. He grabbed the doorknob, threw the door open, and plunged outside, his heart pounding.

"Stop, thief!"

Dick was driving home when he heard Curtis shouting outside the store. He spotted Alan charging into the midst of traffic.

Tires squealing, a Datsun ground to a stop, its driver screaming, "Watch where you're going! Are you crazy?"

Alan raced on without a backward look. The shrill clangor of Curtis's alarm pursued him up the street.

Dick got out of his car and asked Curtis what happened.

"He switched bracelets on me, ran off with the genuine one."

It sounded like The Man was behind this job, too. Dick ran after the thief, who was bounding up the steps of a library. Alan barreled into a line of borrowers and dashed out the back entrance. Puffing and gasping, he made for a bus that was just pulling out. Over his shoulder, he saw Dick pursuing him.

Alan pounded desperately on the side of the bus as it drew away from the curb. To his surprise, the driver brought it to a wheezing stop, and Alan ran for the entrance. Breathless, he leaped on board.

At that moment, Dick caught up with him and dragged him off the bus. Alan put up a fight, but Dick clamped a hammer lock on him, forcing him to his knees.

"Let go!" Alan cried in pain. "You're breaking my arm!"

"Not until you talk. Who put you up to this? Was it The Man?"

The color left Alan's cheeks. "I don't know what you're talking about. Ow!" he screamed as Dick tightened his hold.

"Spill it or you'll talk to the police."

"Ow! I can't. He'll kill me if he finds out."

"Who? What's his name?"

"All right! All right! Let go of my arm!"

Dick released him.

Alan rubbed his sore shoulder. "I didn't want to steal the damn bracelet. He made me."

"Who?"

A shot rang out from a car speeding by. Alan slumped to the ground, blood flowing from his scalp. The car zoomed off before Dick could get its license number. It turned a corner and disappeared.

Dick knelt down beside Alan, who was still conscious. He rolled out a handkerchief and pressed it firmly against Alan's wound. Then he looked inside Alan's wallet for his ID.

A man pushed his way through a gathering crowd. "I'm a doctor. Let me through." he examined the wound. "He's lucky. The bullet just grazed his skull. There could be a light concussion. He may be dizzy for a while."

Alan motioned to Dick to move closer. He spoke with difficulty. Dick bent over him, his ear close to Alan's mouth.

"Six—teen," Alan stammered.

"Sixteen?"

"Cr-Crescent."

"Sixteen Crescent? What about it, Alan?"

Alan struggled to speak. His eyes suddenly glazed and his head pitched forward. He was unconscious.

An ambulance soon arrived and took him to the hospital.

"Sixteen Crescent," Dick repeated to himself. "Was it The Man's address?"

Burning with curiosity, Dick got into his car and drove downtown.

VII

Crescent Street was in the heart of the business district. Sixteen Crescent turned out to be a restaurant. The Regency hardly looked like the headquarters for a dope ring. Maybe he'd misunderstood Alan's words. But having come this far, he was not about to leave without further investigation. He parked the car up the street and doubled back to the restaurant. Entering the lobby, he found himself in a well-appointed, though hardly plush establishment. The dining room was paneled in pale cypress and illuminated by apricot lights. Dick followed the headwaiter to a corner booth. Selecting the least expensive dish, he ordered a hot roast beef sandwich and a Coke.

As the waiter left, Dick glanced about the place. The patrons were mostly middle-aged, with a smattering of young couples in conventional dress. No one remotely resembling a drug addict. Snatches of conversation drifted over to his table. It consisted of the usual topics: family, friends, the mortgage, rising prices. Hardly a den of iniquity, Dick thought. Unless the operation was a front.

At the far end of the room, two swinging doors, IN and OUT led to the kitchen. To his left was the lounge and rest rooms; to his right, a short flight of stairs rising to a door marked PRIVATE. At the back of the room an ornamented doorway marked CLOSED led down a flight of steps to a lower level. Dick supposed it was the cellar. Everything seemed on the up-and-up. All very innocent-looking. Yet Dick wished he could look behind the closed doors, if only to put his mind at ease.

The waiter returned with his order. "The floor show will start soon," he remarked.

"Floor show?"

"Didn't you know? We have a show four times a week: Monday, Wednesday, Friday, and Saturday."

As the waiter was conversational, Dick tried a long shot, "A friend of mine recommended this place."

"Oh yeah? What's his name? Maybe I know him."

"Alan."

The man's eyebrows rose. *I may have hit pay dirt*, Dick thought.

"Alan who?"

"Spencer."

"Never heard of him," the waiter answered too quickly. He left abruptly.

He was lying. Dick was sure of it. He suppressed his excitement as the man walked up the short flight of steps and knocked on the door marked PRIVATE. Out of the corner of his eye, Dick saw the waiter turn in his direction. He felt the man's eyes on him.

He did know Alan. Though Alan didn't fit in with the surroundings, he somehow belonged. As unlikely as it seemed, Dick had found the correct address. The Regency. On the face of it, it made no sense. This was no sleazy dive off the main strip. It was a neat, respectable establishment.

If he'd really located The Man, Carol would finally be free of him. So would all the other kids under his thumb.

Howard Goldsmith

If only he could take a peek behind the doors marked PRIVATE and CLOSED. One of them might contain the answer. If the CLOSED door led to a cellar, it might be large enough to house a number of people. Dick looked down at the floor. He might be sitting right above them. There must be a cellar entrance at the back of the restaurant, Dick reasoned. He was about to leave, with the idea of returning to investigate the rear of the building, when a spotlight flashed on. It illuminated a slightly elevated stage in the center of the floor.

A dapper man dressed in dark evening clothes emerged from the PRIVATE room and crossed to the stage. Dick stiffened in his chair.

He was gray at the temples, of medium height, with an erect, self-confident bearing. He fitted Carol's description of The Man. But then so did a lot of men.

His speech was crisp and aggressive, his voice resonant. It easily penetrated the farthest reaches of the restaurant without a microphone. "How do you do, ladies and gentlemen. My name is Julian Richter. Regular patrons are familiar with my work. But to the uninitiated, let me introduce myself. I am co-owner of this restaurant and a sometime hypnotist. 'Sometime' meaning whenever people let me perform."

There were a few chuckles in the audience.

Dick sat riveted, his eyes following riveted, his eyes following Richter like a cobra.

"One of the advantages of being a co-owner is that I can hire myself at low wages. I don't have an 'act,' in popular parlance—but find that people are amused and instructed by my hypnotic demonstrations. Now—do we have a hardy soul among you who will volunteer as a subject?"

His invitation was met with nervous titters.

Command Performance

"Come, come, don't be afraid. I'm not going to eat you. How about you, young man? You there in the corner booth."

Everyone turned toward Dick, who was caught off guard. "No thanks," he answered.

"No? You disappoint me. You look strong and brave for someone your age. How old are you?"

"Sixteen."

"May I ask your name?"

He hesitated, "Dick Grayson."

"Dick Grayson," Richter repeated. "It seems to me I've heard that name just recently. Are you the same Dick Grayson who wrote the article about drug abuse?"

"Yes." *If this is The Man, I've fallen right into his lap,* Dick thought.

"For those of you who haven't seen the article, Dick is a reporter for the Gotham High *Clarion*. The paper is featuring a series of articles about drug traffic in Gotham City. Don't you think that's commendable? Give the boy a hand."

They all clapped good-humoredly.

"Your reticence is unbecoming in a fearless reformer. Let's see if we can coax Dick up to the stage." He gestured to the audience.

They obliged with more applause. When Dick shook his head, some people shouted:

"Come on, Dick."

"Don't be shy."

"Be a sport."

Richter stepped down from the platform and approached Dick's booth. Gripping Dick firmly by the arm, he said, "Come with me. I will escort you personally. Don't let us down, Dick."

Howard Goldsmith

Yielding, Dick stood up and accompanied Richter to the stage. The patrons laughed and cheered.

You're not going to hypnotize me, Dick silently vowed.

"Stand over here, Dick. I'd like to test your suggestibility." Richter stood behind Dick, his hands on both shoulders. "Now I'm going to blindfold you. Don't be alarmed. Just relax." Richter took a black handkerchief and wound it around Dick's eyes. "Can you see anything, Dick?"

Dick shook his head.

"I thought not." He gently pressed his fingertips to the center of Dick's back. "You're beginning to feel off-balance. Your body is swaying."

Dick stood ramrod-straight, refusing to yield to Richter's suggestion.

"At the count of five, you will fall forward. Have no fear, I will catch you. You won't be hurt. One...two. You're feeling slightly dizzy. You can't control your body's motion. Three. You're falling forward."

Lurching, Dick caught himself and snapped back on his heels. Perspiration broke out on his forehead.

"Four. You're about to fall, Dick. Don't be afraid. I'll catch you. You're teetering now, on the edge of a precipice."

Dick's entire body vibrated like a taut spring. *Don't listen to him. Block out his voice.*

"You're tipping over, Dick. Five. You're falling. Let go. Don't fight it. I'll catch you."

Dick began to tumble; at the last second, he pulled himself erect, standing at rigid attention. *How do you like that, Richter?*

"Obviously, Dick doesn't relish the prospect of falling off a precipice."

The audience laughed.

Command Performance

He removed the blindfold. "But the point is made, I think. In response to my verbal suggestions, Dick pitched forward, on the verge of falling. But he refused to yield to my final command, perhaps afraid I wouldn't catch him. You don't trust me, do you, Dick?" He grinned wolfishly.

Dick didn't answer.

"Well, we'll see if we can do something about that," Richter said. "You can trust me, Dick. Sit in this chair and make yourself comfortable. Relax and let your mind float. Your tension is dissolving."

Dick felt more tense than ever. An experienced hypnotist, Richter noted the rigidity of Dick's arms and decided to make use of it. "Extend your arms straight before you, with your hands tightly clasped."

Dick kept his arms at his sides.

"Come, come, Dick. Follow my directions. There's no need to convince me that you are still not hypnotized. I haven't attempted to put you under. Extend your arms, please."

Dick complied.

"I am going to recite the alphabet. When I reach the letter D—for Dick—you will be able to unclasp your hands, A...B. Tight, tight, tight. C. Tighter, tighter...."

Dick's hands were rigidly locked. He tried with all his might to separate them.

"D. Tighter still. You cannot unlock them. Try."

Flushed and perspiring, Dick struggled to open his hands, without success. They were welded together.

Triumphant, Richter chopped down on Dick's wrists. "Open."

Dick's hands slipped apart, as if greased with melted butter.

"I hope you learned a lesson, Dick. It's pointless to resist my commands."

Dick decided to play along with him, doubtful that he could stand up to Richter's repeated suggestions. But if he could simulate a trance, his mind would still be in control of his actions. *When he hypnotizes you, don't fight him. Make him think you've gone under very rapidly.*

Richter flashed a coin under Dick's eyes. "Concentrate on this golden coin. It's a talisman from the mystic Orient." Richter twirled the coin. "You see nothing but this coin. It occupies your entire field of vision. It is growing larger and larger. Keep staring at it. Its brilliance is dazzling. You cannot keep your eyes open. Your eyelids are growing heavy. A warm, drowsy sensation is creeping over your entire body." Dick's head nodded.

"When I snap my fingers, you will be asleep."

Snap. Dick's head fell forward against his chest.

"The subject is fully asleep now," Richter gloated.

Dick's body felt torpid, but his mind was still clear.

Richter held up a hatpin. "I'm going to stick a pin into your finger, Dick. Don't be afraid. You will feel no pain. You are armored against pain." He raised Dick's right hand—Dick steeled himself—and jabbed the pin into his thumb until it drew blood.

The pain was sharper than Dick expected—but his dreamy expression never wavered.

"This is an example of hypnotically induced analgesia," Richter told the audience. "Loss of pain sensitivity. Now, it has been demonstrated that a subject cannot lie under hypnosis. He becomes compulsively truthful. Let us test this. Dick, how old are you?"

"Sixteen."

"Do you like school, Dick?"

"Most of it."

"Do you like me?"

Dick hesitated. "No."

Command Performance

Everyone laughed.

Richter smiled thinly. "I guess I asked for that. This is your first visit here, isn't it, Dick? I don't remember seeing you here before."

"That's right."

"Did you discover us on your own, or did someone recommend you here before."

"Someone recommended it."

"Would you care to tell us who? Perhaps some of us know him. Or is it a secret?"

"No. It was Alan Spencer."

"A friend of yours?"

"An acquaintance. I hardly know him."

"Did he tell you anything about me?"

"No."

"He just mentioned the restaurant. Nothing else?"

"Nothing else."

"I see. Alan comes here often. I assure you *he* likes me."

The audience laughed.

"In time you'll come to like me, perhaps—once you become a part of my circle."

Circle! Keeping a tight lid on his emotions, Dick forced his features to remain impassive.

"Now we'll try some definitions," Richter said. "This is always fascinating to me, for it tells something about how the mind works. We may stumble upon some interesting subconscious associations. Dick, what is a circle?"

"A round shape. The area of a circle equals pi times the square of the radius."

"Very good. Does the word 'circle' mean anything else to you?"

"A social group."

"Any particular group?"

Dick hesitated. "Any social group could be called a circle."

At that moment a young man entered the restaurant and signaled to Richter. Richter nodded. "Ladies and gentlemen, I must end this demonstration now. Business calls. I trust you enjoyed yourselves."

They gave him a round of applause.

"I'll bring Dick out of it now. Dick, when I clap my hands, you'll be wide awake. You'll feel rested and perfectly relaxed, remembering nothing of our conversation." He clapped his hands.

Opening his eyes, Dick gazed about the restaurant, yawned, and stretched.

"How do you feel, Dick?"

"Just fine. Is it all over?'

"Yes."

"Was I hypnotized?"

Everyone laughed.

"I assure you, you were. You proved a good subject. Now return to your seat and order anything you like. It's on the house."

"Thank you," Dick said, stepping off the stage.

As Dick returned to his booth, Richter marched to the back of the restaurant, walked down a short flight, and entered the room marked CLOSED. He shut the door behind him, locked it, and entered a larger room, which was the headquarters for the Circle.

VIII

Soon afterward, Richter heard raised voices at the rear of the restaurant. As he moved toward the back door, it sprang open.

Command Performance

Two young men entered, prodding someone with their guns. "Come on, you!" they ordered, pushing their captive into the cellar.

"We found this guy poking around outside, boss," one of them said.

Richter's lips twisted into a predatory smile. His arms opened in a gesture of welcome. "How nice of you to join us, Dick Grayson."

Dick's eyes swept the cellar. "Carol!" he cried. She sat with her hands tied to the back of a chair.

Lashing out, Dick knocked the guns from both teenagers' hands. As he dove for a gun, a bullet exploded an inch from his outstretched hand. Dick straightened up to see a puff of smoke rising from a pistol in Richter's hand.

"Tsk, tsk. I had hoped you would become one of us, Dick. But you deceived me. You weren't hypnotized at all, were you?"

"Almost," Dick conceded.

"I give you credit—you had me completely fooled. It took poise to carry that off, plus unusual powers of resistance. It's a pity you didn't join our side. I could have used you."

"The way you've used the others."

Richter smiled. "Your fierce independence makes it impossible for me to release you. You see that, don't you? You know too much for your own good. Ergo, you must die, together with Carol."

"No!" Carol cried. "Please don't do it. I swear I didn't tell the police a thing!"

Richter looked at her contemptuously. "I realize that, or the police would have swooped down on us. We'll make sure your silence is permanent, my dear."

Carol cringed in her chair, her eyes wild with fear.

Howard Goldsmith

"How did you capture her?" Dick asked, with a flash of anger.

"As she was being escorted to the police psychologist's office a block from the jail. It was simply a matter of careful planning and waiting for the right opportunity. Unfortunately, a police officer was shot in the fray."

Richter reached for a hypodermic needle. "I hadn't bargained on a twin execution."

"Please!" Carol cried. She burst out sobbing.

"You will go first, you pathetic sheep. I'm sick of your whining. But I assure you, your deaths will be quite painless. The police will think you overdosed on morphine. Naturally, your bodies will be found far from this place."

"The police will connect us," Dick said. "I participated in your little demonstration, remember? There were witnesses. You gave my name to your audience."

"Quite right. But Julian Richter is a respectable restauranteur. Customers saw you leave this place in good health and good humor. So far as the police are concerned, The Man is still Mr. Anonymous. There's nothing to connect me with your rapidly approaching demise."

"Devil!" Carol cried.

"Shut up!" Richter exploded. "Let's get this over with." He turned to one of the gang members. "Fred, roll up their sleeves."

Fred cautiously unbuttoned Dick's sleeve, remembering how easily Dick had disarmed him before. His friend, Brad, pressed a gun to Dick's temple. Then Fred bent over Carol, huddled limply in her chair, and untied her hands. Carol collapsed weakly into Fred's arms.

There was a knock at the door leading to the restaurant.

"Who is it?" Richter demanded.

"It's Joe, the waiter."

Command Performance

"What do you want?" Richter growled. "I'm busy."
"There's a package for you. Registered mail. They need
your signature."

"Sign it for me, idiot!"

They heard the waiter conferring with someone. "The
guy says the sender requested your personal signature,
boss. Or he has to take it back."

"Very well. One minute." Turning to Fred, he whispered, "Gag them. Brad, keep them covered."

Fred tied handkerchiefs around their mouths. Then
Richter unlocked the door.

Dick cried out in a muffled voice. Brad jabbed a gun to
his back. "Shut up," he whispered, "or I'll plug you."

"Hand it over," Richter said, reaching for the parcel.
The waiter fell forward unexpectedly, and Richter reeled
backward. Batman loomed up behind the waiter. A club-
bing blow sent Richter crashing into Brad, who dropped
his automatic. Dick swooped down, picked it up, and leveled it at Fred.

"All right, drop your gun!" Dick ordered Fred. Before
he finished the sentence, Batman had already twisted the
gun out of Fred's hand.

"Raise your hands and face the wall! All of you," Batman ordered. "You too, Richter."

Richter meekly obeyed.

They heard footsteps charging down the stairs to the
cellar. Policemen appeared in the doorway, their guns
drawn.

"I notified the police before barging in," Batman whispered to Dick.

The police searched and handcuffed the gang. "All
right, take them away," Lieutenant Ross called out.

As the police led them out, Richter managed a defiant
smile. "You can't prove a thing against me. I have wit-

nesses who will swear I haven't left the restaurant all week. You'll never make the charges stick."

"Oh yes they will," Carol shot back. "With my testimony and Dick's."

Richter glared at her, his eyes full of menace.

"And I'll show the police where the junk is stashed," Carol added.

Richter's mouth fell open.

"For once he's speechless," Dick said, as a policeman led Richter outside.

"But how did you find this place?" Dick asked Batman.

"I did a little investigating on my own," Batman answered. "One of our first hunches was that The Man might be a professor adept at hypnosis. A teaching post would be the perfect cover. I looked up an instructor at Gotham U. who remembered a man fitting Carol's description. He was kicked off the faculty for illicit manufacture of psychedelic drugs. Afterward, Richter changed careers and bought an interest in the Regency, where he performed as hypnotist."

After the police put the gang in a van, they began a thorough search of the premises. Carol knew of glassine packets of heroin concealed in ceiling pipes. They found other packets in cans buried behind the brick and mortar walls of the cellar.

"This evidence will help put Richter away for life," Ross said.

"What about the rest of the gang?" Dick asked.

"The ones who abducted Carol will be held for kidnapping and attempted murder. We'll try to rehabilitate the others, beginning with medical treatment for their addictions. It won't be easy, but they're young, and there's always hope."

"What about me?" Carol asked.

Command Performance

"I haven't forgotten you, Carol. You'll be glad to learn that the department store has dropped its charges against you."

"That's great!" Dick said, hugging Carol.

"Your parents are waiting for you at the police station," Ross added.

"How can I ever thank you?" Carol said, clasping his hands. "And you too, of course, Dick and Batman. I'll never forget what you did for me."

"All in a day's police work," Ross said.

"All in a day's investigative reporting," Dick echoed.

Batman started for the door. "I have to leave now. Anyone want a lift?"

"Going my way?" Dick said, with a wink. "It's not every day a reporter gets chauffeured by Batman."

Subway Jack

A Batman Adventure

JOE R. LANSDALE

OLD GOTHAM CITY CEMETERY (early October)

The moon...

The cemetery was at the top of the hill and dead center
of the hill was the grave. It was marked by a stone cross
covered in dark mold and twisting vines. There were
other graves, of course, and all of them in a state of equal
disrepair, but this was the one Jack Barrett wanted.

He climbed to the top of the hill and leaned on his
shovel with one hand and held his flash with the other.
The beam played across the stone marker but revealed little. Age and mold and vines had taken care of the writing
there. Still, Jack had researched enough to know this was
the spot.

He turned off the flash, put it in his coat pocket, and
looked around. The hill the grave was on was high enough
that it stood above the stone walls of the cemetery and
afforded a look at the city; the city that had grown up
around it over the years and now blinked its neon eyes
over this pile of dirt and stone and bones.

Subway Jack

Jack could hear the cars roaring along the city streets, and he thought he could hear the rumble of the subway nearby. To the left of the hill was a great, brittle-looking oak, and he looked up through the branches to watch the moon coasting through the sky behind a veil of clouds. A cool wind blew through the cemetery, rattled the limbs of the tree, ruffled Jack's hair, and blew leaves before it.

Jack took a deep breath, put the shovel to the dirt and began to dig. The sound of the wind, the cars, and the subway died for Jack, and all he heard was the whistle of the shovel sliding into moist earth.

He dug until he came to a cracked stone slab about which were wrapped some rusty chains held fast by a corroded padlock. He put the shovel to the chains, and they snapped as easily as if they had been twine. He worked the point of the shovel into a crack in the slab and lifted out huge chunks until he revealed a short row of dark, narrow steps.

He put the shovel aside and took out his flashlight and went down the slick steps and into the tight, dank tomb. He played the light on a rise of stone covered in dust with a collapsed skull on one end of it and a small, rectangular, metal box on the other. There were a few fragments that might have been bones lying about the stone platform.

He went over and took hold of the box. In spite of the rust that covered it, it felt firm and heavy. He shook it gently and felt and heard something move inside. He put the box in his huge, coat pocket and climbed out of the tomb.

He put the flash in his other coat pocket, and then grabbed the top of the cemetery wall and pulled himself over. He scrambled down the narrow, gravel path that led through a clutch of brush and trees and delivered him to the sidewalk. He walked along until the sounds of the city filled his ears and the lights filled his eyes.

Joe R. Lansdale

He walked on faster, his hand in his coat pocket, caressing the box there as gently as he might a woman's thigh.

JAMES W. GORDON, Police Commissioner (mid-October)

It was only natural that the whole bad business would blow into Gotham City like an October wind with ice on its tail, and I guess you could say it was only natural a dark-minded guy with dark-minded plans would take to the subway the way he did; take to it and do what he did.

So this cold wind blew into Gotham and women started dying—bag ladies, those who hugged the underground for warmth and scrounged or begged for the things they needed.

As if things weren't bad enough for them, along came this guy with a plan and a blade he knew how to use. He cut up women so they didn't look like women anymore; didn't look like much of anything human anymore. Then when he finished with them, he dipped his fingers in their blood and wrote on the subway walls: COMPLIMENTS OF SUBWAY JACK, then the number of the victim.

When he wrote Number 3, I got a firsthand look at his business. I was home in bed when the phone jangled me out of the blankets and into the kitchen to talk on the extension there. A beat cop named LoBrutto said, "Detective Mertz told me to call. Said you wanted to know if there was another one. Said you wanted to check things firsthand."

"Send a car," I said.

I had some instant coffee, then the black and white came and drove me over there. The subway entrance was marked off and there were a few people milling around and a lot of uniforms trying to turn them back. A couple of good detectives, Mertz and Crider, were waiting out front.

Subway Jack

Mertz took me by the elbow and we went down the subway steps and walked along for a ways, and I could smell the vomit and urine smells that were always there, and something else too.

Blood.

When we got to the body it was covered by a yellow tarp and was lying against the subway wall.

"We got photographs and everything," Mertz said. "Not a thing you can mess up if you want to take a look. I've had all I want."

I went over and pulled back the tarp and held my breath. It's bad enough seeing this kind of thing in photographs or in the morgue, but to see it on cold concrete, the blood still drying, the stench of death in the air, well, it gets you, gives you the willies, and I don't care if you've seen death a thousand times. It gets to you if you're normal.

Then too, I'd never seen death quite like this; never seen this kind of violence done to a human being. Maybe someone run through some kind of machinery could be expected to look this bad, but....well, you get the picture.

"All the king's horses and all the king's men...." Crider said. He wasn't looking at the body. He had his back to it. Mertz was over by a concrete support smoking a cigarette and looking out at the subway tracks.

The coffee moved around in my stomach and turned sour and rose up, but I fought it down. I've had some experience.

I got down on one knee just outside the circle of drying blood and looked the body over, trying to be as cool and objective about it as I could. When I was through with that I looked up and took a breath and read what was writ-

ten in blood on the subway wall: COMPLIMENTS OF SUBWAY
JACK. NUMBER 3.

Crider glanced over his shoulder at me and said,
"Shame he didn't put his address there, huh?"

I pulled the tarp over the body and got a cigar out of
my coat pocket, and when I lit it with my lighter I saw my
hands were shaking. I got a good snootful of smoke to
dilute the smell of blood and walked over to where I could
look down at the tracks with Mertz. Crider joined us. He
got out his pipe and lit up. We stood there smoking for a
while, then I said, "Don't guess anyone saw this happen?"

"Just like the others," Crider said. "Wasn't that many
people around to see anything, but there was some. Seems
like they'd have at least heard a scream. Guy can't do what
this guy's doing without taking some time. You'd think
someone would walk up on him."

"Might be best they didn't," I said.

"Yeah, but you'd think so," Crider said. "Hell, it isn't
even that dark over there, a little shadowy maybe, but not
that dark. Wasn't like he did this in hiding. Guy must
move like a rocket and be made of smoke."

"Any idea who the victim is?" I said.

"Bag lady probably," Mertz said. "But who can tell
looking? A scrounger found the body. We've run him in
for vagrancy and petty theft coupla times in the past.
Name's Bud Vincent. Says he was walking along and
found a shopping cart full of stuff, and he admits he was
going to steal it, but he hadn't pushed it far when he came
on the body. He called it in then, and I guess a guy like
this calling in just shows how bad it is. These people don't
usually want anything to do with us, not in any kind of
way. In their book we're the bad guys."

"Until this fella showed up," Crider said. "He sort of
put bad into perspective."

Subway Jack

"You believe this Bud Vincent?" I said.

"Yeah, we believe him," Mertz said.

I didn't go home then. I had a black and white take me to my office. I went in and sat behind my desk in the dark, looked at the hot-line phone on the left of my desk. Looked at it a long time.

The files on the ripper case were locked in my desk drawer; I got my keys and unlocked it and got the files out. I spread the files in front of me and turned on my desk lamp. What I had there was on the first two victims, of course, but I assumed when the information on the third victim was put together, it would say pretty much what was said here about the first two. That the victim was a woman, a street person, that she had been cut to pieces with a sharp instrument and that the killer was very strong. Lastly, clues to the killer's identity would be minimal to none. So far, all we had was a little clay that we had found at the site of the first murder, maybe off the killer's shoes, and maybe not. It could have been from a passerby, and it wasn't really that much help anyway. It was a fairly common kind of clay.

I closed up the file and turned off the light and sat looking at the hot-line, thinking that this Subway Jack stuff was stranger than usual. I could feel it in my bones like some kind of cancer, and when you got into the territory of the strange, you got into Batman's territory.

I guess I didn't call because of a kind of pride. There had been serial murders before, and there would be again. The department had solved most of them, and sometimes they had just stopped. Maybe the killer moved on, maybe he or she died—but women were dying and that had to stop, and if anyone could stop it, Batman could. All I had to do was reach over and pick up the phone and it would ring, and without bothering to answer, he would come.

Joe R. Lansdale

BRUCE WAYNE (Batman)

The bullet.

It tumbled.

It shone in the street light like a silver rocket out of control.

The bullet. The first of two.

Bruce tried to freeze it with his mind and succeeded. It stopped tumbling. It froze in midair. But he couldn't hold it. It began to push at his will and move again, and this time, no matter how hard he willed it back, it tumbled onward.

It was going to happen again.

He was just a boy and moments before he had been happy, but now the bullet would end all that. Lord have mercy, it was going to happen again.

He and his parents had come out of a revival movie theater where they had seen *The Mark of Zorro*, and around the corner of the theater, waiting in the dark with a gun and no patience, was a thug who cut short their talk and laughter and sent Zorro from their heads with a demand for money.

But before his parent's could comply, the thug got nervous and pulled the trigger and the bullet leapt out.

The bullet.

It tumbled.

Bruce was amazed he could see the bullet. It was very clear; slow motion. He was also amazed that this time he had been able to stop it, but his will was not strong enough to maintain the situation. The bullet started to move again. Slowly forward, and now no matter how hard he willed it to stop, it kept straight on toward his mother.

His father stepped in front of her and took it and went down and didn't move, then his mother screamed and the thug fired again and the bullet split her pearl necklace and the pearls went in all directions and his mother fell across the body of his father.

Bruce looked up, and discovered he was in a balcony seat, like the one in the theater where they had watched *The Mark of Zorro.* He was watching the murder of his parents play out in the street below. He could see them lying dead and he could see himself standing there, stunned. The would-be robber panicked, turned, and fled down the street and was swallowed up by darkness like a fish sliding down the throat of a whale.

Bruce realized there was someone in the balcony with him. Someone breathing hotly against his neck, leaning forward to put a heavy arm across his shoulders. Then a voice that seemed to come from a great distance through a pipe said, "You are *mine,* and you will become me...I am your *true* father...and you are my *son.*"

Cheeks wet with tears, Bruce whirled and saw the speaker had tall, leathery ears and a face full of long, sharp teeth. The arm around his shoulders moved away and it was attached to a dark serrated wing. The thing's fingers were tipped with great claws.

It was an enormous man-bat.

It beat its wings, rose from the balcony and into the upper shadows as Bruce sat up in bed and screamed. The shadows in the balcony were pushed aside by the softer shadows of his bedroom, they in turn split by a golden wedge of light split by a long, thin shadow that said, "Are you quite all right, sir?"

"Alfred?"

"The dream, sir?"

"Same one. Only this time I could see the bullets coming out of the gun, and it looked as if I could freeze them, stop them from killing my parents. But it still happened.

Joe R. Lansdale

Even in a dream I couldn't make things come out the way
I wanted."

"The man-bat again, sir?"

"In a balcony this time, overlooking the street."

"I'm quite sorry, sir."

"I'm learning to live with it. At least the dreams vary
a little."

"Not just the dreams, sir. I was coming to wake you
when you screamed."

"The hot-line?"

"Yes sir."

"Good."

SERIES OF PANELS, RICH IN SHADOW AND MOVEMENT

(1) BATCAVE—INTERIOR

Background: Blue-black with stalactites hanging
down from the cave roof like witch fingers. There's enough
light that we can see the wink of glass trophy cases. Their
interiors, except for two—one containing a sampling of
the Penguin's umbrellas and another containing Robin's
retired uniform—are too dark for us to make out their contents. But we can see the larger, free-standing trophies: a
giant Lincoln head penny from the "Penny Plunder's"
case. The life-size mechanical dinosaur from the "Dinosaur Island" case, and the mammoth playing card bearing
the likeness of Batman's arch enemy, the green-haired,
white-faced Joker.

Foreground: Batmobile, long and sleek, a dark needle
to sew through the night. Tinted bubble glass to hide the
driver from view. Great fin attached to the rear. A large
triangular bat head ornament attached to the front. The

headlights bright as minature suns. Motion lines on either side of the craft to show us it's really moving.

(2) BATCAVE—EXTERIOR—NIGHT

Background: Full moon rising above the scene like a burnished shield. Tufts of dark cloud threaten to roll over it. Full view below of secret batcave entrance/exit as a mechanical door with its facade of rocks and brush is closing down; interior of the cave is as dark as a witch's heart.

Foreground: Batmobile (right angle, right side of panel) racing from the cave, looking very much like a prehistoric fish.

(3) GOTHAM CITY STREETS

Background: Straight view of the street, bordered by tall, dark buildings. Street is uncommonly empty. Moon rising dead center at the rear of the street, looking more like a gold ballon now than a burnished shield. No clouds threatening anymore. Clear, dark sky.

Foreground: Street split by the Batmobile racing forward, spreading wind lines before it like straw. A newspaper has blown across the street and stuck to the left headlight. Visible across the face of the headlight is part of a headline that reads: SUBWAY JACK.

JAMES W. GORDON

Batman opened the door to my office and stood framed in the light from the hallway. His costume never fails to strike me with a feeling of awe. The dark cowl with its tall ears and connected cape swirled around him like something alive. I saw the golden circle with a flying bat in the

Joe R. Lansdale

middle centered on his chest. I saw the man himself. Big, real big. Muscled. Yet lithe as a gymnast.

He closed the door. He didn't turn on the light. He likes it dark. He came over and sat down in the chair in front of the desk and smiled. That smile of his could be a frown upside down. He said, "My guess is Subway Jack."

"Good guess."

"I was going to get in on it anyway."

"I thought you might."

"I've been reading about it in the papers, seeing it on the news."

I slid the files across to him and turned on the lamp and positioned it where he could see. "There's extras there if you want them," I said. I leaned back and got out a cigar and lit it.

He reached out with a gloved hand and took a file and opened it and without looking up said, "Nasty habit."

"It's this Subway Jack stuff," I said. "Got me puffing my pipe more than usual, smoking these cigars. I'm nervous as a long-tailed cat in a roomful of rocking chairs. I'll be chewing and dipping next. I saw number three tonight, and I'll tell you, you saw what I saw, you might be taking up some things yourself. Those photos in there don't do these murders the bad justice they deserve."

"Just the same, Jim, I'd prefer not to breathe your smoke."

"You probably eat just the right amount of bran and prunes too, don't you?"

"Just the right amount."

I put out the cigar.

When he finished reading I said, "And number four probably won't be much different."

"Always the subway," he said. "Always bag ladies."

Subway Jack

"Shrink might have something to say about that. We don't have a psych file on him yet. It could just be the subway's close and the bag ladies are easy prey.... But I tell you, there's something different about this one. Something odd. I feel it in my bones."

"Could be rheumatism, Jim."

"That's funny." He put the lamp back the way I had it and turned it off and stood up. He took spare copies of the files and stuck them somewhere in his cloak. "We'll get him."

"Yeah," I said, but I had my doubts. They never got Jack the Ripper. They haven't got the Green River Killer yet. There's some doubt they got the right man for the Boston Strangler crimes.

Sometimes they got away.

"They got a sample of that clay for you down at the dispatcher's office. You want it, they're supposed to give it to you."

"Thanks, Jim." He went out then. I had a sudden urge to tell him to be careful, but he had moved too fast. I got up and went over and opened the door and looked down both ends of the hallway.

He was gone.

He always did move like a ghost.

OLD GOTHAM CITY CEMETERY (after third murder)

Jack went out there after each of the murders and tried to put it back, but it wouldn't let him. Each time he went into the tomb and put the box down, the razor would cut through the metal and cut his hand. It would sing to him, high and pretty, and he knew he couldn't put it back. It owned him, and in the fleeting moments when his mind was his own and he could think clearly, he thought of the damnable book and how it had led him here.

Joe R. Lansdale

He had gone to Gotham City Library to do research on his criminology paper, "The Psychopath and Modern Society," and while searching through the reference section for *Psychopathia Sexualis* by Richard Von Krafft-Ebing...

FLASHBACK: SERIES OF PANELS, DARK AND FOREBODING, ANGLES SHARP AS BLADES

(1) GOTHAM CITY LIBRARY—INTERIOR—DEEP IN THE STACKS

Background: Not much. Rows and rows of books disappearing into darkness.

Foreground: Prominent is Jack (tall and lean with a blond brush-cut, dressed in stylish white, high-top, tennis shoes, slacks, and a red-and-white-striped, long-sleeved shirt) standing on tiptoes reaching for a book. His hand is on the spine of one, but the book next to the one he wants has dislodged and is starting to fall.

(2) LIBRARY FLOOR

Closeup: Jack's hand reaching for the fallen book, which has landed spread open, spine up. The book is old and gray in color and on the spine in dark letters is *Followers of the Razor* by David Webb.

(3) LIBRARY

Closeup: Jack standing, holding the book open. We have a thought balloon that reads: "My God, a book on ripper murders that goes back to the 1800s. I didn't know there was such a thing."

(4) LIBRARY

Overhead (Bird's-Eye) View: Jack seated at a long, wooden table, stacks of books at his right elbow, his head bent over the one he picked up from the floor. Long view of him at the table is the central focus of the panel, but as we move to the edges of the panel, it darkens. The shelves of books that surround him can be made out, but they are shadowy and appear to lean toward him, as if they are living things sneaking a peek over his shoulder. There is a large yellow caption box at the top of the panel that reads: BY THE TIME THE DAY SLID INTO NIGHT, JACK HAD MADE A REMARKABLE DISCOVERY. Within the panel itself is a thought balloon coming from Jack. "Man, what a research paper this will make."

FROM JACK'S JOURNAL (destroyed later by James Gordon)

(Entry written mid-September)

Wow, have I come across something that will make old Professor Hamrick pass out. This should be the research paper to end all research papers. It's got your true crime, it's got your hint of the mystical, it's got your weird legend that can tie in with all kinds of mythology and famous murders. And ultimately, what we're talking here, is a serious high mark on the old research paper for yours truly.

Strikes me it might be a good idea for me to synopsis what I remember from my reading here and now, so I can get down my hotter impressions, then later when I outline the paper, I can review this and transfer those impressions to my paper. And besides, have I ever denied myself what I'm excited about by not writing it down in this journal? The answer to that is, No Sir.

I found this book and it's called *Followers of the Razor* and it was written by this guy named David Webb in the early 1900s, and he had been researching it all his life. He

Joe R. Lansdale

was kind of ahead of his time on his interest in this sort of thing, but his conclusions are a little screwy to say the least. Still, it makes fascinating reading, and he has an interesting bibliography of books and articles and interviews he draws from. I looked at some of those things when I was in the library, and since the Webb book, and the most interesting of the ones he cited, *The Book of Doches*—which is some old English book written in the 1600s—couldn't be checked out, I sort of borrowed them by taking them out under my coat. When I finish my paper, I'll return them.

Webb's theory is that the world we know is occasionally crossed up with other worlds, or dimensions, and this is where we get our ideas about gods and monsters, and it explains some disappearances. Seems this dimension he's referring to is populated with all sorts of horrible people and critters. He explains the disappearance of the *Mary Celeste* crew this way, suggests that the murders Lizzie Borden were blamed for were committed by someone, or something, from this other dimension, which possessed and used her. He claims the same for Jack the Ripper.

But I'll come back to that. Let me note one of his more interesting ideas, the tying of witchcraft to mathematics, geometry, and the movement of the planets and the moon.

He talks about this character that through the centuries has been referred to as the God of Swords, the God of Blades, and during the time he was writing, as the God of the Razor. He says this thing isn't really a god, but a powerful being from this other dimension, and for some reason, when certain mathematical symbols are drawn up, it can open the gate to this world of his, and he can escape from it to possess someone and make them do his bidding.

There's this crude drawing of this dude in the Webb book, and I'll tell you, I wouldn't want to meet him in a dark alley, or a lighted alley for that matter. But the written description Webb gives creeps me even more. He says it's varied a bit over the centuries, but it's pretty much like this: The God of the Razor is very tall and broad and wears a kind of top hat

Subway Jack

(a helmet in some accounts), has a metal hat band and needles or daggers for teeth, wears human skin and human heads for shoes—has little cloven feet that fit right down into the mouths.

Anyway, these mathematical symbols can call him up if blood is involved. He also claims that there's a blade from this other dimension that can open the gate. Says it was once a sword but was somehow broken and made into two daggers, and later on one of the daggers turned up made into a barber's razor and the ivory sword hilt had been made into the razor's sheath or handle. On it are written these mathematical symbols, and if the blade tastes blood, and it doesn't kill who it cuts, then that person is possessed by the God of the Razor and the razor becomes his instrument of destruction. It sucks blood and makes whoever is possessed a berserker. (He ties this in with the Vikings and their wild madnesses in battle.)

Let's see, what else. Oh, Webb says Excalibur, King Arthur's sword, was originally from the same dimension as the God of the Razor, and that it belonged to him. He claims that this is the sword that got broken and made into a razor. (I wonder what happened to the rest of the blade.) He says that eventually the razor fell into the hands of this barber in London, and that the barber accidentally cut himself with it and the God possessed him and made him commit the murders in Whitechapel.

Webb suggests that this possessed man may actually have died or committed suicide, but not before the razor was somehow passed into other hands. He shows evidence of similar murders throughout the U.S. right after those in London, and the last murders he records in his book end right here in Gotham City in 1904.

And get this. His final verification is that he actually saw the God of the Razor with his own eyes, and that he and a policeman managed to dispatch the old boy, which of course freed the man possessed, but also led to his death. He says they were able to defeat the God when the moonlight was

Joe R. Lansdale

affected by cloud cover, one of the few things that dilutes the monster's strength. I guess I should add to this that he says that they did not actually kill the God, merely dismissed him to his own dimension.

Final bit of neato material here is that the murderer Webb claims was possessed by the God of the Razor is buried right here in Gotham City in the Old Gotham Cemetery. According to Webb, the razor was put in a metal box and buried with this fellow so that it will forever be out of the hands of man.

If Webb had thought things through, if he really believed this razor had power, he wouldn't have mentioned that in his book. Because eventually someone is bound to try and find out if there really is a razor in that grave. Someone like me. But maybe as a writer he just couldn't resist telling all he knew.

Might be the razor has already been stolen from the grave. Or perhaps the book has been thought fiction or the ramblings of a madman, as they say in all the gothic horror fiction.

But if there is a razor, think of the kind of presentation I could make. My paper on the God of Razor, and a little bit of show and tell to go with it.

(Entry written early October)

From the book I've figured out which grave the body of the possessed man and the razor is in. Webb never comes right out and says where he's buried, but there are enough references there, that I think I've narrowed it down.

I'm going to get a shovel and go back and dig that grave up. I was a little worried about how I could walk along with a shovel without being noticed, as I figure grave robbery will not be looked upon lightly, but then I realized that in this city a man with a shovel may be a bit unusual, but nothing compared with the stuff you see every day. Besides, if the cops ask I can say I'm taking it to pawn or something. Not the best story in the world, but who's to prove otherwise.

Subway Jack

(Entry next day)

When I opened the grave, I was amazed there really was
a razor. That's what I wanted to find, but I guess a part of me
thought I was being silly. But when I found that box where it
was supposed to be and got it back here and opened it and
found the razor, I got a case of the spooks, you know. Not
that I believe the razor is the door to another dimension and
will let this demon into the body of whoever is cut and
doesn't die from the would, but hey, Webb thought that, and
there really is a razor....

I'm trying to figure a way around the grave robbing angle
now. If I'm going to use this for show and tell, I can't admit
I went out there and dug up a grave to get it.

Man, that razor is sharp and bright. You wouldn't think it
would be after all this time. I figured it would be rusted to
almost nothing. I guess I didn't have a hold of it good,
because when I opened it, it shifted in my hand and I slid a
finger onto the blade and knicked myself. Nothing bad, but
I hardly touched it. It sure does sting.

(Entry written later that day)

Thought about the razor all day. Was terrible in class.
Didn't get a third of the notes Professor Hamrick gave. My
finger hurt like hell, and still hurts. Razor and paper cuts
are the worst.

Decided to take the razor back. Couldn't think of a satisfactory way to explain possession of it. Besides, I don't like
it. Guess Webb's book is getting to me. I'll still do the paper,
but without show and tell. Sooner I get rid of the razor, the
better.

(Entry written later that night)

Carried the razor with me in the box. I walked part of the
way then caught the subway over to Center Station and got
off since it's not too far a walk to the cemetery from there.
When I got off at Center, I saw all these homeless people

Joe R. Lansdale

hanging around. I've always felt sorry for them, especially the bag ladies. But today I got to thinking different. There's really nothing that can be done for them. They really shouldn't be allowed on the street. They ought to be run in, or maybe put to sleep, like a sick dog or something. Isn't that what we do when the animal population gets out of hand? We exterminate the strays. I keep thinking of what it would be like to... well, we've all had those kind of thoughts from time to time, haven't we?

When I got to the cemetery the razor sang to me. It wouldn't go back in the tomb. It cut me through the box. I rode the subway back and it sang to me all the way. I don't think anyone else can hear it. Just me. It sings very pretty. It has suggestions. My cut finger hurts so badly right now I can hardly write; it throbs like a blister and from time to time it opens up and bleeds.

Need to get some sleep. All for now.

(Last entry, mid-October)

Webb was right. I'm not myself. The singing is louder and more frequent; the songs tell me to do things I don't think I want to do. Can't be clear on that. I find my thoughts and his mixing together. Makes a bad jumble. Moment ago I took a sheet of paper and pulled it over my bare legs until I had a dozen paper cuts. Can't fathom why, unless it's the singing making me do that. The cuts hurt so good.

There's a full moon tonight; the singing told me that. Told me too that the razor's edge is the mouth of the God of the Razor and that the mouth needs feeding.

I think about the bag ladies a lot.

THE BATCAVE (day after meeting in James Gordon's office)

"Excuse me sir, I've brought your tray."

Bruce Wayne looked up from the computer screen. "Thanks, Alfred, but I'm not hungry."

Subway Jack

"You asked me to prepare your dinner and bring it to you, sir."

"I did?"

"You did. Said you wanted to eat down here, that you had some work to do. Now please eat the clam chowder so I won't be inclined to break the bowl over your head, Master Bruce."

"Put it here and I'll get to it."

"Yes, put it there. That way you can appease poor old Alfred, but you'll leave it set and it'll get cold, then you won't eat it. Matters not that I've worked my fingers to the bone—"

"You opened a can for this."

"Well, yes sir, I did, but I pinched myself on the can opener. Making headway, Master Bruce?"

"Maybe. That clay they found. I ran it through my lab, analyzed it, and I've been running cross checks on it, and Jim was right."

"Common as dirt."

"A little joke, Alfred?"

"A small one, sir."

"But the thing is, common as dirt—clay actually—is, there really aren't that many places in the city it could have come from. I'm going to cross-hatch information in the computer, find all the spots closest to the city where the clay might have been picked up, and try to narrow the list from there. You see, it was carried in on the murderer's shoes."

"Thank you, sir. I thought perhaps he brought it in in a parcel."

"I don't mean to patronize you, Alfred."

"Of course not, sir."

"It's just that to narrow this down, to take the Sherlock Holmes approach, you determine where the clay might have come from and—"

Joe R. Lansdale

"This last murder, sir...all the murders. They occurred at Center Station, did they not?"

"Yes, but it's the clay I'm concerned with. That's what—"

"The location of the murders is not too terribly far from the Old Gotham City Cemetery, sir. The murderer might well have gotten the clay on his shoes there. It seems a logical possibility to me. Or am I being too presumptuous in my untutored way to suggest such a thing? What he might have been doing there I've no idea. A picnic, perhaps.... You have a very ugly look on your face, Master Wayne."

"That will be all, Alfred."

"Yes, sir, eat your clam chowder. I'll come for the tray after awhile. Shall I serve tea in your study later?"

"I don't think so."

"Very good, sir." Alfred walked to the elevator that led up to Wayne mansion.

Bruce said to the old butler's back. "You're a smart aleck, Alfred, but I couldn't do without you."

Alfred stepped into the elevator and clasped his hands in front of him, and just before the elevator door closed, said, "Of course not, sir."

BATMAN CASE FILE A-4567-C, informal notes (computer entry—October 20)

In the late afternoon I got in contact with Jim and picked him up at his home and drove him over to the Old Gotham City Cemetery. We climbed over the wall because the gate was locked with a chain and padlock and I didn't want to pick the lock because it looked old and I thought it might go to pieces. Jim fussed when I boosted him over the wall. He claims I pushed his face into the wall to smash his cigar. I told him it was an accident. I told him he should look at photographs they've taken after autopsies of smoker's lungs. I told him the nicotine stains his mustache. He told me to go to hell.

We looked around and found a shovel and an open grave. I couldn't make out much about the marker, but the clay there was the kind found at the murder sites; I ran it through lab work when I got back. I bet Alfred's guess was correct, that the murder site clay came from the cemetery. Its close proximity to the murders was just too much of a coincidence. Add to that the uncovered grave, and I thought we'd got some interesting connections.

I got the grave marker cleaned off with some mild acid from my utility belt while Jim held the flashlight for me and cursed. Patience is not one of Jim's virtues. I worked on the marker until I could make out a name—Rufus Jefferson.

Jim promised to run it through his computer at the station and I came back here and did the same. What we both came up with was that Rufus Jefferson died in 1904 at the hands of a Gotham City policeman after committing the fourth of a series of murders, all of them quite like those being committed now by Subway Jack.

Jim said that when his computer records played out, he went downstairs and checked through the old files, the ones not on the computer. He found out that Jefferson was tracked down by a Sergeant Griffith and was aided by a writer named David Webb who later wrote a book that contained his experience in the matter. The book was titled *Followers of the Razor*.

I checked with the public library, as well as some of the smaller libraries in the city, and Gotham City Library said that they had a copy listed in their files, in the reserve section, but that it was missing—stolen perhaps.

Curiouser and curiouser.

Joe R. Lansdale

I got back on the computer and tied in with libraries across the country and found that Stephen F. Austin University Library in Nacogdoches, Texas, had a copy of the book in their rare book section. I have made arrangements through Jim to have it sent to us by overnight mail.

Maybe there's something there that can help us, something that might explain our current murderer's connection with that old grave and Rufus Jefferson.

(Excerpts from later A-4567-C file entries—October)

...book is fascinating, and in spite of its incredible subject matter, is convincing. Up to a point. I'm not sure I'm ready to accept a dimensional murderer, but I've seen some pretty strange things, and if nothing else, there may be a psychological tie-in with...

...the librarian said that after I called she started a little investigation of her own. She says that a young man by the name of Jack Barrett checked out a lot of books in that section, and told her he was looking for material on psychopathic killers for a research paper. She said she wasn't accusing the young man, but I might want to check him out and ...

...discreet inquiries show that Jack Barrett has been an excellent student, until this month. His professor in criminology told me in confidence that he had been acting strangely, and suddenly started cutting classes. He thought it might be problems at home or with a girl...

...University has provided Jack Barrett's address, and I plan to notify Jim so we can follow and check out...

JAMES W. GORDON (one week later)

I have a feeling we're both right and wrong about this Barrett guy, but can't explain it. There's been something funny about this case, right from the start.

Subway Jack

We stationed men outside Barrett's apartment and we've been following him around all week. Batman's working the rooftops a lot. When Barrett goes out, Batman moves across the tops of the buildings like a shadow, like a spider... well, like a bat.

What we got here is a guy that doesn't do much. He's quit the University, and about all he does is walk to the subway entrance and ride the subways all day. He goes over to Center Station and stands around and looks at people, especially the bag ladies.

That part is interesting, of course, but there's a look about this guy like he really doesn't want to be there, that it's all against his will. He walks like his knees are being lifted by puppet strings, and until he gets to the subway he doesn't notice much.

Then he notices plenty about the bag ladies, and he seems to have a thing about the moon. It's always dark when he comes back, and he often stops to look at it. Or what he can see of it. It's been cloudy lately and the clouds cover the moon most of the time. It's little more than a sliver anyway, but he stares at it like he hates it. He keeps one hand in his pocket at all times.

Batman says he thinks he's waiting for a clear night. The idea of the moon being bright ties in with Webb's writings in *Followers of the Razor*. He says the weather report says tomorrow will be a little better, especially early morning—some clear moments with a slight threat of rain. He feels things just might break tomorrow.

I don't know about the moon stuff, but I have a feeling he's right—just one of those gut things. If Barrett does make his move tomorrow—if he is in fact Subway Jack— I hope we'll be ready.

Joe R. Lansdale

GOTHAM CITY STREETS (2 a.m., October 31)

Jack Barrett came out of his apartment and down the steps and onto the street. The tension inside him beat like a drum. He tightened his hand around the razor in his coat pocket and looked at the late night (early morning) moon. It had grown brighter and slightly thicker, and tonight the cloud cover was thin, though the forecast called for rain. The air had a mild tang to it, like the sting of a too-close shave.

He went down the street, walking briskly, not looking at much, except the moon from time to time, and then he heard a horn blare and he turned and looked at the street. There was a taxi rolling along slowly and the window on the passenger side was down. The driver leaned across the seat and called, "Looking for a ride somewhere?"

Barrett shook his head.

"Bad night for walking. Might get wet. You'll sure get cold."

"No money," Barrett said, and walked faster.

The taxi kept coasting. the driver said, "Heck with it, buddy. I hate to see a man walk on night like this, and I'm not getting any action anyway. This one's on the house if you want to get in. What am I doing anyway, huh?"

Barrett stopped walking and the taxi stopped moving Barrett looked at the moon. It was clear now, and he felt the urge swelling up inside him. The taxi would be better than grabbing the subway at Maynard Street and taking it over to Center. It was still a long walk to Maynard. He looked at the driver and said, "All right." He got in the back of the taxi and took a sideways look at the driver. He was big, old guy with a touch of gray whisk-white hair, a rubbery mouth, and wrinkles deep enough to hide quarters in. Maybe he reminded the old guy of his grandson or something. "Take me to Center Station, if that's okay."

Subway Jack

"I invited you," the driver said, and pulled away from the curb. He glanced in the mirror at his passenger and said, "You look a little under the weather, buddy. You been sick?"

"I been sick all right," Barrett said. "You wouldn't believe how I been sick."

"Another reason not to walk. Nights like this are criminal."

"Tell me about it," Barrett said as he leaned back and closed his fevered eyes.

"You know," the driver said, "You got some problems, there's guys you can see. If it's not just physical, there's people you can talk to."

Barrett didn't hear him. He was thinking of the bad things he had to do, and of the ultimate darkness on the other side, a darkness split by the shine of a razor.

"Center Station," the driver said. "Hey, Center Station."

Barrett opened his eyes. He didn't feel rested. His heart was beating faster. He was hot and his head was full of fuzz. He put his hand in his pocket and felt the razor. It was warm. It was starting to sing. He knew the driver couldn't hear it. It only gave its notes to him.

He wanted to take the razor out of his pocket and throw it away. He wanted to take it and slash someone—the driver maybe. He wanted to do all those things, yet none of them.

He said, "Thanks," and got out of the taxi. He went down the subway steps and out of sight.

The taxi driver drove around the corner, found a spot with a few shadows, and parked there. He took off his face by grabbing his hair and ripping up. The mask came free with a sound like a grape being sucked. He ran his hand through his dark hair and over his handsome features; the mask had pinched his face some. He slid out of his jacket and pulled at the tear-away pants and kicked off his shoes. He pulled the cowl over his head. He leaned back in the seat and opened the glove compartment and took out a walkie-talkie, switched it on and said, "He's down there, Jim. He looks rough. I tried to get him to talk. Thought he might spill his guts and I could get him to give up. No soap. You can almost feel the heat coming off this guy, and I got a feeling tonight's the night. If he's the one, and I think he is, and if he's going to do it, I've put him right in your lap."

"We're waiting," Gordon said.

Batman clipped the walkie-talkie to his belt, got out of the taxi and stood leaning against it. He wanted to go down there after Barrett, but he had made a promise to Gordon to try not to get involved. If possible, it was a promise he wanted to keep.

JAMES W. GORDON

I was dressed like a bum. I hadn't shaved in a few days, and my hair was mussed and the overcoat I was wearing had been in police storage so long it smelled mildewy. To add to that, I had poured a little Mad Dog 20/20 over the front of it. The stink of the mildew and the wine gave me motivation for my role. Maybe I could start a new career in the movies. I could play winos. The hours couldn't be any worse.

I put the walkie-talkie in my coat pocket and got out one of my cigars and lit it. Maybe a bum ought not to have a good, whole cigar, but you got to draw the line somewhere. It was either smoke some of my rope, or start pacing.

Subway Jack

I thought of Batman topside, and wished suddenly we hadn't made a deal for him to try to stay out of things so the department could claim the collar. Now and then I got the heat from the folks upstairs saying we relied on Batman too much. Could be.

Anyway, I had just gotten the cigar lit good when I saw Barrett coming down the steps, into the subway. He was weak and tired and sick-looking. He wore a ring of sweat beads around his forehead like a band of pearls. He staggered a little. He looked mostly at the ground.

I leaned against the subway wall and tried to appear drunk. He went on by me without looking up. I let him go on a ways before I took a gander and saw him walking along the edge of the subway landing. I kept thinking he might fall over onto the rails.

Still, there was something about him, a kind of mood in the air that made me reach inside my coat and touch the butt of my .38 for luck. I make a quick, soft call on the walkie-talkie, warned my people up ahead, then went on behind him at a distance, moving as smoothly and silently as I could.

Finally, I saw the bag lady pushing her shopping cart, coming about even with Barrett, humming to herself. Mertz looked good in the disguise, if a little bulky and broad-shouldered for a washed-out bag lady. He had his head down and the gray wig hung around his face and his constant five-o'clock shadow.

I went over behind one of the concrete supports, leaned against it, spat my cigar out, and stepped on it. I peeked around the edge of my hiding place and put my hand in my coat and felt the .38, then waited.

Barrett went right on by Mertz.

Well, we had another "bag lady" plant on down a ways, and Crider had the far end cut off with three plain-

Joe R. Lansdale

clothes if things got nasty. I have to admit, I was disappointed. I didn't get out in the field much these days, and when I did, I was there because I expected something to happen. I began to think that mood I had felt in the air was old age.

I was about to step from behind the support and start walking toward Mertz when Barrett turned abruptly and started back.

Mertz pretended not to notice, but I knew he had because he stopped pushing the cart and put his hand inside it, burying it under the junk he had there. I assumed he had a hold of his revolver.

I was about to pull my head back out of sight when I saw something that kept me from it; something that froze my eyes to Barrett and his shadow.

His shadow jutted out long and thick to his right, and suddenly Barrett fell to the left, flat as a cardboard cutout, and the shadow rose upright to take his place—only it wasn't a shadow anymore. It was a huge, top-hatted figure with a face as dark as tailpipe corrosion, eyes that sparked like shorted-out electrical sockets and this mouth overpacked with teeth as thin and sharp as knitting needles.

His loose coat and pants were ragged and the color of water-stained rawhide. He was wearing human heads for shoes; his ankles tapered like those of a goat and slid snuggly into the open mouths. When he walked, the heads came down on the cement with a noise like overripe fruit falling. To his left, floating flat against the cement, was a pale, pink shadow with the general appearance of Jack Barrett; it twitched in mimicry of the dark man's moves.

The dark man's right arm went up and I could see a flash of metal in his jug-size fist. The arm came down as Mertz jerked the revolver from the cart, turned, and fired.

Subway Jack

The dark man soaked the bullet up and kept coming. The razor flashed and I saw Mertz's hand fly onto the subway tracks. It twitched there momentarily like a spider trying to crawl.

Then the world went hot and kaleidoscopic. There was a sensation of reality collapsing in upon itself, of a malig nant universe pushing into our own, like a greased weasel attempting to navigate a tight tunnel.

Blood spurted from Mertz's wrist, made an arc, and hung in the air like a twisting tube of red neon. Shadows fluttered damply and the light flowed as if it were boiling honey. The subway rails quivered and writhed. The support I was leaning against turned soft as a sponge. The inside of my head was on fire and I was melting. The air screeched.

Then it all went away. I felt solid again. The rails quit moving. Shadows ceased to flutter. The light was firm and bright. Blood from Mertz's wrist shattered its neonlike tube and splattered to the cement and blossomed into rosy puddles.

The razor wove through the air like a conductor's baton during a tense musical movement. Mertz, without time for so much as a wimper, went to pieces.

Then the dark man came for me. I pulled the revolver and snapped off six shots. It didn't bother him. I fumbled for my speed loader and pushed in six more. I shot straight at his face now, all six, rapid fire. I could see where the loads were striking him on the cheeks and chin and below the nose, but the holes closed up rapidly as if his flesh were quicksand and my bullets were no more than a series of sad little victims who had stumbled in.

He was so close I could smell him. An odor like exhaust fumes, factory smoke, and open sewers.

Joe R. Lansdale

The razor went up and caught the light. I ducked low, leaped, and rolled and tumbled over the subway landing, hitting my back across one of the rails. The impact sent a jolt through my spine, and momentarily I was paralyzed. I expected to look up and see the leering face of that big bastard looking over the landing at me, showing me his razor.

That didn't happen. I felt a vibration in the rails that told me a train was coming. I managed to get up and limp to the far side, nestle myself into an indention there with my back against the wall.

I still had my .38, but I was out of shells, and besides, what did it matter? As a matter of habit, I put it in its holster.

Crider and the three plainclothes had heard the shots and they came running. They were almost on the big guy. They were firing their guns, and not having any better luck than I had.

I yelled, "Run for it," but they didn't hear me above the shots and the thunder of the oncoming train. Just as that top-hatted behemoth grabbed Crider by the throat and lifted him above his head and slashed at one of the plain-clothes with the razor, the train jetted in front of me and all there was for me to see was its metal side and its many lighted windows—a rickity-tick-tack of glass and steel.

I pushed back as tight as I could against the wall and felt the wind from the train and heard the screech and rattle of the rails, trying not to imagine what horrors were occurring across the way.

It seemed like a century, but the train finally went by and I saw that the big man was gone from the landing. Crider and the plainclothes were spread all over it. It looked like a slaughterhouse floor. On the wall, written in large, bloody letters was: COMPLIMENTS OF SUBWAY JACK—5

Subway Jack

MORE AND THAT MAKES 8. I DON'T JUST DO THE LADIES. Some distance away, heading topside up the steps, I could see Barrett. He was stumbling. The razor dangled from his hand as if it were a long, silver finger.

I got out the walkie-talkie and tried to make my voice firm. "Batman. He's coming up. He's Barrett now. It's like that book says. It's for real. He changes."

"I got him, Jim."

Under most circumstances I would have believed that. I've seen Batman take some weird ones. But this time...even Batman might not be enough.

I got my feet under me and went across the rails and pulled myself onto the landing, then started toward the steps after Barrett.

BATMAN (topside)

Batman, he's thinking about what Jim said, about how Barrett changes, about that book, *Followers of the Razor* and about the God of the Razor; he's thinking if Jim says it's so, then it's so, and he feels something rare for him, something that matches the moments in his dreams when he sees his parents die and feels the presence of the man-bat at his back, and that rare thing is almost impossible for him to identify—but that rare thing is fear. A quick skuttle goes up his backbone and hits his brain, and then melts away as all his experience and training takes over and he sees Barrett coming out of the subway, wild-eyed, looking up at the sky, trying to spot the moon.

Instinctively, Batman cranes his neck and sees that the moon is behind those rain clouds that were promised, and then he looks back at Barrett who is racing across the street at a lumbering run that makes him look like a puppet being jerked along by strings.

Joe R. Lansdale

Traffic is nonexistent at this early morning hour, and Batman crosses the street easily, making good time and gaining on Barrett. Then everything becomes lighter, touched with silver, and Batman knows the moon is out. He sees that when Barrett puts his right foot forward it is dressed not in a shoe but in a head, and then the left foot goes forward and it is the same, and then the man running before him, moving much faster, is not Barrett, but the dimensional creature Webb called the God of the Razor.

The God of the Razor leaps more than he runs, and Batman thinks of the legends of Spring-heel Jack, then pours it on, trying to close, wondering in the back of his mind what he'll do with this thing if he catches it.

Up they go, the God of the Razor leading Batman through a narrow, twisting path that winds its way through brush and shrubs and trees, and Batman knows they are fast approaching the top of the hill where the walls of Old Gotham Cemetery stand.

The God is really moving and he's almost to the cemetery wall, and with a flex of his whip-thin legs he leaps up and out and over it, effortlessly as a kangaroo, and the weak little shadow of Barrett follows after him and slips over the wall like a wet, pink sheet.

Batman reaches the wall, jumps and grabs and swings himself over. And the clouds have done their trick again. Standing by the stone cross that marks the grave of Rufus Jefferson—the dark open tomb yawning to his right—is Barrett, head hung low, the razor held loosely against his leg.

"It isn't me," Barrett says, his voice weak as a signal from space. "I got no control. Nothing stops the power of the moon but the clouds. Just the clouds. Long as he's got the moon and the need, he's got control. You got to know it's not me. It's him."

Subway Jack

Barrett waves the razor at the God's shadow that is thin and watery, bent, and partially out of sight down the open grave.

"I know, son," Batman says, and he moves quickly toward Barrett. "Give me the razor and we'll set you free."

"Not like that," Barrett says. "Can't give it to you. Not the way you want anyway. Not the way I want. Just the way he wants. I..."

The clouds twirl away from the face of the moon.

JAMES W. GORDON

I saw Batman cross the street and head toward the brush and trees that bunched at the bottom of the cemetery hill. I went after him.

I couldn't keep up with him, he was moving too fast. The cigar smoke that lived in my lungs wasn't helping either. When I got to the cemetery wall I saw the last of Batman's cape going over. Then I saw Barrett topping the rise of the hill inside the cemetery; the hill that was higher than the cemetery walls.

My back was killing me. My sides felt as if they were being skewered. I couldn't help myself. I dropped to one knee and tried to get my wind.

When the skewers quit twisting, I got up, staggered to the wall, and dragged myself over.

When I hit the ground it wasn't Barrett standing on the hill, it was the big top-hatted monster. The little pale shadow of Barrett was thin as watered milk and getting thinner. I guess the God of the Razor was growing stronger and stronger, and Barrett weaker and weaker, with every transformation.

Batman was charging up the hill with his head slightly bent, charging like a locomotive. His cloak fanned out high and wide behind him like a Japanese fan. Then he

Joe R. Lansdale

ducked and the cape dropped down some and I could see the faces of the monster and the flash of his razor as it sliced off part of Batman's cape and sent it fluttering away. Then Batman leaped high as the big guy bent low and swiped back at Batman's ankles. When Batman came down, he brought his fists together at the back of the big guy's head.

It didn't seem to do much. Maybe it made him mad. The big guy jerked upright and his top hat didn't even sway. He raised his arm above his head and brought the razor down like a hammer.

Batman shot out a hand and grabbed the big wrist, stopping the blow. The big guy used his other hand to grab Batman's throat and—

SPLASH PANEL

Complete Side View Body Shots of Batman and the God of the Razor: The scene is dark, but not too dark. (Don't forget that cold slice of moon.) Batman's head is being pushed back and his teeth are clenched and we can see the muscles swelling in his jaw. His muscles push out his costume in the shoulders, arms, and legs. He has his left hand up, holding back the hand with the razor, and he is using his right hand to push at the God's other wrist, trying to break the strangle hold the God has on his throat. Batman's cape is twisted and we can see it hanging limp and touching the ground as his knees are bent and he is forced back.

The God of the Razor looks happy as a winning politician. His smile is so wide his teeth are brushing his ear lobes. His left eye (the only one visible to us) appears to be lit from within by a hot, red bulb. His ragged coat is bulging with muscles. His thin legs are knotted with the same, and his prominent head-shoe is splitting across the forehead and teeth are popping out of the mouth like popcorn because of the pressure of his left-leg-forward stance. Barrett's pathetic, near colorless shadow is flowing loose and distorted into the darkness of the open grave.

In the background is a great oak tree. Through its naked branches we can see the silver curve of the moon, and to the right of that, a dark cloud.

A yellow block at the bottom of the panel alerts us to what Batman sees as his head is being slowly pushed back:

IN WHAT SEEMED LIKE HIS FINAL MOMENTS, BATMAN SAW A DARK RAIN CLOUD ABOUT TO SLIDE OVER THE FACE OF FRAGMENTED MOON LIKE A WOOL MASK.

JAMES W. GORDON

—I pounded up the hill toward them and dove for the big guy's leg, grabbing him just above the knee.

I might as well have been a flea. He kicked me off and I tumbled away.

I was on my hands and knees, about to try it again, when suddenly it grew darker, and in that same instant, Batman, still clinging to the big guy, dropped to his right side and stuck out his foot to catch the creep's knee and send him flipping forward toward the open grave.

Just before he disappeared into the darkness, I saw that it was Barrett falling, the big guy's shadow following after him like black silk sliding over polished bone.

From inside the tomb came a snapping sound, and Batman rolled to a squatting position and produced from his utility belt a little penlight. He shone it into the grave. I went up the hill and stood behind him and looked down into the little pool of light. I watched as Batman moved it up and down Barrett's body.

Joe R. Lansdale

Barrett lay face up with his back across the steps. His head was pointing down, and his legs had swiveled so far his buttocks were pointing up. You didn't have to be a doctor to know his spine was snapped.

His right hand was outstretched and open. The hilt of the razor was in his palm, the blade gleamed against a damp, moss-covered, stone step.

It started to rain.

BATMAN CASE FILE A-4567-C, last of the informal notes (computer entry—November 1)

The Barrett boy was boxed up and sent home to his parents. I don't know what Jim told them—an accident of some kind, I think. Whatever he said, it wasn't enough. No one could say enough, but at least Barrett won't be charged for his crimes. It won't look good on Jim's record that Subway Jack got away. The files will read OPEN, but that's fair play for Barrett. The killings have stopped and it wasn't Barrett anyway. It was the God of the Razor, and he's gone to his dimension to wait for some other fool to let him loose.

That won't be as easy next time.

Jim and I carefully stored the razor in a metal box and hid it. After Barrett and what was left of Jim's men were hauled away, we took the box and put it in a metal drum and filled the drum with concrete. We let it set and harden. The next night we met at the docks and took a police launch out to the middle of Gotham Bay and pushed the drum overboard.

It's deep there. I like to think that's the end of the bad things the razor can do. It won't bring Jim's men back, and it won't bring those bag ladies back, and it won't bring Jack Barrett back, but at least it's out of sight and grasp of others.

Subway Jack

When we were through we sat there on the boat and looked at the water, watching the bay gather in drops of rain. I thought about my parents and how their deaths had led me to become Batman. I thought about my strangest cases. I thought about the God of the Razor, over there safe and happy in his wild dimension. I thought about a lot of things.

Then, just before morning, the light rain stopped and I looked out at the water where we had pushed over the barrel, and there on the face of the bay was the wavering reflection of

the...

...moon.

This story is for Keith Lansdale

Northwestward

ISAAC ASIMOV

homas Trumbull said to Emmanuel Rubin in a low
voice, "Where the devil have you been? I've been
trying to reach you for a week."

Rubin's eyes flashed behind the thick lenses of his
spectacles, and his sparse beard bristled. "I was away at
the Berkshires for a week. I was *not* aware I had to apply
for permission to you for that."

"I wanted to speak to you."

"Then speak to me now. Here I am. That is, supposing
you can think of something intelligent to say."

Trumbull looked about hastily. The Black Widowers
had gathered for the monthly banquet at the Milano, and
Trumbull had managed to arrive on time because he was
the host.

He said, "Keep your voice down, for God's sake,
Manny. I can't speak freely now. It's about," his voice
dropped to a mere mouthing, "my guest."

"Well, what about him?" Rubin glanced in the direction of the tall, distinguished-looking elderly man who
was conversing with Geoffrey Avalon in the far corner.

Northwestward

The guest was a good two inches taller than Avalon, who was usually the tallest person at the gathering. Rubin, who was ten inches shorter than Avalon, grinned.

"I think it does Jeff good to have to look up now and then," he said.

"Listen to me, will you?" said Trumbull. "I've talked to the others, and you were the only one I was really worried about and the only one I couldn't reach."

"But what are you worried about? Get to the point."

"It's my guest. He's peculiar."

"If he's your guest—"

"Sh! He's an interesting guy, and he's not nuts, but you may consider him peculiar and I don't want you to mock him. You just let him be peculiar and accept it."

"How is he peculiar?"

"He has an *idée fixe*, if you know what that means."

Rubin looked revolted. "Can you tell me why it's so necessary for an American with a stumbling knowledge of English to say 'idée fixe' when the English phrase 'fixed idea' does just as well?"

"He has a fixed idea, then. It will come out because he can't keep it in. Please don't make fun of it, or of him. *Please* accept him on his own terms."

"This violates the whole principle of the grilling, Tom."

"It just bends it a little. I'm asking you to be polite, that's all. Everyone else has agreed."

Rubin's eyes narrowed. "I'll try, but so help me, Tom, if this is some sort of gag—if I'm being set up for something—I'll stand on a stool if I have to, and I'll punch you right in the eye."

"There's no gag involved."

Rubin wandered over to where Mario Gonzalo was putting the finishing touches on his caricature of the

Isaac Asimov

guest. Not much of a caricature at that. He was turning out a Gibson man, a collar ad.

Rubin looked at it, then turned to look at the guest. He said, "You're leaving out the lines, Mario."

"Caricature," said Gonzalo, "is the art of truthful exaggeration, Manny. When a guy looks that good at his age, you don't spoil the effect by sticking in lines."

"What's his name?"

"I don't know. Tom didn't give it. He says we ought to wait for the grilling to ask."

Roger Halsted ambled over, drink in hand, and said in a low voice, "Tom was looking for you all week, Manny."

"He told me. And he found me right here."

"Did he explain what he wanted?"

"He didn't *explain* it. He just asked me to be nice."

"Are you going to?"

"I will, until I get the idea that this is a joke at my expense. After which—"

"No, he's serious."

Henry, that quiet bit of waiter-perfection, said in his soft, carrying voice, "Gentlemen, dinner is served."

And they all sat down to their crableg cocktails.

James Drake had stubbed out his cigarette since, by general vote, there was to be no smoking during the actual meal, and handed the ashtray to Henry.

He said, "Henry's announcement just now interrupted our guest in some comments he was making about Superman, which I'd like him to repeat, if he doesn't mind."

The guest nodded his head in a stately gesture of gratitude and, having finished an appreciative mouthful of veal marengo, said, "What I was saying was that Superman was a travesty of an ancient and honorable tradition.

Northwestward

There has always been a branch of literature concerning itself with heroes; human beings of superior strength and courage. Heroes, however, should be supernormal but not supernatural."

"As a matter of fact," said Avalon, in his startling baritone, "I agree. There have always been characters like Hercules, Achilles, Gilgamesh, Rustum—"

"We get the idea, Jeff," said Rubin, balefully.

Avalon went on, smoothly, "Even half a century ago, we had the development of Conan by Robert Howard, as a modern legend. These were all far stronger than we puny fellows are, but they were not godlike. They could be hurt, wounded, even killed. They usually were, in the end."

"In the *Iliad*," said Rubin, perfectly willing, as always, to start an argument, "the gods could be wounded. Ares and Aphrodite were each wounded by Diomedes."

"Homer can be allowed liberties," put in the guest. "But compare, say, Hercules with Superman. Superman has X-ray eyes, he can fly through space without protection, he can move faster than light. None of this would be true of Hercules. But with Superman's abilities, where is the excitement, where's the suspense? Then, too, where's the fairness? He fights off human crooks who are less to him than a ladybug would be to me. How much pride can I take in flipping a ladybug off my wrist?"

Drake said, "One trouble with these heroes, though, is that they're musclebound at the temples. Take Siegfried. If he had an atom of intelligence, he took care never to show it. For that matter, Hercules was not remarkable for the ability to think, either."

"On the other hand," said Halsted, "Prince Valiant had brains, and so, especially, did Odysseus."

"Rare exceptions," said Drake.

Isaac Asimov

Rubin turned to the guest and said, "You seem very interested in storybook heroes."

"Yes, I am," said the guest, quietly. "It's almost an *idée fixe* with me." He smiled with obvious self-deprecation. "I keep talking about them all the time, it seems."

It was soon after that that Henry brought on the baked Alaska.

Trumbull tapped his water glass with his spoon at about the time that Henry was carefully supplying the brandy. Trumbull had waited well past the coffee, as though reluctant to start the grilling, and even now the tinkle of metal against glass seemed less authoritative than customary.

Trumbull said, "It is time we begin the grilling of our guest, and I would like to suggest that Manny Rubin do the honors."

Rubin favored Trumbull with a hard stare, then said to the guest, "Sir, it is usual to ask our guest to begin by justifying his existence, but against all custom, Tom has not introduced you by name. May I, therefore, ask you what your name is?"

"Certainly," said the guest. "My name is Bruce Wayne."

Rubin turned immediately toward Trumbull, who made an unobtrusive, but clear, quieting gesture with his hands.

Rubin took a deep breath and managed a smile. "Well, Mr. Wayne, since we were speaking of heroes, I can't resist asking you if you are ever kidded about being the comic-strip hero, Batman. Bruce Wayne is Batman's real name, as you probably know."

"I do know," said Wayne, "because I *am* Batman."

Northwestward

There was a general stir at the table at this, and even the ordinarily imperturbable Henry raised his eyebrows. Wayne was apparently accustomed to this reaction, for he sipped at his brandy without reacting.

Rubin cast another quick glance at Trumbull, then said carefully, "I suppose that, in saying this, you imply that you are, in one way or another, to be identified with the comic-strip character, and not with something else named Batman, as, for instance, an officer's orderly in the British army."

"You're right," said Wayne. "I'm referring to the comic-strip character. Of course," and he smiled gently, "I'm not trying to convince you I am literally the comic-strip Batman, cape, bat symbol, and all. As you see, I am a three-dimensional living human being, and I assure you I am aware of that. However, I *inspired* the existence of the comic-strip character Batman."

"And how did that come about?" asked Rubin.

"In the past, when I was considerably younger than I am now—"

"How old are you now?" asked Halsted, suddenly.

Wayne smiled. "Tom has told me I must answer all questions truthfully, so I will tell you, though I'd prefer not to. I am seventy-three years old."

Halsted said, "You don't look it, Mr. Wayne. You could pass for fifty."

"Thank you. I try to keep fit."

Rubin said, with a trace of impatience, "Would you get back to my question, Mr. Wayne? Do you want it repeated?"

"No, my memory manages to limp along satisfactorily. When I was considerably younger than I am now, I was of some help to various law enforcement agencies. At that time, there was money to be had in these comic strips

Isaac Asimov

about heroes, and a friend of mine suggested that I serve as a model for one. Batman was invented with a great many of my characteristics and much of my history.

"It was, of course, distinctly romanticized. I do not go about with a cape and never have done so, or had a helicopter of my own, but I did insist that Batman be given no supernatural powers but be restricted to entirely human abilities. I admit they do stretch it a bit sometimes. Even the villains Batman faces, although they are invariably grotesque, are exaggerations of people with whom I had problems in the past and whom I helped put out of circulation."

Avalon said, "I see why Superman annoys you, then. There was a television Batman for two seasons. What about that?"

"I remember it well. Especially Julie Newmar playing Catwoman. I would have liked to have met her as an opponent in real life. The program was played for laughs, you know, and good-natured fun."

"Well," said Drake, looking about the table and carefully lighting a cigarette now that the meal was over (and cupping it in his hand in the obvious belief that that would trap the smoke), "you seem to have had an amusing life. Are you the multimillionaire that the comic-strip Batman is?"

"As a matter of fact," said Wayne, "I'm very well off. My house in the suburbs is elaborate, and I even have an adjoining museum, but you know, we're all human. I have my problems."

"Married? Children?" asked Avalon.

"No, there I also resemble my alter ego—or he resembles me. I have never been married and have no children. Those are not my problems. I have a butler who tends to my household needs, along with some other servants who are of comparatively trivial importance."

"In the comic strip," said Gonzalo, "your butler is your friend and confidant. Right?"

"Well—yes." And he sighed.

Rubin looked thoughtful, and said, "Tell us about the museum, Mr. Wayne. What kind of museum is it? A headquarters for science and criminology?"

"Oh, no. The comic strip continues successfully, but my own day as an active upholder of the law is over. My museum consists of curios. There have been a great many objects made that have been based on the Batman cartoon and his paraphernalia. I have, I believe, at least one of every single piece ever made in that fashion, Batman notepaper, large-scale models of the Batmobile, figurines of every important character in the strip, copies of every magazine issue featuring the character, cassettes of all the television shows, and so on.

"It pleases me to have all this. After all, I am sure the strip will survive me, and it will be the part of me that will be best remembered after my death. I don't have children to revere my memory and I have done nothing very much in my real life to make me part of history. These evidences of my fictional life are the best I can do to bring myself a little nearer to immortality."

Rubin said, "I see. Now I'm going to ask a question that may cause you to feel a little uncomfortable, but you must answer. You said—Oh, for God's sake, Tom, this is a legitimate question. Why don't you let me ask it before you start jumping."

Trumbull, looking both abashed and troubled, sank back in his chair.

Rubin said, "A little while ago, Mr. Wayne, you said that you too have your problems and, almost immediately

Isaac Asimov

afterward, when you mentioned your butler, you looked distinctly uncomfortable. Are you having trouble with your butler?—What are you laughing at, Tom?"

"Nothing," said Trumbull, chuckling.

Wayne said, "He's laughing because he bet me five dollars that if I just answered any questions about me, and did so naturally and truthfully, the Black Widowers would have this out of me within twenty minutes, and he's won."

"I take it, then, that Tom Trumbull knows about this."

"Yes, I do," said Trumbull, "but I'm dealing myself out of this one for that reason. The rest of you handle it."

"I would suggest," interposed Avalon, "that Tom and Manny both quiet down and that we ask Mr. Wayne to tell us his troubles with his butler."

"My butler's name," began Wayne, "is Cecil Penny-worth—"

"Don't you mean Alfred Pennyworth?" put in Halsted.

"No interruptions," said Trumbull, clinking his water glass.

Wayne said, "That's all right, Tom. I don't mind being interrupted. Alfred Pennyworth was indeed my butler originally, and with his permission, his name was used in the strip. However, he was older than I, and in the course of time, he died. Characters do not necessarily age and die in comic strips, but real life is rather different, you know. My present butler is Alfred's nephew."

"Is he a worthy substitute?" asked Drake softly.

"No one could ever replace Alfred, of course, but Cecil has given satisfaction—" here Wayne frowned "—in all but one respect, and there my problem rests.

"You must understand that I sometimes attend conventions that are devoted to comic-strip heroes. I don't make a big issue of my being Batman, and I don't put on a cape or anything like that, although the publishers sometimes hire actors to do so.

"What I do is set up an exhibition of my Batman memorabilia. Sometimes my publishers set up the more conventional items for sale, not so much for the money that is taken in as for the publicity, since it keeps the thought of Batman alive in the minds of people. I have nothing to do with the commercial aspect. What I do is exhibit a selection of some of the more unusual curios that are *not* for sale. I allow them to be seen and studied, while I give a little lecture on the subject. That has its publicity value, too.

"Needless to say, it is necessary to keep a sharp eye on all the exhibits. Most of them have no intrinsic value to speak of, but they are enormously valuable to me and sometimes, I'm afraid, to the fans. While the vast majority of them wouldn't think of appropriating any of the items, there are bound to be occasional individuals who, out of a natural dishonesty or, more likely, an irresistible desire, would try to make off with one or more items. We have to watch for that.

"I am even the target for more desperate felons. On two different occasions there have been attempts to break into my museum; attempts that, I am glad to say, were foiled by our rather sophisticated security system. I see you are smiling, Mr. Avalon, but actually my memorabilia, however trivial they might seem, could be disposed of quietly for a considerable sum of money.

"One item I have *does*, in fact, have a sizable intrinsic value. It is a Batman ring in which the bat symbol is cut out of an emerald. I was given it under circumstances that, if I may say so, reflected well on the real Batman— myself—and it has always been much dearer to me for that reason than because of the value of the emerald itself.

Isaac Asimov

It is the *pièce de résistance* of my collection, and I put it on display only very occasionally.

"A year or so ago, though, I had promised to appear at a convention in Minneapolis, and I did not quite feel up to going. As you see, I am getting on in age, and for all my fitness program, my health and my sense of well-being are not what they once were.

"I therefore asked Cecil Pennyworth to attend the convention as my substitute. On occasion I have asked him to fill in for me, though, till then, not at a major convention. I had promised an interesting display, but I had to cut that to Cecil's measure. I chose small items that could all be packed systematically—so they could be quickly checked to make sure the display was intact—in a single good-sized suitcase. I sent Cecil off with the usual unnecessary admonition to keep a close watch on everything.

"He called me from Minneapolis to assure me of his safe arrival and, again, a few hours later, to apprise me of the fact that an attempt had been made to switch suitcases.

" 'And failed, I hope,' I said.

"He assured me that he had the right suitcase and that the display was safe and intact, but he asked me if I really felt he should display the ring. You see, since I was sending only small items, I felt that I was, in a way, cheating my public, and I therefore included my ring so that at least they could see this rarest and most valuable of all my curios. I told Cecil, therefore, that he should certainly display the ring, but keep the sharpest of eyes upon it.

"I heard from him again two mornings later, when the convention was drawing to a close. He was breathless and sounded strained.

" 'Everything is safe, Mr. Wayne,' he said, 'but I think

Northwestward

I am being followed. I can duck them, though. I'm going northwest, and I'll see you soon.'

"I said, rather alarmed, 'Are you in danger?'

"He only said, 'I must go now,' and hung up.

"I was galvanized into activity—it's the Batman in me, I suppose. I threw off all trace of my indisposition and made ready for action. It seemed to me that I knew what was happening. Cecil was being tracked by someone intent on that suitcase, and he was not himself a strong person of the heroic mold. It seemed to him, therefore, that he ought to do the unexpected. Instead of returning to New York, he would try to elude those who were after him, and quietly head off in another direction altogether. Once he had gotten away from his pursuers, he could then return to New York in safety.

"What's more, I knew where he was going. I have several homes over the United States, which is the privilege of one who, like myself, is quite well off. One of my homes is a small and unobtrusive place in North Dakota, where I sometimes go when I feel the need to isolate myself from the too-unbearable insinuations of the world into my private life.

"It made good sense to go there. No one but Cecil and me and some legal representatives knows that the house in question belongs to me. If he got there safely, he could feel secure. He knew that to indicate to me that he was going northwestward would have complete meaning to me, and would mean nothing to anyone who might overhear him. That was clever. He had to hang up quickly because, I presume, he was aware of enemies in the vicinity. He had said, 'I'll see you soon,' by which, it seemed to me, he was begging me to go to my North Dakota home to join him. Clearly, he wanted me to take over the responsibility of defense. As I said, he was not the heroic type.

"He had called me in the morning, and before night fell, I was at my North Dakota house. I remember being grateful that it was early fall. I would have hated to have to go there with two feet of snow on the ground and the temperature forty below."

Rubin, who was listening intently, said, "I suppose that your butler, in weather like that, would have chosen some other place as a hideout. He would have told you he was going southeastward and you would have gone to your home in Florida, if you have one."

"I have a home in Georgia," said Wayne, "but you are correct otherwise. I suppose that is what he would have done. In any case, when I arrived in North Dakota, I found that Cecil was not yet there. I got in touch with the people who care for the place in my absence (and who know me only as a 'Mr. Smith'), and they assured me that nobody, to their knowledge, had arrived. There were no signs of any very recent occupancy, so he could not have arrived and been waylaid in the house. Of course, he might have been interrupted en route.

"I spent the night in the house, a very wakeful night as you can imagine, and an uncomfortable one. In the morning, when he still had not arrived, I called the police. There were no reports of any accidents to planes, trains, buses, or cars that could have possibly applied to Cecil.

"I decided to wait another day or so. It was possible, after all, that he might have taken a circuitous route or paused on the way, 'holed up,' one might say, to mislead his pursuers, and would soon take up the trip again. In short, he might arrive a day late, or even two days late.

"On the third morning, however, I could wait no more. I was certain, by then, that something was very wrong. I

Northwestward

called my New York home, feeling he might have left a message there, and was rather berating myself for not having made the call earlier for that purpose; or, if no message had been received, to have left the number at which I could be reached when the message came.

"At any rate, on the third morning I called, and it was Cecil who answered. I was thunderstruck. He had arrived on the afternoon of the day I had left. I simply said I would be home that night and, of course, I was. So you see my difficulty, gentlemen."

There was a short silence at the rather abrupt ending to the story, and then Rubin said, "I take it that Cecil was perfectly safe and sound."

"Oh, yes, indeed. I asked him about the pursuers, and he smiled faintly and said, 'I believe I eluded them, Mr. Wayne. Or I may even have been entirely mistaken and they did not really exist. At least, I wasn't bothered at all on my way home.' "

"So that he got home safely?"

"Yes, Mr. Rubin."

"And the exhibition curios were intact?"

"Entirely."

"Even the ring, Mr. Wayne?"

"Absolutely."

Rubin threw himself back in the chair with an annoyed expression on his face, "Then, no, I don't see your difficulty."

"But why did he tell me he was going northwestward? He told me that distinctly. There is no question of my having misheard."

Halsted said, "Well, he thought he was being followed, so he told you he was going to the North Dakota place. Then he decided that either he had gotten away from the pursuers, or that they didn't exist, and he thereupon

Isaac Asimov

switched his plans, and went straight to New York without having time to call you again and warn you of that."

"Don't you think, in that case," said Wayne, with some heat, "he might have apologized to me? After all, he had misled me, sent me on an unnecessary chase into North Dakota, subjected me to a little over two days of uncertainty during which I not only feared for my collection, but also felt that he might be lying dead or badly injured somewhere. All this was the result of his having told me, falsely, that he was heading northwestward. And then, having arrived in New York, he might have known, since I wasn't home, that I had flown to the North Dakota house to be with him, and he might have had the kindness to call me there and tell me he was safe. He knew the North Dakota number. But he didn't call me, and he didn't apologize to me or excuse himself when I got home."

"Are you sure he knew that you were in North Dakota?" asked Halsted.

"Of course I'm sure he knew. For one thing, I told him. I had to account for the fact that I had been away from home for three days. I said, 'Sorry I wasn't home when you arrived, Cecil. I had to make a quick and unexpected trip to North Dakota.' It would have taken a heart of forged steel not to have winced at that, and not to have begun apologizing, but it didn't seem to bother him at all."

There was another pause at this point, and then Avalon cleared his throat in a deep rumble and said, "Mr. Wayne, you know your butler better than any of us do. How do you account for this behavior?"

"The logical feeling is that it was just callousness," said Wayne, "but I don't know him as a callous man. I have evolved the following thought, though: What if he had been tempted by the ring and the other curios himself? What if it was his plan to dispose of them for his own benefit? He could tell me that he was being pursued, and that would send me off on my foolish mission to North Dakota so that he would have a period of time to put away his ill-gotten gains somewhere and pretend he had been robbed. See?''

Rubin said, ''Do you know Cecil to be a dishonest man?''

''I wouldn't have said so, but anyone can yield to temptation.''

''Granted. But if he did, he resisted. You have everything. He didn't steal anything.''

''That's true, but his telling me he was going northwestward and then never explaining why he had changed his mind tells me that he was up to skulduggery. Just because he was too fainthearted to go through with it this time doesn't excuse him. He might be bolder the next time.''

Rubin said, ''Have you asked him to explain the northwestward business?''

Wayne hesitated. ''I don't like to. Suppose there is some explanation. The fact that I would ask him about it would indicate that I didn't trust him, and that would spoil our relationship. My having waited so long makes it worse. If I ask now, it would mean I have brooded about it all year, and I'm sure he would resign in resentment. On the other hand, I can't think what explanation he might have, and my not asking him leaves me unable to relax in his presence. I find I am always keyed up and waiting for him to try again.''

Rubin said, ''Then it seems that if you don't ask him, but convince yourself he's guilty, your relationship is ruined. And if you do ask him and he convinces you he's innocent, your relationship is ruined. What if you don't ask him, but convince yourself he is innocent?''

''That would be fine,'' said Wayne, ''but how? I would

love to do so. When I think of my long and close associa-
tion with Alfred Pennyworth, Cecil's uncle, I feel I owe
something to the nephew—but I must have an explanation
and I don't dare to ask for it.''

Drake said, "Since Tom Trumbull knows about all
this—What do you say about it, Tom?''

Wayne interposed. "Tom says I should forget all about
it."

Trumbull said, "That's right. Cecil might have been so
ashamed of his needless panic that he just can't talk
about it.''

"But he *did* talk about it," said Wayne, heatedly. "He
casually admitted that he might have been mistaken about
being pursued, and did so as soon as I got home. Why
didn't he apologize to me and express regret for the
trouble he had put me to?''

"Maybe *that's* what he can't talk about," said
Trumbull.

"Ridiculous. What do I do? Wait for a deathbed confession? He's twenty-two years younger than I am, and he'll
outlive me."

"Then," said Avalon, "if we're to clear the air between
you, we must find some natural explanation that would
account for his having told you he was heading northwestward and that would also account for his having failed to
express regret over the trouble he put you to.''

"Exactly," said Wayne, "but to explain both at once is
impossible. I defy you to.''

The silence that followed endured for quite a while
until Rubin said, "And you won't accept embarrassment
as an explanation for his failure to express regret?''

"Of course not.''

"And you won't ask him?''

Northwestward

"No, I won't," said Wayne, biting off the remark with decision.

"And you find having him in your employ under present conditions is wearisome and nervewracking."

"Yes, I do."

"But you don't want to fire him, either."

"No. For old Alfred's sake, I don't."

"In that case," said Rubin, gloomily, "you have painted yourself into a corner, Mr. Wayne. I don't see how you can get out of it."

"I still say," growled Trumbull, "that you ought to forget about it, Bruce. Pretend it never happened."

"That's more than I can do," said Wayne, frowning.

"Then Manny is right," said Trumbull. "You can't get out of the hole you're in."

Rubin looked about the table. "Tom and I say Wayne can't get out of this impasse. What about the rest of you?"

Avalon said, "What if a third party—"

"No," said Wayne instantly. "I won't have anyone else discussing this with Cecil. This is strictly between him and me."

Avalon shook his head. "Then I'm stuck, too."

"It would appear," said Rubin, looking about the table, "that none of the Black Widowers can help you."

"None of the Black Widowers seated at the table," said Gonzalo, "but we haven't asked Henry yet. He's our waiter, Mr. Wayne, and you'd be surprised at his ability to work things out.—Henry!"

"Yes, Mr. Gonzalo," said Henry, from his quiet post at the sideboard.

"You heard everything. What do you think Mr. Wayne ought to do?"

"I agree with Mr. Trumbull, sir. I think that Mr. Wayne should forget the matter."

Isaac Asimov

Wayne rolled his eyes upward and shook his head firmly.

"However," Henry went on, "I have a specific reason for suggesting it, one that perhaps Mr. Wayne will agree with."

"Good," said Gonzalo. "What is it, Henry?"

"I couldn't help but notice, sir, that all of you, in referring to what Mr. Pennyworth said on the phone, mentioned that he said he was going northwestward. That, however, isn't quite so. When Mr. Wayne first mentioned the phone conversation, he quoted Mr. Pennyworth as saying, 'I'm going northwest.' Is that correct?"

Wayne said, "Yes, as a matter of fact, that is what he said, but does it matter? What is the difference between 'northwestward' and 'northwest'?"

"A huge difference, Mr. Wayne. To go 'northwestward' can only mean traveling in a particular direction, but to go 'northwest' need not mean that at all."

"Of course it needs to mean that."

"No, sir. I beg your pardon, Mr. Wayne, but 'to go northwest' could mean one's intention to take a plane belonging to Northwest Airlines, one of our larger plane lines."

The pause that followed was electric. Then Wayne whispered, "Good Lord!"

"Yes, sir. And in that case, everything explains itself. Mr. Pennyworth may have been mistaken about being followed, but, even if he thought he was, he was not sufficiently worried over the situation to follow any circuitous route. He told you he was taking a Northwest airplane, speaking of the matter elliptically, as many people do, and assuming you would understand.

"Despite the name of the plane line, which may have been more accurate at its start, Northwest Airlines serves

Northwestward

the United States generally and you can take one of its planes from Minneapolis to New York, traveling eastward. I'm sure that but for the coincidence that you had a home in North Dakota, you might have interpreted Mr. Pennyworth's remark correctly.

"Mr. Pennyworth, under the impression he had told you he was flying to New York, said he would see you soon—meaning, in New York. And he hung up suddenly probably because his flight announced that it was ready for boarding.

"Good Lord!" said Wayne, again.

"Exactly, sir. Then when Mr. Pennyworth got home and found you had been to North Dakota, he could honestly see no connection between that and anything he might have done, so that it never occurred to him to apologize for his actions. He couldn't have asked you why you had gone to North Dakota; as a servant, it wasn't his place to. Had you explained of your own accord, he would have understood the confusion and would undoubtedly have apologized for contributing to it. But you remained silent."

"Good Lord!" said Wayne, a third time. Then, energetically, "I have spent over a year making myself miserable over nothing at all. There's no question about it. Batman has made a terrible mistake."

"Batman," said Henry, "has, as you yourself have pointed out, the great advantage, and the occasional disadvantage, of being only human."

Museum Piece

MIKE RESNICK

CATALOG

Special JOKER Exhibition in the Batman Hall of the Gotham Museum

(Catalog Notes by Richard Grayson, Esq.)

Exhibit I:

Lethal 10,000-volt "joy buzzer" with which the notorious Clown Prince of Crime dispatched five different people, including two members of his own gang.

Exhibit 1A:

Rubber gauntlets and thick-soled rubber boots created especially for the Batman by Reuben Kittlemeier (deceased). By allowing the Joker to think him unprepared and helpless, the Batman was able to get close enough to arrest him while the electric charge passed harmlessly through the safely grounded crime fighter.

Exhibit 2:

This was a two-headed coin (note that both heads are defaced) that the Joker had manufactured during the brief period of time that he allied himself with Two-Face, another criminal kingpin. Two-Face was known to always flip a coin when deciding between mercy and brutality, or even committing a crime versus obeying the law, and the Joker managed to plant this coin on Two-Face's person so that he would always elect to follow in the Joker's criminal footsteps.

Exhibit 2A:

This coin seems identical to the coin in Exhibit 2, but there is one vital difference: this coin, created by the Batman, is weighted so that, when flipped in the air, it will always land on its edge. The coin, which the Batman managed to substitute for the Joker's coin, so unnerved Two-Face that he turned upon his former ally, and during the confusion the police, under the leadership of Commissioner James Gordon, were able to capture both villains.

Exhibit 3:

This is the automatic pilot mechanism from the *Pagliacci*, a blimp that the Joker loaded with a deadly gas and aimed at the Thomas Wayne Memorial Stadium during the fourth quarter of the Gotham Bowl on New Year's Day.

Mike Resnick

Exhibit 3A:

This is a child's bow and hunting arrow with which the Batman improvised his last-second response to the Joker's threat. The blimp, struck in midair, dispersed its gas over the sea, and not a single member of the crowd of 75,000 was harmed.

Exhibit 4:

This normal-appearing fountain pen actually releases an ultrasonic blast that temporarily paralyzes its victim, and was used on the Batman when the Joker disguised himself as an autograph seeker.

Exhibit 4A:

This is a mask of the Joker's first known murder victim, which the Batman wore beneath his cowl as a safety measure during that period of time when the Joker publicly threatened to reveal his secret identity. When he was momentarily overcome by the ultrasonic fountain pen (Exhibit 4), it was this mask that the Joker revealed beneath the Batman's cowl. The shock of seeing his long-dead victim caused the Joker to go into a near-catatonic trance, a condition that persisted until hours after the Batman regained consciousness and returned his arch-enemy to Arkham Asylum.

Exhibit 5:

Remains of exploding baseball, capable of killing everyone within a radius of fifty feet, which the Joker substituted for the normal baseball that the mayor was supposed to throw out on Opening Day.

Exhibit 5A:

This is a chemically treated catcher's mitt that the Batman, disguised as the catcher for the Gotham Giants, used to muffle the explosion just prior to apprehending the Joker.

Exhibit 6:

This earthen jar holds the contaminant with which the Joker planned to poison Gotham City's water supply.

Exhibit 6A:

These eyebrows, blue-tinted contact lenses, false nose, and blond wig formed the disguise the Batman used to impersonate the Joker's henchman while substituting half a gallon of perfectly harmless Vitamin C for the contaminant.

Exhibit 7:

Clipping of hair, purportedly taken from Robin's head. The Joker, aware that Robin had been called out of town on a case while the Batman was otherwise occupied, used this in an attempt to entrap the Batman by convincing him that Robin was his prisoner.

Exhibit 7A:

Electron microscope with which the Batman analyzed the clipping in Exhibit 7, and proved that the hair came from a dog infested with a certain species of flea that could only come from Olson's Kennel on the shore of the Gotham River. He relayed this information to the police,

Mike Resnick

who, led by Commissioner James Gordon, broke into the kennel and captured the Joker's entire gang.

Exhibit 8:

Coffin used by the Joker when he faked his own death to gain access to the North Gotham Mausoleum.

Exhibit 8A:

Sound detector with which the Batman detected the Joker's heartbeat in the mausoleum where the criminal's loot from the Gotham Diamond Exchange robbery was hidden.

Exhibit 9:

Juggling balls filled with knockout gas, which the Joker used during his attempt to steal more than $200,000 of gate receipts from the Gotham Circus.

Exhibit 9A:

False clown nose worn over breathing filter by the Batman, who masqueraded as a Gotham Circus clown to apprehend the Joker.

Exhibit 10:

This mounted snake is a rare South African variety whose poison leaves victims with a grotesque smile on their faces. This is not the actual snake used by the Joker, but is a member of the same species. (Courtesy of Gotham Museum of Natural History.)

Exhibit 10A:

"Trump," the mongoose that Batman borrowed from the Gotham Zoo to dispatch the Joker's killer snake. ("Trump" is on loan from the Gotham Zoo. Please do not feed him or insert fingers into his cage.)

Exhibit 11:

This is the phony television camera the Joker used when masquerading as a member of the media during an inaugural dinner for the mayor. The small red button on the left fires the handgun that is hidden beneath the lens.

Exhibit 11A:

The lens from the Joker's false television camera (see Exhibit 11). The Batman, suspecting just such an attack, had Robin sneak into the Joker's headquarters and replace the original lens with this specially treated lens, which distorts the user's perceptions and causes him to fire eighteen inches to the left of his target.

Exhibit 12:

Membership card to the exclusive Gotham Millionaires Club, made out to one Joe Ker. With this card, the Joker gained access to Gotham's richest men and women, whom he planned to hold for ransom.

Exhibit 12A:

Gold-plated honorary membership card to the Gotham Millionaires Club, offered to the Batman by unanimous vote of the membership after the Dark Knight had foiled the Joker's scheme. He declined membership, and donated the card to the Gotham Museum.

Exhibit 13:

This final exhibit is the cannister of lethal gas with which the Joker planned to kill himself after his most recent capture by the Batman.

Exhibit 13A:

Laughing-gas cannister substituted for Exhibit 13 by the Batman, which left the Joker laughing all the way to Arkham Asylum, where he currently resides. It is rumored that he is laughing still.

Wise Men of Gotham

EDWARD WELLEN

Bruce Wayne wore a bemused smile as he mingled with the other guests aboard billionaire real estate developer Jack King's luxurious yacht. He also wore his Batman outfit.

It seemed a risk worth taking, for this was a costume ball—and he had already spotted three other Batmen. And—truth to tell—his outfit, somewhat the worse for wear after his latest adventure, looked the least authentic of all.

That, however, was not the cause of his bemusement. It had suddenly struck him how ironic it was that such a glittering occasion had such a sad cause.

Jack King and his wife Queena were throwing a benefit bash for the homeless of Gotham City.

On his way here to the yacht basin, under the neon that fogged the stars, Bruce Wayne had passed many ragged shapes huddled in stinking doorways or nestled in cardboard cartons or crumpled over steaming sidewalk grates, and he had dropped here a dollar and there a dollar. He looked around now at the other guests; they too had seen the homeless—but the homeless seemed already far away and forgotten in the babble and clink and band rhythm.

All about him in the dazzling ballroom, the men as well as the women flaunted their jewels and stuffed their faces. All appeared well-clothed, well-fed, well-housed.

Handsome Jack King and beautiful Queena King most of all. He knew them behind their gem-encrusted masks. Jack was the eye-patched pirate and Queena was the harem slave.

Others of the elite were also easy to spot. Hizzoner the Mayor moved about, glad-handing. Mayor Ned Notts and developer Jack King were at political odds, and had had their shouting matches by way of newspaper headlines and talk shows. However, the plight of the homeless— toward which neither had demonstrated any particular sensitivity—now drew them together in this fleeting show of care. Their teeth gleamed in big smiles at one another for the benefit of press flashbulbs and television lights. The charity ball brought Jack King favorable publicity to offset the bad, such as evicting the poor—and so adding to the homeless—to make way for his grandiose projects, and no doubt allowed him to charge off considerable expenses against taxes. The charity ball afforded Mayor Notts, who was running for re-election for the nth time, a welcome opportunity to put a new gloss on his tainted administration and to shore up his eroding popularity.

Keeping close company with Hizzoner were his political backer, Rudolph Newkirk, the newspaper magnate; Hizzoner's crony Housing Commissioner Sam Rubin; and Hizzoner's temporary ally in the election campaign, environmentalist Glenn Dubois.

Wayne marveled at the rampant hypocrisy. It seemed an ego thing between Nott and King, because Mayor Nott

Edward Wellen

had cosied up to other developers of luxury housing; Nott and King each appeared to covet the role of Numero Uno in Gotham City. Newkirk's papers were doing a hatchet job on King, printing exposés of King's projects, hinting at big bribes for permits and tax abatements, and interviewing the poor harassed out of buildings standing in King's juggernaut path—while Newkirk himself was an insatiable gobbler-up of papers and television stations. Commissioner Rubin had done little to rehabilitate abandoned buildings to house uprooted families; for some unfathomable reason he found it more practical to cram them into rundown-but-expensive, rat-and-roach-infested, single-room-occupancy hotels. Environmentalist Dubois had stood in the way of building out into the bay because of what that would do to the fish population, but had offered no alternatives. And here all of them joined with the Kings to raise money for the homeless.

Another personage Bruce Wayne easily picked out was his old friend Police Commissioner Gordon. Gordon's presence took away much of the bad taste in Wayne's mouth.

Commissioner Gordon had come as a musketeer, but security seemed too much on his mind to let him play the part with ease. He kept up the pose with gallant flourishes and courtly bows whenever he met someone he knew, or was introduced to someone new. But his knuckles were white on his sword as he checked the placement of his men and women, and he jerked around whenever a voice grew too shrill or a glass suddenly crashed to the ballroom floor.

Wayne smiled wryly. He knew what preyed on Gordon's mind. This past week the media had been full of the fevered auction at which King outbid even the Japanese for a Rembrandt. The battered gavel had finally knocked the masterpiece down to King for eighty-six million dollars.

Commissioner Gordon's big fear had to be that someone would use the swirling confusion of the charity ball to steal the Rembrandt from under his patrician nose, for the famous painting hung in a stateroom here aboard the *Île de Joie.*

Some of the secrecy about it evaporated for a favored few. Wayne grew aware of this when he realized that Jack and Queena King were taking turns leading the more privileged of the guests—identified by discreet face-card pins that had been sent along with tickets when those invited to the ball RSVP'd with a fat check made out to the charity—on guided tours of the yacht's treasures, of which the Rembrandt was the highlight.

Bruce Wayne sported such a pin, and now found himself tapped by Jack King personally for such a tour. King patted him on the shoulder and nodded toward an elevator.

Wayne found himself matching stride with a sweaty musketeer wearing a face-card pin as they followed King to the elevator.

"Enjoying this nice little party, Commissioner Gordon?" Wayne asked.

The musketeer shot the Batman a sharp look. "Is that you, Bruce?"

Wayne nodded.

Gordon sighed almost explosively. "How I wish you were the real Batman instead of ..."

"Instead of a useless rich idler?"

"I didn't say that."

"No, you bit your tongue. But no matter. What's got you wishing for Batman's help?"

Edward Wellen

Gordon leaned close. "Let's keep this hush-hush—I don't want to panic all of Gotham City. Riddler's back in town."

Wayne's senses quickened at the mention of his old foe. The pointy ears of his cowl seemed to stand up on their own. "How do you know?"

Gordon drew a color photo from the pocket of his cloak. "Here's his handiwork. An unidentified corpse found floating in the harbor. One of his damnable riddles tattooed on the body."

Wayne took the gruesome picture and stared at a naked chest and read the rhyme printed on it. The period at the end of the rhyme was a lurid bullethole.

Art thou?
How now!
Art not
When shot.

—Yours truly, the Riddler

Wayne handed the photo back and they caught up with the small party and remained silent in the full elevator as it descended two decks.

They brightened a bit at sight of the treasures King guided them by. Few monarchs had in their lifetimes garnered so great a hoard. King's prizes would outlast him, but while he held them he took full pride in them.

The Rembrandt drew the greatest hush. It hung in a well-lit alcove; a velvet rope kept viewers at a distance.

It was the famous *The Would-Be Bride*, sometimes called *The Coscinomancer*. The painting showed a young girl seemingly in the first awareness that her sexuality gave her power—and finding it both exhilarating and frightening. She held a pair of shears with a sieve hanging from the points of the blades, and she stood frozen hopefully, prayerfully apparently having just called the name of a suitor and now waiting to see if the turning of the sieve would tell her he was the one for her.

The viewers stood similarly frozen by the power of the painter.

SSWISSHHH-THUNNKK!

A blow dart whizzed through the open doorway and into the masterpiece, landing dead center on the robust breast. A note was impaled on the shank of the dart.

Wayne whirled with a black flutter and dashed to the doorway. Too late—a like black flutter had vanished up the companionway at the far end of the passage.

He turned back to the room. No one else seemed to have glimpsed the black-caped vandal. At least, no one spoke of having seen another Batman blow the dart and flee. Wayne breathed thankfully.

Commissioner Gordon had produced a walkie-talkie and was calling for assistance.

Wayne shot a glance at King. It seemed to him that King looked singularly unperturbed for one whose eighty-six-million-dollar prize possession had just sustained damage.

But he had no more time to ponder that. Gordon's call had brought a plainclotheswoman who swung into action Wayne closely observed.

Plainclotheswoman! Detective Sergeant Heather Mortimer, as Gordon introduced her, wore an elegant Empire gown, and more than fulfilled her role.

She swung briskly into action. From somewhere on her person she produced plastic gloves and put them on. Carefully, she removed the dart from the painting. She had

Edward Wellen

to pull hard to free the dart, and in doing so rubbed her
forearm against the canvas. As her hand came away with
the dart gripped firmly in it, Wayne noticed a faint
smudge on her bare forearm. The smudge might have been
there beforehand, but he doubted that. Forensics might
find spittle on the dart and from it determine the blood
type, and even the DNA pattern, of the vandal. Before putting it into an evidence bag, she slipped the note off the
shank. She slid the note into a clear plastic envelope and
handed the envelope to her boss.

Wayne read the note over Gordon's shoulder.

The sage—so-called—
Of Brought-Home-the-Bacon
Will drop off to sleep
And never awaken.

   —Yours unruly, the Riddler

He imprinted it in his memory.

Wayne smiled crookedly. So that had been the Riddler
he had glimpsed—and wearing a Batman outfit! But vil-
lainous as the man was, the Riddler had not pinned the
vandalism on Batman. The Riddler had too much ego to
give credit to another for anything he himself had done.

Gordon's detail, and King's own security people, had
sealed off all exits, but Wayne felt sure the Riddler had
already made good his escape—had found some way off
the yacht or some hiding place aboard it.

And so it proved.

After his own identity had been checked—and
vouched for by Police Commissioner Gordon himself—
Wayne descended the gangway and headed thoughtfully
home. The Riddler had given him much to think about.

Wise Men of Gotham

Alfred, the English butler, shook his head mournfully as he put the Batman costume away. He tsk-tsked and tut-tutted at its deplorable state.

"I feel dreadful about having let you go out in this, sir. I did do my best, though, on short notice."

"Yes, I'm afraid I waited till the last minute to advise you of the ball."

Alfred, once started, had to finish his bill of particulars. "I bespoke a dozen new outfits from our Saville Row tailors—using the safe address for delivery—but they were booked solid. Meanwhile I thought to make do locally; I tried all the costumers in the yellow pages, sir, but it seems they had rented out every one of their Batman suits."

From the bedroom window of the penthouse suite, Bruce Wayne could make out the lights of the *Île de Joie* at its slip in the yacht basin. "Somehow I guessed that might be the case, Alfred."

"If I may say so, sir, I'm afraid you have only your own popularity to blame for that."

Wayne turned from the window to eye Alfred. "Alfred, let me pick your brains."

Alfred looked alarmed. "Beg pardon, sir?"

"Tell me about Gotham."

Alfred's alarm increased. He looked out the penthouse window at the millions of lights. Where to begin? What to describe? How could he possibly do Gotham City justice?

Wayne followed Alfred's glance and laughed apologetically. "I mean the English Gotham, the place our Gotham gets its name from. The Wise Men of Gotham and all that."

Edward Wellen

"Oh, *that* Gotham, sir." Alfred looked first relieved, then severe. "That Gotham is a village in Nottinghamshire. I've never been there myself." He conveyed that he wouldn't be caught dead there. "'Wise Men' is a misnomer, sir. A jest, as it were. The Gothamites appear to have been quite a collection of fools." By his tone he washed his hands of them.

"Hmmm. And that's all you know?"

"Afraid so, sir. Will there be anything else?"

"Just wake me early tomorrow."

"As you wish, sir."

Alfred winced as the master crunched the toast so thoughtfully that crumbs spilled all over everything.

As soon as the hour approached decency, Wayne dialed Dr. Amicia Sollis and invited her to breakfast. She accepted sleepily, seeming both pleased and puzzled.

He picked her up at Gotham City University and took her to the Skyways Building and to the restaurant atop it.

They talked of this and that as they ate—Amicia seeming as always to seek some glimpse into the true nature of Bruce Wayne, for it was clear she did not take him at face value but sensed some depth to the shallow man-about-town. At last she shoved the dessert plate aside and put hand on chin and elbow on table and looked into his eyes.

"Time for me to sing for my lunch. What's the tune?"

So, while the restaurant revolved high above the streets of midtown Gotham City, he told the sleek, dark-haired professor of linguistics about the Riddler's having pinned a note to the Rembrandt. He recited it to her.

"That's scary," she said. "What do you make of it?"

He frowned. "'Brought-Home-the-Bacon' seems an obvious play on 'Got-ham,' and it follows that the Riddler

is threatening the lives of the Wise Men of Gotham—whoever *they* may be. I've heard about the Wise Men of
Gotham—the Nottinghamshire Gotham, I mean—but I
don't know the story behind them. You're the authority on
folklore, so give."

She took a moment to gather her thoughts before she
answered. "Some say it goes back to King John in the
1200s. This was the tricky, greedy, cowardly king who was
forced to sign the Magna Carta. The story goes that King
John planned to seize some of the Gothamites' land for a
hunting ground and to cut a highway across their pas-
tures. That would have been bad enough, but in addition
the people would be expected to provide services to the
court and to the flock of courtiers. The townspeople got
together and plotted to change King John's mind. They
engaged in idiotic pursuits to fool the king's messengers
into thinking the local yokels would make unsuitable
neighbors. Things like trying to drown an eel in a pond;
burning down a forge to get rid of a wasps' nest; hoisting
a wagon to the top of a barn to shade the roof; planting
a hedge around a cuckoo's nest—or, in another version,
joining hands around a thornbush—to shut in a cuckoo
so it would sing all year long."

"And it worked?"

"It worked. At least, so far as I know, there's no royal
hunting lodge at Gotham." She smiled. "That's the legend.
But the real source of tales about the fools of Gotham may
have been the absurd customary services attached to land
tenure there."

"Such as?"

She shrugged. "I can't tell you off the top of my head.
Perhaps such things as still obtain right in our own neigh-
borhood. Do you know that in one of the suburbs of *this*
Gotham, the town must come up with 'one fatte calfe'

Edward Wellen

each year forever if the descendants of the original owners of the land demand it?"

They had finished the meal but she had given him much to chew on.

He drove her back to the campus. As he watched her walk gracefully into the gothic building he felt his face burn. His Batman preoccupations got too much in the way of Bruce Wayne's life. Why hadn't he thought to invite Amicia to attend the ball with him? Why had he thought of her only after the fact? Not only did she deserve better of him but it was his great loss. Next time...

He phoned Commissioner Gordon's office and got through to Gordon, though the man sounded bothered and beset.

"Afraid I don't have much time, Wayne. Another of Riddler's notes."

"A threat?"

"A particular threat—but I don't think I should say any more about it. If only I could get word to Batman."

"You have some way of signaling to him, don't you?"

"Yes, but how can I be sure he's on the lookout for it?"

"He has a bat's radar. Anyway, you have no choice but to try."

"True." Gordon sighed. "I'll get on it." Then he said wearily, "did you have something you wanted to speak to me about?"

"Nothing that can't wait. You have enough to worry about. Let me get out of your hair. Goodbye."

"Thanks for being so understanding. Goodbye."

Wayne had a weather eye out to the night sky and Commissioner Gordon did not signal in vain.

Wise Men of Gotham

Sitting out on the terrace of his penthouse suite though March made itself felt, Wayne spotted the searchlight beam. It swept the heavens with a bat silhouette. The bat flew due east, then south–southwest. That formed a 7, and meant a rendezvous at the corner of Seventh Avenue and Seventh Street at seven p.m.

Wayne checked his watch. He had a half hour to get there.

The beam had switched off at the end of the 7; it switched on again and repeated the figure. It would keep on doing that until seven o'clock, when Gordon would give up if Batman failed to keep the rendezvous.

Wayne leapt inside. "Alfred!"

Alfred was ready, the Batman outfit folded on his arm. He helped Wayne get it on. Alfred had done his best, laundering and steampressing the cowl and the cape, but was still disdainful of the outfit's shabbiness.

Batman smiled to himself. Clothes did not make the bat.

Commissioner Gordon started as the black figure slid from the shadows. Then he gave a groan of relief. "Batman!"

"It's about the Riddler?"

"How did you know?"

"Bats have good ears."

"That's almost what Wayne said."

"Who?"

"Never mind. He doesn't really matter. Nice fellow and all that, but..."

"I know the type." Batman grew brisk. "What's our old friend the Riddler up to now?"

For answer, Commissioner Gordon drew three pictures from an inner pocket.

Edward Wellen

Batman unclipped a penlight from his belt and examined the topmost photo. It showed the punctuated message tattooed on the torso of the floater.

"We've identified him as a promising young art student," Gordon said. "Classmates told our homicide detectives that he had been flashing money and dropping hints about having received some mysterious commission. Then he himself suddenly dropped out of sight."

"Ah! That explains the 'Art thou?' and 'Art not.'" Batman's mouth went grim. "The Riddler, with his twisted logic, took someone whose subject was art—and made him into an object of art!"

Batman turned to the second photo. What it showed was also familiar, but he let Gordon explain it.

"This is a picture of a note Riddler pinned to the famous Rembrandt on Jack King's yacht."

Batman nodded. "Here he's threatening the Wise Men of Gotham."

Gordon stared at Batman's shadowy face. "Amazing! It took the best brains of the Department all night and all day to figure that out!"

Batman gave a modest wave of dismissal and concentrated on the third photo.

"That," Gordon said, "is a copy of Riddler's latest message." His voice shook with mixed rage and fear. "I found it on my own desk in my own office at headquarters. How he could penetrate that fortress—"

"Every fortress is penetrable," Batman said absently. He was busy with the message.

Smoking the beehive is best
For combing out honey.
Burning both house and wasps' nest
Is stupid but funny.
  —Yours bluely, the Riddler

Wise Men of Gotham

Gordon was peering at him prayerfully, as one hoping for a miracle. In a hushed voice Gordon asked, "Well, Batman? Do you have any idea what this means?"

"It means trouble," Batman said. Then, with a smile, he lifted Gordon's gloom. "Yes, I have a pretty good idea what it means."

Before Gordon could ask further, Batman took a step back and was one with the shadows.

The Valley Forge Club was the last stronghold of male elitism, an exclusive organization with a policy of admitting none but White Anglo-Saxon Protestants.

A meat truck was making a delivery. The driver and his helper were unloading it. Batman waited his chance to shoulder a ham, and bent under it so that it obscured his face and upper body as he walked inside. He jettisoned the ham before he reached the meat locker, leaving it for others to wonder how it had got into the chef's clothes closet.

Batman flitted unseen through the corridors, looking for sign of the Riddler's machinations.

Nowhere did he find anything to back his hunch, though this *had* to be the latterday counterpart of the forge and the wasps' nest in the legend of the original Gothamites as told to him by Dr. Amicia Sollis.

He reached the head of the fire stairs on what sounds told him was the floor housing the game room and the smoking lounge. He cracked the door open and sneaked a look down the hallway.

A man in blue paced away from him. Batman raised an eyebrow. Had Commissioner Gordon reached the same conclusion—that the Valley Forge Club was the Riddler's target—and provided protection?

Edward Wellen

Batman was about to call to the policeman, with the object of joining forces, when—*BONNGGGG!*—an alarm went off in his head.

It had struck Batman that the man in blue was not so much patroling as prowling. Batman, himself prowling, knew the difference.

The next minute he was not so sure. For a pair of members, cocktail glasses and cigars in hand, emerged from a room and the man in blue straightened up and gave them a snappy salute that they casually returned. Batman recognized one of them as environmentalist Glenn Dubois. If these men accepted the policeman's presence without question...

But after they had crossed the hall and vanished into a room that emitted the clicking of billiards, the man in blue once more looked on the prowl. Batman's gaze hardened.

A man in blue had entry everywhere—even into the Police Commissioner's inner sanctum.

And the Riddler had signed his challenge "Yours *bluely.*"

A shiver passed through Batman. The avenger of evil knew evil when he saw it—though it were clothed in the vestments of good!

But he bided his moment to see what the Riddler meant to do.

The man in blue came to a stop at a point where a shelf jutted from the wall. He looked around, then slid open a small door just above the shelf. Batman realized that this was the opening of a dumbwaiter. The false cop lifted a jerrican down out of the dumbwaiter.

Quickly he uncapped the jerrican and splashed its contents along the hall toward the door of the game room.

Wise Men of Gotham

Batman caught the odor of gasoline and waited no longer.

Before the Riddler could finish emptying the jerrican and strike a match, Batman had hurled himself from the stairwell, straight at the arsonist.

"Hold it right there, Riddler!"

The Riddler froze. Then his face twisted in a sneer, and he whipped out a knife.

"Steel *this* thunder, Batman!"

SWOOOSSHHHH! The Riddler's knife slashed Batman's cape. Batman felt anger on Alfred's account. Alfred would be really put out.

Batman smiled fiercely. "Close—but no scar!"

Then, launching a savage attack of his own, he kicked the Riddler's wrist and the knife flew flashing out of his hand. But as he moved to grab the Riddler, he slipped on a gasoline slick. The Riddler took advantage of this and pulled the dumbwaiter box higher so that it cleared the shaft. Then he dived into the opening and escaped down the rope.

Batman had to comfort himself with the knowledge that he'had foiled the Riddler's attempt on this one of the Wise Men of Gotham.

They met at the corner of 11th Avenue and 11th Street at 11 p.m.

"Great work, Batman!" Commissioner Gordon said, but worry and foreboding overlay his pleasure and gratitude. "Do you think you can pull it off again?"

"Another Riddler threat?"

Gordon nodded and produced a photocopy.

Batman—with the Riddler's knife slash in his cape neatly stitched, though Alfred had bitten off the thread

Edward Wellen

with a most unbutlerish snarl—stepped out of the shadows to examine the latest challenge from the Riddler.

High now chuck the wain
To shade the roof.
Why not the mare, too,
In its behoof?

    —Yours coolly, the Riddler

Batman felt a chill sharper than the night's. The outmoded word *wain* for *wagon* had struck home.

Could the Riddler have pierced Batman's identity, Bruce *Wayne*, or was it merest and purest coincidence?

"Are you feeling all right, Batman?"

Batman looked at Gordon's worried face, made ghastly by the streetlight, and forced a smile. "I feel fine."

He had to put thoughts of his own peril out of his mind. He had to fix his wits on puzzling out the threat to another Wise Man of Gotham.

With a swirl of his cape, he melted into the darkness.

Unaware of affronting Alfred, Wayne let the breakfast crepes grow cold while he rifled through the morning papers. The Riddler appeared to be targeting public figures on the order of environmentalist Glenn Dubois, whose life Batman had saved...together with the lives of many innocents who would have perished had the Valley Forge Club burned down. What were the latest doings of such public figures?

Wayne frowned as he scanned the pages. The words *chuck* and *wain* had suggested to him that *chuck wagon* might be the key to what the Riddler had in mind. Wayne perused the columns in hopes of coming across some public event involving something even faintly hitched to a chuck wagon—a rodeo, Meals on Wheels, a dude ranch, a new fast-foods eaterie...

BINGO!—and none of the above.

This very afternoon, Hizzoner, the Mayor, would be attending the opening of a new display at the Planetarium.

That started a whole new line of thought, and prompted a call to Dr. Amicia Sollis.

She seemed not to mind that this was getting to be a habit. She smiled across the restaurant table at him. "Yes, 'Chuck' is a recognized nickname for 'Charles.' And yes, there is such a thing as 'Charles's Wain.' Though I hardly think the 'mare' in the rhyme would be a Charley horse."

Wayne nodded. He thought it likely that "Mare" was a play on "mayor." But he did not voice the thought, he merely gestured for Amicia to go on.

Which she did after taking a sip of claret to moisten her lips. "Let's stick to 'Charles's Wain.' Some say it's named for Charlemagne, some for Charles I of England. In either case, it refers to the group of seven stars in the constellation of Ursa Major, which we in the U.S. call the Big Dipper. That group of seven stars is supposed to resemble a cart without wheels, but with a shaft horses could be hitched to." She tilted her head. "Does that help you?"

It did.

Afternoon outside, but midnight inside.

Edward Wellen

Batman lurked in the darkness under the great starry dome. His gaze roamed the auditorium, with special attention to the section reserved for the mayoral party. Grimly, he noted that those seats were directly beneath the stars of Charles's Wain.

An agitated huddle of Planetarium officials drew Batman's attention. He slipped nearer to listen and caught mention of the air-conditioning system. From what they said, it was malfunctioning. Indeed, now that his attention was on the condition of the air, the place did seem stuffy.

Just then a coveralled figure bustled up to the group.

The Planetarium director heaved a sigh of relief. "It'll be all right. The air-conditioning serviceman is here."

Batman narrowed his eyes in thought. *Air conditioning.* The Riddler had signed his challenge "Yours *coolly.*"

"I'll have a look at the vents on the roof." The voice of the coveralled figure sounded familiar.

The mayor's party arrived just then, and the officials went to greet Hizzoner. The coveralled figure stood watching until Hizzoner was seated, then made for a door marked MAINTENANCE.

Batman gave him a moment, then followed him through the door into a dimly lit space between the inner and outer shells of the great dome. The place hummed with machinery and smelled of grease. Batman caught sight of the coveralled figure already halfway up a ladder that climbed the inner shell of the dome. Batman waited at the foot of the ladder until it stopped vibrating, then climbed it in turn, careful not to shake it and give away his presence.

He reached the top in time to see the coveralled figure fit a wrench to a nut on a bolt and begin to loosen it. No doubt about it—this was the Riddler at his deadly work!

Wise Men of Gotham

From the care with which the Riddler worked the wrench, and from the give of the whole section as the nut on the bolt loosened, Batman could tell that the Riddler had previously loosened most of that section of the dome and that it would plummet to crush the mayoral party once this last bolt came free.

"Hold it, Riddler! You're one nut too many!"

The Riddler froze. Then, with a curse, he flung the wrench at Batman.

Batman did not flinch or duck. Instead, he made a neat one-handed catch. In almost the same motion with which he plucked the wrench out of the air, he hurled the wrench back at the Riddler.

BONNKK! The boomeranged wrench glanced off the Riddler's skull and caromed downward with a heavy clatter.

"Seeing stars, Riddler?"

If the Riddler was, he quickly shook off his daze and pushed himself away from Batman's—and the ladder's— side of the dome and with a prolonged and pronounced *Y-E-E-E-O-W-W-W!!!!* slid and slithered down the curve of the dome to the bottom. There was a *SPLAT!*, then silence.

By the time Batman scrambled down the ladder the Riddler was gone.

Alfred would find the grease stains on Batman's cape highly lamentable.

They met at the corner of First Avenue and First Street at one a.m.

Commissioner Gordon jumped a foot in the air. "Batman! I was expecting you, but not swooping down the guywire of a crane."

Edward Wellen

"Sorry." Maybe he should've been direct instead of derricked, but it had seemed a good idea to get a bird's-eye view of the rendezvous area beforehand and make sure they would be alone.

"Quite all right." Gordon harrumphed. "Thanks to you, Batman, Mayor Notts is still around. He had a severe heart attack when he learned of the close call. That made it another close call. But he'll pull through."

"Glad I could be of help. But you didn't summon me here so that you might deliver a bulletin on Hizzoner's medical condition. It's the Riddler again?"

Looking hopeful, Commissioner Gordon handed Batman a photocopy of a note in rhyme.

Have you heard the lewd word?

What does the cuckoo sing?

Is the wing on the bird—

Or the bird on the wing?

> *—Yours billet-doux-ly,*
>> *Yours bill-and-coo-ly,*
>>> *The Riddler*

Batman frowned but not too severely. Once again he needed Amicia's expertise.

"What's your interest in these riddles, Bruce? Are they merely an intellectual exercise?

"That's how it started out, Amicia. But my findings got passed along to Batman, who appears to have made good use of them."

Wise Men of Gotham

"You make quite a team, don't you? She leaned forward avidly over the avocados. "What's Batman really like? I'd love to meet him."

Wayne smiled. "I'm the last one to tell you what he's really like. Commissioner Gordon has yet to introduce us. But if we do meet, I'll be sure to mention your interest."

Amicia flushed. "Don't you dare!" She spooned up the last of her dessert, then touched her napkin to her mouth. "I sing for supper, the cuckoo sings for summer. The Cuckoo Song is the oldest English song set to music." She sang softly in a voice that did not reach the other diners.

"'Sumer is icumen in,
  Lhude sing cuccu!'"

She smiled. "*Lhude* doesn't mean 'lewd'; it means 'loud.' But the Riddler seems to be leering. The female cuckoo lays her eggs in the nests of other birds, who hatch them and rear them. That's how 'cuckold' came to denote the husband of an unfaithful wife. Centuries ago, in England, people would call out 'cuckoo!' to warn a husband when a known adulterer came near. Somehow, the term stuck to the husband."

Wayne leaned back. "Ah. Then I—rather, Batman—would have to look for adultery."

"You won't have to look far," Amicia said. "I'm afraid the avocados were adulterated."

Alfred woke up Wayne. "Precisely seven a.m., sir."

Wayne opened one eye and cocked it. "How do you know—*precisely?*"

Alfred gestured to the French windows giving on to the terrace. "The clock tower of the Nest Egg building, sir."

And Wayne heard the last dying note of the chimes.

Edward Wellen

He swept the covers aside and leapt to his feet. He pressed his nose to the glass and stared at the clock tower that shouldered above the clinging mists of morning. *Nest Egg*...

The Nest Egg Investment Corporation, a subsidiary of Fidelity Trust, ranked among Gotham City's most respected institutions, financial or other. The Riddler surely would count its head among the Wise Men. Foster Cavendish, the Nest Egg's CEO, had to fit the Wise Man profile—a citizen of standing and power. Was Cavendish involved in adultery? Was the Nest Egg clock a cuckoo clock?

"My Batman costume, Alfred."

"But, sir. Do you really care to be seen in it? Shouldn't you prefer to await the bespoke costumes?"

"My Batman costume, Alfred."

"Sir, do you realize this is Easter Sunday and all will be attired in their best?"

"Alfred, my Batman costume."

"Very good, sir."

Batman was a creature of the night, but the canyons of Gotham City afforded shadow by day. And where that shadow did not reach, the latest model Batmobile, with its chameleon paint and dark windows, afforded cover and concealment for stakeouts. So it was that Batman found it feasible to pick up and tail Foster Cavendish without arousing Cavendish's suspicions.

The Foster Cavendishes lived in a high-rise condominium on fashionable Eden Avenue. At half past ten a.m., Foster Cavendish emerged from the elegant front entrance and the doorman hailed a cab. Just before stepping in, Cavendish looked back and up, shifted his carry-on to his other hand, and waved. From a window near the top, a wide-sleeved arm returned the wave.

Batman followed the cab to Fitzgerald Airport and watched Cavendish pick up a ticket to Red Wing, Minnesota, then board the plane a good ten minutes before take-off. Batman smiled.

The bird would be on the wing and away from danger at the hands of the Riddler, for the Riddler would want—as a matter of pride if not honor—to carry out his threats within the borders of Gotham City.

Then Batman thought again. A bomb set to go off while the plane was still in Gotham City's airspace would fulfill the Riddler's self-imposed guidelines.

Batman had no certain knowledge that the Riddler had planted a bomb on this flight—but then he had no certain knowledge that the Riddler had not planted a bomb.

Better to be safe than sorry, as his parents had been wont to tell him before their untimely deaths at the hands of a holdup man—his eyewitnessed event that had turned him into the fearsome Batman striking terror into hearts of criminals.

He darted to a pay phone, beating out a yellow-bonneted, green-gowned woman. She folded her Easter parasol and hammered his shoulders with it while he dialed 911, but when she heard the word "bomb" in his anonymous tip she shrieked—OOOOHHH!!!—and let up.

Batman, again in the Batmobile, watched the plane disgorge its passengers and crew, a pale and trembling Cavendish among them.

ULPULPULPULPULP!!! EEPWEEPWEEPWEEPWEEP!!! The bomb squad arrived in its ululating van and searched the plane with dogs and electronic sniffers.

No bomb.

Edward Wellen

But the nonevent had shaken Cavendish. After a few drinks at an airport lounge, he got himself and his carry-on into another cab and headed home.

Batman followed, weighed down with responsibility. The anonymous tip had backfired, putting Cavendish squarely back in danger of death at the Riddler's hands. Now Batman would have to stay almost as close as Cavendish's skin if he were to protect him from the Riddler.

While the doorman assisted Cavendish and his carry-on out of the cab and into the building, Batman scooted around to the back and let himself in through the basement door. He had counted the stories to the window Mrs. Cavendish had waved from, and knew what button to press. The freight elevator took Batman to Cavendish's floor before the passenger elevator arrived.

With seconds to spare, Batman located the Cavendish nameplate, drew a lockpick from his belt, opened the door, and slipped inside.

He squeezed inside the hall closet, behind raincoats and boots. He had barely done so when the front door opened again, this time with the rattle of keys and a loud BANG! as it slammed shut and the THUMP! of the carry-on hitting the floor.

From a rear bedroom came a banshee wail. EEEEEE!!!

"It's only me, honey," Cavendish called out. "I just had a bad scare."

"You had a bad scare? What do you think this was?"

Batman peered out cautiously and glimpsed a frizz of hennaed hair and a filmy peignoir.

"Wait till I tell you, Bathsheba. Mine was a bomb scare. I let the plane take off without me. Brrr. Boy, I could use a stiff one."

Bathsheba's voice turned concerned. "Poor baby. Go into the living room and I'll pour you a tall glass."

Wise Men of Gotham

Batman waited until they had gone into the living room, then he stole out of the closet and prowled the apartment in search of a better hiding place, one that would allow him to keep a lookout for the Riddler.

As he stepped into the bedroom Bathsheba had come from, he stopped dead in his tracks. His senses told him of another presence.

He attuned himself and caught muffled breathing from beneath the king-size bed.

Moving softly, he drew near enough to the bed to grip the footboard, then with a sudden jerk and thrust he swung the bed in an arc. Then he pounced upon the form thus laid bare, before it could move.

"Got you, Riddler!" he gritted through clenched teeth as he tightened a chokehold on the man beneath him on the floor.

"Aarghh!" The man was trying to tell him something. To deny being the Riddler.

Batman took his first good look at the man, eased his grip, and slowly got to his feet. The man was Housing Commissioner Sam Rubin.

Batman quickly recovered. Rubin was sitting up, gently massaging his throat where wheals showed. He looked around and started to croak something. Batman spotted a shirt and trousers on a chair. He shoved Rubin flat, tossed the clothes onto him, and swung the bed back into place.

He owed Rubin nothing, not the covering up of Rubin's cuckolding of Foster Cavendish, not even the saving of Rubin's life—it seemed clear now that the Riddler's target was not Cavendish but Rubin. Batman would do whatever fell in with foiling the Riddler.

A buzzer sounded, and Batman listened to talk over the intercom. The doorman announced a postman with a

Edward Wellen

special delivery package for Bathsheba Cavendish that she had to sign for, and Cavendish told the doorman to let the man in.

Batman's heart pounded. *This was it!* The Riddler had signed his challenge "Billet-doux-ly"—and here came a letter carrier. It must indeed be a special delivery that brought a letter carrier on Easter Sunday.

The doorbell rang.

"I'll get it, dear." That was Bathsheba.

Batman debated with himself whether to act now or to hold off until the Riddler made his move. He decided to hold off.

The door opened.

"Why, what a lovely package!" Bathsheba called over her shoulder. "Thank you, dear. Here, you take it and open it."

"Sign here, ma'am."

"I didn't send it. You must have an unknown admirer."

"Sign here, ma'am."

"And wouldn't that be nice. Open it. I want to see what my secret lover sent me."

"Sign here, ma'am."

Before Batman could shout not to open the package, he heard paper rip.

"It's a big chocolate Easter egg!"

"How sweet!"

He did not hear another "Sign here, ma'am."

Evidently the Riddler had chosen not to wait.

Batman hurtled into the living room, grabbed the chocolate egg from Foster Cavendish, and dashed out of the apartment.

TICK-TICK-TICK-TICK-TICK

The egg was clutched close to his heart, which went *thumpthumpthumpthumpthump.*

Wise Men of Gotham

Foster Cavendish stared at Bathsheba Cavendish. "With *Batman?*"

Bathsheba stood with folded arms and lifted her chin.

Oblivious to this byplay, Batman raced down the hall with the Easter egg as though heading for a touchdown. The Riddler, dressed as a letter carrier, was alone in the cage. Their eyes met as the door closed.

Batman skidded to a stop, and with one arm forced the sliding door open enough to drop the chocolate egg through; the egg fell toward the top of the descending elevator cab. Batman pulled quickly back and flattened against the wall. Even so, he found himself flung to the floor while splinters of wood and steel pierced his cape.

B-A-R-O-O-M!!!

Then SWOOSHHHH-THUDD!!! as the blast severed the steel cables and dropped the cage several floors to the basement.

A singed and battered postman limped out past the doorman and hobbled away.

A quarter hour later, Sam Rubin slipped out from under the bed and pretended to have come with the police and fire personnel now swarming the scene. Foster Cavendish was touched that Rubin had responded to the news of the explosion—not just as a Housing Commissioner concerned about damage to habitable buildings, but as an acquaintance concerned about the Cavendishes. Cavendish hadn't realized how good a friend of the family Rubin was.

Batman dreaded the thought of facing Alfred with the cape in the state it was.

Wayne phoned Sollis. "Do you happen to know how many Wise Men of Gotham there were?"

Edward Wellen

A pause, then Amicia said, "I could journey to England and look up Gotham in the Domesday Book, and in the Pipe Rolls that carried on the census, but I doubt I'd find a breakdown of the male population into wise and foolish."

A pause at Wayne's end, then he said, "You're taking me too literally. I'm talking about the Wise Men in the legends, not necessarily about men who lived and breathed."

"You're right, Bruce. I ought to lighten up. Let's see...Well, there *is* a nursery rhyme:

'Three wise men of Gotham
Went to sea in a bowl.
If the bowl had been stronger,
My story had been longer.'

But it doesn't say 'The three wise men.' So that leaves it open-ended."

"What I was afraid of," Wayne said.

Even though Bruce would have continued cause to consult her—which she didn't mind at all—Dr. Sollis shared his fear.

"You have to go out again, sir? I haven't finished spotting the cape." Alfred reluctantly fetched the Batman costume. He hesitated before handing it over. "If I may suggest, sir, mightn't you wear Master Dick's Robin costume while he's in England on his Rhodes scholarship?"

Wayne worked his shoulders. "It wouldn't hang right." He patted Alfred reassuringly. "Don't fret, Alfred. Darkness covers a multitude of sins."

Wise Men of Gotham

Alfred remained stiff. "I thought it was Charity, sir, that did the covering."

"We're told to do good deeds in secret, aren't we? That's darkness." Batman flung this and his cape over his shoulder and did not wait for Alfred's comeback.

They met at Fourth Avenue and Fourth Street at four a.m.

"That was a near thing with Foster Cavendish," Comissioner Gordon said.

"That it was," Batman said. He did not add that not Cavendish but Rubin had been the Riddler's target. He said quickly, "The Riddler again?"

Gordon nodded grimly. "He keeps bouncing right back." He handed Batman a photocopy of a rhymed note.

Fool's cap for a crown,

Would'st see the dunce drown

An eel in a pond?

Then come and be conned.

> *—Yours cruelly, the Riddler*

Like a cold cold finger the word "cruelly" touched Batman's spine to ice. The Riddler seemed bent on making up for the past near-misses. Batman did not let Gordon see the dismay he felt. He smiled, then faded to black before Gordon could tell the smile was frozen.

Dr. Amicia Sollis had words for the words. "'Foolscap' is a size of writing paper large enough to twist-and-paste

Edward Wellen

into a dunce cap. It gets its name from a watermark in the
form of a jester's cap with bells. 'Drown an eel in a pond'
is of course the Gothamites' playing at being fools. 'Come
and be conned' invites Batman to be suckered by a con—
or confidence—game. Then, too, there's 'conn' with a
double en, from cond for conduct; 'to take the conn' is to
take over the steering of a vessel, to watch its course and
direct the helmsman."

"Then Batman has only to find the fool, the eel, and
the pond."

"You got it." Amicia dug into the sole. "This is
delicious."

But Wayne had lost his appetite. Glumly, without
thinking, he sipped water.

CLICK! A light bulb went on in his head.

He held the glass to the light of the chandeliers. Water
was the key.

Could the Riddler's "pond" be the yacht basin? Could
the Riddler's "eel" be the *Île de Joie*? Could the "fool" be
Jack King?

Batman would go and take the conn.

Alfred looked flushed but defiant. "Master Dick is in his
room unpacking."

Wayne shot Alfred a look and made for his protegé's
room. Dick Grayson looked fit save for signs of jet lag.

They thumped one another, then Wayne eyed Dick
keenly. "I thought you planned to hike through the high-
lands on your Easter holiday. What gives?"

Dick shrugged. "Alfred called me last night and said
that you had let yourself go in your preoccupation with
the Riddler. I figured you could use my help, so I Con-
corded right over."

Wise Men of Gotham

"I'll speak to Alfred later. But I must admit I feel surer and stronger now that you're here. Let's change, and I'll fill you in on our way to the yacht basin."

Batman pedaled to the Batmobile's metal. The sleek vehicle whizzed through Gotham's canyons.

SCREEEECHHH!!!

Only their seat belts saved them.

Robin turned to stare at Batman. "Why did you brake?"

"It hit me. I *am* being conned by the Riddler. Jack King is not his target. In fact, Jack King is the mastermind behind the Riddler's attempts on the Wise Men of Gotham."

He ticked off on black-gloved fingers, "First, the floating corpse with the tattooed Riddler rhyme had been an art student mixed up in something mysterious at the time he turned up missing. That mysterious something could well have been the copying of a particular painting—the $86 million Rembrandt. Second, that would explain Jack King's curious composure when the Riddler vandalized *The Would-Be Bride*—Jack King was exhibiting not the original but a recently painted copy. Because, third, I noticed a faint smudge on Detective Sergeant Heather Mortimer's forearm after she pulled the dart from the canvas. The paint had not yet dried hard! Four, the Riddler found it awfully easy to get on and off the *Île de Joie*. Five, the Wise Men the Riddler has been after have all stood in Jack King's juggernaut path."

Batman made a fist. "It adds up."

Robin nodded. "Seems to. But now what?"

Batman eased out of the Batmobile. "You cover the *Île de Joie* just in case the Riddler is pulling a double con."

Robin shifted to the driver's seat. "While you—?"

Edward Wellen

"Look for the right eel in the right pond."

"Good fishing!"

Robin's voice thinned away on the Batmobile's exhaust.

Batman moved to the sidewalk, looking for a news-stand—a bit late, now, to be scanning the paper for some hint as to where the Riddler might strike.

Robin slowed as he neared the yacht basin. He spotted the *Île de Joie* and parked the Batmobile in a space preserved by fluorescent-orange traffic cones. It struck him that they looked like dunce caps.

"Keep the change," Batman said absently. He was already perusing the paper.

"Gee, thanks Batman!" the blind newsstand operator said.

Batman gave a start. "How do you know who I am?"

"Who else wears a cape these days? I heard the swirl."

"Oh." Batman moved away, reading as he walked.

The paper was thicker than usual for a weekday. It had a special Boat Show section.

Batman stopped in his tracks.

"You all right, Batman?" the newsstand operator called.

"Fine, fine." Batman hurried away.

He headed for Exposition Center, the venue of the Boat Show.

It all fell into place. "Fool's cap for a crown." Foolscap was paper. Gotham City's leading newspaper, the one in

Wise Men of Gotham

Batman's hands, was the crown of Rudolph Newkirk's media empire. Rudolph Newkirk stood in Jack King's way, therefore representing a Wise Man for the Riddler to bump off. According to the special section, which must have brought the paper millions in advertising revenue, Rudolph Newkirk would be at the Boat Show this evening.

Batman quickened his pace.

Exposition Center had ways of ingress unknown to ticket buyers.

Batman made entry into the labyrinthine basement of the complex. Others had done so before him. As he moved through the vaulted chambers he glimpsed shadowy forms in the dim recesses. Scores of the homeless had taken up residence here.

He moved carefully and quietly to keep from disturbing them. Even so, some stirred and muttered at his passage.

"YOWW!" Skeletal hands with dirty claws waved threateningly in his face, red eyes glared into his, and foul breath assailed his nostrils. A ragged figure, thick with layers of clothes rather than with meat on its bones, had sprung out of an alcove at him. The raspy voice followed up on its shout. "Stay away! This is my place!"

Batman gestured placatingly. "Right! It's all yours!"

He made to pass by, but the claws gripped his cape at the throat and held him fast and the red eyes bored into his. "You wear a mask, but I've seen those eyes. Where have I seen those eyes?"

Batman tore free and shoved the man as gently as he could back into the precious alcove. "I don't know, my

Edward Wellen

friend. We'll have to puzzle that out another time. Right now I'm on urgent business." He hurried on toward stairs going up.

He did not notice that the ragged figure followed him, fear and fascination in its bloodshot eyes.

On the exhibition floor, a vast arena filled with boats of all sizes and decked with flags and bunting, Batman hid himself from the crowd behind a motorboat booth and studied a program sheet he had picked up. Rudolph Newkirk's name jumped out at him. The publisher was scheduled to award best-of-show trophies at ten o'clock— a quarter of an hour from now. The handing out was to take place at the Caribbean display.

The reverse of the program sheet had a map that showed the Caribbean display to be a detailed scale model of the Caribbean area—clay islands in a steel-framed pool of water. Batman stretched to see over the crowd and found the display where the map put it—at the other end of the hall.

Batman consulted the program again. Just before Rudolph Newkirk's big moment, an expert from Anguilla in the Leeward Islands would demonstrate spearfishing in the same display. Batman's synapses sparked. Anguilla meant eel or snake. L-e-e was e-e-l backwards...

Crews from the local channels were already setting up lights and television cameras, clearing space for the thick cables snaking across the floor.

Nearby, on a bench for the weary of soles, a woman sat embroidering away with a long-eyed sharp needle and worsted yarn, as if waiting patiently for her man to get his fill of the exhibits.

Wise Men of Gotham

Batman only had eyes for the Anguillan spearfisher, a bronzed man wearing goggles and swimming trunks. Speargun in hand, he waded calf-deep into the pool, stirring up the live fish swimming there. He mounted the replica of his native island, and balanced on this tiny foothold. Now Batman saw Newkirk arrive with an entourage and stand in the wings. How easy it would be for the spearfisher (the Riddler in disguise?) to kill Newkirk as the one left the spotlight and the other entered it!

Batman edged around to the Caribbean display. He stood next to the bench where the woman—who might have been Mme. Defarge knitting as the guillotine lopped heads—sat working needle and yarn through an embroidery hoop.

A sprightly program chairwoman introduced the spearfisher as Captain Jacoby. In an accent of the Islands, Captain Jacoby described the technique, then speared some half-dozen wriggling blowfish in rapid order.

To a smattering of applause, Captain Jacoby splashed out of the Caribbean Sea. Greater applause attended Newkirk's introduction.

One eye on the spearfisher, who stopped by the side of the pool to towel his legs, Batman watched Newkirk goodsportedly take off shoes and socks and roll up trouser bottoms before stepping into the pool.

Newkirk lifted one foot into the pool and then the other. Batman tensed. Now the Riddler would make his move.

Captain Jacoby straightened and turned to look at Newkirk. Batman set himself to leap at the spearfisher.

But the move came from the woman knitting. She rose from the bench, dropped her crewel embroidery, and bent to pull the male plug of a floodlight from an extension

Edward Wellen

cord snaking from the wall socket. She whipped the
female end of the extension cord at the pool.

Crewel...cruel...flashed through Batman's mind. The
Riddler!

Everyone stood stunned as the length of cord, like
some slick-backed electric eel, arced toward the water.
Everyone but Batman.

He lunged for the extension cord, grabbed hold, and
pulled it from the wall socket just as the other end was
about to hit the water with a terrible hissing and sparking.
Newkirk stood frightened but unharmed.

With a curse, the Riddler—with wig askew, his identity now clear—dove for the embroidery, grabbed the
crewel needle, and thrust the sharp point straight at Batman's heart.

A ragged figure hurled itself between the needle and
Batman.

Batman let others give chase to the Riddler. He bent to
the ragged figure that had taken the deathblow meant for
Batman.

He strained to hear the homeless man's last gasps. The
man stared into Batman's eyes.

"The eyes...the eyes of the kid...who watched
me...knock off his folks...in the stickup..."

It took a moment to sink in, then Batman felt a rush of
rage. But the man's eyes had closed. The man was past
Batman's hate, past everything except, perhaps, peace.

Bruce Wayne held a sort of postmortem, a gathering of
himself, Dick Grayson, Commissioner Gordon, and Dr.
Amicia Sollis.

Alfred had a riddle of claret at the proper temperature,
and they were doing justice to at least the magnum.

Wise Men of Gotham

Batman's string of victories over the Riddler had had swift and amazing consequences.

Gordon looked darkly through his half-full glass. "Jack King overreached himself—with no golden handshake at the end. When the Wise Men of Gotham lived to frustrate his grandiose project, his whole house of cards collapsed. Even his Swiss and Caribbean assets were frozen, and the *Île de Joie* was attached for back taxes, together with all its treasures—including the *real* Rembrandt discovered rolled up in the wall safe."

Dick said, "I happened to be at the yacht basin at the time news of the attempt on Newkirk came over the radio. I happened to see Jack King leave the *Île de Joie* and zoom away in a speedboat. I'm surprised he didn't take the Rembrandt with him."

"Had other things on his mind," Wayne guessed.

Amicia smiled wryly. "He didn't think to take Queena with him. I hear Queena filed for divorce, asking huge alimony. Fat chance she'll collect, with all his creditors—wolves, sharks, and vultures—seeking him by land, sea, and air, but at least she has all her jewels."

"A Wise Woman of Gotham?" Wayne asked. He looked at Amicia. "I know a wiser."

The Police Commissioner and the Avenger of Evil met one more time about the affair of the Wise Men of Gotham, just that Gordon might thank Batman—and update him on the hunt for the Riddler.

"He's escaped us again. We've looked high and low. First place, of course, was low—the basement of Exposition Center." He shivered. "What a pesthole! It'll take some doing to clear those creatures out of their nests and burrows and to squatter-proof the place."

Edward Wellen

Batman put a hand on Gordon's arm. "Let them be. From what I hear, Jack King will be needing somewhere to lay his head."

Robber's Roost

MAX ALLAN COLLINS

The rain that lashed Gotham City was as dark and relentless as the living gargoyle that perched on the flat roof of a glass-and-steel structure whose architect never imagined so gothic an ornamentation.

Like a large bird of prey, cape gathered around him like wings, the Batman waited and watched. On a night like this, in a storm so unremitting, most birds had sought shelter. Not this one.

Nor one other: a jailbird called the Penguin.

Across the way was the rear of the apartment building where that human bowling pin was said to reside, if one could believe the information Oswald C. Cobblepot (for that was the Penguin's real name, unlikely as it sounded) had provided the parole board. The only reason Batman believed it, was that he'd seen the Penguin enter the building the day of his release, stepping from the cab that had brought him here from the state pen.

On that sunny fall afternoon, the Batman had been

waiting, like a hostile, masked doorman, to greet his old adversary.

"I don't believe I've ever seen you in gray before, Penguin," he'd said, sarcasm like a knife blade in his voice.

The Penguin—who was wearing a baggy gray prison-issue suit, a gift from the state upon departing their care—sneered and squinted, the monocle digging into his flesh.

"My manservant will have dress tails awaiting me." The Penguin beamed arrogantly, rocking on his heels like a child's top. "Freshly pressed. What brings you by, my dear old friend? To wish me luck, now that I've turned over a new leaf?"

"With a crook like you, it'll be a gold leaf. No, Penguin, I'm not here to wish you luck—I'm here to let you know I'll be watching you . . . like a hawk."

The eyebrow above the monocle arched, but the glass stayed in place. "That's what my parole officer is for."

"Government officials are overworked. From time to time, concerned citizens need to lend a hand."

And the Batman laid his massive gloved hand on Penguin's shoulder and squeezed; Penguin swallowed, his face turning as pale as a chicken egg.

"If you harass me . . ."

Beneath the mask a smile curled. "What? You'll get me fired? I'm not in the law-enforcement business, Penguin. I deal in justice."

"Awk!" Penguin sputtered. "Justice as *you* see it!"

Batman thumped the little man's overstuffed chest with a thick forefinger. "That's why we've been 'friends' for so long, Penguin . . . we understand each other."

He'd been keeping watch for over a month now, but

it had been a necessarily sporadic thing: he had other responsibilities, among them the shifting patrol of the city that the newspapers referred to as Batman's "spot check" on crime. Bad as things were in Gotham City, its crime statistics were lower than any other major metropolitan area in the nation—due in some part, he hoped, to these efforts.

So he'd hardly been keeping a constant watch on the Penguin: It was possible Mr. Cobblepot had managed to break his parole in some manner that had escaped Batman's notice. Bt at least the local crime reports bore no trace of Penguin's distinctive M.O.

A resourceful thief displaying a surprisingly homicidal streak at times, the Penguin had several recurring motifs—notably, umbrellas and birds—that often manifested themselves in his heists. His elaborate attempted robbery of a fabulous display of Fabergé Eggs at the Gotham Institute of Art had incorporated both of his favorite themes, as he drifted down through a skylight on an electronically controlled umbrella, weaving skillfully through a network of light beams, wearing an infrared monocle that charted his path.

The umbrella would have worked just as well lifting him off the ground as it had as a parachute, had not the Batman interrupted his efforts, streaking downward through that same skylight like a dark comet, setting off alarms, placing a well-aimed boot heel on the butlerlike burglar's pointed chin.

That had been the crime that sent Penguin to the pen.

Now, out on good behavior, the Penguin waddled the streets a free man. The downside of what Batman had bragged about to the Penguin—that he was not a government official, that his interest was that of a "concerned citizen"—had been all too apparent at the Cobblepot parole-board hearing.

The grim manner in which the panel of five faced him immediately made Batman feel that he was the one whose behavior was being judged.

"We're only giving you a hearing because Commissioner Gordon requested it," the stern-faced schoolmarm of a chairperson informed him, in a chalk-on-blackboard voice. She peered over wireframe glasses, a birdlike woman in a severe dark gray suit over an unconvincingly feminine ruffled blouse.

"I appreciate you granting me this forum," Batman said, standing erectly before them, feeling oddly guilty—about nothing in particular, just guilty. It was as close as Batman had ever come to identifying with the other side.

"Before you speak," a thin, bored-looking man in his fifties said patronizingly, "you should understand that several of us have already filed protests against your appearance here."

It had been downhill from there: the word of a "vigilante, albeit a sanctioned one" was deemed to carry "little weight." When the Batman reminded them that Cobblepot was not only a thief, but a suspected murderer, he got only a reprimand.

"We're concerned only with two things, here, sir— the crime for which Mr. Cobblepot was incarcerated, and whether or not Mr. Cobblepot regrets that crime . . . and, of course, on the latter point, whether his behavior while under the state's supervision showed signs of rehabilitation."

Batman had protested any such signs as typical of the Penguin, whose abilities extended beyond theft into the domain of the con man.

Max Allan Collins

"If you believe he's in any way reformed or regretful of his ways," Batman said tightly, "you're the victims of the Penguin's latest 'sting.'"

But the prison psychiatrist had already testified to Mr. Cobblepot's "improved condition." Since the Penguin was a rich man—some years ago he'd inherited a family fortune—his theft was written off by the shrink as a need for "attention" and "approval." His "collecting" (which is to say, theft) was a "simple anal retentive tendency" that could be overcome by continuing, outpatient therapy.

Now that patient was under observation by a "doctor" in cape and cowl. Rain beading off the waterproof surface of battle garb designed to instill fear and blend its wearer into the dark night, the Dark Knight watched the comical figure in top hat and tails and, of course, protective umbrella as he exited the service entry at the rear of the apartment building.

The Batman had expected this—the Penguin would anticipate being watched, and never consider going out the front way, not on any engagement that might find him wandering from the straight and narrow path he was pretending to trod. Or, waddle.

The Penguin caught a cab at the alley's mouth, and Batman swung down on a nylon rope so thin he seemed to be flying. In the next alley waited the dark sleek custom machine the media insisted upon calling the Batmobile, hidden under a canvas tarp labeled DANGER—CHEMICAL WASTE—AUTHORIZED REMOVAL ONLY. He flipped off the tarp, leaving it behind for now, not wanting to lose the Penguin's taxi in traffic.

Only, on this storm-swept early evening, on these black shining streets pelted by God's wet machine-gun

Robber's Roost

fire, there was little traffic to be lost in. In fact, the
Batman had to lay back—his distinctive transporta-
tion was hardly designed for shadowing a suspect.

The waterfront area where the cab deposited its tiny,
eccentric passenger was home to any number of bars;
but this one, the Polluted Pelican, was notorious even
for this neighborhood. The Batman stood on the
sidewalk, sheltered by an awning, and watched
through the corner of a moisture-streaked window
while the dapper little man walked in his side-to-side
manner through a roughneck bar filled with dock
workers and seamen, some of whom would smile and
start to laugh and point at the odd little duck, until
they realized (sometimes having to be told by a neighbor) just who that odd little duck was.

That odd little duck was, after all, the Penguin—and
in the handle of that umbrella could be a blade or a
bullet or a burst of poison gas. So even the toughest
of this tough lot kept their distance. . . .

The Penguin waddled to a corner booth, and the
Batman had to strain to see, but see he did: the two
men Penguin was meeting with were familiar faces—
accomplices, henchmen if you will, who'd been impli-
cated but never arrested in that unsuccessful Fabergé
heist.

With all the criminals that littered his life, Batman
couldn't remember anything but the nicknames of the
pair: Turk and Hawk, making burly bookends in the
booth as they crowded around their boss, who spoke
to them with animated glee.

By consorting with other ex-cons, Penguin was in
parole violation this very moment—with a phone call,
Batman could have the little vulture back in that cage
at the state pen.

Max Allan Collins

But even with parole violation, Penguin would be
out again in another two years, max. And the Batman
was tired of hunting this particular bird. It was his
prerogative, as a concerned citizen rather than an official arm of the law, to stay in the shadows . . . to allow
this scenario to play itself out . . . to give the Penguin
the opportunity to attempt some new crime that would
have him trading his tuxedo for an untailored black-
and-white striped suit and a long, long stay up the
river.

Within half an hour, Turk and Hawk exited, coming
right out the front door of the Polluted Pelican; but
the Batman had dropped back into the alley, just
another of the long shadows he blended with. The rain
was letting up. In dark turtlenecks under down-filled
jackets on whose slick surfaces the water beaded, their
sneakered feet making small puddles out of large ones,
the Penguin's henchmen crossed an empty street to a
late-model Firebird, blue with red-flame decals.

Batman followed. His vehicle bore no such spectacular markings, and was almost lost in the night, its
blackness, its deco lines making ripples in the darkness. When pedestrians would see it pass, particularly
on a night like this, they would wonder if they'd
imagined it.

He again kept well back, and almost missed it when
the Firebird pulled over, in a fire zone, waiting for
something, apparently. Pulling into an alley a block
behind them, Batman watched, on foot, peering around
the edge of a building.

Turk, who was behind the wheel, a weak-chinned,
mustached man in a stocking cap, was looking at his
watch, every half minute or so. This lasted at least
four minutes. . . .

Robber's Roost

Then the Firebird roared back out into the street.

Batman climbed behind his own wheel and took measured pursuit. They seemed headed toward the park. Barely two blocks later, the Firebird pulled up just half a block from the Park Plaza, one of the most exclusive, expensive high-rise apartment houses in the city. Ducking into another alley, the Batman hugged the shadows, crossing to the park opposite, cloaked himself in darkness, and watched.

The Park Plaza's red-carpeted, canopied entrance glowed in the night like a mirage of wealth. Millionaires lived there—billionaires—including real-estate tycoon Roland Crumm, who remained a high-roller despite his publicized financial misfortunes of late.

Barely had the thought of Crumm crossed Batman's mind than the man himself appeared in the doorway, standing under the canopy chatting pleasantly with the uniformed doorman, adjusting his silk scarf, tugging his heavy black topcoat around him, his puffy, almost pretty face peeking out to see if the rain was still coming down.

It was, but just barely.

Apparently Crumm was waiting for his car—his limo and driver, that is. Actually, his car was already there: the Firebird that slid up to the curb, with Hawk leaping out, belting the doorman, who went down like a three-legged card table. Now Turk was out from behind the wheel and aimed a long-nosed dart gun at Crumm and fired, the red-feathered dart-tip quivering as it struck the man in the right thigh. The billionaire—or was it millionaire, now?—struggled briefly, before the tranquilizer kicked in, wrestling out of his coat, which Turk ended up carrying over one arm, as if he were looking for someplace to hang it up.

Then they had him in the car and were gone.

It had happened quickly, and possibly—possibly—Batman could have intervened in time to stop this before Turk and Hawk could drive away.

But he had hesitated. Already, in this concerned citizen's mind, a thought had formed: a kidnapping charge would put Penguin away for a very long time. Maybe forever.

Better, for all concerned (with the admitted possible exception of the kidnap victim himself) for Batman to follow the henchmen to their leader.

Which is exactly what the Batman did.

Back to the waterfront, into a warehouse district, where the Firebird rolled up a ramp to a loading dock into a massive building, and a steel garage door *whang*ed shut, as if a brick beast had devoured them.

Climbing the rear wall of the warehouse led the Batman to a row of windows, one of which was ajar, and he slipped in to find himself in a loft amid boxes and crates. Beyond the darkness of the loft, a central area of the warehouse was lit by several conical hanging lamps, which threw harsh light that created angular, eerie shadows.

A cackling laugh was echoing.

"Roland Crumm!" gloated the Penguin. The kidnap victim in his tuxedo and white scarf lay like a puddle of ink with dabs of Wite-Out on the gray cement floor, where Turk and Hawk had dumped him. "A pity our guest sleeps, or I would welcome him to the festivities we have planned."

At the edge of the loft, having wound his way

Robber's Roost

through the crates and boxes, Batman had to wonder why Penguin had chosen a kidnap victim whose fortunes had fallen so severely in recent times. Hadn't the Penguin kidnapped Crumm about five years too *late*?

No room for such ruminations now, however; the time had come to free Crumm, and cage his captors.

"Didn't you know my hobby was bird-watching, Penguin?" the Batman said casually, standing on the edge of the loft, casting his own ominous shadow across the startled, dismayed trio below.

Penguin's sneer was all the answer he had time for, as Batman leaped toward him, using the fat little man as a mattress to land on.

"Awk!" Penguin squawked, bobbing backward like a boxing dummy, breath knocked out of him, his balance a memory as he flailed on his back on the floor.

Batman was already on his feet again, ready to meet Turk and Hawk. They were twins from the neck down, but Turk's face was weak-chinned, beady-eyed and mustached, whereas Hawk's features were sharp, his eyes piercing below one continuous eyebrow. As the Penguin rolled around on his back like a turned-over turtle, the two henchmen approached the Batman, one from either side. They threw dark, nasty shadows, and their expressions were darker and nastier. . . .

Batman swung a leg around in a martial-arts move so swift Turk didn't blink before it caught his neck and dropped him. Hawk was fumbling under the down jacket for an automatic and didn't quite have it out when Batman butted him in the belly and knocked him into the Firebird parked along one wall.

But Hawk was a tougher customer than Turk, apparently, and even with the wind knocked out of him managed to lash out with the gun, not firing it, but slamming Batman alongside the temple with its barrel. Even with his protctive headgear, Batman was staggered, momentarily.

Hawk managed a body blow before Batman snapped a fist back, almost casually, and put Hawk's lights out.

"And now, Penguin," Batman said smugly, turning easily, "I think it's time you checked in with your parole officer. . . ."

But the Penguin wasn't on his back anymore; he stood near a support beam with his hand on a lever. His sneering smile gleamed, and so did the eye behind that silly monocle.

"Wakk! Wakk! Wakk!" laughed the Penguin.

"What do *you* have to quack about?" Batman asked acidly, striding across the warehouse toward the little thief; the gloved hands were fists.

The Penguin pulled the lever.

Instinctively, Batman jerked his gaze upward and saw the crosshatch of the net grow larger as it came toward him; he tried to run out from under it, but there was no running—he only stumbled, as the heavy, weaved net caught him, and as he went down, on the cement, he hit the same side of his head that Hawk had whacked with the automatic.

Simultaneously, the Penguin fired a tranquilizer dart from the gun that Turk had used on Crumm. The dart quivered from Batman's midsection, but he was already out.

Not from the dart, but from the blow to the head.

But Penguin didn't know that.

Hawk and Turk had recovered, though both were walking like they were a few hundred years old and had just woken from a nap in a hammock.

The Penguin hit a button on the support beam and the net tugged tight as it lifted Batman up near the high, open ceiling.

"Penguin—what's wrong with you?" Hawk said in a voice deep as a well. "We coulda looked under his mask!"

"We'll save that for later." He cackled. "Every great banquet needs a scrumptious dessert—right, boys?"

"But, Penguin!" Turk said, in his whiny nasal way. "Batman's got that utility belt of his on—you better lower that net so we can at least strip *that* off. . . ."

"No. No time for that, and too dangerous. That tranquilizer dart may not have the effect on that mutant bat that it has on a normal human being like our friend Mr. Crumm. Do you want to risk the Batman waking up on us, while we're removing his clothing? Peeking under his mask?"

Turk and Hawk shrugged their reluctant agreement.

"Now, transfer Mr. Crumm to the delivery truck. It's time we *catered* to our guest. . . ."

And with another mutual shrug, the two henchmen carried the slumbering Crumm like a laundry bag to a panel truck in another part of the warehouse; painted white, the truck bore a generic designation, COBBLEPOT CATERING SERVICE.

Before departing with his flunkies, the Penguin paused to smile up at the unconscious Batman, hanging like a weird Christmas ornament from the rafters.

With a sweep of his top hat, the Penguin bowed and said, "Wish I could be a better host, my old friend . . ."

He climbed in back of the truck with the unconscious Crumm.

"But I have a dinner engagement. . . ."

Max Allan Collins

Although he did not know it, Batman awoke only minutes after the Penguin and his boys had left with
Crumm. He had not seen the catering truck, which
had clung to the shadows at the rear of the warehouse.
All he knew, really, was that he was suspended from
the ceiling, wrapped in netting, high over the
warehouse floor.

The catch of the day.

What the Penguin didn't know was that the tranquilizer dart hadn't had any effect on the Batman at
all; its tip had pierced the first thin layer of material
and caught, but the second skin of Kevlar-like body
armor had prevented further purchase.

It was the blow on the head that sent consciousness
rushing from Batman, only not for long. The Batman's
strength of will was at least equal to his physical
power, and a throbbing headache that would send most
people to their knees was to him only the mildest annoyance.

Like captured Kong, the Batman stood in the netting, his hands gripping in and around the dark hemp
crosshatch that was the bars of his swaying prison
cell. He was not, however, protesting his fate: he was
testing the strength, examining the makeup, of the
netting itself.

Then he was kneeling in the net sack, limiting his
movement to keep the pendulumlike motion to a
minimum.

The thickness of the hemp required a tool that could
cut steel, and the small acetylene torch from his utility
belt was just the ticket. The hole he cut in the bottom

of the netting was one he could swing down from, and he dropped nimbly to the floor of the warehouse, a drop that would break the legs of most men, but to this one was like stepping from a bath.

He swiftly searched the warehouse. With one major exception, there was nothing left of the Penguin's presence; that exception, however, was the Firebird (probably stolen) that had brought Crumm here. In the backseat, on the floor, Batman found the topcoat of the kidnapped tycoon, pulled off in the momentary struggle before the tranq had kicked in.

In one pocket was a fancy, engraved invitation.

THE EPICUREAN CLUB
Annual Banquet
Members Only
Cash Only

Batman studied the off-white card. A faint memory tickled his mind, not from his clandestine after-hours life as the Batman, but from his public, daily life as Bruce Wayne, wealthy peer of Roland Crumm. He placed a hand on his jaw and stroked idly, thinking.

Then he returned to the night, running toward the alley where he'd stowed his wheels, cape flapping in the wind, like a wraith pursuing him.

The rain had stopped, but another storm was coming.

The wealthy of Gotham City—men in white tie and tails, women in luxurious fur coats—were filtering into the banquet room on the top floor of the Ritz Hotel for the invitation-only affair. A *maitre d'*, with the proper snobbish air, escorted them to individual tables, where before taking a seat, a male member of each party handed an envelope with cash to the *maitre d'*, who would quickly, discreetly count the bills. Meanwhile, in the candlelit, romantic ambience, busboys and waiters scurried to provide the best of attention.

Not *all* of Gotham City's wealthy were here, of course. Even among the four hundred, the Epicurean Club was exclusive—an annual affair that dated back to the turn of the century, although in recent years a naughty, delicious twist had been added. . . .

A woman in a silver fox stole, her own foxlike face yanked taut by a plastic surgeon, looked about the room and wondered aloud to her porcine husband, "I wonder where our host is?"

"You know Roland," her husband said, and his laugh was as rough as his skin was pink and soft. "That Crumm propensity for making a memorable entrance."

"With some starlet on his arm no doubt," she agreed with a nasty little smile. "No brains, and the best breast implants Roland's money can buy."

The catty remark ignored the thousands of dollars she herself had spent on cosmetic surgery.

Elsewhere, a beautiful young woman in mink hugged the arm of her escort, the silver-haired, weasel-featured CEO of Gotham Chemical.

"Where's that hunk, Bruce Wayne?" she asked. The young woman was a stunning creature with wide, vacant eyes and breathtaking, natural cleavage. Her gown hugged her figure like shimmering emerald paint.

"I don't think he's on the guest list, my pet."

"Oh? Why not? He's so *charming*. . . ."

"He's probably at some Greenpeace fund-raiser. He's such an eco-junkie."

And the CEO laughed, and the young woman laughed with him, her shrill, brittle laughter belying her complete lack of understanding of what her escort meant.

The dinner proceeded with course after course, delicacies that the guests *ooooo*ed and *aahhh*ed over— French stuffed endive, seviche, glazed shrimp aspic, tongue cornucopias, pâté de foie gras. Finally, however, as the moneyed, jewelry- and fur-bedecked assemblage—mouths watering—awaited the presentation of the main course, the chef entered, wheeling a large cart with a huge round gleaming silver serving tray. The expectant faces of the hushed dinner guests were reflected in the tray's rounded metal surface, open mouths, wide eyes, distorted by the curvature.

The chef himself was a little bowling-pin-shaped man with glasses and tiny French mustache and the spotless white apparel and high fluffy hat of his profession.

"Allow me to thank you all for your contributions to the evening's festivities," the chef said. Despite the French mustache, his accent was, if anything, faintly British. "As you know, we have a very *special* entree. . . ."

The chef placed his hand gently on the lid of the serving dish, as if passing a benediction.

Then he seemed to cackle and said, "There *has* been a change of menu, however. . . ."

The crowd stirred; eyebrows raised and nostrils flared. The voices of men used to never being contradicted hurled objections at the little man—no obscenities, but the indignation and contempt in the air was palpable.

"Please rest assured that you will not be disappointed," the chef insisted, the cackle out of his tone. "Tonight's endangered-species main course was to have been Gotham's own speckled owl. We had what may have been the last remaining six such animals in our kitchen, just this afternoon . . . unfortunately, they were stolen. . . ."

Gasps of disappointment and outrage rose in the room.

"Where in hell is Crumm?" demanded the weasel-faced CEO.

The chef ignored the interruption. "So, instead, tonight's ten-thousand-dollar-a-plate entree will be Gotham Speckled Hog, tartar . . ."

And the chef—which is to say, the Penguin—lifted the lid grandly from the giant serving dish to reveal Crumm, naked, on his elbows and knees, trussed up with an apple in his mouth, surrounded by money-color garnish.

There were again gasps, particularly from the women, who at first thought their host was dead; but it became readily apparent he was not. His wide eyes and hysterical expression, around the apple that all but choked him, revealed only humiliation and fright.

"*Bon appétit,*" the Penguin said, and while in the doorway the *maitre d'* kept the crowd covered with an Uzi, Penguin's boys—Turk and Hawk and several others, who moments prior had been serving this crowd as waiters and busboys—began passing amongst the crowd collecting glittering jewelry and Rolex watches.

"Sorry I'm late," a commanding voice said.

All eyes turned to the Batman, who stood in the doorway, next to the *maitre d',* who now sat in an unconscious heap next to his post, weapon tossed to one side. Hands on hips, chin erect, Batman gazed around the room at corporate heads, human jackals who gave a responsible capitalist like Bruce Wayne a bad name, and he felt the same disgust that coursed through him when he bagged a rapist or serial killer.

Only what excuse of heredity and environment did these parasites have? They hadn't grown up in the slums of Crime Alley. And Bruce Wayne, the man beneath the mask, knew damn well that you didn't have to grow up corrupt and venal just because you were born to wealth and privilege.

"Batman!" Penguin squawked. He balled his fists. Looking even more absurd than usual, thanks to his chef's apparel, the Penguin looked like a petulant child about to jump up and down. "Are you going to spoil my evening?"

"Give them their belongings back," Batman instructed the Penguin, raising a scolding finger, casting his hard gaze on the henchmen in their waiter and busboy uniforms.

"There's only *one* of him!" the Penguin shouted. "What are you waiting for? Are you chickens or men?"

Three came at him at once, but the one in the lead—not Hawk or Turk, who were laying back, having had their dose of Batman's medicine for the day—took a foot in the chin and fell backward into a table, glass and china shattering, rich people yelping. The second one went down hard when Batman, his back to the man, sent an elbow into his sternum. The third one proved that drywall isn't all that sturdy, as the Batman hurled him into the adjacent coatroom through a self-made passage in the wall.

Max Allan Collins

The rest of Penguin's men backed away.

Batman stepped forward, raised a forefinger, and soon the henchmen were begrudgingly returning the items to the guests, who beamed.

"The man of the hour!" the weasel-faced CEO said, standing, and he began to applaud.

The others, their smiles as shining as their jewelry, joined in, giving their savior a standing ovation. Several were helping Crumm off the cart, untying him, providing the shaking, shaken millionaire with a tablecloth to wear, like an oversize diaper.

The Batman was ignoring this, as he saw the Penguin ducking into the kitchen. He caught the little man crawling into a dumbwaiter, clutching a briefcase of cash, about to deliver himself to another floor.

He dragged the Penguin back into the banquet room, where the crowd's applause rose to a roar. Batman patted the air with one hand, his other holding the collar of the scowling little crook.

"Throw him in jail, Batman!" the pretty young woman in mink called out gleefully. "Call the cops!"

But the mention of jail and police sobered the rest of the crowd.

And made Batman smile.

"I could call the police," he said. "The sight of you fine citizens being loaded into paddy wagons would do me a world of good. There *is* another option."

The silent, alarmed faces of the corporate heads in the crowd expressed mute interest in that option.

"I can see to it that the money the Penguin collected here tonight is turned over to your friend Bruce Wayne," Batman said, hefting the money-filled briefcase. "As a philanthropist with environmental and related concerns, he would, I feel certain, distribute this wealth among worthy charities . . . including, perhaps, the Humane Society."

The Penguin's sneer turned to a smile. Like another of the Batman's adversaries, he liked a good joke.

"Go home, all of you," Batman said. "Shoo!"

The expressions in the crowd were not uniform—some were chagrined, others angry, still others relieved—but to a man and woman, they filed out silently. And quickly.

The half-naked and completely humiliated Roland Crumm was among them.

"You want everybody to 'shoo'—including me, Batman?" Penguin asked.

"Your boys can flee the coup," Batman said, "but I have something *else* in mind for *you*. . . ."

The following morning the sun turned vivid the fall colors of the forest near the Bat Cave.

"A feast for the eyes, Penguin," the Batman said.

Amid the foliage, the Penguin's tux was out of place; but the Penguin himself, kneeling by the six stacked cages, seemed at home.

"Food for the soul," Penguin said.

"Remember," the Batman said, raising a warning finger, "this free pass I'm extending you is one-time-only: I catch you with your boys again, you're in violation of parole, and it's back to the slammer."

"And you'll be watching, I suppose."

"Bird-watching is a hard habit to break, Penguin."

"Ah . . . isn't it."

And Batman watched as the bird-loving Penguin coaxed the owls from their cages, and both men watched the large birds flutter majestically into the trees and sky.

The Penguin stood, brushed crushed leaves from his black pants. "You surprise me, Batman," he said wistfully. "Imagine *you,* aiding *me* in my vigilante actions. . . ."

"You know what they say about birds of a feather, Penguin," the Batman said.

Brothers in Crime

WILLIAM F. NOLAN

The first thing I noticed when the guard brought him to the cell was his nose. Reminded me of the one that guy Cyrano had, long enough to hang clothes on. Right away, from the nose, I knew who he was. 'Course his white gloves were missing, and they had him dressed in prison stripes, like me, and they'd taken away his monocle and umbrella—but I knew for sure he was the Penguin.

And if that nose of his wasn't enough, there was the lingo he used, right out of a book. Fancy as hell. I'll never forget the way he talked. Once the guard had locked us in together and split, this fat little guy looked me over real careful.

"Hi," I said, putting out a hand. "I'm Fast Eddie Giddings."

"It seems," he said, ignoring my hand, "that a capricious destiny has placed us here together as cellmates. And since I am obliged to share these odoriferous accommodations with a low felon, there are some basic rules I must insist upon."

Brothers in Crime

I let the "low felon" stuff slide past me because I knew I wasn't in his league, but he hooked me with the part about rules. I blinked at him. "What kinda rules?"

"Rule One," he declared, ripping my latest centerfold from the wall. "I shall not permit the brazen display of unclad females. It shall be replaced with a more suitable adornment."

He shook a long tube of paper from his sleeve, unrolled it, and taped it to the wall. It had birds on it, all kinds of birds, big and little, skinny and fat. There were eagles, gulls, owls—even some ugly, red-necked vultures.

"There!" he said. "A panoply of our glorious feathered friends!" He turned toward me again. "Rule Two. You shall never, under any circumstances, mention the name of my prime nemesis."

"You mean the Batman?"

He lunged at me across the cell and pecked me sharply in the chest with his beaked nose. It hurt.

"Never mention him in my presence," he snarled. "Despite the fact that I am by nature overendowed with flesh, you will find that I am expertly trained in the martial arts. I can inflict great pain if I am provoked, so do *not* provoke me."

"Okay," I said. "So I won't mention you-know-who."

"Ah, that such a splendid specimen of nature should be forced to reside in this wretched abode," he said, waddling back and forth in front of me, stroking his chest the way a bird preens his feathers.

"Breaks of the game." I shrugged. "Had me a nice little check-forging racket going till they collared me."

"Rule Three," he said. "Silence is golden. Therefore, you will refrain from speaking to me unless requested

William F. Nolan

to do so. It is vital that a brilliant mind such as mine not be polluted by the witless gibberings of an ape."

That got me sore. "Hey, who you callin' an ape?"

He gave me a cool smile. "Tut, tut, my dear fellow, I merely state the obvious. You have the slope-browed face and wide nostrils of a gorilla."

I glared at him. "With a beak like yours, I wouldn't go talkin' about how somebody *else* looks."

He sighed deeply. "Already I find that we are engaged in vapid and wasteful discourse. I must use my keenly honed wits to devise an escape. To do this, I shall require that we no longer converse."

"Suits me," I said. "If that's how you wanna play it."

So for a solid month we didn't swap a word. He spent most of the time stretched out on his bunk, pudgy eyes closed, with his fat belly poking up like he'd swallowed a basketball. But I knew he wasn't sleeping. He was thinking.

Then, one afternoon, he sat up abruptly on his bunk and said: "I have arrived at the grim and somewhat depressing conclusion that there is no possible way for me to depart these drear premises lacking outside assistance. Might I, therefore, inquire as to the date of your expected departure?"

"Huh?" I said. "I don't read ya."

"Allow me to reiterate. At what point in time do you anticipate a release from your current bondage?"

"You mean, when am I gettin' outta this joint?"

"Precisely."

"I'm only in for nine more weeks," I said. "It's a short rap."

"Splendid!" he said. "Then we shall talk again in two months."

Brothers in Crime

And that's how it went down. He didn't say a word to me until the morning I was due to walk out of prison. Then he talked. And what he came up with blew me away.

"Once you are on the outside," he told me, "you are to contact an uncouth ruffian named Knuckles O'Rourke. He can usually be found in Dirty Sam's, a poolroom of ill repute near the wharf. Despite a shockingly deficient vocabulary, O'Rourke *can* be depended upon. He will take you to my personal headquarters. There you will find—"

"Hold it!" I protested. "What are you leadin' up to?"

"To your achieving my escape from Gotham Penitentiary, what else?"

"Just gimme one good reason I should risk my neck helping you split out of this joint."

"Because, my dear fellow, we are brothers in crime."

"I'm no brother of yours," I snapped.

"Ah, but you are." And he smiled. *"Literally."*

"What's that supposed to mean?"

"I am never imprecise," he declared. "We are genetically linked. The same blood flows in our veins. The fruitful womb from which we were delivered into this discordant world is one and the same, although you emerged at a somewhat later date."

"Are you sayin' that my Ma was *your* Ma?"

"Indeed I am."

"But you called me an *ape*!"

"That is because your father, the man our mother married after my father died, unfortunately provided you with apelike features. I meant nothing personal by my observation."

"You're puttin' me on," I said.

"Not so, dear brother, not so."

William F. Nolan

"Yeah? Gimme some proof."

"Very well," he said with a nod, ticking off the points on his fat fingers. "My name is Oswald Chesterfield Cobblepot. My father called me Ozzie, a name I have always detested. After pneumonia plucked him from this dolorous vale, my widowed mother remarried. Her new husband was Thomas Giddings, your father. You, my fine fellow, are the issue of their loins. Our dear mother, now unhappily deceased, was Elmira Riddley Cobblepot Giddings. We are, therefore, of one flesh."

I blinked at him, stunned. "And you knew who I was from the start?"

"Naturally." He clasped his pudgy hands behind his back. "When my wings were clipped by that miserable bat-creature and I found that I was being dispatched to this wretched place, I arranged, via a simple bribe, to be assigned this particular cell. It was my intention to work out an escape plan on my own, but if I were unable to do so, which, alas, has proven to be the case, I knew I could repair to you for assistance. Blood-to-blood, brother-to-brother."

I shook my head. "I never knew Ma had another kid before she married Pop."

"Our dear mother grew ashamed of me and refused to acknowledge my existence. She had no tolerance for crime or criminals. How ironic that you seem to be following the same dark path."

"How come you need me?" I asked him, "if you got this O'Rourke mug on the outside?"

"I have many outside contacts beyond Mr. O'Rourke," he said, "but only *you* can handle a hot-air balloon."

So that was his game. The Penguin had checked me out and he knew my Pop ran a balloon factory. I'd been

Brothers in Crime

taken up for my first ride when I was seven and I know a lot about handling an airbag. Pop figured I'd go into the business, but when Ma died, I quit school at fourteen and lit out on my own. Maybe that's why I became a crook—because I was the Penguin's brother. Because of genetics. Who knows?

Anyhow, here's what happened...I met Knuckles O'Rourke in Dirty Sam's, and he took me to this weird place full of birds in cages and all kinds of odd stuff, but I didn't get much of a chance to look the joint over since we were on a real tight schedule.

What I'd come for was to handle the balloon my brother had stashed there, get it inflated and into the air. It was shaped like a huge penguin, which figured, since there was a lot of penguin-shaped stuff at my brother's pad. Weird, but colorful.

With me and O'Rourke in the basket, we took off for Gotham prison, floating down into the main exercise yard at the exact time my brother was outside doing knee-bends. Knuckles cut loose with a rapid-fire weapon, spewing rubber bullets, knocking down two of the guards as I hauled my brother into the basket. The guy in the tower swung his weapon in our direction, but Knuckles stunned him with another burst, and we were outta there, soaring upward smooth as you please.

And that was how the Penguin escaped from Gotham Penitentiary.

The job was a lead-pipe cinch. No sweat. And I gotta confess I felt all warm inside, not being alone in the world anymore.

It was good having a brother.

Maybe you're wondering about the Batman—why he wasn't around in his Batplane to chase the Penguin's balloon. Well, on the day we got my brother out, the Batman was busy in the suburbs saving a teenage girl from being kidnapped by a motorcycle gang. I guess ole Bats was plenty ticked off at my brother's escape from the pen because he'd gone to a lot of trouble to send him there in the first place.

They were old enemies, and the Penguin had nearly killed the Batman on several occasions, using his trick umbrellas and stuff. Back at his secret headquarters, after the escape, my brother showed me umbrellas that had swords inside, and some that could shoot poison arrows, and other that could electrocute you if the metal tip of the umbrella touched your skin. One was a flamethrower and another could produce a billowing smoke-screen. I was impressed.

"How'd you ever think up all these wild gimmicks?" I asked.

"Genius, dear brother, sheer unadulterated genius! My awesome powers of invention are infinite." The prison clothes were gone and Mr. P. was dressed in his famous outfit: monocle, white gloves, bow tie, top hat and tails, yellow vest, striped purple trousers, and spats. Lemme tellya, he *did* look like a penguin in that getup.

He talked about how "vastly superior" he was to all the other major criminals in Gotham. "The Joker is a joke," he snapped. "Two-Face is a bumbling idiot. The Scarecrow is witless. The Riddler is a clumsy oaf. And, of course, the Mad Hatter is insane. At least the media jackals acknowledge my rarefied status."

He tossed me the morning *Globe*. The headline called

him a "Master Criminal"—but it was the words *under-neath* the headline that rocked me:

PENGUIN'S BROTHER EFFECTS DARING BALLOON ESCAPE

"How'd they find out we were related?" I asked.

"Because, dear lad, I *told* them. Last night I phoned the editor and revealed our blood-ties. Thus, you are no longer simply Fast Eddie Giddings, a cheap small-time forger. You are, for all the world to envy, the Penguin's brother!"

"Yeah." I grinned. "Guess I've become famous over-night, huh?"

"Indeed you have, dear boy. Indeed you have."

"What's your next caper?" I asked him. "Whatever it is, I wanna be in on it."

"Ah, my dear Eddie," he said, raising a gloved finger. A yellow canary flew over and perched there, singing his little heart out. "I shall naturally allow you to ac-company me on, as you put it, my 'next caper.' Indeed, you shall have the rare privilege of watching the Penguin in action."

"Swell," I said, grinning. "What's the job?"

"You shall see. In due time, you shall see."

And he was off to feed his vultures.

Now, I'm proud to say that I keep up with what's going on in the criminal world, and I've learned enough about how my brother operates to know he usually steals something related to birds. It's his rep, you might say. So next day, when I read in the paper about this new treasure going on display that weekend at the Gotham Museum, I figured he'd go for it. And I was right.

William F. Nolan

"How could I possibly pass up such a fabulous opportunity?" he said. "Rest assured that before the sun rises tomorrow above the towers of Gotham City, the falcon shall be mine!"

He was talking about the jeweled bird know as the Saracen Falcon. It had a long and bloody history.

The newspaper said that the whole routine started way back in the 1100s, with Richard the Lion-Heart and the Crusades. Ole King Richard wanted to get the Holy Land back from the infidels, okay, but he wasn't above going after a bit of booty when it suited his purposes. And when he recaptured Jaffa from Saladin, part of the treasure was a bird made of gold with a bunch of jewels stuck on it from beak to talons. The Saracen Falcon.

When Richard was on his way back to England, Duke Leopold of Austria grabbed him and stuck him in prison. The falcon was lost and nobody knew who got it.

The fancy bird popped up again in Tangiers a hundred years later, where more blood was spilled over it. Finally it ended up in Italy, where a lusty prince gave it to his lady friend. Then a Turkish antique dealer hooked onto the bird and sold it to a rich guy in Constantinople. But not long after that, a Russian general snuffed the rich guy for it. The point is, it was nabbed over and over again down the centuries, including the time it was taken as loot by a member of the French Expedition to Mongolia. (The paper didn't say when *that* happened.)

Anyhow, people kept knocking off other people to get it and somehow the bird wound up in the hands of a billionaire collector in New York named Gino Goularti who was connected with the Mafia. Lord knows who *he* snuffed to get the bird. Well, on his deathbed, Gino decided to donate it to the Gotham City Museum because he'd grown up in Gotham and wanted to do something nice for his old hometown. So here it was.

And now the Penguin had his beak in the game.

I'd read all about the round-the-clock guards they had posted at the museum and about the fact that when the place was closed to the public at night they set these special alarms.

The only thing the Penguin had going for him was the fact that the exhibit room itself, where they had the bird, was empty at night. But that was because they had the floor rigged so that if anybody's foot touched it, a zillion bells would start clanging and the guards posted outside the room would come rushing in—plus another alarm would alert the cops at the station just five blocks away. The floor was so sensitive a butterfly could set off the alarms. (They even had guards on the *roof* of the building!)

"...and besides all this," I told the Penguin, "you just gotta know that the Batman will be hanging around there waiting for you to make your move. He's no sap. He'll figure that this fancy falcon is just the hotsy item you'll go after. I got some advice for you, bro."

The Penguin gave me a scowl. "A common felon of your low station is hardly in a position to give a criminal of my caliber advice," he told me in that croaking voice of his. "Nevertheless, since we *have* shared the same womb, I shall allow you to proceed."

"Wait for a coupla months, till the heat dies down. *Then* hit the joint. Ole Bats will've given up hanging around, and you'll have clear sailing."

"*What?*" He removed his monocle in shock. "Me! *Wait?* And besmirch my sterling reputation for steal-

William F. Nolan

ing the treasures of this world when the spotlight is brightest upon them? Everyone will be expecting me to strike during the weekend, and I shall not disappoint my public."

"But that's *nuts*," I protested. "They'll grab ya for sure!"

He smiled, readjusting his monocle. "Tut, tut," he said, "I am one bird who is not easily netted. Let them try, dear boy. Let them try!"

Just like the Penguin promised, I was in on the whole caper, start to finish. And I had to hand it to my brother, he was one smart cookie. The way he planned the knockover was nothing short of sensational. I'll just run it down for you the way it happened....

The job was set for late that Friday night, after the museum was closed. Knuckles O'Rourke was going up in the Penguin's balloon as a decoy. I told him how to empty air from the bag so as to lower it over the roof— and just how to land it. Idea was, the searchlights would pinpoint him in the sky and by the time the basket touched the roof, he'd be surrounded by about fifty guards with their guns all pointed at him. They'd figure it was the Penguin for sure. And, no doubt, the Batman would be there to welcome him down. Once they saw that he wasn't their boy, they'd know they'd been tricked—but by then it would be too late. The bird would have grabbed the bird, as it were. At least, that's the way the Penguin had it set up. He wouldn't tell me how he planned to avoid all the inside guards or how he'd be able to snatch the falcon over a wired floor. Told me to "observe and learn." Which was okay with me. I like surprises.

Brothers in Crime

Knuckles wasn't too happy to be going up in the balloon. "Dey could shoot me down, Boss!" he rasped. "Dey might not *wait* for me to hit the roof. An' I ain't bulletproof! Besides, I don't got me no chute in case I hafta jump."

"A parachute would be utterly useless at that altitude," my brother told him. Knuckles was big and stupid and he worshipped the Penguin. That's what my brother counted on. "As for your not being bullet-proof, I am outfitting you in my special bullet-resistant suit. Your head will be covered with my newly designed Fibrohelmet. It is impervious to anything short of a ten-millimeter projectile. By the time you have landed on the roof and they have wrestled off your helmet to discover your true identity, I shall have made off with their precious Saracen Falcon." And he let go with his braying bird's laugh.

"I just dunno, Boss." Knuckles shook his head. "I'm gonna feel like a sittin' duck up there."

"Tush and nonsense, lad," said the Penguin. "You'll do splendidly, and I guarantee that not a hair on your loathsome body will be harmed."

"Won't they jug me when they find out I ain't you?"

"For what, pray tell? You'll have broken no law, flying a balloon above the Gotham Museum. They cannot hold you without legal cause."

Knuckles was too dumb to realize that he was wanted for helping the Penguin escape from Gotham Penitentiary in this same balloon. He grinned stupidly as my brother clapped him on the shoulder. "Make me proud of you, Knuckles. Once more into the breech, dear friend!"

"Yuh! Okay. Yuh, yuh! I'll make you real proud of

William F. Nolan

me, Boss." And a tear slid down O'Rourke's grimy unshaven cheek.

Which proved how good the Penguin was at winning
people over. To tell you the truth, it made me a little
sick.

Once Knuckles was launched in the airbag, me and the
Penguin headed for the museum on his Whispercycle.
I mean, it's jet black and you don't hear a sound from
that bike as it glides over the pavement. He did something to the exhaust that makes it silent as a tomb.

We pulled into a lot just behind Rudy's Hardware,
two blocks short of the museum. "From this point we
shall proceed via shank's mare," the Penguin told me.
I knew that meant we'd go on foot. His top hat was
cocked at a jaunty angle and his eyes twinkled. He was
having himself a dandy time.

"We can't just *walk* over there and rob that joint," I
told him.

"Ah, but we can," he told me, "so long as we remain
off the street. Follow me, Edward." (He only called me
Edward when he was real intent, so I knew things were
getting serious.)

He had me pry off a big manhole cover and we went
down a flight of iron steps into an underground tunnel.
It was a storm drain that ran right under the museum.

"The cops must know all about this," I said. "They'll
have the exit guarded."

"Of course they will," he said with a nod. "However,
the guards will be no problem. Trust me." In addition
to his ever-present umbrella, he had a canvas sack
slung over one shoulder, but I didn't know what was in
it.

Brothers in Crime

When we got to the ladder leading up into the museum basement, the Penguin put a gloved finger to his lips. "Quiet now, Edward. The game's afoot!"

I could hear the mutter of voices just above us. At least two guards.

The Penguin climbed the ladder very carefully with me right behind him. I didn't have a weapon, but he told me I wouldn't need one. It was like he said, I was trusting him.

At the top there was an iron grating with round holes in it. My brother reached into his canvas sack and removed two small breathing masks. He handed one to me and slipped the other over his long beak. I put mine on. Then he poked the metal tip of his umbrella through the grating and pressed a stud on the handle. With a hissing sound, a thick blue cloud spouted out, filling the room above us. We heard a kind of gasping, then the thump of falling bodies.

The Penguin smiled, pushing on the grating. "After you, my dear Alphonse!"

Three guards were stretched out on the basement floor, sleeping like babes. I was surprised to see they were all wearing gas masks!

"How come you were able to gas 'em with their masks on?" I wanted to know.

"Indeed, a fair and reasonable question. I have used gas quite often in past escapades, as the Gotham authorities are well aware. Therefore, I assumed that all the guards here would be wearing protective gear. My solution was simple: I prepared a potent new blend of vapor designed to penetrate an ordinary gas mask. And, as you can see, I have succeeded brilliantly.

I was still confused. "What about *our* masks?"

"Perfectly safe. My new sleep gas will have no effect

William F. Nolan

on us. But make certain you *continue* to wear your mask, dear heart. There are many more minions of the law waiting to be eased into the arms of Morpheus."

And that's what happened. Every time we encountered more guards, my brother put them to sleep with his umbrella. Finally, we were outside the main exhibit room. The bodies of snoozing guards littered the hallway. A couple of them were snoring like buzz saws.

The door was made of steel bars, and you could see the golden falcon under a bell jar in the middle of the room. An overhead pinbeam made it shimmer and glow.

"Ah...the moment is at hand." The Penguin sighed. "The fabled treasure awaits me."

"Even if you could melt those bars, we can't go in there," I said. "Once our tootsies touch that floor, all hell breaks loose. When those alarms go off, they'll have half the town here before we can take ten steps."

"True enough," he replied. "Therefore, we shall *not* enter the room."

"Then how are you gonna grab the bird?"

"I will not *personally* remove the falcon from his perch," he said. "I leave that task to my feathered friends."

He took two birds out of his canvas sack. Hawks, with hooded eyes. The hall lights played on their shiny metal bodies.

"They fly by remote control," my brother told me, taking something else from the sack—a small box with buttons on the top. "I shall utilize this to direct them. Observe!"

They slipped easily through the bars, winging over to the glassed falcon.

Brothers in Crime

The Penguin was gloating as we heard the sound of gunshots from the roof. *Knuckles!*

"They're shooting at him!"

"Naturally," said the Penguin. "I expected them to."

"But if they puncture the balloon, he could croak in the fall!"

"Do be quiet, Edward. There is still work to be done here. The most delicate part of my operation is yet to come. Idle chatter is quite out of order."

I shut up—but I didn't like to think about what was happening to poor Knuckles O'Rourke.

He fiddled with the controls and the first hawk clamped its sticker claws onto the bell jar, lifting it clear, while the second hawk neatly scooped up the treasure. Then both hawks winged back in our direction.

"It won't fit through the bars," I said. "The falcon's too wide."

"You spoke of my ability to melt steel." The Penguin smiled. "Indeed, that is precisely what I'm about to do."

He unclipped a small laser pen from his coat pocket and directed its beam at the first bar. The beam sliced through like a blade in hot butter. Within moments my brother had the golden bird in his gloved hands.

"Mine!" he piped, breaking into little hopping dance-steps. "Oh, glory! The Saracen Falcon is mine!"

Which is when the Batman showed up. A door crashed open at the end of the hall—and there he was coming at us like God's lightning. He hadn't been duped by the roof action. Not old Bats! I'd seen pictures of him, but they sure didn't do him justice. I mean, this guy had a body like Arnold Schwarzenegger. He was *all* muscle under that dark costume.

William F. Nolan

"Penguin!" he shouted. "Your game's over. We don't give out free falcons in Gotham City."

That's when the Penguin amazed me. He popped the jeweled bird into his sack and flipped an arm around my neck, pressing the razor-sharp tip of of his umbrella into my ribs. "Stop, or be responsible for this lad's instant demise! The tip of my bumbershoot is coated with a deadly substance that can penetrate to the heart in less than a second. I warn you, stay back!"

The Batman hesitated, fists balled. I couldn't see his eyes behind the dark blue cowl, but I knew they were blazing.

"I intend to exit this building in the same manner I entered it," said the Penguin. "If you attempt to interfere, this poor lad dies. His life rests entirely in your hands."

I wasn't worried. This was a stunt to help us both get away. I knew he wouldn't really hurt me.

"Better do whatever my brother says," I told the Batman.

"He's not your brother, Eddie," declared the dark crime fighter. "The Penguin *has* no brother."

"The foul bat-brute is lying!" shouted the Penguin.

"No, Mr. P., as always, *you're* the liar," countered Batman. "I speak the truth."

And suddenly I believed him. I'd been played for a prime sucker. When the Penguin couldn't figure a way out of stir, he duped me into helping him by feeding me that "brother" line. What a sap I'd been!

"You used me just like you used poor Knuckles!"

"And why not?" mocked the Penguin, tightening his grip on my neck. "Fools such as you are *made* to be used."

Brothers in Crime

That's when I exploded, driving my right elbow into that bloated stomach of his. When he fell back grunting, I ducked under his umbrella and snatched the canvas bag from his shoulder. I had the falcon!

The Penguin's hand darted inside his coat, emerging with a .45 automatic. He fired point-blank at Batman and the caped crusader staggered back, dropping to one knee. Blood pulsed from a nasty wound in his head.

"Now, my freakish bat-friend," cackled the Penguin. "I am about to deliver the *coup de grâce*. In the words of the immortal Bard, 'Good night, sweet prince, may flights of angels sing thee to thy rest!'"

He triggered the big automatic. In that same roaring split second I tossed the canvas bag aside and threw myself in front of his bullet, taking the heavy .45 slug in the chest. It whacked into my body just below the left shoulder. Right away the hall lights began spinning around me in a big circle. Blinking aside a wave of dizziness, I saw the Batman wade into his fat foe. His fists cracked home just as a thick tide of black ink spilled over me.

Then all the lights went out.

Well the doc says I'm going to pull through, that the Penguin's bullet missed my heart. I'm going to be okay again.

That's where I'm dictating this from, a bed at Gotham City Hospital. To a city reporter from the *Globe*. A doll named Vicki somebody. (I've never been much good at remembering last names.)

The Penguin's back in the slammer. Maybe for good this trip. I hope so. He deserves to *rot* in there if you ask me. Knuckles O'Rourke is dead. That fall to the

William F. Nolan

roof killed him. He was just a poor dumb loser who never had a chance.

As for the Batman, he's A-OK. That .45 slug only grazed his skull. Last night he came to see me here in the hospital.

"I computer-checked the Penguin's family tree," he told me. "Elmira Giddings, your deceased mother, was never married to the Penguin's father. That was pure fabrication. In fact, *his* mother is still alive, still a widow. Therefore, you have no Cobblepot blood in your veins."

"That's great to know," I said. "Now I can go straight. Maybe after I get out of jail Pop will take me back at the balloon factory."

"There'll be no jail for you, Eddie," declared the Batman. "Commissioner Gordon has contacted the governor. You are to be granted a full pardon for saving my life."

"Wow!" I exclaimed. "That's terrific!"

"Good luck!" said the Batman—and then he was gone, through the window, a dark shape vanishing into the night.

Well, at least I've learned one thing from this whole crazy caper...brothers in crime aren't always related.

Death of the Dreammaster

ROBERT SHECKLEY

Bruce Wayne would never forget the scene. He saw it again in his mind's eye, the grisly windmill in the low fen country outside New Charity Parish. Bruce himself, as Batman, was there. He was spread-eagled against a wide wooden door, his arms and legs pinioned by steel clamps secured with half-inch bolts. The bodies of the Joker's most recent victims had been stacked roughly against a wall like so much bloodstained cordwood. The torsos were in one pile, the arms and legs in another, the heads in a third. The Joker himself, his thin-lipped grin wider and more hideous than ever, his painter's smock stiff with blood, a bloodstained beret perched on his green-haired head, had just lifted up the last of his victims, little Monica Elroy. The child was still alive, but she had fainted. The Joker tried to slap her into consciousness because death was so much nicer when the victim was awake to appreciate it. Mercifully for her, the child did not respond.

"Well, she's being a poor sport about it," the Joker said. "Might as well finish her and get to you, Batman."

Death of the Dreammaster

The Joker carried the child to the center of the big high-ceilinged room. It was dominated by two enormous grindstones, set on axles contained within an open scaffolding. The great wheels turned slowly, propelled by the wide wings of the windmill outside. They were blood-stained, those wheels. The blood from the victims they had ground into a paste of flesh and bone had stained the granite deeply.

"We'll just feed her in one toe at a time," the Joker said. "Maybe she'll come around in time to say bye-bye."

Batman had been tugging at the clamp that held his right arm to the door. It had a fraction of give to it. Not much, but maybe enough. Enough to give him a chance, faint though it was.

In past years, Batman had learned a precise control of muscles and nerves in his advanced studies in Tibet. He remembered those studies now and forced his concentration to narrow and deepen, ignoring the scenes of horror around him and the overwhelming smell of blood. All his energy had to go into that arm, into his wrist, into the exact point of contact where the clamp pressed. He directed his force outward in a rhythmic fashion, timing it with his pulse beats, and, as he saw the Joker, unconscious child in his arms, mounting the three steps to the platform where the great grindstones touched their rough faces together, Batman drove at the clamp with every ounce of mental and physical energy at his disposal.

For a moment, nothing happened. And then the steel clamp wrenched free from the wooden door with a loud clear ringing sound, and the bolt that had secured it flew across the room as if it had been shot from a slingshot.

The Joker, who had just been lowering the unconscious girl toward the grindstones, was hit on the back of the head. Although the blow did not hurt him, he started vio-

Robert Sheckley

lently, more shock than pain, and the girl fell from his arms. Off balance, he flailed, trying to regain his footing.

One hand, wildly gesticulating in its bloodstained white glove, came up against the grindstones at their point of contact. The hand was pulled in at once. The Joker howled and tried to pull free. The grindstones turned inexorably. The madman screamed and wrenched at his arm, and so violent was his movement that it seemed as if the limb might be pulled from his shoulder. But no such luck. The grindstones continued to devour him, and, as his forearm vanished between the stones and the rest of him was pulled in after it, the Joker, mad with pain, began to laugh, the high inhuman laughter of absolute insanity, and he continued to laugh as his body was pulled between the grindstone wheels, only stopping when his head came apart like a watermelon in a hydraulic press....

And so the Joker was dead.

But was he?

If so, who was that madcap and horrifying creature that Bruce kept glimpsing at the corners of his vision?

Who was Bruce Wayne seeing now, as he walked through downtown Gotham City, on his way to see his old friend Dr. Edwin Waltham?

Bruce Wayne shuddered slightly and resisted the urge to turn. The figure was never there when he turned around.

But he kept on seeing it.

This time, however, was different.

He was at the corner of Fifth and Concord in the heart of Gotham City. Across the street rose the tall tower with the famous polychrome façade that was the New Era Hotel. It was the newest and most sumptuous hotel in the city, built, it was said, by a consortium of foreign invest-

Death of the Dreammaster

ors. It was a place where the rich from all over the world came to look and to be seen, the women to parade in their furs and silks, the men to blow smoke from their fine Havana cigars.

As he stood on the corner across from the hotel, waiting for the light to change, he clearly saw the figure he had glimpsed earlier. The man was long and skinny, dressed in a bottle-green swallow-tailed coat and tattersall trousers like an Edwardian dandy. But that was not what caught Bruce Wayne's eye. It was the man's hair, mossy green above a narrow, long-nosed, long-chinned face. The face looked at Wayne for a split second; the long, red, thin-lipped mouth stretched into a grin. There could be no doubt about it: it was the Joker.

But that was impossible. The Joker was dead. Bruce had seen him die himself; had even had a hand in it.

The Joker, or his look-alike, turned away abruptly, darted across the street, and went into the New Era Hotel.

Bruce Wayne came to an immediate decision. He darted out into the street. Cars screeched, and slewed out of his way. Picking his way across the wide boulevard like a fleet, broken-field runner, Wayne made it to the curb, pushed with unaccustomed brusqueness past a group of gabbling society women, and entered the lobby.

It was like stepping into another world. Outside was the modern-day rush and squalor of Gotham City. Inside, his feet sank into the deep-piled Isfahani rug made especially for the New Era. Overhead the central vault of the ceiling arched upward. Chandeliers, suspended from slender stainless steel threads, glittered with cut glass and blazed with light. The tall windows of the lobby were made of stained glass, giving the place a resemblance to a church for the worship of success.

Robert Sheckley

Surveying the scene, Bruce noticed many men in long flowing Arab robes and headdresses. Some of the women were attired in the heavy veils of those where a form of purdah is still practiced. Scattered here and there were bellboys, smart in their Coldstream Guards uniforms.

Nowhere was there anyone who bore the least resemblance to the grinning figure Bruce had seen only seconds ago.

Bruce hesitated a moment, then went up to the front desk. An assistant manager, a large dignified-looking man in full evening dress with muttonchop sideburns and a bald, gleaming skull, asked if he could be of service.

Bruce described the man he sought.

The assistant manager pursed his lips in an imitation of thoughtfulness.

"No such person of that description has entered here, sir. Not now or ever."

"He might have sneaked in without being noticed," Bruce suggested.

"Oh, I think not, sir," the assistant manager said. He smiled a supercilious smile. "A person of the description you gave us could hardly go unnoticed in a place like the New Era. Green hair and bottle-green coat you said? No sir, not in the New Era."

Bruce felt like a fool. The man was eyeing him as though he were drunk or crazy. Bruce knew very well he was not drunk. As for crazy.... Well, that was one of the things he was going to Dr. Waltham to find out about.

6:15 p.m. Dr. Waltham looked at his watch. Batman was late for his appointment. Waltham had been the Dark Knight's physician for many years. Never before had Batman been this late.

Death of the Dreammaster

Waltham was ready to close up. The physician went to draw the blinds. He heard a low laugh behind him and turned.

"Sorry I'm late," Batman said. "I ran into somebody I thought I knew. Hope you hadn't given up on me."

"No problem, Batman," Dr. Waltham said, peering at the tall cloaked man with the black mask. As usual, Batman appeared seemingly out of nowhere. Waltham had come to expect it—as well as you can expect the unexpected. "Anybody I know?"

"No longer."

"Beg pardon?"

"Nothing, Doc. Shall we get on with the examination?"

It was the time for Bruce Wayne's yearly physical. In his role as Batman, he required absolute physical conditioning of himself. He worked to his own exercise program, and spent hours each week honing his skills in the martial arts. Although he was always in perfect condition, he knew that ailments and conditions could sneak up on you. Hence this yearly physical with his old family friend, Edwin Waltham, one of the top physicians in Gotham City. Waltham was an independently wealthy man who maintained his office and apartment on Starcross Boulevard, one of the best locations in the city. Waltham was small and corpulent, with a head of curly gray hair, a face flushed from good living, and small alert eyes that, behind round glasses, glinted with intelligence. Clever though he was, however, it had never occurred to him that his old friend Batman was the same person as his father's friend, Bruce Wayne.

"You're in great shape, Batman, as usual," Waltham said at the conclusion of the examination as Batman adjusted his tunic. "You've got a heart like a steam locomotive. You'd have to, for some of the things you do."

Robert Sheckley

Batman nodded, frowning slightly. Waltham, who had been his parents' physician, was like most of the people in Gotham City and knew him only as Batman, scourge of criminals and of evildoers everywhere. The doctor was always eager to hear about Batman's cases. There was no harm in it, but there was no need for it, either. Bruce Wayne handled the Batman portion of his life like a state secret.

As he expected, Waltham asked, "Are you working on anything now, Batman?"

"No, I'm still taking it easy."

"I haven't seen you with Vera recently." He was referring to Vera St. Clair, a pretty society woman whom Batman had been seen with.

"She's in Rio. For the Carnival."

"Lucky her! You should have gone yourself, Batman."

"I considered it." Batman didn't know how to tell it to Waltham, but a sort of lethargy had invaded his senses in the last few months. It had begun about the time he began having the hallucinations.

He didn't want to talk about that, but it was one of the reasons he had come to see the doctor.

Seeing him hesitate, Waltham asked, "What is it, Batman?"

Batman decided to take the plunge. "Doc, I've begun seeing things."

The doctor maintained his professional aplomb, but concern glinted from his eyes. "Tell me about it."

The tall, grim-faced masked man described his recent hallucinations. He had had them three times now in as many months. They were usually fleeting, no more than a glimpse of some old enemy from the past, now long defeated and safely buried.

Death of the Dreammaster

Most recently it had been the Joker. Dead, but Bruce had seen him entering the lobby of the New Era Hotel.

Dr. Waltham considered his words carefully. "Batman, I've given you the best physical money can buy. There is nothing wrong with you physically."

"But mentally?"

"I would almost stake my life on your being the sanest man I know."

"Almost?"

"Just a way of speaking. Have you had any unusual concerns on your mind recently?"

Batman shook his head. He couldn't tell Waltham that he had been thinking a lot about the past recently. About friends he had once known, now dead. Robin, Bat Woman, Bat Girl.... And dead enemies, too—the Joker, the Riddler, the Penguin. All of them, friends and foes alike, were his family, those who shared his deeds back when the world was younger.

He was older now. Still perfectly fit, a unique physical specimen. But older.

"No, no particular concerns."

Waltham took off his glasses and wiped them carefully. Before putting them back on he looked at Batman, his eyes a soft, unfocused myopic blue. "Tell me about the most recent."

"On my way here, I thought I saw the Joker."

"Somebody in the crowd, perhaps, a superficial resemblance...."

"No, it was him. I followed him into the New Era Hotel. But he wasn't there. The manager said that no such person had entered."

"A few hallucinations don't matter much," Dr. Waltham said. "You've been through some of the most difficult and terrible experiences known to man. A little

Robert Sheckley

psychomotor activity would not be unexpected. But tell me...is there any chance the Joker is still alive?"

"None whatsoever."

"I don't know the details of his demise, but I would remind you that the Joker escaped from many situations where death seemed certain. Why not this time?"

"I'm sure he's dead," he said.

"Well then, I don't know how to advise you," Dr. Waltham said. "The best thing would be for you to go down to Rio and join Vera. You need to get away, take your mind off these concerns."

"Thanks for the advice," Batman said. "I'll think about it."

"Some tea, sir?" asked Alfred Pennyworth, Bruce Wayne's butler. "It's the special Darjeeling that you like so well."

"Not right now," Bruce said. He had been going over crime reports at the antique table that served him as a desk. There were priceless antiques throughout the big, gracious old mansion that was situated on a landscaped knoll within view of Gotham City. "Is there anything else I can do for you, sir, before I retire?" Alfred asked.

"As a matter of fact, there is," Bruce said. He had been brooding all evening about the events of the day and his visit to Dr. Waltham. Now he had decided to do something. "I want you to pack a suitcase for me immediately."

"Certainly, sir," Alfred said, and his grave expression brightened. "I'll pack your lightweight shorts, sir, and your new tropical suits. Perhaps a mask and snorkel? They say there's good underwater swimming there."

"I beg your pardon, Alfred?"

"In Rio de Janeiro, sir. I assume that is your destination. To join Miss Vera for the Carnival. And if you'll

Death of the Dreammaster

excuse my saying so, it's just what you need, sir. A change, and a little amusement in your life. You have been rather on the gloomy side of late, sir, if you'll permit the observation."

Bruce smiled. "I'm touched by your concern, Alfred, but I'm afraid you've jumped to an erroneous conclusion. I will need no carnival costume where I'm going."

"I apologize for my incorrect assumption, sir. Might I ask where you're going?"

"The New Era Hotel, here in Gotham City."

"Indeed, sir?" Alfred's aplomb was unshakeable. Bruce could have told him he was going to the North Pole and the faithful servant would merely have inquired if he should pack ice skates.

"I'll need about half a dozen evening suits, and some casual clothing for daytime wear, and the usual shirts and socks."

"A wardrobe such as you describe is already packed and ready to go, Master Wayne. I packed the Charlie Morrison wardrobe for you, sir."

"Alfred, you anticipate well."

"Yes, sir. One thing I didn't know, sir. Will you require the Batman Suit?"

Bruce looked up sharply. Somehow he hadn't considered taking the Batman Suit. He hadn't quite brought himself to the point of considering that there were at least two interpretations of his hallucinations. One, that he was going crazy. Two, that someone was planning something clever and criminal and was trying to put a scare into him.

"Yes, pack the Batman Suit," Bruce said. "And put in the small leather bag marked OPS 12. And one of the standard utility belts."

"At once, sir," said Alfred. He didn't bother to mention that he had also packed those things in expectation of just

Robert Sheckley

such a trip. You don't stay Batman's batman for long if you can't anticipate his needs.

Despite all the advantages of his Batman persona, there were a few disadvantages, too. For surprising hoodlums and criminals, the shock value of Batman was great. But for everyday use, it was too noticeable. When it was necessary for him to go somewhere, it was often an advantage to go looking like an ordinary citizen. But there were problems to going as Bruce Wayne, and then suddenly appearing later as Batman. Someone might find it a little more than coincidence that Bruce was around whenever Batman appeared.

Because of this, Bruce had adopted several other personas, to be used when occasion demanded it. The most recent of these, whom he called Charlie Morrison, had been invaluable when Bruce had gone to Europe to detect and foil a counterfeiting ring operating in several cities of northern Europe. Bruce remembered how Commissioner Gordon himself had congratulated him at the end of the case when they met in the mayor's office in Hamburg. Gordon might have suspected that Charlie Morrison was Batman; but that was all right. He was supposed to think that. It helped keep suspicions off Bruce Wayne, the progenitor of both personas.

Working with Lafayette Boyent, one of the masters of classical drama, Bruce had mastered makeup, posture and voice. His impersonations could have earned him a place in the theater if the direction of his life had not been decided long ago.

When Charlie Morrison checked into the New Era Hotel, the assistant manager helped him sign in with no hint of remembering his earlier visit as Bruce Wayne.

Death of the Dreammaster

The assistant manager was cheerful and helpful. Charlie Morrison was a man whose sapphire and ruby American Express card allowed him luxuries unknown to the ordinary citizen. Even among the crowds of visiting oil sheiks and heads of industrial parks, he was a welcome guest—tall, good-looking, quiet-mannered, and renowned for his liberal tips.

The assistant manager brushed back his muttonchop whiskers, a habitual gesture, and swiftly plucked out of a nearby tray a shimmering, plastic oblong slightly larger than a credit card. He held it out to Bruce.

"Your suite is penthouse A2, Mr. Morrison. It is one of our choicest suites, and I'm sure you will find it eminently satisfactory. This card will give you entry to all of the New Era's facilities—the health club, the restaurants and nightclubs, the solarium, the flying room, and so on. There is a complete list of our services in your suite. My name is Blithely. It is my ambition to serve you. If there is any complaint at all, please do not hesitate to call on me day or night."

Bruce thanked Blithely, picked up his key and went to the elevators. There was a special elevator for the penthouse suites. His luggage had already gone up. He pressed the button and stepped in when the heavy, ornate brass door opened. Just as the door was about to close, a woman slipped in with him.

She was tall, sleek and attractive, wearing a frock whose simplicity accentuated rather than belied its price tag. Her dark hair was tied back with a simple ribbon. She carried a small, richly brocaded purse that must have cost plenty, even in Hincheng, China, which Bruce remembered as the home of these objects.

"Yes," she said, following his gaze. "It's Hinchengese. Do you like it?"

Robert Sheckley

Bruce shrugged. "It is quite attractive."

She looked at him boldly. He didn't like the intensity of her inspection. Yet there was something exciting about her, something forward yet subtle, and unashamedly feminine.

"You are also in one of the penthouses?" she asked.

"Yes. And you?"

"Of course. I always stay here when I am in Gotham City." He had detected her faint foreign accent. But what was it? Not German. Something farther east... Czechoslovakia, perhaps. "Dear old penthouse A1 has become something of a home for me. Do you stay here often?"

"My first time," Bruce said.

"You will like it here very much," she said, as the elevator came to a soft stop and the door slid open.

They walked together down the corridor. Penthouses A1 and A2 were opposite each other, the only apartments on the floor. They opened their doors with their cards.

"By the way," Bruce said, "I'm Charlie Morrison."

"Perhaps we will meet again," she said. "I am Ilona." She closed the door softly behind her.

Bruce's clothes were already laid out by the hotel staff, all except the one large leather case to which he kept the only key. In it was the Batman equipment he might soon need, if his instincts were to be trusted.

The suite was indeed beautiful, with a breathtaking terrace view of Gotham City. The city looked magnificent at this hour, a sleeping giant composed of the bodies and minds of its millions of inhabitants.

Was one of those inhabitants the Joker? Impossible. Yet he had seen something.

Or had he?

He sighed and turned away from the terrace.

The living room of his suite was furnished with rare antiques from Eastern Europe and the Near East. There were Turkish wall hangings on one wall, a Picasso on another. A quick inspection told Bruce that the Picasso was genuine, worth perhaps several million dollars. The television was state-of-the-art. The VCR came with a complete tape library, and a catalogue of others that could be called up on a moment's notice. The music console was also impressive.

These things meant little to Bruce, however. This was the same sort of equipment he had at home. He knew from personal experience how difficult it is for the rich to buy anything really special.

He sat in an Ames chair and leafed through a magazine. He was preoccupied, morose. What was he doing here? What could possibly happen in a place like this? The New Era was one of the great bastions of safety with luxury. He was wasting his time.

He called room service and ordered a light dinner: eggs poached in Normandy butter, toast points, slice of Paris ham, fruit cocktail, demitasse. He showered and shaved and dressed in a lightweight evening suit. He had just finished combing his hair when a discreet tap at the door told him the meal had come.

The waiter wheeled the cart, with its high silver-domed salver, to the little table near the balcony. Bruce seated himself and opened the day's newspaper that the man had brought. The waiter deftly laid out the silverware, then whisked the top off the salver and set the plate down in front of Bruce. He bowed, said, "anything else, sir, please call," and started toward the door.

Bruce folded his newspaper and looked down at the plate. His expression froze. There, on the fine Spode china, was a mass of writhing snakes, little green ones and a few red ones. Among them were several small toads. They looked up balefully at Bruce with their evil pop eyes.

"Waiter!" Bruce called out as the waiter was going through the door.

"Sir?"

"What is the meaning of this?"

"I beg your pardon, sir?"

"Come here and tell me how you explain this."

Dutifully enough the man came back into the room. Bruce noticed now that the waiter was almost bald, and that there were faint tattoo marks on his shining skull.

"What seems to be the trouble, sir?"

"Just look here and explain it," Bruce said, indicating his place.

"Yes sir. I'm looking, but I fail to see anything amiss."

Bruce looked down. The snakes and toads were no longer there. What was on the plate now was what he had ordered: ham and eggs by any other name.

"It's the toast points," Bruce said, recovering quickly. "They're soggy."

"They look all right to me, Mr. Morrison," the waiter said, bending down to peer at the golden brown triangles of bread.

"You can see the moisture shining on them. And those eggs are practically hardboiled, not poached at all."

Bruce glared at the waiter, daring him to dispute, but the waiter was not there for that.

"Yes, sir, of course, sir," he said, his tone of voice indicating that he thought Bruce was acting a little peculiar but that he was prepared to humor him. "I'll have the order replaced at once."

Death of the Dreammaster

He wheeled the cart out, closing the door quietly behind him.

It didn't take long to replace his dinner, and this time it underwent no change. Bruce ate quickly. After he was through he wheeled the cart into the corridor. As he turned to return to his room, he saw a figure vanish around the corner at the end of the long corridor. A familiar figure. Tall, emaciated, with green hair and a crazy smile....

It took Bruce Wayne only three strides to reach full sprinting speed as he raced after the figure of his old enemy, who was looking remarkably healthy for one who was well and truly dead.

The corridor was empty. On this side of the hotel there were no suites, no doors at all. The Joker, or whoever it was, had vanished into a blank wall.

Bruce inspected the wall closely. Beneath a light fixture he saw a thin, metal-lined slit. He slipped the card the hotel had given him into it. A panel in the corridor's wall slid back. Retrieving his card, Bruce went through the opening into the darkness within.

The corridor led down a long slope. Bruce hurried down it, just faintly hearing the sound of distant footsteps ahead of him. In another twenty yards the corridor branched. A faint swirling of dust in the left-hand branch told him which way to go. He plunged down a steepening incline. The corridor had at first been lit by fluorescent panels set into the ceiling. As Bruce proceeded, the corridor became dimmer. Some of the panels weren't working. The pitch was so great that he was having difficulty maintaining his balance. There was a blocked-up window ahead of him, dimly perceivable in the gloom. There was

Robert Sheckley

no place to go other than through that or back up the slope. Bruce picked up speed and rammed the window with his shoulder, crashing through it and tumbling into a brightly lit room beyond.

The room was done entirely in white tile and was lit by overhead fluorescents. It was steamy and warm. As Bruce rolled to his feet, he noticed that there were many men in the room, some of them wearing shorts, some towels, a few nothing at all. There were machines scattered around the room. Bruce was familiar with them. They were exercise machines of the sort he had himself in his workout room. He was in the health club.

If there had been any doubt, that doubt would have been cleared up immediately when a short, muscular man with a wrestler's build, wearing white slacks and a white T-shirt that read, New Era Health Club Instructor, strode up to him in a belligerent manner and said, "Say, look here, bub, what's the big idea trying to break in here through the ventilator system?" Then he noticed the card in Bruce's hand. "Oh, sorry, sir, didn't know you were a guest. Our clients usually come through the door."

The instructor was starting to grin. Bruce reached out and took the man's biceps in his hand. It looked like a friendly gesture. And his grip tightened only slightly. But the instructor went pale, tried to pull free, saw it was no use and turned to Bruce with a frightened look on his face.

"Did you see someone just enter?" Bruce asked. "A very tall, thin man with green hair?"

"Green hair!" the instructor said, and seemed ready to laugh. A slight application of pressure to his biceps convinced him that it was not really a laughing matter.

"No sir, I didn't. Really. I'd tell you if I did."

Bruce released the man. A quick glance around the room told him that nobody answering the Joker's description could possibly have come here.

Death of the Dreammaster

Bruce said, "Get me a pair of swimming trunks, please. I think I'll have a dip before I go back up."

"Yes sir," the instructor said. "And which way will you be leaving, sir? Going by the ventilators again?"

"No," Bruce said, "they're only fast getting here."

Bruce felt better after doing a hundred or so laps in his explosive Australian crawl. He returned to his suite.

Mr. Blithely came to visit him a little later. Blithely wanted to know if there was anything the matter. By his expression, Bruce surmised that he really meant, is there anything the matter with you, sir? Bruce merely glared at him. Blithely explained that although it was not so posted, the management encouraged guests to stay out of the ventilation system. Bruce managed to hold his temper. Now was not the time for an outburst.

When the manager had left, Bruce went to the balcony and looked out at the night for a long time. He could hear music from the suite next door, and sounds of laughter and the clink of glasses. It sounded like someone was having a good time.

He was starting to get the idea that something was going on in the New Era Hotel. So far it seemed to be something done especially for him.

It was much later in the night that the noise woke him up. He sat bolt upright, moving instantaneously from deep sleep to immediate alertness. What had it been? A muffled thud from the next suite. It must have been something thrown against the wall, thrown hard enough for the sound to penetrate the soundproofing. Bruce dressed quickly in the dark. He was utterly silent, listening, his senses at full alert. Then he heard a scream. It was from the suite next door.

He hurried out to the balcony. It was about a fifteen-foot jump to the balcony of the next suite. Bruce could do better than that in the standing broad jump, but that was under ideal conditions. Here he would have to crouch on the very edge of his balcony and push off without the benefit of being able to swing his arms. And he would also have to be careful not to let his feet slip on the bevelled facing material.

He leaped. His calculations were not amiss, no matter what else might be wrong with him. His fingers closed crisply around the rail of the next penthouse. He used his back flip to vault neatly over the railing.

The terrace doors to the penthouse were open, but long fluttering white curtains obscured his view within. He moved forward into the darkened room. He felt something soft under his foot and recoiled sharply. Then he had found the light switch and flooded the room with light.

She had been beautiful in life, but death had taken something out of her. She lay with one arm thrown back, the other bent beneath her. Her eyes were open and she seemed to be smiling. This was remarkable in view of the fact that her throat had been cut.

There was nothing to do there. The woman, sole occupant of the suite, was dead. The telephone line had been cut. Her brocade purse seemed to be missing, but Bruce had no time for a complete search. Nor did he know what to look for.

He went back to his own suite. There he made two calls, one to Commissioner James Gordon, the other to

Assistant Manager Blithely. And then back to await further developments.

Soon thereafter, he received a telephone call from the assistant manager. Would Mr. Morrison come to the main office.

Bruce was already dressed. He paused only to check his attire, then went down to the lobby. Although it was the small hours of the morning, there were still many people there milling around. Fun ran late in Gotham City.

Blithely greeted him as suavely as before. But he had a curious expression on his round rosy face as he looked at Bruce. Could it be pity?

Also present in the office was Police Commissioner James Gordon. The tough cop had cooperated secretly with Batman on more than one occasion. Despite Gordon's skepticism, they often teamed up in their fight against crime.

"Hello, Morrison," James Gordon said. "Been quite a while."

"Hamburg, about three years ago," Bruce said.

"Tell me what you saw tonight, Charlie," Gordon said.

"But you've seen it yourself by now."

"Never mind. Describe it for me, please."

Bruce described the scene in the suite.

"OK," Gordon said. "Let's take a look."

Bruce, Gordon, and Blithely took the penthouse elevator to the top floor. There was the same corridor, with Bruce's suite on one side, the other belonging to the woman who had ridden up in the elevator with him.

"Is this the place?" Gordon asked, indicating the door through which the woman had passed.

"Of course it is," Bruce said. "What's the problem?"

Blithely opened the door with his pass card. He entered and turned on the light. The first thing Bruce noticed when he went in was the smell of fresh paint. Under the strong overhead lights, he could see that the whole suite had been freshly painted. Before painting, it had been stripped of furniture. A pile of dropcloths was stacked in a corner. Aside from that, the room was empty.

Gordon and Blithely waited while Bruce inspected the apartment. He checked out all the rooms. In none of them was there any trace of recent occupancy, and even less was there evidence that a brutal murder had been committed less than half an hour ago.

The two men waited while Bruce walked back to them.

Bruce said, "Gentlemen, my apologies. I seem to have been mistaken."

Gordon gave him a curious look and sucked at his unlit pipe. In his own brown gabardine suit and beige trenchcoat he looked like a private investigator of the old days rather than Police Commissioner of Gotham City.

The manager said, "Are you feeling all right, sir? It was a very startling incident you described. I do not wish to pry, but are you perhaps under the influence of alcohol or some prohibited drug?"

"Certainly not," Bruce said, his voice taking on a cutting edge. "Do you want to make charges against me, Mr. Blithely?"

"Heavens no," Blithely said. "I am only thinking of the reputation of the hotel. When a guest starts describing scenes of mayhem that have never taken place.... Well, it makes one fear ever so slightly for the safety of the other guests. That, taken with the various other incidents—"

"What are those?" Gordon asked, interrupting sharply.

Blithely described Bruce's first appearance at the hotel, when he was looking for a man with green hair, and then Bruce's unusual entry into the health club.

Death of the Dreammaster

Gordon nodded when Blithely was through. He took off his heavy horn-rimmed glasses and cleaned them with a crumpled tissue. He put the glasses back on, then broke into a grin.

"Well, Charlie," he said, "you've won your bet." He took a ten dollar bill out of his pocket and handed it to Bruce.

"Thanks," Bruce said, following Gordon's lead, nonchalantly pocketing the money.

"I don't understand," Blithely said.

"I used to tell Mr. Morrison here he was too formal, too uptight. I said he was too well-mannered to start a commotion. Charlie bet me ten bucks he could get the manager of the best hotel in town to call me and complain that he was crazy. I never thought you'd go through with it, Charlie."

"Well, you annoyed me," Bruce said.

"So this has all been a practical joke?" Blithely asked.

"Of course it has," Gordon said. "Does Mr. Morrison look crazy to you?"

"Not in the slightest," Blithely said. But there was still a shade of doubt in his voice.

"Thanks for being such a good sport about it," Bruce said. "There'll be a nice bonus added to the bill for you, personally, for taking this in such good humor."

"Oh, Mr. Morrison, there's no need—"

But Bruce waved him away with a lordly gesture. When Blithely left, even he was chuckling at the joke.

When they were alone, Bruce went to the bar and poured Gordon a shot of bourbon, and accompanied it with branchwater on the side. He poured himself a glass of Vichy. Both men sat down on one of the couches. Gordon sipped his bourbon.

"Damn good bourbon, Charlie," he said.

Robert Sheckley

"They have only the best here," Bruce said.

"So I see. Charlie, what in the name of Sam Hill went on here?"

"Nothing, apparently," Bruce said. "You should have taken me in. I'm obviously 'round the bend."

Gordon didn't reply until he had his pipe going. While malodorous fumes rose in the air, he said, "Even if you were crazy, I'd never let on to a guy like that."

Bruce nodded. "Blithely is not a sympathetic type, is he?"

Gordon shook his head. "I'd arrange to have you committed all by myself, if that was what was needed. Charlie, *are* you crazy?"

"Why ask me?" Bruce said. "How would I know?"

"I've gotten to know you pretty well over the years," Gordon said. "You and I were involved in one of the toughest cases of this century. Charlie, I lost my belief in organized religion a long time ago. And I think I've lost about half my faith in justice, too. But one thing I still believe in is Batman."

Gordon looked up from his drink. He saw that "Charlie Morrison" was smiling at him.

"What's so funny?"

"You. Police Commissioner of Gotham City and you don't even know a loony when you see one. But you know what, Jim? I'm just as bad. I don't believe for a moment I'm crazy. Tonight has proven it to me."

"How's that, Charlie?"

"I've seen the Joker several times in recent months. Just quick little glimpses, then he vanishes. It had me worried. I followed him into this hotel, or so I thought. I decided it would be worthwhile to check in myself and see what was going on. All these incidents, all in one night, convince me that someone is trying to put some-

thing over on me. I don't know how, or why—not yet—
but I'm going to find out."

"Frankly, I'm glad you're doing this," Gordon said.
"We've been getting a lot of rumors recently, nothing we
can pin down, but stuff that keeps on popping up. About
something going down that's both criminal and political.
Something involving important people. Something involving the New Era Hotel."

"Interesting," Bruce said. "Anything else?"

"Nothing definite. Just a lot of ominous-sounding
rumors. You always hear these crazy stories about new
criminal combines from foreign countries. This time there
just might be something to it."

"I'm going to see what turns up," Bruce said.

"I'm glad. The way I see it, we've got just one thing to
worry about."

"What's that?" Bruce asked.

"I know you're sane and you know you're sane. But
what if we're both wrong?"

Two days passed without incident. Charlie Morrison did
all the things a wealthy young bachelor might do in a
hotel like the New Era. He sampled all their nightclubs
and watched the shows. He listened to the comedians and
laughed as heartily as anyone else. He tasted the gourmet
specialties in several exquisite restaurants. He drank spar-
ingly and turned down the offers of drugs and women
from the bellboys.

Early on the evening of the third day he saw her again.
She stepped out of the New Era beauty parlor just as he
was coming out of the magazine shop. It was her unmis-
takably, Ilona, the woman he had ridden up with in the
elevator and later seen murdered in her suite.

Robert Sheckley

She wore a dark silk dress, and had a turquoise scarf knotted carelessly around her neck.

"Excuse me, Ilona," he said. But she ignored him and hurried through the lobby, going through a door marked PRIVATE. Bruce followed. He was in a corridor that seemed to lead to the kitchen area. The lighting was bad, and there was deep dust on the floor: the New Eras spick-and-span look did not extend to the off-stage areas. Bruce decided he wouldn't eat here any more if this was a sample of their true housekeeping. He rounded a corner, and there she was.

"Stop following me!" she said.

"Just a couple of questions," Bruce said.

"Oh. Well, if that's all...." She smiled, then opened her purse and took out a cigarette. She found a small golden lighter in her purse. She flicked it once and a cloud of yellow gas sprayed into Bruce's face. She dropped the lighter and fled as soon as Bruce hit the floor.

You can fool all of the superheroes some of the time, but you can't fool any of them all of the time. Especially not Batman. Lacking Superman's invulnerability, Batman had to rely on cunning, foresight, and his preternaturally keen eyesight. He had seen at once that the object Ilona took from her purse was no ordinary lighter. Her very air of unconcern gave her away. He guessed what it was, but did not let on that he knew. He was holding his breath when she sprayed him. He fell to the floor and was gratified to hear the tinkle of the little gas container as she dropped it beside him.

He got up and picked up the little metal case. It was cunningly fashioned, turned on a metal lathe with a jeweler's precision. The curves of its surfaces were deep and complex. All in all it was one of the finest bits of machine work he had seen in a long time. And he was one to know: Bruce Wayne, Batman, had his own tool shop and his own metal-working equipment. He knew good work when he saw it.

Good work, yes. But who's work was it?

He didn't know. But he had an idea where to go to find out.

First, though, a change of attire.

Night fell, deep and dangerous, on Gotham City.

Darkness came down over the Northside docks, where sailors of a dozen nations traded with whores from half the continent. The gin mills of Gotham City were notorious from Montreal to Valparaiso. Recent defense contracts in Subiuz County adjoining Gotham City had brought many new people into the city. They came to work in the Subiuz County defense plants. At night, after finishing their shifts, they wanted some fun. They were not particular about how they got it.

Fun tended to get rough in the more noisome parts of Gotham City such as Limehouse. A man could get knocked on the head and rolled with little difficulty. If he was smart, he took his lumps and went away, a sadder but wiser man. If he tried to do something about it, he was due for an even more unpleasant surprise—such as waking up to find himself wearing lead-filled skiboots and sinking in the garbage-strewn waters of the Limehouse River in the company of eels and crabs.

Limehouse was an old industrial slum, a dark and dangerous place. The more upright inhabitants had been trying to get the street lighting back on for a long time, without success, because of a corrupt city administration that sold all the lighting fixtures to a Mexican entrepreneur.

Darkness bred crime in the stews of the city.

Darkness bred all creatures of the night.

Especially bats.

It was close to midnight, and Limehouse was just coming into its fullest flower. The drunken and motley crowds of sailors parading the streets did not notice a shadow that passed briefly across the huge lemon moon before it dipped down to ground level and came to rest in one of the narrow backyards.

Batman, in full uniform and mask, folded the small batwinged Batcopter and stowed it in its compact carrying case. With a small but powerful Batlight he briefly consulted a map of his own devising. It was a flat tablet about the size of a sheet of typing paper, and less than an inch thick. Illuminated from beneath, it could be scrolled to reveal highly detailed maps of any part of Gotham City.

Batman checked his coordinates again. Yes, he was in the right location. It had been almost two years since he had come to this particular address. He hoped that Tony Marrotti was still in business.

Orienting himself, Batman moved silently to the back door of the sagging one-story frame house nearby. He moved like a shadow. The full moon picked up the white glints of his eyes beneath the black mask. That was all that was visible as he jimmied the door and slipped inside.

The house was divided into several rooms, just as he had remembered. He was in the rearmost, the storage room. Here, neatly laid out on greasy steel shelving, was a variety of metal tubing, cogwheels, nuts and bolts in steel bins, reels of electrical wire of various gauges, and many other things of similar nature. The door to the outer rooms was closed, but a yellow oblong of light shone from beneath it. Batman listened at the door. He could hear a radio softly playing jazz, and the scrape of footsteps as a man moved around within.

A few minutes' listening convinced him that only one man was inside. Batman opened the door and stepped into the room.

The man had been working at a small lathe. He looked up abruptly as Batman came through, his hand diving toward a rear pocket. Before he could draw the gun he kept there, Batman was across the room and had taken the weapon out of his hand.

"Not so fast, Marrotti," he said. "You don't want to plug your old friend Batman, do you?"

"Sorry, Batman," Marrotti said. "Didn't know it was you. I went for the rod before looking to see who it was."

"Do you usually shoot first without looking to see who it is?"

"When they come through my storage room after midnight, yes. But you're very welcome here, Batman. Can I get you a drink?"

"Not while I'm on duty," Batman said.

"But this is something special. My uncle, Lou, you remember him, don't you, sent over this bottle of liqueur from the old country. Try a shot with me for old time's sake."

"A sip, no more," Batman said.

Marrotti crossed the room and went to a cupboard. He took out a large long-necked bottle with a florid Italian label on it.

Marrotti was a short man, bull-chested and thick-necked. His head was round and covered in crisp black curls. He had a wide, generous mouth and clever, shifty eyes. He walked with a noticeable limp, a souvenir of the time some years ago when Batman had managed to save

Robert Sheckley

him from a gang that had trapped him on a tenement roof near his pigeon coop and shot out his kneecap.

"Good to see you, Batman," Marrotti said. "Whatcha been up to? Haven't seen any newspaper writeups about you in quite a while."

Batman ignored that. "How have you been keeping, Marrotti?"

"Pretty well, Batman, pretty well."

"Is crime still profitable?"

"Aw, come on, you know I don't do that stuff anymore."

"I know that you do," Batman said. "But I'm not here about that. You're not big enough for me to go after. No insult intended, but I need to reserve my time for the really big ones."

"I know that," Marrotti said, "and I respect it."

"I need some information."

"Sure," Marrotti said. "Shoot. Only kidding, I mean, what about?"

Batman took a pouch out of one of the pockets on his utility belt and opened it. He removed the small cannister with which Ilona had tried to gas him earlier and handed it to Marrotti.

Marrotti looked at it and seemed about to ask a question. Then he changed his mind, fished a pair of granny glasses out of a greasy vest pocket, put them on and studied the cannister carefully.

"Where'd you get this?" he asked.

"Never mind. Tell me who made it, and who for. I thought this might have been your handiwork."

Marrotti shook his head. "This is high-class machining. Takes better equipment than I've got to do this. See this beading? You need a zero-null drill press and hoe-line redactor to do that. I don't need that for my line of equipment."

"Can you identify it for me?" Batman asked.

"Maybe. Mind if I cut it apart?"

"Go ahead," Batman said.

Marrotti limped across the room and adjusted the overhead floodlights so that he could get a good look at what he was doing. He set up the casing in a vise, then cut it apart with a diamond-toothed saw. He examined the interior of the two hemispheres, frowning, then looked at them again with a magnifying glass. After studying both carefully he discarded one and turned his attention to the other. He gave a grunt when he found what he wanted.

"Look here, Batman. See this symbol?"

Batman peered through the magnifying glass and made out a tiny V with a crossbar stamped into the metal.

"That's a manufacturing symbol," Marrotti said.

"Do you know whose it is?"

"I've seen it somewhere but I don't remember. But I must have it here somewhere."

Marrotti went to a sagging bookshelf and pulled down a thick book. "Manufacturers' symbols," he explained. He leafed quickly through, his fingers going deftly to the right page.

"Here it is. One of the trademarked symbols of ARDC. That stands for Armadillo Rex Development Corporation. Says here they're based in Ogdensville, Texas. The plant manager and chief stockholder is Rufus 'Red' Murphy."

"Do you know anything about these people?" Batman asked.

"ARDC designs and sells special arms. They specialize in exotics, as they're sometimes called in the trade. They turn out anything from miniature spy stuff to complete missile launch systems."

Robert Sheckley

Marrotti took off his glasses and put them away in a worn case. Then he turned to Batman and said, "What was in this cannister? Some kind of tear gas?"

Batman shook his head. "A gas evidently designed to make a man sleep. Or possibly kill him. I didn't inhale it to find out."

"Very wise."

"Do you know anything about this?"

Marrotti went to his jacket, hanging from a wooden peg on a wall, and fished out a cigarette. He fired up and said, "There's been talk about new development in anti-personnel gases. In some compounds they can put a man out for twenty-four hours without harming him. Change the formula slightly and you kill the man dead. All without telltale odor, mind you. In another formulation, LSD extracts are used to make a hallucinatory gas designed to disorient an enemy."

"Interesting, " Batman said. "Is that of interest to the criminal element?"

"You can bet on it. Can you think of a better way to stage a bank robbery? Get everybody tripping and seeing visions or horrors while you walk away with the loot. But nobody's got any of the stuff yet. Otherwise you'd be hearing more about it."

Batman could testify that someone, at least, had some of that gas. But there was no need to tell Marrotti that.

Bruce Wayne, disguised as Charlie Morrison, was at the Gotham City Municipal Airport at nine o'clock the next morning. He was booked first class to Ogdensville, Texas, with only one brief stop in Atlanta. His two suitcases of equipment made him overweight, but he was able to get them on the same flight. There was no inspection for in-country luggage, but even if an inspector had looked into it, he would have seen cases of industrial samples. Only when they were assembled would they constitute the essential equipment Batman found useful on many of his cases.

Atlanta was bright and steaming. Bruce had time for a coffee in the first-class lounge, and a look at the newspaper. Then it was time to board again. Miraculously, the flight was nearly on time.

The trip passed uneventfully. It was mid-afternoon, Central Time, when the big Boeing 747 put down at Staked Plains Airport serving Ogdensville and Amarillo. A telex sent earlier had alerted Finley Lopez, an investment consultant on energy and defense matters, with his main office in Houston. He was one of the foremost investment consultants in the Southwest, and someone Bruce often worked with in his Morrison persona. Lopez had taken a local flight to Ogdensville and was at the airport to meet him.

"How good to see you, Mr. Morrison!" Finley Lopez was a large man, suave and easy-mannered, his complexion a light olive. He had a narrow black moustache and bright brown eyes with dark pouches under them. A small scar above his left eye was the last reminder of a tough childhood growing up in the barrios of Brownsville.

"You're looking well, Finley. Not letting the señoritas take up all of your time, are you?"

Lopez grinned. His reputation as a lady's man was known from Bayou City, Louisiana, clear west to Albuquerque. "Not quite all, Mr. Morrison. Business comes first. But I could show you one fine old time if you'd let me."

"Good of you to offer," Bruce said, "but I'm afraid I'm here this time on business."

Robert Sheckley

"So let's get it done, then we can paint the town red. Or maybe you'd like a real old-style Texas barbecue at my ranch. My wife Esmeralda has a special way with beef ribs."

"I remember Esmeralda's cooking well," Bruce said. "Please give her my love. But I'm just here for the day. I return to Gotham City tonight."

"Well, tarnation," Lopez said with mock annoyance. "Can't get you to have any fun at all. What can I do for you, Mr. Morrison?"

"I'm interested in the ARDC corporation."

Lopez nodded. "Good solid output with a first-class reputation. Red Murphy's the chief ramrod on that spread, Mr. Morrison. You'd like him. He looks a little like Spencer Tracy, only not so pretty."

"I'd like to meet him. Today."

"Let's find a telephone," Lopez said.

Lopez found a phone in the airport and called. He left the booth shaking his head.

"I don't know what's getting into Murphy," he said. "Must be getting old."

"What's the matter?" Bruce asked.

"I spoke to his personal secretary. She said that Murphy isn't seeing anyone at the moment."

"For how long?"

"She couldn't say. Just that he was very occupied with important matters." Lopez scratched his chin, thinking. "Let me make another call."

Ten minutes later he had further news.

"I called Ben Braxton. I don't think you ever met him, Mr. Morrison. He's chief editor of the main newspaper here, *The Ogdensville Bugle*. I've done him a few favors in my time and he was glad to fill me in on Murphy. It's all public knowledge anyhow, but it saves us from having to dig it out of the newspaper's morgue. It seems that Murphy has been acting oddly for the past several weeks. He has a suite in the factory complex, you know, and he moved in there recently, him and his wife. Her name's Lavinia. She's a fine woman, Mr. Morrison."

"So they're both living in the ARDC factory complex?"

"That's right. And they haven't come out. They talk to family members by telephone from time to time. But they haven't been seeing anyone. Not even their son, Dennis, who was in town recently on his way to South America. He's a fire-fighting specialist and spends most of his time on the road. But Murphy wouldn't even see him. It's very curious."

"Curious indeed," Bruce said. "Well, Finley, let's have some lunch. I'll just have time to catch the evening flight back to Gotham City."

"You're going to come and go just like that? Come on, Mr. Morrison! Why don't you tell me what this is all about."

"It isn't about anything," Bruce said. "I've gotten some information about ARDC and I was considering making a large investment in the company. I thought I'd talk to Murphy, see what I think of him, before tying up capital. But if it can't be done at this time, it'll keep. You got any place good to eat around here?"

"Indeed we do!" Lopez said. "I hope you like barbecue, Mr. Morrison, because one of the finest restaurants in the state is just a few miles outside of town."

The restaurant, Las Angelitas de Tejas, was a beautifully restored building in Spanish colonial style. They ate on the broad terrace, overlooking the formal gardens that the restaurant maintained at great expense. Bruce ate enough of the fiery and savory barbecue to satisfy his host. Bruce's own taste was more for diets high in fiber and

Robert Sheckley

nuts, with plenty of salad and vegetables on the side. But he didn't want to insult Lopez's native cuisine.

Lopez drove him back to the airport and saw him aboard the four p.m. flight to Gotham City with a stopover in Kansas City.

When the plane reached Kansas City, Bruce got off and booked a private plane to take him back to Ogdensville. He arrived just after dark. His luggage was still there, in the locker where he had left it.

The ARDC complex occupied several hundred square acres of flat desert close to Ogdensville. It was surrounded by a double barrier of electrified fence. Armed guards patroled the perimeter at all hours.

At night, the place looked uncanny with its guard towers spaced every hundred yards, the entire line of fence brilliantly illuminated by searchlights. It looked like a concentration camp in the American desert.

Bruce Wayne, who had been Charlie Morrison, now became Batman. And Batman was not too impressed.

In his line of work, fighting some of the most ingenious and well-financed criminals the world had ever known, he had on many occasions had to get into places of strong security; places whose owners had gone to considerable expense and ingenuity to make Batmanproof.

ARDC would not be easy, but it was a long way from impossible.

Batman's first attempt was on the north side of the complex. Here, several of the floodlights had gone out; a sign of carelessness that might in itself mean something. Carrying a heavy suitcase of equipment with him, Batman observed the guards' routine for a while. Blending perfectly into the night, and with the gift of total immobility when he so desired, Batman watched for almost two hours.

He concluded that it would be difficult to get through the wire without someone noticing. The guards' paths meshed too well to allow even the ten minutes or so he would need to neutralize the electricity and get through the wire.

He turned his attention to burrowing beneath. Taking a small but powerful mass detector from his suitcase, he took an underground profile of the surrounding land to a depth of a hundred feet.

As he had feared, the ARDC security people had invested in an advanced sensing alarm system, which would detect movements in the earth to a depth of fifty feet. He would have to give up any thought of going under the wire. He would need earthmoving equipment if he wanted to get below the level of the detectors.

He decided that this break-in might not be as easy as he had expected.

He stood in the darkness and thought for a while, a tall, awe-inspiring figure dressed in black from head to toe. Even the little peaked ears of his costume seemed to be standing stiff in concentration.

At last he made up his mind. It was risky, but he had undergone worse.

Billy-Joe Namon and Steve Kingston were on the northeastern quadrant that night. Even in their dark blue guards' uniforms they looked like what they were—out-of-work cowboys filling in the time between rodeos with any work they could find. Guarding the place for Old Man Murphy was not bad work. Murphy was a fair man and he paid a decent wage. The only trouble with the job was,

Robert Sheckley

it was boring. So highly evolved were the protective systems that surrounded the factory that no one ever tried to
get in. Night after night it was the same: the soft hiss of
the desert wind, the occasional howl of a coyote, and
nothing else. Ever.

Except for tonight.

Tonight was different. It began with a loud hissing
sound that seemed to come from the desert.

"You ever heard anything like that?" Billy-Joe asked.

"Might be a gut-shot bear," Steve said.

"I doubt it. Not this far south."

They listened. The sound increased in intensity. Then
a light appeared in the sky in front of them. It pulsed, a
bright electric violet, unlike anything either man had ever
seen before.

"You know," Billy-Joe said, "I don't like this one little
bit."

"What's it up to now?" Steve asked.

The violet light had begun to move, traveling in easy
swoops back and forth across the sky, coming closer and
closer to the perimeter fence.

"You think we should shoot it down?" Steve asked. He
had already cleared his sidearm.

"Don't go gettin' nervous," Billy-Joe said. "Ain't even
nothin' to shoot at yet. Let it get a little closer."

They watched as the brilliant violet light advanced
toward them. Billy-Joe had picked up his submachine
gun. He clicked off the safeties as the violet light came
directly overhead.

Then it burst into dazzling light like the simultaneous
bursting of a million flashbulbs. At the same time it gave
off a deafening noise like a howitzer going off about five
feet from them.

Both men fell down, stunned and blinded. They got to their feet quickly, rubbing their eyes and trying to regain sight.

There was a field telephone ringing nearby. It was from the southern quadrant guardpost, several miles away on the other side of the perimeter fence. The guards there had picked up the noise and flash and wanted to know what was going on.

Billy-Joe pulled himself together enough to make a report.

"Cal," he said to the southern quadrant guard, "I hate to tell you this because you're going to call me a liar, but I think we just saw a UFO close up."

"My aunt May saw one of those last year," Cal said. "They are the dangdest things, aren't they?"

"Cal, I'm telling you, that's what we saw near as we can tell."

"Oh, I believe you," Cal said. "But I guess we'd better go on full alert just in case you boys been hittin' the bottle or chewing on devil weed."

Four Jeeps full of armed men roared out of the motor pool. They raced around the inner perimeter, helping out the Jeeps' headlights with handheld searchlights. They came across plenty of tumbleweed but nothing else.

Nothing they were able to spot, that is.

Darkness and silence again. No sounds but the moaning desert wind and the occasional call of a coyote.

No movement on the fenced-in land of the inner perimeter except for the wind, rippling the grass that the ARDC Corporation maintained at so high a cost.

Grass rippling in the dark.

Something flowing across the dark grass.

Robert Sheckley

Something dark, shapeless, large, moving in a zigzag fashion, coming closer and closer to the main buildings.

In the high watchtower, Steve was watching the grass. There was something a little funny about it tonight. But that was the wind, blowing it back and forth in sudden flaws, taking unexpected turns and reversals, until you could almost swear there was someone or something moving through it.

But that was crazy.

Nothing could get through the fence.

"What you looking at?" Billy-Joe remarked beside him.

"Just watching the grass," Steve said.

"Old buddy," Billy-Joe said, "we're paid to look outside the perimeter, not inside. We already know there's nothing inside."

"Nothing except us chickens," Steve said, grinning.

Us chickens. And a very large bat.

Promptly at midnight, the Captain of the ARDC guards, Blaise Connell, a former Texas Ranger, reported to Red Murphy in his suite.

"Everything OK, Mr. Murphy."

"Thank you, Blaise. What was that bright flash a couple of hours ago?"

Although Murphy's suite was deep within the ARDC complex, and had no window to the outer world, Red Murphy had picked up the flash on one of the banks of tv monitors that were the eyes of the perimeter surveillance system.

"Couple of the boys think it was flying saucers," Connell said. "But that's crazy. I really don't know what it was, sir."

Death of the Dreammaster

"Does the perimeter fence show any signs of breaching?"

Connell shook his head. "Integrity intact."

"I guess we won't worry too much about it," Murphy said. "Good night, Blaise."

When his guard captain had departed, Red Murphy went to the sideboard and poured himself a drink. He'd been going to the bottle a little too much recently. He knew that, but he was under heavy stress. The worst of it was having to keep it all to himself. At least he could share it with his bottle, even if that was not such a great idea.

The apartment was furnished plainly in a typical Western motif. Piebald cowhides covered the chairs. The couches and tables were simple but well made. There were two original Remington oil paintings on the wall, the only touch of ostentation in the room. Aside from them, everything was plain and serviceable, even though the suite was larger than usual. Red Murphy was a man who didn't like to feel hemmed in. The Remingtons, with their sense of wide spaces and western subjects, helped him forget the reinforced concrete on all sides.

He held the shotglass up to the light and squinted at it. He had a tough square face, tanned to the color of saddle leather and seamed by many hours in the fierce sun and driving wind. Murphy was short, and so big in the chest and shoulders that he looked almost misshapen. He had done all the oil field jobs—roustabout, gantry walker, puddler, valve wiper. For years his hobby had been riding around the scrub country west of Ogdensville in his battered old land rover. Folks thought he was a touch loco, spending all those hours just aimlessly riding around the desolate land. They thought he was crazy for sure when he put up every cent of his earnings to take out a drilling

Robert Sheckley

lease on the old Double "O" Field. It had gone dry ten years before, and even though new deposits had been suspected in the area, not a drop had been taken out of it.

Red Murphy got up the money to hire an oil rig. He surprised everybody by first bulldozing the shack and corrals that had marked the headquarters building of the Double "O" Enterprise. Then he'd sunk his bits into a point not more than ten feet off the center of what had been the living room.

The ensuing guster was a beauty.

He'd found the basin. Just as his studies of the surrounding countryside, carried out during those so-called idle trips in the land rover, had predicted. The oil was there, in sufficient quantity to let him begin to build a fortune that was soon to be legendary even in this country of big men with big bankrolls.

When the bottom dropped out of the oil business in Texas, he anticipated it by almost six months. He got his money out and bought the ailing ARDC corporation.

ARDC had a list of bad debts as long as a polecat's shadow on Sadie Hawkins' Day, as the wits at Bernigan's Saloon and Pool Hall in Ogdensville used to say. Its machinery was out of date and mostly falling apart, and its senior personnel had given up on the company long ago, keeping their jobs for the paychecks, but looking around for something more interesting to switch into.

Against all these liabilities, the company had only two assets: a potentially lucrative assortment of defense contracts, and a team of the country's best weapons systems engineers.

Murphy thought he could parlay those into something interesting. He rebuilt the factory, replaced the worn-out machinery, fired the time-servers and gave wage increases

and incentive bonuses to the ones he kept. When he hired
new men, he hired the best.

Soon, ARDC, under its dynamic new management,
was turning out some of the best weapons systems in the
world. Their small arms division attracted the attention
of the British and French secret services, who were eager
to buy some of the products. And the Department of
Defense was very interested indeed. As were the police
chiefs of America, who saw in ARDC one of their best
hopes in the endless war against crime.

Red Murphy was liked and respected in business
groups all over the country. He was welcome in high circles in Washington. He used to attend Washington's special functions frequently.

But for the past months he had not been seen in his
usual haunts. He had begun staying in the factory suite,
talking to business associates, friends and relatives by
telephone. Only Blaise Connell the security chief saw
him. People wondered about it, but eccentricity is part of
the Texas tradition. As long as a man doesn't hurt people
or walk around naked, he can act as weird as he pleases.
Nobody's going to pay any attention.

Practically nobody.

Murphy finished his drink and quickly poured
another. He held up the shotglass and looked at the room
through its amber transparency. The room looked distorted. Murphy laughed and tossed down half the drink.

Then he heard a sound behind him and stiffened.

There was nothing there but the big double closet
where he stored his hat collection and his golf clubs.

"Somebody in there?" he said aloud.

There was no reply.

Murphy put down the shot glass. He reached to his
back and took out, from beneath his flowing Hawaiian

Robert Sheckley

shirt, a chromed .44 Magnum automatic with rosewood handles. He cocked it and walked toward the closet.

"Come on out," he said. "This is the only time I'll say it."

No reply.

He leveled the big gun and pulled the trigger. Slugs blasted apart the light wooden closet door. A pile of hats tumbled out, some of them ragged from being shot through the headbands.

Murphy cursed softly when he saw what he'd done.

He was even angrier when he saw that he'd put a slug through his Ben Hogan Memorial Classic sets of woods.

"Damnation!" he said.

"Don't worry," a voice said behind him. "You only punctured the bag."

The sparse hair on Murphy's big skull lifted as he heard a voice from where no man could be. A tremor of fear swept over him. He forced himself to turn and wasn't surprised when the automatic was plucked out of his hand.

His second shock came when he faced the owner of the voice. He was looking at a tall man dressed entirely in black and gray. A wide cloak with many points flowed from the man's broad shoulders. The man wore a cowl and a half mask. On top of the cowl-like covering, there were small pointed ears.

"Batman!" Murphy cried, clutching at his chest. The pain had just hit him, the almost-forgotten pain in his chest and neck that he used to get before the triple bypass; the sudden attack brought on by the shock of seeing the legendary figure here, in the midst of his fortifications; the pain brought on by long anxiety and a guilty conscience.

Murphy collapsed suddenly, and wasn't aware that blue-gauntleted arms caught him before he hit the floor.

Death of the Dreammaster

Murphy's eyes fluttered, then opened wide. "You still here?" he asked.

He was stretched out on the bed. His tie had been loosened and his shoes taken off. The tall figure of Batman stood near the bedside.

"Yes, I'm still here," Batman said. "How are you feeling?"

"Not bad, for a man who didn't expect to open his eyes this side of the Jordon. What'd you do?"

"I gave you an injection of hectomorphinate. It's one of the antidotes I carry in my utility belt. I couldn't be sure, but it seemed that you were having a heart attack."

"And what does this hecto whatever-you-call-it do?"

"It acts on the blood vessel walls, taking them out of the fatal spasms that presage death."

"My doctor never mentioned this stuff to me."

"He will. It will be coming on the market in the fall."

Murphy sat up cautiously. "I guess I don't have to ask who you are. I've heard about you for years, but never thought I'd meet you. I did meet Superman once, at a fund raising for crippled children in Washington. Seemed like a nice fellow."

"Superman's OK," Batman said. "But I didn't come here to discuss superheroes with you."

"I didn't think so. Do you think I can walk all right? No, don't help me. If I can't make it to the liquor cabinet myself, I'm washed up anyway."

He moved in a slightly creaky fashion to the liquor cabinet and poured himself a double shot of bourbon. It steadied him so nicely that he immediately poured another.

Robert Sheckley

"Hitting that stuff a little hard, aren't you?" Batman said.

"So what are you? Murphy said belligerently. "An advanceman for the WCTU or something?"

"Just a concerned bystander," Batman said. "I need an explanation from you, Mr. Murphy."

"About what?"

"This." Batman produced the two halves of the little hemisphere with which llona had tried to gas him.

Murphy examined it. "Yeah, that's our trademark. Where'd you get this?"

"Somebody tried to use it on me."

"So? Is Colt responsible for every revolver that gets used on somebody?"

"That's beside the point," Batman said. "I know you know something about this because other weapons like this have been turning up. They've been traced to your factory."

"You can't prove a thing," Murphy said.

"Maybe I can't," Batman said. "Not yet. But I will."

"Go ahead and try," Murphy said, and put away half the shot, looking up startled when Batman slapped the glass out of his hand.

"What's the big idea?"

"Get hold of yourself, Murphy," Batman said. "You've got quite a reputation in this country. People consider you a brilliant operator and a straight shooter. You've always had a reputation for being forthright, accessible. Now suddenly you're hiding inside your own factory, you've got the place guarded like it was Hitler's hideout, and you're drinking heavily. You've got troubles, Murphy; something's turned your life around, and I want you to tell me about it."

"Why should I?"

Death of the Dreammaster

"Because you've got to tell somebody, otherwise you'll explode. And why not me? If you can't tell your troubles to a superhero, whom can you tell them to?"

Murphy stared at him, open mouthed.

"And anyhow, Red," Batman said, "maybe I can help. I'd like to try."

Murphy continued to stare at him. Suddenly there were tears in his eyes.

He said, "When I was a kid, I loved the superheroes and wanted more than anything to be like them. Tarzan was the first for me, and then there were a lot after that. You were always special for me, Batman. I liked you because you were more human than most of them. For a while I tried to be like you....Funny, isn't it? You ought to get a good laugh out of this."

"I'm not laughing," Batman said. "And I don't look down on you. Talk to me, Red. Tell me what's going on."

Murphy looked uncertain. "I could get killed for talking to you."

"You're killing yourself by not talking to me."

"I guess that's so," Murphy said. "Yes, I'm in trouble, Batman. It all started about a year ago..."

Murphy told about how, a year ago, when ARDC went public for the first time, Teufel Corporation, a big Swiss-based corporation, made hidden purchases all over the world through designated nominees and acquired a controlling share of ARDC's outstanding stocks. Teufel had taken over ARDC, and they had the right to retire Red Murphy if they so desired. Murphy didn't figure out for a long time how it had happened. It all took place so rapidly that he was shocked and apathetic at a time when all his senses should have been on alert. The new owners never appeared. Operating behind on screen of lawyers, they proposed to allow Murphy to continue running

Robert Sheckley

ARDC. They even promised him a chance to buy back a majority interest in the stock, and so reacquire his own company. But first, for a while, he had to do things their way.

"Several of my people warned me about them," Murphy said. "I should have listened. Especially when they started screwing up the research and production divisions. But I thought that playing along would get me back in control faster. I figured that with their sloppy methods and inadequate quality control they'd fail, you see. I didn't know then what they were really up to."

He reached for the bourbon bottle. Batman pushed it gently out of his reach.

"Might as well give it up now, Red. You can't keep on hiding here forever and drinking. You'll never find a better chance to quit than now."

Murphy looked at Batman and knew that the masked man spoke the truth; you don't get a superhero telling you to quit the booze every day.

Murphy reached out and grabbed the bottle. He threw it against the wall as hard as he could. It made a satisfying sound as it shattered.

Soon after that his telephone rang. Murphy answered it. "Blaise? Yes, I'm fine. Yeah, that was me firing the .44 earlier. And breaking the bottle now. I was having a little celebration. Yeah, sure, all by myself. Me and my bats. The bats in my belfry, I mean. Sure, I'm fine, see you in the morning."

He hung up the phone and said to Batman, "Suppose I make us some coffee. We've got a lot of talking to do, and not much time to do it in."

"What do you mean?" Batman asked.

"The Joint Chiefs are about to sign a contract with ARDC for a new computerized weapons system."

Death of the Dreammaster

"What's so bad about that?" Batman asked.
"Let's get that coffee and I'll tell you."

In the morning, Red Murphy surprised his staff by announcing that he was going to Lake Sarmatian, the manmade lake that had been created by the recent damming of the North Pecos River. He had his staff pack the new Carliño–Gar Wood monohull, still in its packing case, onto the back of his heavy-duty pickup. The gates opened and Murphy sped through, waving to his guards.

Twenty miles down the road there was a grove of cottonwood trees used by the local high school and bible college for barbecues and song fests. It was deserted now. Murphy negotiated the steep dirt road and pulled out of sight of the highway. He got out and went back, pry bar in hand, to open the packing case.

Batman, who had been secreted within the packing case, had already worked his way out and was sitting under a tarpaulin, reading a plane schedule with a little penlight.

"Hope it wasn't too uncomfortable for you," Murphy said.

"I've been in worse," Batman said. "It was easier than breaking out of your factory again."

"What do you want me to do now?" Murphy asked.

"I'd like to leave you here for a while," Batman said. "I'll drive your truck to the airport alone, and arrange to have someone drive it back here."

"That's fine with me," Murphy said. "Lucky I brought along a newspaper. But why can't I drive you to the airport myself?"

"When I reach the airport," Batman said, "I will have changed clothes and become someone else."

Robert Sheckley

"And you don't want me to know who that someone else is?"

"That's it. Please understand, it's not that I don't trust you. But it should be obvious that there's no sense being an anonymous figure if everyone knows who you are in real life."

"Makes sense," Murphy said.

"Sometimes," Batman said, "the costume changes are more difficult to arrange than solving the case."

"I can imagine," Murphy said. "Here, Batman." He handed the masked man the car keys. "Is there anything else I can do for you?"

"Just a final point or two. You said that the Joint Chiefs are about to sign the contract with ARDC?"

"I got confirmation of that only yesterday. It ought to be signed into law by tonight."

Batman nodded. "I think there's still time to do something. I'm glad you let me have the facsimile plans for your production models. I'll have a chance to study them on the plane to Washington."

"My competition would do a lot to get their hands on those blueprints."

"Don't worry. I'll destroy them when I'm finished with them. Now, these people who took over your company. You really have no idea who is in control of them?"

"None at all. Whoever it is, they seem to have some friends in high places. I've never seen a contract go through so smoothly."

"One more question. Do any of your weapons systems make use of hallucinogens?"

Murphy looked surprised. "How did you know? That's the tightest secret of the century."

"I learned it from a man with green hair," Batman said.

"Come again?"

"Forget I said it. Goodbye, Murphy."

"Good luck, Batman."

"Thanks," Batman said. "I suspect I'm going to need it."

Batman drove another five miles down the highway. No cars passed him in either direction. That was just as well; your average cowboy might become curious if he passed a new red pickup driven by a man over six feet tall dressed as a bat. Not that that was likely. Batman had taken the precaution of spraying the windshield and windows of the pickup with a glare-resistant compound that did not impede vision from inside the vehicle but rendered it opaque from the outside. He had neglected to tell Murphy that the compound washed off with soap and water—an uncustomary lapse, but no doubt Murphy could figure that out for himself.

Batman stopped the pickup on a turnout and quickly changed to the sober and well-tailored suit of Charlie Morrison. He packed up the Batman gear in the folding valise he had brought along for that purpose, and went on to the airport.

Bruce decided not to take a commercial aircraft, since none were scheduled at a suitable hour. He quickly arranged to charter a plane for the trip to Washington. Although he was an experienced pilot, he also hired a pilot. It was simply easier that way.

The Batman gear, the two suitcases of special equipment, and the utility belt fit nicely into the Lear jet he had rented.

He had time for a quick brunch while the pilot fueled up and made out a flight plan. He had a small green salad and a side dish of guacamole, accompanied by plenty of

Robert Sheckley

strong black coffee. He had just paid his bill when he
remembered a phone call he had to make. He telephoned
Commissioner James Gordon in Gotham City and told him
briefly where he was going. That was necessary in case
anything happened to him. If Robin could be killed, then
Batman could be killed, too. But crime fighting had to go
on.

Then he went to the Personal Services Booth and
arranged for a chauffeur to take Red Murphy's pickup to
where he was waiting, reading a newspaper under the cot-
tonwoods. And then it was plane time.

It was early evening when the quick little Lear jet flew
into Washington's Reagan airport. The evening lights were
on in the city; twinkling little fairy lights belying the
skullduggery that went on in the nation's capital.

In the airport, taking a private booth in the first-class
lounge's men's room, Bruce dressed again in the Batman
outfit. This time he left off the mask and cowl, concealing
his costume under a long camel's hair overcoat. He was
going to need both of his identities if he hoped to get this
job done.

When he emerged, he looked like any well-dressed
young man.

The overcoat was loose enough to conceal the bulky
utility belt. It was difficult to know in advance exactly
which piece of equipment he would need.

He caught a taxi into Washington proper, directing the
driver to take him to Old Edward's Chop House on Fifth
and Ohio. It was a popular dining place for Washingto-
nians. It also was just across the street from the Gaudi
Building, where, in the General Procurement offices on

the fortieth floor, the contracts for ARDC were to be signed.

The Gaudi Building was not a simple glass tower like so much of the recent construction in Washington. It had been done in a florid neo-Baroque style, with pediments and gargoyles and odd curves and unexpected angles. The architect, Nino de Talaveres of Barcelona, the eccentric Spanish mystic who had won the Prix de Rome for architecture two years running, had predicted, accurately, as it turned out, that the Gaudi Building would introduce a new and popular style into the sterile skyline of the nation's capital.

This unique and unexpected building was liked by many.

Batman was not one of them.

Batman's judgment was not aesthetic, however. It was purely functional. He had worked out long ago a system and the necessary equipment to scale glass towers with great speed and sureness. Now, faced with a brand new version of an outmoded architectural schema, he saw that he would have to improvise.

The porous Carrara granite offered unreliable purchase for the quick-release suction cups that he usually relied on.

The laser glasscutters he had used so often to gain entry through the gigantic picture windows would do no good with windows shaped like slits and barred with wrought iron bars.

He sighed. It was hard enough staying up with new technology without having to reinvent ways of scaling ancient buildings.

Robert Sheckley

He could try to get in through one of the entrances, of course. The thought was attractive, but impractical, he decided after giving it a moment's thought. There was an unusual flurry of activity around the building tonight. The streets were full of police SWAT teams. There were also a lot of men lurking around in simple seersucker suits and rep ties with bulges in their jackets. These, Batman knew from previous experience, were apt to be Secret Service men.

Had Murphy talked to the people who had such a hold over him? Had he given Batman away?

Batman thought not. But they might have become curious about Murphy's unusual actions of the night before, firing off his .44 Magnum and then, in the morning, driving out in his pickup. They would have to be extremely obtuse not to relate these discrepancies. Would they have time to do anything about them? He would have to wait and see.

Batman had had a chance to study ARDC's plans on the trip to Washington, concealing them within a newspaper so that the pilot, a cheerful Tennesssean named Cohen, would not get curious.

Bruce Wayne had a fair technical background. He augmented it with a great deal of mathematical and scientific reading.

He was able to supplement his insights now by using his laptop computer, built to his own specifications at high cost, but with the power of a third generation mainframe.

The insights he had gained into the blueprints had been eye-opening, to say the least.

If that contract were signed into law...

He studied the building again. Getting into it was never going to get much easier than it was right now.

Death of the Dreammaster

He finished his meal at the chop house, paid his bill, went to the rest room, and slipped out the back way.

He was in a noisome alley. Yowling cats slunk around overflowing garbage cans. The zebralike combination of strong lights and impenetrable shadows made the perfect milieu for a man on the run—or a bat in flight.

Within the Gaudi building, on the fortieth floor, in a special amphitheater with recessed lighting, the Joint Chiefs were meeting to consider the ARDC contract proposals. Admiral William Fenton was chairman for tonight's session. He was a squarefaced old seadog with iron gray hair and a bulldog mouth. General "Flying Phil" Kowalski, Commandant of the Air Force, sat at his right hand. Kowalski was tall and slim; his baby face, tousled blond hair, and easy laughter belied the fact that he had been an ace during the recent incident in the south Caribbean, piloting his own Thunderclap-class all-weather interceptor and shooting down four Trinidadian jets before it was discovered that the U.S. was not at war with Trinidad. Beside him was General Chuck Rohort of the army, his short, heavily built body displaying the concentrated attentiveness that a really good tank commander needs.

"Well," Admiral Fenton said, "we might as well call this meeting to order. I propose that we waive the reading of the minutes of the last meeting. There are entirely too many important decisions to make tonight without having to rehash any old ones. No objections? Good, let's go on. I believe that General Kowalski has a somewhat unusual request to make."

Flying Phil stood up, grinning pleasantly, twirling his goldleaf encrusted hat in his hands in an awkward motion that he had studied with some care.

Robert Sheckley

"As I understand it, this meeting is to decide the issue of the ARDC contract, docket number 123341-A-2."

"That is correct," Admiral Fenton said. "As you would know if you had attended yesterday's meeting, those of us present weighed the pros and cons of the new ARDC system. Since we will be supplying these weapons to our own troops as well as our allies, I need hardly mention to you the seriousness of this contract."

"I know the weapons are good," said General Rohort, shifting his heavy body in an alert manner. But can ARDC be relied upon to deliver?"

"I think we need have no doubts about that," Fenton said. "But as a final witness, I have taken the liberty of calling in James Nelson, Deputy Director of the CIA."

Fenton gestured and a yeoman opened the door to the outer office.

In walked a tall tan man dressed entirely in shades of tan. Even his fingernails were tan; an extremely light tan, but a tan nevertheless.

Only his teeth were white; his teeth, and the whites of his eyes.

General Kowalski wondered if it meant anything that the first thing he noticed about James Nelson was the whites of his eyes.

"Good evening, gentlemen," Nelson said. "Please excuse my tan. I'm just back from Florida where I have been supervising our counterinsurgency program designed to bring Columbian cocaine dealers in line with current clandestine drug pricing policies."

"Have they been undercutting the government drug-supply programs again?" General Rohort said, a frown on his tanklike face.

"Indeed they have," Nelson said. "The loss of revenue for the government's various clandestine services has been severe. And of course there is the loss of quality experienced by the end users."

"That foreign stuff doesn't meet FDA regulations," Admiral Fenton growled. "There really ought to be a law against it."

"The President believes in free trade," Nelson said. "Within limits, of course." He ignored the No Smoking sign and lit a cigarette. The faint yellow cast of the tan cigarette contrasted subtly with the faded rose tan of his lips.

"Well, never mind," Kowalski said. "It's none of our business what anyone does about drugs. We're here to do something about this contract. I must say, Nelson, I've had my doubts about a few of the details."

"Set your mind at rest," Nelson said. "This is one of the best and most constructive contracts the U.S. government has ever entered into with a company from the private sector. What makes it even nicer is that several of our foreign allies will also profit from the contract and give this move a lot of good publicity."

A copy of the contract was taken out and passed around. The Joint Chiefs peered at it and passed it around.

"Well, gee," Kowalski said. "I'm still unsure."

"Let me reassure you," Nelson said. "The President himself wants this bill to be signed into law."

"Then why doesn't he tell us so?" Kowalski asked.

"Gentlemen, that is just what he is going to do. The President is coming here to witness your signatures and congratulate you on doing your patriotic duty."

"The President? Coming here?" said Chuck Rohort.

"You got it, Chuck," Fenton said.

"Then let me waste no further time," Nelson said. "Gentlemen, the President!"

Robert Sheckley

He nodded to the yeoman. The yeoman gulped and opened the door. In walked Marshall Seldon, the tall, stooped, gray-haired man with the lopsided grin known in every home around America.

The Joint Chiefs rose so as to crowd around the President. Nelson made them stay back.

The President held up a hand. Soon they heard his familiar tweedy tenor.

"Gentlemen, I have many important matters to attend to. Please sign the treaty, and let us get on with the business of confounding our enemies and comforting our friends."

The Joint Chiefs crowded around, each pushing to be first. They were interrupted by a clear baritone voice as the door opened again, this time without any assistance from the yeoman.

"Before you sign that piece of paper, gentlemen, I'd like a word with you."

They all fell silent. Even important men like generals and admirals were likely to give Batman a chance to speak.

Nelson was an exception to that rule, by virtue of his unique position. It was his duty not to be seduced by other men's words. He knew that Batman did not belong there. He pretended to listen, but all the time his right hand was snaking toward his belt, where a two-shot derringer, disguised as a Hickok belt buckle, awaited his touch.

Batman had had no insurmountable difficulties scaling the Gaudi at first. He hadn't been able to use the means that had gotten him over the ARDC fence. In that instance he had employed a whiz-bang, a simple enough contrap-

Death of the Dreammaster

tion designed to make brilliant flashes of light and strange, unsettling noises, and to do so long enough to allow an attack to be launched from another quarter. The attacker had been Batman himself, climbing up and over the fence, protected from the electrical current by his insulated gloves and boots. For a moment he had blotted out the stars as he came over the fence and down the other side. During that brief time, Billy-Joe and Steve were blinking into the flash of the whiz-bang, blinded and deafened for critical moments necessary for Batman to land safely and secretly on the other side.

No such diversion could be used here. No distraction could be counted on to rivet the attention for the long minutes that would be needed to scale the Gaudi, and nothing in Batman's bag of tricks could propel him to the fortieth floor.

Luckily, there was a brilliant gibbous moon that night. It bathed one face of the building in its cold white light, but left the other faces in darkness. Using spring-driven crampons of his own devising that permitted him to get footholds on granite, the Masked Man swarmed up the dark side of the building. When he reached the fifth floor, where there was a row of gargoyles, an expedient presented itself. The next level of gargoyles was on the tenth floor, and each five floors after that. The Batarang presented a feasible opportunity, tied to a light line on the end of a coiled line. Batman was an expert at throwing the curiously shaped Batarang, similar to a boomerang but infinitely more useful in terms of angles that it could be projected along.

Batman's first cast was a few feet high. He retrieved the Batarang and threw again, cautioning himself not to overdo it—precision was called for, not brute strength.

Robert Sheckley

This time the Batarang flew true and coiled around the neck of a stone devil.

To climb forty stories up a rope is, in its quiet way, a greater feat than many others the world deems more spectacular. Luckily, Batman had along a BatHoist to assist him on vertical assents by rope. The little device, powered by a miniature atomic motor, and operating through a cunning set of gears, was able to pull a man's weight up a rope at a steady four miles an hour.

When Batman gained the fortieth floor, he used a hand-held punch to take out the exterior window fasteners and let himself in. He took care not the drop the window, and refastened the fasteners again from the inside, reversing the hand-held punch and tapping the rivets in with great delicacy. After that, it was easy enough to skulk down the hall and find the main conference room where the Joint Chiefs were meeting.

"What is the meaning of this?" Admiral Fenton said. "I've heard of you, of course, Batman. It is said that you serve some good causes. But if you think your reputation is going to intimidate me, you've got another thing coming."

"I had no such thought," Batman said. "I merely wanted to present a few facts about the ARDC weapons systems with which you are proposing to arm our forces."

"You've got a lot of nerve," Fenton said, "trying to teach us our business. We've checked out those weapons to the hundredth decimal point. They're the bes I've ever seen."

"Perhaps," Batman said. "But have you also checked out their computer-supported operating systems?"

"It's a new system," General Rohort said. "Supposed to be the best the mind of man has come up with."

Death of the Dreammaster

"I'd advise that you look again," Batman said. "I have some documents I think you'll find interesting."

"What are you getting at, Batman?" Fenton said. "You don't expect to stop us, do you?"

The Masked Man did not answer.

"This place is filled with our men," Fenton went on. "You can't hope to delay us from signing for long. And to think you'd try something like this with the President here."

President Marshall Seldon had been standing at the far end of the room throughout this exchange. Now, smiling slightly, he said, "Let him show us his documents. This will be amusing."

Batman pulled his cloak close to him, and, from a pocket deep in its fold, he extracted a wad of computer printouts. They showed complex circuitry and were filled with tiny numbers and Greek letters.

"Gentlemen," Batman said, "please take a look at these."

Kowalski was the first to reach for one. "What are these?"

"Schematics for the main computer circuitry for the ARDC weapons."

Kowalski looked through them, his curly blond hair tumbling boyishly over his forehead. "Yes...yes, it all looks all right so far...Yes, that's a standard Sliger circuit....But what's this, it's tied into a resonator with a provision for switchable mirror reflectivity.... Hell, I see what you mean!"

"What is it?" the other chiefs asked, not being as adept at computer schematics as was the tall, young Air Force general.

Kowalski looked up and his face was grim. "You tell them, Batman."

Batman said, "I believe you've all heard of computer viruses."

"Of course," Fenton said. "They are those specially designed programs that some madmen or malcontents devise to feed into computers and so render them inoperative, sometimes for long periods of time, until a killer program can be devised and introduced to get rid of them again. Sometimes the computer virus program is so deeply ingrained that even the metals of the affected computers must be changed due to imprinting error. But nobody is going to introduce any viruses into these programs, Batman. This is a whole new generation of program and it is virus-resistant except to an as yet undevised new generation of computer viruses."

"That is true," Batman said. "But you miss the point."

"Which is?"

"The software for the ARDC programs is designed to generate its own virus which will first pervert its functioning, then destroy it."

"Create its own viruses?" General Rohort said. "Like tadpoles hatching out of mud?"

Kowalski nodded grimly. "It's there in the specs, general. We just overlooked it—as we were intended to do."

Rohort turned to Kowalski. "You understand these matters, Flying Phil. But I can hardly believe it. Can what the masked man is saying be true?"

"It's true, all right." Kowalski said, a note of iron underlying the lightness of his voice. "That's exactly what it is."

"Gentlemen!" It was the voice of President Seldon, and it brought every man in the room to attention—and the yeoman, too.

"Yes, Mr. President?" said Admiral Fenton.

Death of the Dreammaster

"First of all, I want to thank Batman," the President said, "for having brought this matter to our attention. As a matter of fact we have already corrected the design flaw, Batman, and now there is nothing standing in the way of the Joint Chiefs signing it."

"That document must not be signed," Batman said. "And these men must no longer take their orders from you."

"Why do you say that?" the President asked. "Stop this senseless charade now, Batman, and I think we can arrange a medal for you. How would you like an official position in my cabinet? Presidential Advisor on Superheroes. How does that sound to you?"

"It's fine, Mr. President," Batman said. "Except for one thing." He stepped forward suddenly, walking directly toward the President. Even Nelson of the CIA was caught off guard for a moment. He drew his sidearm quickly, not the beltbuckle derringer but a heavy Browning automatic that he reserved for dire emergencies. But by then Batman had stepped up to the President....

And then, in another step, he had walked *through* the President.

And the President continued smiling.

The Joint Chiefs stared at Batman, slack-jawed. Nelson stood with the gun at his side, momentarily frozen.

"The trouble is," Batman said, "I don't see how you can do anything, Mr. President. Because you're not the President at all."

"What in God's name is it?" Fenton asked, long-suppressed superstition bringing his voice to a reedy tenor. "A ghost?"

"Not exactly," Batman said. "It's a hologram."

Fenton was trying to understand. "How did you know?"

Robert Sheckley

"Because the same people who produce this," Batman said, jerking a gloved thumb at the still smiling hologram of President Selden, "have also been throwing holograms at other people."

"Who are these people?" Kowalski asked.

"I think," Batman said, "that Deputy Director James Nelson here has the answer to that one."

Nelson looked at him with pure hate.

The image of the President winked out abruptly.

Deputy Director Nelson had come into prominence about six months before, when James Tolliver, respected head of the CIA, had fallen ill to an as yet unidentified virus that even the best specialists had been unable to cure. The disease had taken a great toll on Tolliver's strength and vitality. Bedridden, kept alive on support systems, Tolliver had been forced to turn over the day-to-day running of the agency to his assistant, Nelson.

Nelson was known as an extremely capable man with a grandiose personality. He had a reputation for ruthlessness, and more recently, and almost paranoid self-assurance. He had been known to take the law into his own hands when he thought he knew what to do better than his superiors. This, Tolliver would not tolerate.

There had been rumors that Tolliver had been planning to fire Nelson, or force him into early retirement. But now Tolliver was able to do nothing but lie in an oxygen tent and fight for his life.

Some in Washington circles considered Nelson more than a little dangerous, and more than a little crazy.

Like many another crazy and dangerous man, he had gathered a small circle of CIA operatives around him,

Death of the Dreammaster

whom he had seduced to his view. They were fanatical in
their devotion to him. They would follow his every order.

These were the men who came into the meeting room
now, moving slowly and alertly, hands near their concealed weapons.

"That contract is going to be signed," Nelson said.

"You must be mad," Admiral Fenton said. "You can't
expect us to sign it after all this."

"I can, and you shall. But you needn't bother doing it
in person, gentlemen, I have expert forgers who can do a
better job on your signatures than you can do yourselves."

"What are you going to do with us?" Rohort asked.

"You will be given heroes' burials," Nelson said. "We
have already established that Batman has been having hallucinations. His misadventures with Ilona and others in
the New Era Hotel are on film. The public will believe it
when we tell them that he massacred all of you before
we could get here and kill him. We will release our news
shortly before Super Bowl time, when no one will pay it
any attention anyhow."

"And what about me?" Batman asked.

Nelson gave a short, unhappy laugh. "I tried my best
to keep you out of this, Batman. I decided to work on you.
With the aid of my organization I discovered your true
identity. You are Charlie Morrison!"

The tall hooded figure stirred slightly. A smile
appeared on the masked man's grim lips.

"Is that why you showed those holograms to Charlie
Morrison in the New Era Hotel?" Batman asked.

"I was trying to convince you to stay out of this."

"Your sense of psychology," Batman said, "is as flawed
as your sense of strategy. How could Batman resist a challenge like that? You set up your own defeat, Nelson."

"But Nelson, why are you doing this?" General Kowalski asked. "Why do you want us to sign the contract? The ARDC weapons system is obviously flawed. And it is vulnerable to infiltration by enemy computers. As soon as our enemies get wind of this, they can attack our weapons system with impunity. When we try to fight back, our own weapons will be programmed to act against us."

"That's what Tolliver said when I showed him the plan," Nelson said. "He couldn't see that its weakness was only the outer layer of a deeper scheme. Yes, our enemies will certainly learn about the deficiencies in our plans and try to make a profit from our weakness. But we also have another program, this one really secret, which turns our enemy's apparent gain into our advantage. It's a built-in computer-killing program that is initiated when they try to crack our codes. When our enemies try to stab us in the back by reprogramming our weapons systems, they'll find they've introduced the seeds of destruction into their own systems."

"Interesting," Batman said. "Ilona was a plant, I suppose?"

"Of course," Nelson said. "We faked her death."

The Joint Chiefs looked at each other in astonishment. Finally, Fenton said, "Nelson, this whole thing's crazy! Your plan is crazy! What if our enemies also discover the scavenger program?"

"We have other secrets!" Nelson cried. His eyes were quite mad. "You don't know how many secrets we have! Only my followers and I are aware of the power we can wield and the influence we can have upon events!"

Batman said, "What I do know is, you and your little clique stand to make a lot of money out of this contract. You are the secret shareholder behind the buyout of ARDC. Isn't that so?"

Death of the Dreammaster

Nelson shrugged. "It doesn't matter that you know that now. There's nothing you can do about it. This contract is going through."

"Oh, I don't think so," Batman said.

James Nelson looked at the hooded figure and laughed. "Are you going to stop us? According to the standard biographical material, you are vulnerable to human weapons, unlike your hardshelled friend Superman."

"I puncture as easily as other men," Batman said. "But first you have to hit me."

Nelson raised his gun. Batman opened his hand. A flock of tiny motes flew out of the capsule at the end of his little finger which he had managed to puncture while Nelson was ranting. The motes flew toward the light sources. The lights flashed crazily, dimmed, and went black.

"Chinese light-suckers!" Nelson exclaimed. "You *are* clever, Batman. But it will do you no good. Shoot, men!"

The CIA men swung into action. Shots crashed through the room, ricocheting off filing cabinets, screaming off the hardened plastic walls like a swarm of enraged hornets. But Batman was already moving, an inky shadow in the darkened room. The Joint Chiefs, too, had dived under tables and were answering the CIA fire with their own sidearms.

The outcome was never really in doubt, but perhaps it was just as well that James Gordon at the head of platoon of New Gotham's finest burst through the door just then. The hard-bitten boys in blue made short work of the seersuckered government operatives.

"Gordon!" Batman said. "What are you doing here?"

"After you called me, I figured you might need a little backup," Gordon said. "So I brought a platoon of my Gotham City boys for a tour of Washington."

Robert Sheckley

"Don't kill Nelson!" Batman said.

"The rat deserves it," Gordon said, but held his fire.

"I know he does," Batman said. "But he has to take us to wherever he's hidden the President."

Nelson, in handcuffs, led them to a small storage room in the basement. There, haggard and unshaven, they found President Marshall Seldon.

"Batman," Seldon said. "I might have guessed it'd be you."

"I thought I had taken care of you, Batman," Nelson said. "I seem to have been mistaken." The tan man bit down hard and grimaced, then slumped to the floor. The acrid odor of bitter almonds filled the room.

"A cyanide capsule," Batman said. "Poor deluded fool. It's all over now, Mr. President. But I think you're going to need a new deputy director."

Back at his house in Gotham City, Bruce Wayne was reading the newspaper in the drawing room when Alfred came in with a letter on a silver tray. "For you, sir. From Miss Vera."

Bruce opened it and scanned it quickly. "She says she's having a wonderful time," he said, "but misses me and wishes I would join her."

"A very good idea, sir," Alfred said from the door.

Bruce Wayne needed less than a second to consider and make up his mind. "Alfred, pack my tropicals and book me the next flight to Rio."

"Very good, sir!" the butler said, smiling despite his

best efforts to maintain a grave face. "And the Batman Suit, sir?"

"Don't pack it. This time I'm really going to take a vacation."

On a Beautiful Summer's Day, He Was

ROBERT R. McCAMMON

A boy.

Junior was smiling, and the sun was on his face. He was fourteen years old, it was the middle of June and summer looked like a long sweet road that went on and on until it was out of sight, swallowed by the hills of autumn a hundred miles away. Junior walked along the street two blocks from his house, his hands in the pockets of trousers that had patched knees, his fingers clenched on bird bones. The warm breeze stirred through his shock of brown hair, and in that breeze he smelled the roses in Mrs. Broughton's garden. Across the street, Eddie Connors and a couple of his buddies were working on the engine of Eddie's red, fire-breathing Chevy. They were big guys, all of them eighteen years old, already getting beer guts. Junior lay in bed at night and listened to the racket of Eddie's red Chevy roaring up and down the street like a tiger looking for a way out of a cage, and that was when the shouting rose up from the Napier house like the wrath of God and—

Eddie looked up from the work, grease all over the

On a Beautiful Summer's Day, He Was

front of his sweat-soaked T-shirt, a smear of grease across his bulbous nose like black war paint. He nudged the guy next to him, Greg Cawthen, and then the third of them, Dennis Hafner, looked across the street and saw Junior, too.

Junior knew what was coming. His feet in their bright blue Keds stuttered on the broken pavement, where bottle shards caught the summer sun. He was a tall boy for his age, but gaunt. His face was long, his chin pointed. His eyebrows merged over a thin, sharp nose. *Know why your nose is in the middle of your face?* his father had asked him once. *Because it's the scenter. That's a joke, Junior. It's a joke. Get it?*

Smile, Junior!

SMILE, I SAID!

The corners of Junior's mouth upturned. His eyes were dark, and his cheeks strained.

"Hey!" Eddie shouted. His voice came at Junior like a freight train, and Junior stopped walking. Eddie nudged Greg in the ribs, a conspiratorial nudge. "Where y goin', gooney?"

"Nowhere," Junior answered, standing on shattered glass.

"Yes, you are." Eddie tapped his beefy palm with a socket wrench. "You gotta be goin' somewhere. You're walkin', ain't you?"

Junior shrugged. In his hands he worked the bird bones deep in his pockets. "I'm just walking."

"Gooney's too stupid to know where he's goin'," Dennis Hafner spoke up, from a mouth that looked like a puffy red wound. "Skinny little fruit." His ugly lips spouted a sound of disgust.

"Hey, Gooney!" Greg Cawthen said, his face square

and ruddy under a crewcut of red hair. "Your old man home?"

Junior squinted up at the sun. A bird was flying in the sky, alone in all that stark blue expanse.

"We're *talkin'* to ya, numb nuts!" Eddie said. "Greg asked if your old man was home!"

Junior shook his head. His heart was beating very hard, and he wished he had wings.

"Yeah, right!" Dennis nodded, and punched Greg on the shoulder. "They've got Gooney's old man in the crazy house again. Didn't you hear?"

"Is that so?" Eddie stared balefully at Junior. "They got your old man in the crazy house again? They got him locked up so he can't hurt nobody?"

Junior's mouth moved. "No," he answered. He felt cold inside, as if his guts were coated with ice.

"Why'd they let him out, then?" Eddie Connors went on, his eyes narrowed into fleshy slits. "If he's crazy, why'd they let him out?"

"He's not . . ." Junior's voice was weak, and he stopped speaking. He tried again: "My dad's not crazy."

"Sure!" Dennis let out a mean yawp of laughter. "They only put sane people in the crazy house!"

"It wasn't . . . wasn't a crazy house!" Junior said; it came out louder and harder than he'd wanted. "It was a hospital!"

"Oh, yeah! Big difference!" Eddie said, and again his elbow found Greg's ribs. Greg was grinning, his teeth big and white. Junior wondered if Greg Cawthen's bones were as white as his teeth. "So they put him in a *hospital* for crazy people!"

"My dad's not crazy." Junior looked back the two blocks to his house, the one with a big elm tree in the front yard. All the houses in the neighborhood were alike:

wooden structures with narrow front porches and small, square lawns, most of the houses in need of painting, the grass dried and burnt, the trees throwing blue shadows that moved with the sun. Clothes hung on backyard lines, garbage cans stood dented and beaten, and here and there stood the hulks of old cars waiting to be hauled off to the junkyard. Junior returned his gaze to Eddie Connors, as his fingers played with the bird bones—the bones of a blue jay, to be precise—in his pockets. "He had a nervous breakdown," Junior said. "That's all."

"That's *all*?" Eddie grunted. "Hell, ain't that enough?" He walked out into the street, still popping his palm with the wrench, and he stopped about ten feet from Junior. "You tell your old man it's a free country. You tell him I can drive my car anytime I want, day or night, and if he wants some trouble he ought to call the cops again. You tell him if he wants some trouble, I'll give it to him."

"Nervous breakdown," Dennis said, and he laughed again. "That's just another way of sayin' *crazy*, ain't it?"

"Get outta here!" Eddie told the boy. "Go on, Gooney! Move it!"

"Yeah!" Greg added. And couldn't resist another sharp shot: "I'll bet your old lady's crazy in the head, too!"

"MOVE IT!" Eddie shouted, king of the block.

Junior began walking again, in the same direction he'd been going, away from the house with the elm tree in its dried-up yard and paint peeling in strips from its front porch. His father's voice came to him, and he remembered his father sitting in front of the TV, scribbling on a yellow pad and saying this: *Know what a nervous breakdown is, Junior? It's what happens when you spend half your time keeping your mind on your work and the other half keeping your work on your mind.*

That's a joke. Get it?

Smile, Junior.

Junior did.

"Skinny little fruit!" Dennis Hafner shouted at Junior's back. And Eddie Connors called out, "It's a free country! You tell him that, you hear me?"

Know what normal is, Junior? It's somebody before a shrink gets hold of him.

Smile, Junior.

He walked on, along the street layered with sunlight and shadows, his fingers grasping the bones in his pockets and his heart dark as a piece of coal.

But he was smiling, on this beautiful summer day.

Junior turned right at the next block. Ahead of him, shimmering in the heat, was the last remaining wooded hillside in this suburb. It was green and thick and held secrets. It was a wonderful place, and it was his destination.

Before he reached the end of the street, where a rugged trail led up the hillside, Junior heard the noise of sneakers on the pavement behind him. Somebody running. His first thought was that Eddie Connors had decided to chase him down, and he spun around to face his attacker and try to bluff his way out of a bloody nose. But it wasn't Eddie Connors, or any of his ilk, at all. It was a gawky, frail-looking boy with curly brown hair and glasses, a dumb grin on his face. The boy wore a T-shirt, short pants that exposed his skinny legs, black socks, and sneakers, and he stopped just shy of running into Junior and said, "Hi, Junior! I saw you from over there!" He pointed at a house further up the block, near the intersection where Junior had turned. The boy aimed his dumb grin on Junior again. "Where you goin'?"

"Somewhere," Junior said, and he kept walking toward the hillside.

On a Beautiful Summer's Day, He Was

"Can I go with you?" Wally Manfred began to lope alongside. He was ten years old, his blue eyes magnified behind his glasses, and he needed braces in the worst way. Junior thought of Wally Manfred as a little dog that liked to chase cars and follow strangers, eager to be petted. "Can I, huh?"

"No."

"Why not? Where you goin'?"

"Just somewhere. Go on home, Wally."

Wally was silent. The noise of his sneakers on the pavement said he was still following. Junior didn't want him to see the secret place. The secret place was his alone. "Go home, Wally," Junior repeated. The beginning of the forest trail was coming up pretty soon.

"Aw, come on!" Wally persisted, and he darted in front of Junior. "Lemme go with you!"

"Ixnay."

"I can if I want to!" Wally said, a note of petulance in his voice.

Junior stopped. This wouldn't do. It wouldn't do at all. "Go *home*, Wally!" he commanded. "I mean it!"

Wally had stopped, too, and he looked as if he might be about to burst into tears. Junior knew Wally lived with his mother, in a house even smaller than his own, and Wally's father had gone out for a pack of cigarettes a year ago and never come home. Or that was the story, at least. Junior had overheard his parents talking about it, when they thought he was asleep. Parents had their secrets, just like kids. "I mean it," Junior said. "I don't want you to go with me."

Wally just stared at him, as the summer sun beat down on both of them.

"Go find somebody else to bother," Junior told him.

Wally took a backward step. His eyes looked wet

behind his glasses. "How come you don't like me?" Wally asked, and something in his voice was terrible. "How come nobody likes me?"

Junior strode past him, and began walking alone again.

"I like *you!*" Wally called out. "How come you don't want to be friends?"

Know what a friend is, Junior? It's somebody who has the same enemies as you.

Smile, Junior!

He went on. He started up the path, and about fifty yards into the woods he hunkered down and waited to see if Wally Manfred was following. "I don't care!" he heard Wally shout from the street. "I still like you!"

Junior waited for about ten minutes, there in the underbrush. When he was sure Wally wasn't coming after him, he stood up and continued on his way.

The trail led through the last of the neighborhood's woods. Trash and bottles littered the ground, proof that others had followed this path, but Junior's secret place was up higher on the hillside and about a quarter of a mile away. The trail steepened and became a rough climb, and Junior had to struggle up by grasping onto tree roots that emerged from the dirt. He left the last of the trash and bottles behind, and climbed up through green woods. The secret place was well-hidden, and he'd only found it himself by accident, a couple of years before on one of his long solitary treks.

At last, there it was. A rusted, brown water-tank that rose about sixty feet from the crest of the hill and was all but obscured by trees. A ladder led up, and Junior began to ascend with a quick, easy grace. The ladder took him to the top of the tank, where he stood up and looked to the northeast.

The gray towers of Gotham City loomed before him,

On a Beautiful Summer's Day, He Was

and in the valley below were thousands of houses and buildings that radiated out from Gotham City on its maze of streets. There seemed to be nothing green in there, nothing but concrete and brick and stone. Factories stood between him and the central city, and the haze today was a pale, shimmering brown that clung close to the earth. One of those factories was the chemical company where his dad used to be a shift manager, last year, before his nervous breakdown. His dad still worked with the company, but now he was a salesman and he was on the road a lot. The factory was the one with the six tall chimneys, and today white streamers of smoke were rising from them into the brown air.

Junior felt like the king of the world, looking down from this height. But he had the bones in his pockets, and there was work to be done.

He went to the tank's hatch, where there was a flywheel. The flywheel had been tough to crack open. He'd had to bring a can of Rust-Eater—one of his dad's products—and a hammer, and even then it had been a hard task to loosen the wheel.

Junior bent down and began to turn the wheel. It was still a tough job that he had to put his shoulders into. But the hatch was coming open, and in another moment he lifted it and looked down the hole. Another ladder led into the empty tank. Hot, dry air rose into Junior's face. He let most of the heat out, and then he eased down into the hole and began to descend the ladder, eagerness working in his brain like a hot little machine full of oiled gears.

He was happy for a while, industrious amid his toys.

He emerged when the afternoon had cooled. His pockets were empty. He resealed the water tank, went back the way he'd come through the woods, and headed for home.

Robert R. McCammon

Eddie Connors and his buddies were no longer in sight, but the red Chevy was still there. Junior stopped at Mrs. Broughton's and leaned over her fence to smell a rose, and his gaze ticked back and forth, looking for Eddie or the others. A few beer cans lay on the street near the car. Junior stared at them, and began to shred the petals from a yellow rose. Then he crossed the street to the Chevy, took a handful of dirt and grit from the Connors' yard, and opened the Chevy's gas portal. In went the dirt, quick as you please. He washed it down with some beer left in a can, and then he closed the gas portal and returned the beer can exactly as it had been.

He went home smiling.

And there he found his mother, on her knees in the front room, scrubbing the threadbare carpet around the easy chair that faced the television set.

"He's coming home!" Mom said, and her eyes were wild in her pallid face. "He called! He'll be home by six o'clock!"

Two hours. Junior knew the routine. There was no time to be lost. He shoved down the terror that threatened to rise up within him, and he caged it. Then he hurried past his mother into his small dark room, and he began to straighten his shelves of books and put them all in alphabetical order. If there was one thing his father demanded, it was order in this chaotic world.

Oh yes: and one other thing, too.

Smile, Junior! Smile, Wifey!

SMILE, I SAID!

When Junior was finished with his books, he worked on his closet. Blue clothes together, white clothes together, garments with red next, then with green. Laces tied in all the shoes. Socks balled up, just so. A place for everything, and everything in its place. "Help me!" his mother called, her voice getting frantic. "Junior, help me mop the kitchen floor! Hurry!"

"Yes, Mother," he said, and he went into the kitchen where his mother was working on the yellow linoleum tiles that would never fully be clean, never, never in a hundred years of scrubbing even with Stain-Away.

At four minutes before six o'clock, they heard his car turn into the driveway. They heard the engine stop, and the driver's door open. They heard him coming, and mom said to her son, "Daddy's home!" She clicked on an awful smile, and went to the front door.

"Darling!" she said, as the tall, slim man in a dark brown suit came into the house, carrying his briefcase of samples. She hugged him stiffly, and drew away as soon as she could. "How was your trip?"

"It was," Dad answered. "Thank you. This is the only job I know of where you can have breakfast in Lynchton, lunch in Harrisburg, and indigestion in Fremont." His eyes, darker than his son's, searched their faces. "That's a joke," he said. "How about a couple of smiles?"

Mom gave a bright, forced laugh. Junior stared at the floor, and smiled with aching jaws.

"Come give me a hug," Dad said. "Know what a hug is? The freedom of the press."

Junior walked to his father, and hugged him with labored arms.

"Good boy," Dad said. "Know what a boy is? An appetite with a skin pulled over it. What's for dinner, Wifey?"

"I was going to put some turkey dinners into the oven."

"Turkey dinners." Dad nodded. "Okay, that's all right. It's a good night for the funnies. Turkey: that's a bird who'd strut a lot less if he could see into the future."

Their smiles weren't quick enough. Dad slammed his briefcase down into his easy chair, and the noise made both mother and son jump. "Damn it, where's the happiness around here? This isn't a funeral home, is it? I've seen bigger smiles on dead people! That's no wonder, since the dead don't have to pay taxes! What's wrong with you two? Aren't you *happy*?"

"We're happy!" Mom said quickly. "We're real happy! Aren't we, Junior?"

Junior looked into his father's face. It was a tight face, with hard, sharp cheekbones. His father's eyes were dark and deep-set, and down in that darkness there was a rage coiled up and waiting. It flew out without warning, but most of the time it lay inside Dad's head and simmered in its stew of perpetual jokes and gritted-teeth smiles. Where that rage had been born, and why, Junior did not know, and he figured his father didn't know either. But jokes were its armor and weapons, and Dad wore them like metal spikes.

"Yes, sir," Junior answered. "I'm happy."

"Remember what I told you." Dad placed a finger against his son's chest. "People like to smile. If you can make people smile, you'll be a success. People like to hear a joke or two. They like to laugh. Know what a laugh is? It's a smile that's exploded." The finger moved to one corner of Junior's mouth and hitched it up. Then to the other. "There," Dad said. "That's what I like to see."

Mom turned away and walked into the kitchen to put three turkey TV dinners in the oven. Then Dad began his weekly inspection of the house—a wandering from room to room as he spouted off jokes and comments he considered funny, punctuated by the opening of drawers and cabinets. The rest of the evening would be spent with John in front of the TV set, watching the sitcoms and scribbling down on his yellow pad jokes and repartee that particularly caught his interest. *Grist for the grin mill,* he called it.

That's a joke, Junior.

Smile.

Sometimes between the third and fourth comedy show of the night, Junior opened a door and went down the stairs to the dirt-floored basement. He switched on the light bulb, picked up a flashlight, which was always in its proper place, and went to the far corner at the rear of the basement. He lifted a cardboard box and watched roaches scurry in the flashlight's beam.

The ants were swarming. They'd done a good job. The chipmunk was almost down to the bones, and most of the kitten's bones were showing now, too. It wouldn't be too much longer. But Junior was impatient for his toys. The basement was very damp, the walls mildewed. He wondered if he'd have skeletons faster if he put the dead things in a dryer place. He lifted a second box, looking at his newest acquisitions. He'd found the dead bat in the abandoned house near the church three blocks away, and the robin had been snatched from a cat's jaws just yesterday. They weren't going to smell very good soon. The smell would rise into the house, as the beautiful summer days got hotter. Junior had been wanting to kill a full-grown dog or cat and watch its skeleton come out, but that smell would get up into the house for sure and his mother might come down here and find everything. His father he didn't worry much about; nothing pulled his father away from the comedies and the yellow joke pad.

But if he was going to start finding bigger playthings, maybe he needed somewhere else to keep them.

At nine-forty, Junior was sitting in the living room watching his father snore in his easy chair. His mother was on the telephone in the kitchen, talking to her friend Linda Shapona, who lived a few streets over. They'd gone to high school together, and Linda owned the beauty shop on Kerredge Avenue. Mom was usually on the telephone most of the evening; it was her only route of escape. The television was on, the last of the night's comedies. The yellow pad had slipped to the floor, and Junior picked it up to see what his father had written there.

It was hard to read the writing. The pen had attacked the paper. Junior could only make out a few of the mass of scribbled jokes and puns, the writing running together and overlapping like a nest of thorns.

Boss. A big noise in the office but at home a little squeak.

What's a diplomat's favorite color? Plaid.

Heaven's where God pays all the bills.

A father always no's best.

Middle age is the time in life when a girl you smile at thinks you know her.

"It's late."

Junior looked up. His father's eyes were swollen, and he was peering at his wristwatch under the dim lamplight. "Gosh. I went to sleep, didn't I?"

"Yes, sir." Junior put the yellow pad down beside his father's chair. His father stretched, and his joints popped.

"I get tired early, I guess. I didn't even know my eyes closed."

"Yes, sir," Junior said.

Dad picked up the yellow pad and examined it. The way the light caught his face made him look very old, and the sight made Junior think of the collection of skulls at the Gotham Museum, one of his favorite places to spend a Saturday. "People like to smile," Dad said, in a quiet voice. "They like a man who tells jokes. A happy man."

On a Beautiful Summer's Day, He Was

Junior suddenly tensed, because he heard the sound of a car's engine racketing. Dad stared at the front door, as if he expected Eddie Connors's red Chevy to come roaring up the porch steps and into the house. Eddie revved the engine a few times, getting ready to lay rubber on the street right in front of the house—and then the car began to pop and sputter, and after a few seconds of that the engine died.

"Thank God," Dad said, and let out the breath he'd been holding. "I can't stand that noise. It makes my head hurt."

Junior nodded. Eddie Connors wasn't going to be tearing the street up tonight.

Dad was looking at his son. They stared at each other, their faces similar constructions of flesh and bone. The people in the situation comedy prattled on, and the canned laughter filled the room. "You're my boy, aren't you?" Dad asked.

"Yes, sir."

"My boy," Dad repeated. "And you're not going to be one of those people who think the world owes him a giving, are you?"

"No, sir."

"That's a joke. Smile."

Junior did, on command.

His father leaned toward him. Closer. And closer still. Junior could see pinpricks of sweat glistening on his father's cheeks and forehead. His father's skin had a sour smell, and the man's eyes were like black glass. "Junior?" his father whispered. "I want to tell you a secret. Know what a secret is? It's anything a woman doesn't know. But I want to tell you, because you're my boy." His father's face floated before him in the dim light, half of it in shadow like a waning moon. "I'm afraid," Dad whispered.

He swallowed thickly, as the canned laughter swelled. "I'm afraid I'm getting sick again."

Junior didn't speak. A small vein was beating very hard at his right temple, and his lips were bloodless.

"Sometimes," Dad said, "I feel like the world is spinning so fast it's about to throw me off. Sometimes I feel like the sky is so heavy it's crushing me down, and I can't get a breath. They gave me a second chance, at the company. They said I was good with people, and I could make people smile so I ought to be able to sell things." A grin flickered across his mouth like quicksilver, but his eyes remained black. "A salesman. That's somebody with two feet on the ground who takes orders from a person with two feet on a desk."

Junior did not smile.

"I feel like . . . the wind's about to take me away, Junior. I feel like I can't get steady. I don't know why. It's just . . . I can't stay happy."

Junior didn't move. He could hear his mother, talking on the telephone. He thought of the toys in the basement, slowly being whittled down to the bones by ants and roaches, a little more hour after hour.

"I can't go back to that hospital," his father whispered, right in his face. "I couldn't stand that place. They don't know how to smile there. That's what Hell would be for me, Junior. A place where people wouldn't smile. If I had to go back there . . . I don't know what I might do."

"Dad?" Junior's voice cracked. "I . . . wish you wouldn't . . . talk like this."

"What's wrong with wanting to be happy?" his father asked. The whisper was gone. "Is it a sin to be happy? Is it a damned sin?" His father was getting louder, and he drew his face back from Junior's. "You know, that's what's wrong with this world! They take everything away from you, and then they try to cut the smile off your face! Well, I won't let them! I'll see them in Hell before they break me down! They broke down my old man, and he was crying with that bottle in his hand and I said I'll make you smile again, I will, I'll make you smile, I'll do anything to make you smile, but the world broke him down! Because a man who smiles is a dangerous man! They want to cut the smile off your face, and make you weak! But I won't have it. I swear to God I won't have it! And you're part of me, Junior, you're my boy, you're my flesh and bone!'' One of Dad's sinewy hands grasped his son's shoulder. "The world's not going to break us down, is it?''

"No, sir," Junior said, lifelessly, but in his chest his heart was pounding.

"Junior?" It was his mother. She was standing in the doorway between the front room and the kitchen, and her hands had seized the wall like white spiders. Her eyes tracked back and forth from the boy to his father, and over the noise of the television laughter Junior could hear his father's harsh, slow breathing. "Why don't you get ready for bed? All right?"

A silence stretched. And then Dad said, "Mom's the word," and released his son. As Junior walked toward the hallway that led to his room, his father said, "Know what a mother is, Junior? It's a woman who spends twenty years making a boy into a man so another woman can make a fool of him in twenty minutes." Junior kept going, his insides quaking. He had taken three more steps when his father said, easily, "Lock your door tonight."

Junior stopped. Terror had crippled him. Those words were not said very often, but Junior understood them. He looked at his mother, who seemed to have diminished in size, her skin turned a sickly gray.

"Lock your door," Dad repeated. He was staring at the television screen. "Say your prayers, will you?"

"Yes, sir," the boy answered, and he went to his room and locked the door. Then he lay in bed and stared at the ceiling, where cracks riddled the plaster.

In the morning, he could pretend he had had a particularly terrible nightmare. He could pretend he had not heard, as the clock's hands crept past midnight, the muffled noise of his father's voice beyond the wall, speaking stridently—commanding—and his mother's weak begging. He could pretend he had not heard his father shouting for her to laugh, to laugh, to fill the house with laughter. To laugh and laugh until she screamed. And there was the slapping noise of the belt and a lamp going over and the bed creaking savagely and his mother's sobbing in the silence that followed afterward.

Smile, Junior.

SMILE, I SAID!

His teeth gritted in a rictus, he lay with night pressing in on the house and darkness coiled within.

When he got out of bed, the sun was shining again. His father was gone, and so was the briefcase and the yellow pad. His mother made him breakfast. She had a split lip, but most of her bruises never showed. She smiled and laughed, a brittle sound, as she moved around the kitchen, and when she asked Junior what he was going to do today he said he had plans.

He left home early, bound for the secret place. He passed Eddie Connors's red Chevy, a deballed stallion at the curb. It would take more than a wrench to get the fuel line unclogged. He continued along the street where sunlight and shadows intermingled, and he went his way alone.

Atop the water tower on the high hill, Junior stood

staring toward the spires of Gotham City. The chimneys of the factories were pumping out smoke, the arteries were clogged with traffic, and life went on whether your old man was crazy or not.

Junior opened the tower's hatch, and that was when he heard the voice.

"Hey, Junior! Hey, I'm down here!"

He walked to the edge, looked down at the green earth, and there stood Wally Manfred in his T-shirt and shorts, this time wearing purple socks with his sneakers. Wally was grinning, and the sun sparked off his glasses. Wally waved up at him. "I see you!"

Junior felt his eyes narrow. Felt his face tighten, around the bones of his father. Felt rage open inside him like the unfolding of a dark flower, and black seeds spewed forth.

"I followed you!" Wally said. "Fooled you, huh?"

Junior trembled. It was a quick trembling, over and done with, but it was like an inner earthquake and left cracks in his foundation.

The secret place had been found. His haven of solitude was no longer his. And what did he own on this earth, except the toys that were stored within?

"What're you doin' up there?" Wally called.

Junior made his face relax. He made a smile rise up, through the hot flesh. He opened his mouth, and he said, "Climb up."

"Is this where you go all the time? It sure is high!"

"Climb up," Junior repeated. "The ladder's strong."

"I don't know." Wally kicked at a stone with the toe of his sneaker. "I might fall."

"I won't let you fall," Junior said. "Honest."

"Maybe I can come up halfway," Wally said, and he started up the ladder.

Robert R. McCammon

What he was going to do about this, Junior didn't know. Sooner or later, Wally would tell somebody else about the secret place. Wally might even come up here alone, open the hatch, and see what was inside. Wally might go tell his mother, and then his mother might tell Junior's mother, and then . . .

They might get the wrong idea. They might think he was like his father. They might want him to go to that hospital where his father had gone, and where his father would be returning to soon. They might think something was wrong with him, and that something had been wrong with him for a long time but he'd been very good at hiding it.

"I'm halfway up!" Wally called out. He sounded scared. "I'd better stop!"

Junior was staring toward Gotham City, a garden of stones. "Come on the rest of the way," he said quietly. "I've . . . got a joke to tell you."

"I'd better get down!"

"It's a good joke. Come on up, Wally. Come on up."

Silence. Junior waited. And then he heard the noise of Wally climbing the rest of the way up, and Junior said, "That's a good boy. Know what a boy is? An appetite with a skin pulled over it."

Wally reached the top of the tank. There was sweat on his face, and his glasses had slid down to the end of his nose. He was shaking as he got off the ladder and stood up.

"There's a good view of Gotham City from here. See?" Junior pointed.

Wally turned to look at the city. "Wow," he said, his back to Junior.

One push.

Sixty feet down.

Drag Wally into the bushes. Hide him. Who was Wally,

anyway? He was a little nothing, and he should never have sneaked up here to the secret place. One push, and the secret would be a secret again. But Junior didn't move, and then Wally turned around again and saw the open hatch. "What's in there?" he asked.

And it all came clear to Junior, what should be done, like a burst of brilliant light in his brain.

"Want to see?" Junior asked, smiling. He was cold, even standing in the sunshine, and he trembled though he could feel sweat on his back.

Wally walked carefully to the hatch and looked in, but it was dark in there and he could see nothing. "I don't know."

"I'll go down first. I've got a light in there. Want to see?"

Wally shrugged. "I guess."

"Just come down the ladder slow and easy," Junior told him. "Wally? You like me, don't you?"

"Yeah." Wally nodded, but he was looking at the open hatch.

"Follow me down," Junior said, and he slid into the hatch and descended the ladder.

In another moment, Wally Manfred followed. Junior reached the bottom and picked up a flashlight he'd brought from home. He didn't switch it on yet, and Wally said nervously, "Where's the light?"

"I've got it. Just come on down."

"It smells bad in here. It's hot, too."

"No, it's not," Junior said. "It's just right."

Wally reached the tank's floor. His hands found Junior's arm. "I can't see anything."

"Here's a light," Junior said, and he switched it on. A heat was building in his skull, and his temples were pounding. "See my toys?" he asked, as he swung the light slowly back and forth. "I made them, all by myself."

Wally was silent.

Wires dangled from pipes overhead, and from those wires hung the bones.

There were over a hundred. Constructions of wire and small skeletons—birds, kittens, puppies, chipmunks, squirrels, lizards, mice, snakes and rats. Junior had not killed all of them himself; most of the carcasses he'd found, on his long solitary treks. He'd only killed maybe forty of them, the kittens, puppies, and some birds with broken wings. But the skeletons had been reformed, with wire and patience, into bizarre new shapes that did not resemble anything that had ever lived. There were birds with the skulls of kittens, and kittens with wings. There were comminglings of rats and puppies, squirrels with beaks, and other things with eight legs and three heads and ribcages melded together like strange Siamese twins. There were things freakish and hellish, constructed from Junior's imagination. And here, on these wires, was the result of the only thing that excited Junior and made him truly smile: Death.

"I . . . think . . . I'd better go home," Wally said, and he sounded choked.

Junior's hand closed on the boy's wrist, and held him. "I wanted you to see my toys, Wally. Aren't they pretty?" He kept moving the light, going to one grotesquerie after another. "It takes hard work to do this. It takes a careful hand. Do you see?"

"I've gotta get home, Junior! Okay?"

"I do good work," Junior said. "I make things that not even God can do."

"Junior, you're hurtin' my arm!"

On a Beautiful Summer's Day, He Was

"You like me, don't you?" Junior asked, as he moved the light from monster to monster.

"Yeah! I like you! Lemme go, okay?"

Junior swallowed thickly. His face was damp with sweat, his heart racing. "Nobody who likes me," he said, "is worth anything."

He let Wally go, and he picked up the hammer that lay near the bottom of the ladder, next to the coil of wire, the wire-cutters and glue and the can of Rust-Eater. Wally was pulling himself up on the first rung of the ladder, but Junior grinned and swung the hammer and as the hammer crunched into the back of Wally Manfred's skull, Junior was filled with a blaze of joy.

Wally gave a little cry, and he fell backward off the ladder. In the wind of his passage, the freakish skeletons danced. Wally tried to get up to his knees on the floor, and Junior watched him struggle for a moment. The red was coming out of Wally's head.

Junior thought of his father, scribbling fevered jokes on the yellow pad. He thought of his mother, and how she sobbed through the wall on the nights when Junior locked his door.

Smile, Junior.

SMILE, I SAID!

Wally was mewing, like a wounded kitten.

"Know what a laugh is?" Junior asked.

Wally didn't answer.

"It's a smile," Junior said, "that explodes."

He hit Wally with the hammer again, in the back of the head. Again. And again. Wally was on his stomach and he was making no noise. Junior lifted the clotted hammer to strike Wally Manfred once more, but he stopped himself.

There was no use breaking the skull anymore.

Junior sat down beside the corpse, making sure not to

get any blood on his clothes. He listened to the rustling of his toys overhead. The secret place was a secret again, and all was right with the world.

After a while, he prodded dead Wally with the hammer. Poked him all over, seeing how much meat there was on the bones. Wally was a skinny kid. It wouldn't be long. Wally had never known he was a walking Erector Set, with so many different neat parts.

Junior switched off the flashlight and he smiled in the darkness.

He was a happy boy.

He left the hammer in its proper place. Atop the tank, he sealed the hatch good and tight. Maybe he'd come back in a month and see how things were going. It would be like opening a Christmas present, wouldn't it?

Junior stood up and stared toward Gotham City with dark, hollowed-out eyes.

The chemical factory's chimneys were spouting a mixture of white, reddish-brown, and pale green smoke. The haze filmed the sky between him and Gotham's towers, and it shimmered like a mystery on this beautiful summer's day.

Junior descended the ladder to the earth and started walking home through the woods. The replay of a hammer striking flesh reeled itself over and over in his brain, and it got better every time.

On the way home, he came up with a joke of his own that he'd have to tell his father: *Why is a dead person like an old house?*

Because they're both morgue-aged.

Smile, Dad.

The Joker's War

ROBERT SHECKLEY

There was a flash of white light, brief, brilliant, blinding. The man sitting at the writing table blinked and looked up irritably. "What was that?" But there was no one in the room to answer him. He frowned, the lines on his long white face turning down. Whatever it was, it had passed. Outside his cabin, he could hear the ship's horns and sirens hooting. He was aboard the German ship *Deutschland*. It was March 13, 1940. The steamship had just finished docking at Hamburg.

There was a discreet tap at the door. The man turned. "Who is it?"

"Ship's steward, Mr. Simmons. We are ready to disembark. Please have your passport ready."

"Thanks. I'll be there soon. Oh, Steward. Did anything go wrong with the lighting?"

"No, sir. Is something the matter?"

"No, everything's fine. Send some porters to take my bags."

"Yes, sir!"

The man stood up and took off his dressing gown. He

dressed in his usual outfit—purple formal jacket, trousers with black pinstripes, green shirt with purple string tie. He added an orange vest. Black shoes with white spats came next. Finally, since it was a chilly day outside, he put on his lavender overcoat. Pausing, he looked at himself critically in the mirror.

Although he traveled under the name of Alfred Simmons, his clothing and appearance proclaimed him none other than the Joker. He studied his green hair, red lips, and long face. His face split into an impossibly wide smile. The Joker was happy. He had waited a long time for this. Now one of his old dreams was going to come true. He was going to get extremely rich, and he was going to have a lot of fun doing it.

The Joker was the focus of all eyes as he sauntered down the gangplank. Hamburg was gray and cold that March morning, and recent raindrops glistened on the old gray walls of the big old buildings. There was a platoon of S.S. troops just behind the immigration booth. Police in their distinctive red-collared uniforms and small peaked slate-blue caps stood around looking sullen and violent. Enormous signs in gothic black letters proclaimed many things *Verboten*. The sky was gray and storm-tossed. Vehicles were crowded into the landing area, and there were tanks and armored cars there, too.

The Joker breathed it all in, expanding his chest as he stood on the soil of Nazi Germany. Yes, it was just as he had thought it would be.

He walked up to the immigration booth. The official examined his passport and peered at him suspiciously. "Herr Simmons? You come to Germany at a strange time. We are at war, you know."

"Yes, I know," the Joker said. "Against France and

Robert Sheckley

England. Nothing to do with us Americans. Anyhow, there's not much happening yet, though, is there?''

"We conquered Poland last month!" the official said.

"Big deal." The Joker smirked.

The official stiffened. His eyes narrowed. "I could have you arrested for a remark like that. I have a good mind not to let you into Germany."

"Read the note in back," the Joker said, flicking his finger toward his passport.

The official opened the passport and took out a piece of paper. He unfolded it and read it, once, then twice. He looked at the Joker and his jaw fell open.

"But that signature—"

"Yes," the Joker said. "Are you satisfied? I'll be off, then." The Joker retrieved his passport with a quick movement of his purple-gloved hand, and walked through the barrier to the waiting cars outside.

One of those cars was an enormous Mercedes-Benz, gunmetal gray, imposing. The chauffeur came over, clicked his heels, bowed. "Herr Simmons? I will attend to your luggage. Please get in."

The Joker settled down in back. His trip was starting well.

Soon the limousine had left the gray city of Hamburg under its haze of smoke, mist, and rain. They were on the *Autobahn* now, moving at high speed to the south. There were thin dead woods on either side. Nothing was in bloom yet. The trees looked unreal in the thin shimmering mists that clung to them.

After a while they were in the Black Forest. Here the limo turned off onto a side road, and then another side road. At last it went through an open gate onto the wooded estate of the Bad Fleishstein Spa.

The proprieter, Herr Gerstner, a small, balding, worried-looking man in a tuxedo, hurried out to open the limo door and greet the Joker personally. "Herr Simmons! So very happy am I to greet you and welcome you to our spa. We had received Herr Obermeier's phone call alerting us to the imminence of your arrival. We have prepared our finest chalet for your occupancy. It is called "The Kaiser' and your driver can proceed to it and unload your luggage."

"Great," the Joker said. He turned to the chauffeur. "Go do that, Hans, and I'll accompany Herr Gertie here to the spa."

"You must have a glass of cherry liqueur with me," Herr Gerstner said. "It is the finest in all Germany. *Heil Hitler!*"

The Joker smirked but did not reply. The two men strolled up the curving path that led to the main building. There was only a scattering of people around, since it was still early for the spa season. But those the Joker saw were well-dressed and had a prosperous, self-contented look. The Joker decided at once that this was one of the nice things about dealing with cultured and wealthy people. They looked good and they had money.

After drinking a glass of cherry brandy with Herr Gerstner, the Joker strolled through the woods to his chalet. Hans had hung up his clothing, but following orders, hadn't touched several suitcases with special locks on them.

"OK," the Joker said, "you go find yourself a place to stay in the village we passed. Telephone your number to Gertie when you're settled. Be prepared to move at any time."

Hans saluted and left. The Joker made several telephone calls from the chalet, one of them long-distance to Rome. Then he went outside and strolled around the chalet, knocking off the heads of early spring flowers with his walking stick. Going back inside, he unlocked a small pigskin case and took out several sheets of paper. He studied them carefully, then locked them away again. By then it was time for dinner. He checked his appearance critically in a tall mirror, and substituted a floppy silver and mauve cravat for his black shoestring tie, and strolled back to the main building.

Herr Gerstner had given him a table to himself beside one of the long French windows. The Joker ate the soup and salad without comment. But when the waiter brought him a plate of greenish brown things curled into circles and swimming in a suspicious-looking sauce, he bent over it apprehensively, smelled it, and tapped with his knife on a wineglass to get the waiter's attention.

"What is this?" he asked.

The waiter, a tall blond boy with a bad foot, which had kept him out of the military service so far, blushed and said, "*Rollmops*, sir."

"And what exactly," the Joker asked, "is *rollmops*?"

"It is herring, Meinherr," the waiter said. "It is a special delicacy here in our great country. The sauce is light and contains vinegar—"

"*You* eat it," the Joker said. "What else have you got?"

"The main course is roast pork with prunes, sir."

"I don't eat prunes. Haven't you got any real food?"

By then Herr Gerstner had seen that something was wrong and came hurrying over.

"What is the trouble, Herr Simmons? How may I serve you?"

"That's easy," the Joker said. "Have somebody clear away this slop and bring me some real food. I was assured when I made my booking in this joint that you could cook food of any nation."

"I assure you, we can. Our chefs are world-famous! What would you like?"

"A hamburger steak, medium-well done with plenty of fried onions, french fries, coleslaw, and the trimmings."

"Trimmings?" Gerstner asked, struggling with the idiom.

"Excuse me, gentlemen, perhaps I could help." A woman dining alone at a nearby table had overheard the conversation with considerable amusement. Now she swiftly told Gerstner what to bring, breaking off to enquire of the Joker, "Would you like to finish with apple pie and vanilla ice cream?" The Joker nodded, staring at her. The woman completed the order. Herr Gerstner bowed and went away.

"Where'd you learn about American food?" The Joker asked. "You've got a good accent but you're not American, are you?"

"No, I am not," the woman said. "But I have relatives in America. I visited them on their estate outside of Philadelphia a few years ago, before the war. I am the Baroness Petra von Sidow."

"And I am Alfred Simmons," the Joker said, smiling his smile that split his face laterally from ear to ear. The Joker's smile was a sight that, under other circumstances, had made strong men flinch and had given women nightmares. But the Baroness Petra seemed not to be disconcerted by it.

The Joker looked at her and saw a young woman

dressed in the latest Parisian fashion. She was not exactly pretty; her features were too severe for that. But she was as handsome as a young lioness, and looked about as dangerous. Her ash blonde hair was pulled tightly back. Her blue eyes were outlined in a dark red lipstick. Her blue eyes were highlighted by dark makeup. Her off-the-shoulder dress displayed her magnificent shoulders and bosom.

"Perhaps you would care to join me for dinner, Herr Simmons?" she said.

"Only if you permit me to buy a bottle of the finest champagne," the Joker said gallantly.

The dinner went well. The Joker was amazed, because he had never been much of a ladies' man, certainly not since the death of Jeanne and his bath in the chemical vat while making his escape from Batman. The immersion in the hellish mix of chemicals had resulted in permanently dying his face dead white, his lips red, and his hair green. But Petra didn't seem to mind. After dinner there was a dance in the spa's grand ballroom. The Joker hadn't planned on attending. But Petra wanted him to go. He accompanied her to her room so she could get a light stole.

Her room was a suite on the spa's top floor. Petra let them in with her key. The first sight that greeted their eyes was a little chambermaid in black costume and frilly white cap asleep in one of the big armchairs.

The Joker found this amusing. Not so Petra.

"Asleep?" she cried. "How dare she sleep when she should be tidying up my things!"

Petra looked around furiously as the maid stumbled to her feet babbling apologies. Petra's gaze fell on a riding crop hanging from the wall. She seized it and flailed furiously at the maid, once, twice, three times, reducing her to tears.

The Joker's War

"Now, little fool," Petra said, "find me my stole and don't let me ever find you sleeping in here again!"

The maid hurried off and returned a moment later, wiping her tears with the stole. It was at that moment that the Joker fell in love with Petra.

That evening, dancing with Petra under the stars, on the balcony of the hotel, was the most romantic evening the Joker had ever spent. Petra seemed to be taken with him, too.

"I hope to see you again," the Joker said, when the evening was at an end.

"But of course! We are staying in the same hotel, after all."

"Unfortunately," the Joker said, "I must leave tomorrow on business. But I'll be back in a day or so."

"You have not told me what is your business, bad boy," Petra said.

"I'm a businessman," the Joker said, "I get things and sell things. You know how it is with business."

"I have always thought business was very dull," Petra said. "But perhaps that is because my family has not had to engage in it. We have lived from the income of our family estates in East Prussia for hundreds of years."

"You got a good thing going," the Joker said.

She shrugged. "East Prussia is home, of course, but I have always wanted to travel. I enjoyed my stay in America, but there is another place I want to go to."

"Where's that?"

"Rio de Janeiro!" Her eyes gleamed. "I have relatives there. They tell me it is the most fabulous life. And I simply love to samba!"

Robert Sheckley

"I've got some contacts there, too," the Joker said. "Look, Petra, we must talk more about this."

"I would be delighted," Petra said. "Good night, Herr Simmons. Or should I say—Herr Joker!"

The Joker returned to his chalet. He was walking on air. It took an effort to remind himself that he had come to Europe for a purpose, and that the time for action was almost at hand.

Early the next morning his chauffeur arrived punctually at the chalet. The Joker had him put two suitcases into the trunk, and then told him to drive to Flugelhoff Airport, the nearest international airport to the spa. Arriving, he saw that most of the field was taken up with military activities. There were two squadrons of Heinkel bombers parked wing to wing at one end of the field. Security was tight. But the Joker's passport and the letter in it from Obermeier were more than sufficient to get him through. Soon they were in the air. The Joker watched through the window as they crossed the Alps and began the journey down the Italian peninsula.

Despite the air of ingenuousness that he put on, the Joker was very well aware that there was a war on. It was inescapable, even far away in America. He had followed Hitler's progress, taking the Rhineland, the Sudetenland, then launching the blitzkrieg against Poland. The Poles had resisted gallantly but couldn't stand up to the German army of more than a million men and the great panzer divisions that raced on ahead of the troops. Norway and Denmark had fallen. Britain and France were in a state of war with Germany, but so far little had happened. Both sides, Allies and Axis, mobilized, but the French stayed behind the Maginot Line, the Germans behind the Seigfried Line. And the world waited to see what would happen next.

The Joker was a master criminal. He knew that war brought great opportunities for those who could move fast, fearlessly, and with imagination. Those were his qualities. A scheme had lain in the back of his mind for a long time. The present state of upset in Europe made it the perfect opportunity. Now he was doing it.

The German plane flew down the Po Valley and at last began the descent at Rome's Leonardo da Vinci Airport. Customs and immigration were simple. The Joker had several letters of introduction. And he had a well-filled wallet and spread money around liberally among the delighted customs and immigration people.

He went through the formalities quickly and there was a chauffeur to meet him just outside the customs area.

"Signore Simmons?"

"You got it," the Joker said.

"Giuseppe sent me," the chauffeur said. "I am Pietro. I am to take you to where the others are awaiting your arrival."

"Sounds good to me," the Joker said. He let Pietro open the door for him. The vehicle was an old but immaculate Hispano-Suiza, the deluxe model with gold fittings.

"Nice bus," the Joker commented.

"Nothing but the best for you, Signore," Pietro said. "That is what Signore Giuseppe said."

They drove off into the streets of downtown Rome. It was late afternoon. The brilliance was just going out of the sky. By the time Pietro had fought the traffic and brought them to Trastevere, it was early evening.

Evening in Trastevere. The skies of Italy were as brilliant as those of Germany were gloomy. The streets were filled

Robert Sheckley

with banners from a recent Fascist rally. Huge portraits of
Il Duce hung from the sides of the tall terracotta buildings.
The limo pulled up in front of a large restaurant. There
were potted palms in front. Several men in business suits
lounged in front of the entrance. From the sag in their
pinstriped suits, the Joker could tell they were armed. He
had no doubt they were the guards for Giuseppe Scuzzi,
his contact in Rome for the coming operation.

The Joker emerged, and his bizarre and colorful appearance gave pause for the moment even to these hardened
criminals. They didn't let their awe show for long. One of
them said, in broken English, "You are the Signore Joker,
eh? They are inside, waiting for you."

The Joker swept inside past the guards. The restaurant
was large, but it was nearly empty. All the tables were
neatly stacked, with chairs on top of them. Only one table
was filled, and that was at the rear. There, a group of about
a dozen men sat over straw-covered bottles of Chianti and
little plates of *calamari*, deep fried to a golden brown.
They were arguing together in low ominous voices, but
looked up when the Joker pranced in. One of them, a short
rotund man sitting at the head of the table, stood up. This
was Scuzzi himself, mastermind of mafia operations in
the Rome area.

"Eh," Scuzzi said, "that's-a da Signore Joker!" He
stood up, the white-and-black check suit emphasizing his
girth. He swept the broad-brimmed Panama hat off his
head and made a mock bow. "Long have I heard of your
fame, Joker, since it stretches to the four corners of the
Earth, and beyond! It is a privilege for me and my associates, poor hoodlums though we are, to be permitted to

assist you in what our associates assured us would be the caper of the century!''

The Joker smiled his ghastly smile. He had no difficulty detecting the note of irony in Scuzzi's gallant speech. The other mafia men at the table were grinning and nudging each other.

"And how is our mutual friend?" Scuzzi said. "I refer, of course, to Antonio Patina, the famous *padrino* of Gotham City?''

"Patina is well," the Joker said. "As you know, he is presently behind bars in Gotham Penitentiary on a trifling charge of income tax evasion. We are working night and day to get him off, and expect to succeed in the near future. Patina sends you his great love and asserts again that you are to obey me in all things during the course of this job."

"Of course!" Scuzzi said, his grin too broad to be convincing. "You are a world-famous figure, Signore Joker. It brings great honor upon us to serve you in this. There also is the matter of the division of the booty."

"That has already been arranged," the Joker said. "Half for you and your men, half for me."

"That is correct," Scuzzi said. "We are only poor mafiosi, we are of course content with half to be divided among us. The rest goes to you, eh, Joker?''

"I need a full half," the Joker said. "I would remind you that I have been setting up this scheme for a long time. I have had high expenses, traveling to Europe, bribing people, either buying or making special equipment. Are you dissatisfied, then?''

"Not at all!" Scuzzi said, with too great heartiness. "It is only fair, as you point out. And now, perhaps you will favor us with the knowledge of what this job is. We have noted that you did not entrust us with the secret of your

Robert Sheckley

destination before now. Are you going to tell us, or do we go into the job blind?''

"There has been a need for secrecy," the Joker said. "As long as only I knew, there was no chance of anyone else finding out. I do not talk in my sleep, gentlemen! But yes, now is the time and now you shall know." The Joker opened his briefcase and took out a large folded sheet of paper.

Next day, early in the morning, the crowds came across the Vittorio Emanuele Bridge and onto the broad Via della Conciliazione. There were no French or British tourists in that war year, but they were more than made up for by the crowds of German and Austrian tourists, plus the Italians, of course, and a large group of Spaniards and Portuguese. They were like sightseers at any time and any palace; they stopped to peer at the Swiss guards in their traditional uniforms of red, yellow, and blue stripes, carrying their ceremonial halberds. They stood for a while in Saint Peter's Square, each group gathered around his docent. Lectures in many languages were carried on near the big ranks of tourist buses. There were many independent tourists as well; they flocked up the stairs, leaving the Arco delle Campane on the left, with the Vatican Palace and museums and the Sistine Chapel on the right. There were many native Italians among the sightseers, some seeking audience with the pope, others merely passing a mild day in mid-March.

Within Saint Peter's Basilica they went, clustering around the great statues, especially the great bronze Saint Peter by Cambio, where many stopped to kiss its foot.

Inside they scattered in many directions, some explor-

ing the transept and apse, others examining the tombs of
Pius VII and the monument of Leo XI.

All of this was under the watchful eye of guards. Those
within were armed with pistols. There were many guards,
because within these walls were some of the costliest as
well as holiest treasures in Europe.

All day the tourists came and went. By five in the
afternoon the last of them had left, ushered out by the
guards. A careful double check was made to be sure that
no one had been left behind. Despite its holiness, it was
considered unlucky to be locked into Saint Peter's at
night. Some said that the ghosts of early martyrs still
walked these marble halls.

By nine in the evening everything had been carefully
locked up. The alarm system was tested. A last examination of the galleries was made. And at last Saint Peter's
was ready to settle down for the night.

Dark and mysterious, night came again to Rome. Lights
were burning late in nearby Castel Sant'Angelo, where the
pope worked late with his assistants, trying to bring some
sense and order to a Europe gone mad with war.

Guard dogs prowled the grassy walks and the colon-
aded aisles. A special patrol of *carabinieri* made their
rounds and declared that all was well. The Vatican was
safe again for the night. Or so it seemed.

Dim lights glowed in the great art galleries. Saint
Peter's chair glowed with the color of soft gold. Michelangelo's *Pietà* seemed like old ivory in that subdued lighting.

In the picture galleries, bearded popes and antique
saints looked down from their golden frames. In the Vatican Picture Gallery there were row upon row of them.

Not all the paintings were of religious subjects, however. Here and there was a portrait of a shepherd. And at
the far end of one gallery, life-size, was a portrait of a

Venetian reveler. He wore clown's costume, a white satin outfit with dark blue polka dots. A domino half mask covered his eyes, and his lower face showed a smile that stretched from ear to ear and seemed to mock the somber religious paintings on all sides of him. He was perfectly immobile, a strange figure in his finery.

The Lateran clock struck midnight. The figure of the Venetian clown moved, stretched, and stepped out of its frame.

The Joker stretched luxuriously, then walked quickly toward Leo the Great's monument. He moved behind it and located the little door set in the stone, sealed many years before. He had a knapsack under his white gown. Taking from it a small amount of plastic, he patted it quickly into place. Then he looked up. He could hear footsteps approaching.

Two *carabinieri* came, walking their rounds. The Joker made no attempt to conceal himself. He had been expecting these men.

"Hi, fellows," he said.

The guards looked up unbelievingly.

The Joker grinned even wider, advanced toward them, saying, "Look, guys. I can explain everything. It was a bet, you understand what I mean? Look, I got something for both of you. . . ."

He reached them and opened his hands. A cloud of dust flew out. The guards coughed, sneezed, and then slumped to the floor.

"You'll be OK," the Joker said to their recumbent bodies. "Just a slightly altered formula of my Joker venom, in handy powder form. Sweet dreams, fellows."

The Joker moved swiftly through the basilica. He had memorized its layout, back when he first conceived this idea. He remembered the time well. He had been reading about the Huns and how they had marched down the Italian peninsula and sacked Rome. The Joker had always admired Atilla. There was a man for you! And the Joker had thought to himself, anything Atilla can do, I can do, too. And I don't need a million Huns to help me.

Just a few mafiosi, who, according to the plan, ought to be outside waiting to be let in.

The Joker went out into the soft Roman night. He went past the tall poplars to the gate on the left side. This was a small gate, solidly barred. The Joker met two more guards on his way there. Swiftly he put them to sleep with his patented gas. A plastic explosive was enough to blow open the lock. He swung the gate open, hearing it make a soft screeching noise.

"Come on out, fellows," the Joker said.

A group of shadows detached themselves from the dense shadows along the Vatican wall. It was Giuseppe, and a dozen of his men. They looked in awe at the open gate, hesitated before going in.

"Well, whatsa matter?" the Joker asked. "This is what we agreed on, isn't it?"

"I just never thought you could bring it off," Giuseppe Scuzzi said. "Come on, boys!"

They hurried into the Vatican.

Spreading out, they went about their tasks like a well-oiled machine. The Joker had shown them on a map of the Vatican which were the paintings to take, the ones which were small enough to be portable but worth a lot of money. They hurried around to the rooms while the Joker himself went to the crypt.

The door did not hold him up long. He went down, following the strong yellow beam of a flashlight he'd had under his clothing.

There was deep dust on the steps. They had been a

Robert Sheckley

long time unused. The flashlight threw great shadows
over suits of armor, great chests, more paintings. The Joker
went to one side of the room and searched more carefully.
Yes, here it was, just as his researches in America had
shown him. The never-used doorway into the secret underground crypt.

Working more quickly now, the Joker found the ring-
bolt in the floor. With the aid of a miniature fulcrum of
his own invention he hoisted it up. The trapdoor, which
was a slab of marble half a foot thick, yielded grudgingly.
The Joker finally had it levered up and pushed aside. He
went down into the subcellar.

He was in a sort of underground dungeon. Skeletons
hung in chains from the wall. A scurry of movement
proved to be rats, scrambling back to their holes. The sight
of them amused the Joker.

"I won't disturb you for long, fellows," he said. The
Joker had always felt a kinship with rats.

In a far end of the dungeon he found what he was
looking for: a small coffer, about two feet long by one foot
wide and a foot deep, made of rare enameled wood, now
dusty and with no shine. He pried it open. Yes, just as he
had been told, here was a box full of the rarest treasure—
great pearls, some lustrous white, others dusky. There
were diamonds and rubies, too, some of them set in red-
gold, others loose. There were ornaments—brooches and
pins, all made of pure gold and crusted with precious
stones. This take alone was worth millions.

The Joker glanced at his watch and saw that it was
almost time to go. He hurried back to the inhabited levels,
closing the vault behind him. He lugged the casket outside. The mafiosi had been busy and efficient. They had
rolled out the great sheet of reinforced canvas he had had
them bring, and in the middle of it dumped the paintings

and statuary he'd told them to take. Everything was inside the great square of canvas. And now Giuseppe Scuzzi came up to him.

"But tell me this, Joker," he said, "how are you going to get this stuff outside? You didn't tell me that part of your plan."

"One part at a time, that's my motto," the Joker said. "Never fear, I have my methods. Now, tell your boys to fold over the edges so we can make one nice pile of it."

"You must have hired a truck," Scuzzi said, giving the orders to his men. "But I didn't see it around. Come on, Joker, what did you set up?"

"Don't worry about it," the Joker said. "You'll see when it's time."

"I think we have to see now," Scuzzi said. The Joker looked at him and was not entirely surprised to find a gun leveled at his chest.

"Scuzzi," the Joker said sadly, "I thought we were friends?"

"Of course we are," Scuzzi said, "But you're the sort of friend I don't really trust. I don't think you have anything worked out beyond this, Joker. I think you mean for us to carry it out through the gate. That's not a bad idea. Then we can load it into our cars."

"That's not what I had in mind, at all," the Joker said. "And I will thank you to point that gun in a different direction."

Scuzzi laughed. The rest of his men had gathered around now. They all had their guns drawn. They were all pointing at the Joker.

"Don't try any funny stuff," Scuzzi said. "I saw what you did with the guards. Nice work, Joker, but you're not going to get us that way."

"What do you intend?" the Joker asked.

Robert Sheckley

"I'm afraid this is the end," Scuzzi said. "The end for you, Joker. Thanks for leading us to this haul. But I really don't think I can afford to have you take half. Ready boys?"

The Joker stepped into the middle of the treasure. He had the two ends of the rope that bound the ends of the bundle together. He began to laugh.

"What in hell are you laughing at?" Scuzzi snarled.

"You, my friend! I'm thinking what a nice headline this is going to make in the morning newspaper!"

"What're you talking about?" Scuzzi asked.

"Look on the wall," the Joker suggested.

Scuzzi and his men did so. There, lined up five feet apart, were at least fifty *carabinieri*. Their guns were at the ready.

"Where'd they come from?" Scuzzi cried.

"I thought the police might like to take care of this," the Joker said. "It saves me the trouble." He whirled and raised his arms. A gas bomb concealed on his person exploded, emitting a thick cloud of yellow smoke. It billowed up around him, hiding the Joker from their view. The mafiosi began firing, but the police were ready and started firing back. Men started to curse and fall. Above it all could be heard the Joker's high uncanny laughter.

"Maybe they'll get us," Scuzzi said, "but they'll get you, too!"

"Oh, I think not," the Joker said.

Scuzzi tried to take aim at him, but the Joker was invisible in the clouds of yellow smoke. Then Scuzzi saw a sight he wouldn't have believed possible.

The great square of canvas, with the Joker in the middle of it, had suddenly drawn together. As he watched, incredulously, he saw the entire mass, the canvas, the treasure, the Joker within, drawn straight up in the air.

For a moment he thought his eyes were failing him. Then, looking straight up, he saw, almost invisible in the gloom, a small dirigible. It had come down low over the Vatican, a free-swinging hook catching the ropes that bound the treasure, and now it was being drawn straight up into the air.

"I'll get you!" Scuzzi screamed. "I'll get you! Boys! Shoot down that blimp!"

But the mafiosi were having their own troubles. Shots from the *carabinieri* had already decimated their ranks. Scuzzi saw that he was going to have a lot of trouble saving himself. He rushed toward the exit, straight into the arms of a waiting group of policemen.

"What about him?" he asked the lieutenant of police who put the cuffs on him.

"Him? Who do you mean?"

"The Joker, you idiot! He's making off with the treasure!"

The lieutenant looked up in the direction Scuzzi was pointing, saw the great canvas bag swing into the air. Before he could call his men's attention to it, it was gone.

The pilot of the dirigible let the lighter-than-air craft steer itself while he guided the canvas load onto a platform beneath the operator's cupola. The Joker stepped out and made the load secure, then joined the pilot in his compartment.

"Thanks, Chang," the Joker said.

The pilot removed his goggles, showing his Mongolian features and thin moustache. He grinned at the Joker.

"Went good, didn't it?"

Robert Sheckley

The dirigible continued north to Germany, piloted by Chang, personal pilot to one of the Joker's friends, Fu Yu, the Mongolian warlord with whom he had made a deal earlier. So careful had the Joker been of this operation that he hadn't wanted to use a European. Fu Yu had been amenable to a deal, and had had one of his air units stationed in Albania, part of a complex deal he had been putting together.

Assisted by the dirigible's powerful pusher engines, they were back over Germany before daylight.

As the dirigible hovered, the Joker said, "I've already put aside the art treasures I promised your master. You can look them over and see that everything is correct."

The Mongolian pilot shrugged. "If you say OK, is OK. You'd have to be crazier than I think you are to double-cross my master. He isn't soft like those mafiosi."

"I didn't double-cross them, Chang," the Joker said. "They double-crossed me. I just happened to have an ace up my sleeve."

"You called the cops on them."

"Precisely. Because I knew they were going to double-cross me."

"But what would you have done if they hadn't double-crossed you?"

"I would have figured out some way to get them out," the Joker said. "I'm an honest criminal, at least that's what everyone says. You can put me down here. My chalet is right down there."

"You've got it," Chang said.

"My regards to General Fu Yu," the Joker said.

"Thank you, Joker," Chang said. "I will tell him."

Before dawn brought curiosity-seekers, the Joker was able to put the treasure away in the spare bedroom of his

The Joker's War

rented chalet. He stacked the paintings carefully. Some of those Michelangelos and Raphaels were priceless; or so the wealthy South American collectors who had contracted with him had told him. This done, he showered and changed, and looked over the casket of treasures. He selected one particularly nice piece—a genuine Cellini, to judge by the long wavy lines on the side of the brooch. It was a magnificent piece, a sculpture of a sea horse done in amber and covered in precious stones. Smiling to himself he slipped it into his pocket. Next he needed a few hours' sleep. But the excitement was too high in him to permit him to rest for long. Instead he took a drug that had been specially developed for him by a black-market genius. It gave great clarity and intellectual acumen and wiped away the effects of sleeplessness. The only trouble with it was that repeated use tended to rot the brain stem and send a person into delirium tremors. The Joker thought it was a small price to pay for feeling good.

Now that he had the treasure safely stored away in his chalet, the Joker had but to complete his arrangements to get it out of Europe, to the wealthy and unscrupulous men who had contracted with him for it. He could still remember the oily smile of old Soao Goncales, in his planter's white drill uniform, with the bullwhip in the pant loops instead of a belt. "These paintings will serve me well," he had told the Joker. You have seen my house here in the outback. It is very fine, no? With paintings on the wall, my new bride Miriam Da Silva, whom I imported from Portugal, will have something to look at during the day when I am away sweating the rubber planters to keep up their pace." And the other planters had felt the same way, too. They were a long way from civilization, far even

Robert Sheckley

from the dubious thrills of Manaus on the Amazon. With
these treasures they could at least play at being European
grandees. And since they had the price, the Joker was
willing to oblige.

The Joker was well content with himself. As evening
approached he telephoned the hotel and made a reserva-
tion for two. He had been unable to get Petra out of
his mind. Few women had ever affected him so deeply.
Looking at her, he could conjure for himself a life beyond
crime, a life lived with a beautiful blonde wife whose
tastes seemed so clearly to coincide with his.

But what did she think of him? That was still unan-
swered. He would learn that this evening.

He put the Cellini brooch in his pocket, first wrapping
it in a piece of Kleenex to keep from scratching it. He then
dressed carefully in his green tuxedo, brushed back his
dark green hair, grinned at himself in the mirror, and
walked over to the hotel.

Petra was glorious in an off-the-shoulder silver lamé evening gown. The waiters did not have to be told to bring
the strange American his favorite hamburger steak. And
this time, wonder of wonders, Herr Gerstner had managed
to find a bottle of genuine American ketchup! And, remembering what he had read of American dietary habits,
he had caused to be cooked a quantity of onions with the
hamburger steak. Petra looked on fondly as the Joker
gorged, murmuring, "Eat, eat, my green-haired wolf." It
was about as domestic a scene as the Joker had known in
quite some time.

Later, the orchestra played Viennese waltzes.

Though the Joker was not much of a dancer, he managed to galumph around the floor in credible fashion.

The Joker's War

When they sat down again, over chilled champagne, he thought the time was right to give her the present.

"I have something for you, Petra," he said. He took the brooch out of his pocket and handed it to her. She peeled back the Kleenex and exclaimed when she saw what lay within it.

"But my dear Joker!" she exclaimed. "It is perfectly splendid. The workmanship is very fine."

"It's a genuine Cellini," the Joker said. "You can tell by those wavy lines on the side. Do you like it?"

"*Ach*, but I adore it! And what shall I give you in return? She leaned toward him, bosom heaving against the silver material of her dress. "Perhaps a kiss, yes?"

"That's always good for openers," the Joker said.

She made an expression of mock dismay and tapped him on the arm with a forefinger. "Oh, but you are naughty! We have punishments for naughty boys! Would you like me to punish you?"

"We'll get to who does what to whom a little later," the Joker said. "Listen, Petra, all fooling aside, I'm crazy about you. You've got class and breeding. You're sophisticated, beautiful. And I am the master criminal of this age, and perhaps any age. Don't you think we would make a nice couple?"

"Herr Joker, what are you suggesting?" There was a hint of amusement in her corn-blue eyes, and a hint of intrigue as well.

"I want you to go away with me," the Joker said. "Come with me to America. Or maybe South America would be better. I'm rich now." He gestured at her brooch. "There's plenty more where that came from. We could start a new life together in Rio."

"Rio!" she murmured, and there was the scent of hibiscus in her voice.

Robert Sheckley

"Sure, Rio, why not?" the Joker said. "A new place for us both. What do you think?"

She looked at him, then at the brooch. Her eyes fondled the ornament while her fingers stroked his arm. "You tempt me very much! But it is impossible."

"Why?" the Joker asked. "It's my green hair, isn't it?"

"Not at all! I love your appearance! I would love to run away with you, and to live with you in a tropical paradise far from the concerns of old Europe. But it cannot be."

"So why?"

"Because there is a war on. Much as I care for you, I care yet more, greater, for the Fatherland."

"The Fatherland," the Joker mused. "I suppose you are referring to Germany?"

"I am speaking," she said, "of our glorious Third Reich and its great leader, Adolf Hitler!"

She raised her voice when she said this, and several diners at nearby tables automatically said, "*Seig Heil!*"

She let the Joker accompany her to the door of her suite. But no further.

"It is not because I don't want to, dear Joker," she said at the door, her voice husky. "But I could not trust myself with a man such as you. And it must not be. It is written in the stars that I am to belong to one who does a great deed for the Fatherland."

"You're sure of that, huh?" the Joker said.

"Yes, I am. Hitler's own astrologer, Herr Otto Obermeier, read the cards and told me so."

That gave the Joker quite a lot to think about. In the morning, he telephoned Obermeier in his Munich apartment and got an appointment for that afternoon.

The Joker's War

Munich was adazzle with Nazi flags. Armored columns filled the streets. Hitler Youth marched on the broad boulevards. The famous beer halls were filled with soldiers. The Joker went to Obermeier's address and instructed his chauffeur to pick him up soon after. He rang the bell and climbed the three flights of stairs of Obermeier's atelier.

Obermeier answered the door himself. Despite being Hitler's astrologer, he lived modestly, ploughing back all his earnings into a great project. He was convinced that Frederick Barbarossa and his knights still lived somewhere in a deep ice cavern under a river in Germany. When not prognosticating the future, Obermeier went off on expeditions to find the lost cave of Barbarossa. This used up a lot of his earnings. More went to maintain his daily diet of pâté de foie gras and champagne, which his physician, Dr. Faustus, had prescribed for him as the only diet for visionaries. Obermeier was short and round and pink, with albino-white hair and thin reddish eyebrows. He was overjoyed at the Joker's visit.

"I am your greatest fan!" he declared, ushering the Joker into his living room. "I follow all of your exploits, Herr Joker, and I have told the Führer more than once that if Germany had a regiment of men such as yourself the war would soon be over."

"Even a platoon would help," the Joker said. "But it's tough; there's only me and none like me."

They talked idle talk for a while. The Joker expressed his gratitude for the letter Obermeier had sent him. It had opened many doors for him in Germany. Their talk turned inevitably to the war. Obermeier was vehement in his objection to the slow course it was taking.

"Look at our lightning victories in Norway, Denmark, Poland! We have the mightiest war machine the world has ever known. All Europe stands ready to fall at our feet. Our thousand-year Reich is ready to take over. But what are the generals doing? They sit timidly behind the defenses of the Siegfried Line, waiting. Hitler has the right instinct. He wants to attack through the Ardennes, throw his troops through Belgium. It is the Schlieffen Plan, which almost won the First World War for us. It would be bound to win the Second."

"And why is this plan not put into action?" the Joker asked.

Obermeier shrugged and made a comical-sad face. "It is the conservatism of the generals. Although the Führer has supreme power, yet he still listens to those bemedaled idiots. I try to advise him, but although he listens to me, he still waits and hangs fire."

"You're pretty sure this plan would succeed?" the Joker asked, studying the map which Obermeier had opened in front of him.

"Certain of it! And the man who convinced Hitler of it would be a hero of the Reich."

"Is that a fact?" the Joker said. "Let's just go over the whole plan once more. . . ."

The Brownshirt rally had been a great success. Adolf Hitler had stood on the little balcony on the third floor of the Chancellery in Berlin and harangued the crowd for the better part of four hours, often repeating himself for greater emphasis. Now, as the applause died down and then rose again, he came in from the balcony, wiping his brow with a large handkerchief. Although it was a cool day, he was perspiring. These speeches took it out of a man.

He threw himself into an armchair, moodily pushing

back the fold of dark hair that had become his trademark. Then he looked up abruptly. He suddenly knew, with a sixth sense that rarely failed him, that he was not alone in the room.

"Who iss dass?" he asked, his voice harsh.

There was a movement to one side of him. A tall figure in clown's costume stepped out from behind a drapery. The man had green hair, red lips, a dead-white face. He was grinning—a horrible rictus of a smile that stretched his face from ear to ear.

"Hi, there," the Joker said brightly, stepping out into the middle of the room.

"It iss dass Joker!" Hitler exclaimed. "Herr Obermeier told me that you were in Germany and wanted to see me. I agreed. But this is not the usual channels. . . ."

"No, it's not," the Joker said. "You've heard of me, right?"

"Of course!" Hitler said. "I love the way you constantly confound that beefy Batman and his catamite boyfriend Robin! I follow all your exploits! It is a pleasure to meet you, even if the circumstances are unorthodox."

"Unorthodoxy is what is needed to fight a war," the Joker said.

"Exactly what I have told my generals," Hitler said. "But they just snicker and say, 'Leave the fighting to us, mein Führer; war is for professional men.' "

"But you know better than that, don't you?"

"Of course I do!"

"And I know it, too," the Joker said. "Listen, Adolf, I've been studying this Shuffling Plan—"

"You mean the Schlieffen Plan," Hitler said.

Hitler seemed almost mesmerized by the tall grinning figure. He followed as the Joker led him to the desk. Taking a large map out from his cape, the Joker unfurled it.

Robert Sheckley

"Now look here. This shows present positions. Don't worry about how I got this! Your secrets are safe with me! Now then, look, you've got Manfred's divisions here and here, and Von Rundstedt is sitting on his ass over here near the Swiss border, and Keitel is larking around in front of the Maginot Line. Well, why not pull them all out, except for Keitel near the Swiss border. He can make a diversion, make them think you're going to hit elsewhere. But you take all these guys, and the motorized panzers, and push them straight through here." The Joker's gloved hand came down hard on Belgium and Holland.

"It is what I want to do," Hitler said, almost in a whisper. "But if it goes wrong . . ."

"Adolf," the Joker said, "I've been doing stuff like this for quite a while. I've got something to tell you."

"I'm listening," Hitler said. "But can I get you a drink?"

"Later. For now, pay attention. You have to put your mind into an outrageous scheme and then do it without looking back. You got me?"

"Yes, yes, it is what I want to do. But the generals—"

"Who rules Germany? You or the generals?"

Hitler looked up. His eyes were on fire. His hands trembled as he seized the Joker's hands in both of his and shook them fervently. "Joker, I'll do it! This is too big for generals to sit back advising caution. I would probably have done it anyhow. But you have convinced me that now is the time. Joker, how may I reward you?"

"Just scratch a few words on a piece of paper telling what I've done for you and for Germany," the Joker said. "I want to show it to my girlfriend."

On May 9, the Joker visited Hitler again to make sure that the Führer had everything straight. Hitler was glad to see

The Joker's War

him. He had been haranguing his generals and setting up the new plan. There were a few details he was unsure of, however. The Joker was able to clear these up for him. On the Joker's advice, Bock's army group B was combined into two armies rather than its former unwieldy three. The detached army, the 18th under General George van Kuchler, was detailed to attack the Netherlands. Runstedt's army advanced on May 10. They were on a broad front between the middle Meuse and the Moselle. They drove forward with forty-six divisions, seven of which were armored. On the Joker's insistence, they were backed by twenty-seven divisions. While they were preparing for the attack, Von Leeb's army group C, composed of two armies, threatened an attack on the Maginot Line, thus pinning down large numbers of French troops.

Von Runstedt's forces rumbled forward in the blitzkrieg. It brushed aside the weak Belgian resistance in the Ardennes and fought through two understrength French armies still equipped with horse cavalry.

Hitler didn't like to have the Joker around his headquarters because the man's crazy smile unnerved his staff, and there was always the fear that the generals would think their leader too much under the influence of an American crazy. The Joker grinned when Hitler told him this, saying, "Hey, I know when I'm not wanted," and took up residence at the Princeknacht, the best hotel in Berlin at that time. There he had a direct line to Hitler, who also picked up all his bills.

By mid-May the die was cast. The Allied armies were retreating in confusion, German tanks were completing a huge envelopment, and the British Expeditionary Army was retreating to the dead end of Dunkirk. It looked like the war was over not long after it had properly begun.

The Joker returned in triumph to the spa in Bad Fleish-

Robert Sheckley

stein; back to his stolen art treasures, and Petra. In his
pocket was a letter signed by Hitler, praising the part he
had played in the glorious victory and declaring him a
Friend of the Third Reich, First Class.

Back at the spa, the Joker went straight to his chalet. He
saw the first sign of trouble as he approached. There were
several armored cars packed in the grass around his house.
When he came in, he found Germans in air force uniforms
taking out his treasures. They had found it without difficulty. There aren't a lot of places to hide a huge assortment
of paintings, statuary, and jewelry in a small rented chalet.

"What do you guys think you're doing?" he asked.

A young lieutenant came up to him and snapped his
heels as he saluted.

"Lieutenant Karl von Krausner, at your service," he
said. "How may I serve you?"

"Easy," the Joker said. "You can tell your goons to put
all of my stuff back where they found it."

"You claim this as your treasure?"

"Of course I do! It's been in the family for years!"

"And do you always travel to Europe with uncounta-
ble millions of dollars' worth of Italian art treasures?"

"You're damned right I do," the Joker said. "I like to
have good art around me, not these tacky magazine re-
pros." He gestured at the artwork on the chalet's walls.

"There is nothing I can do," Lieutenant von Krausner
said. "These objects are confiscated under the direct orders of Field Marshal Goering himself."

The Joker cooled off immediately. He recognized the
name of the second in command in Germany, and head of
the Luftwaffe, Germany's air force.

"There must have been some mistake," the Joker said. "I have permission from the highest authorities."

"I know nothing of this," the lieutenant said. "You will have to take it up with the Reichs Marschall himself."

"Where'll I find him?"

"He is presently a guest at the spa."

The Joker hurried back to the hotel and asked the manager where Goering was.

"He is in his suite," Gerstner said. "But he left orders not to be disturbed."

"Big deal," the Joker sneered, and hurried off despite Gerstner's protests.

The Joker bounded up the stairs, pushing people aside as he hurried down the hall. He reached the door of the special suite. There was something familiar about it. Yes, of course, this was Petra's suite! The Joker was getting really angry now. What were these people trying to put over on him? There was a German soldier with a Schmeisser machine pistol on guard at the door. The Joker pushed past him, ready to knock.

"Nein!" the soldier shouted. He fumbled for his gun.

"Cool off, baby," the Joker said to him, and, reaching into his pocket, took out a handful of a white substance and threw it into the soldier's face. The guard sneezed violently, three times, then sagged to the floor unconscious.

"The new Joker sleeping venom always works," the Joker mused. "He'll wake up in a couple hours with a hangover and a memory of snowflakes." He tried the door. It was not locked. He opened it and barged in.

Robert Sheckley

Inside the room he heard the sounds of laughter from the bedroom. One of the voices had a high-pitched, slightly hysterical voice. Petra. The other was deep and gruff and weird. That had to be the Field Marshal. The Joker walked into the bedroom.

There he saw Goering sitting in an easy chair. He was a huge fat man with a particularly obnoxious expression. His sleeves were rolled up revealing forearms like hamhocks. His military jacket with the many rows of medals had been hung neatly over a chair. The Field Marshal was just leaning forward to pour champagne into two tall glasses when the Joker entered. Petra was also in the room. She was wearing her negligee, her blonde hair unbound and falling loosely around her shoulders. On the bedside table next to the champagne there were various drugs and little bottles with syringes. A phonograph was playing a German army march. The midday sun, streaming in through the venetian blinds, showed the craters and pits in Goering's face. It was said that he suffered from many different diseases, all of them brought upon by drugs and unhealthy living.

Petra was the first to react. "Why, Joker, I thought you were still away. I would like you to meet my very good friend, Field Marshal Hermann Goering."

"I have heard of you," Goering said. "You are the crazy American who has been advising the Führer. Though, of course, the Führer needs no advice."

"He needed some when I saw him last," the Joker said.

"The Führer never needs advice," Goering said. "To say otherwise is treason."

"I've got a signed letter from him thanking me for my help and declaring me a hero of the Third Reich. And now you go stealing my treasures. How did you find out about it in the first place."

"Word gets around," Goering said, giving Petra a side-wise glance.

"I can see that it does," the Joker said. "I want it back."

"Oh, I'm afraid that would be quite impossible," Goering said. "These art treasures that you stole from the Italians are actually German property. We've had a claim on them for over two hundred years."

"Then you should have picked them up yourself," the Joker said.

"Why do that when we had your services to do it for us so much better? No, my dear Joker, they will stay in the army depository at the camp here in Bad Fleishstein. You will be recompensed for your services. Shall we say a thousand marks?"

The Joker sneered. "I've stolen treasure worth millions of dollars and you're offering me a lousy thousand marks?"

"Well," the Reichs Marschall said, "I suppose I could make it two thousand. That's the absolute top."

The Joker paced up and down the room. He was getting agitated. Then he managed to calm himself. He looked at Goering, who had now put on his jacket, buttoned it, straightened the collar, and stood, trying to look every inch a warrior and commander. The Joker remembered what he had heard about Goering; how much the man wanted to excel in martial deeds.

"Listen, Goering," he said, "I want that stuff back. I stole it and it's mine."

Goering shrugged, a gesture that made his belly ripple. "Well, so, what is that to me?"

"Only this," the Joker said. "Maybe we can do a deal. Maybe I can do something for you, and you can give me back my stuff in return."

Robert Sheckley

The fat Reichs Marschall laughed. "What can you do for me? I am the second most powerful man in Germany."

"I'm aware of that," the Joker said. "But your influence at this point isn't quite what it might be. There's something you want, isn't there? Something you want badly, and Hitler won't give it to you."

"Damn you!" Goering said. "How do you know these things? You are a devil!"

"No, I'm a joker," the Joker said. "People like me know all sorts of things. It helps being crazy. You know more that way. I happen to know that you've begged Hitler to let you and your Luftwaffe kill off the British army at Dunkirk, entirely on your own."

"Yes, well, that is so," Goering said. "I've told the Führer over and over again to call off the troops. It's risky to use them against a cornered enemy. We need them for the big onslaught against Russia. And I have the English swine trapped on the Dunkirk beaches. My planes can easily finish them off with no help from anyone."

"Suppose I could set that up for you?" the Joker asked.

"You could do this? But it is quite impossible!"

"But suppose I could?" the Joker asked. "Would you make a deal?"

"Yes, of course I would make a deal. You could have it all, all, and more, if I could just get this opportunity to prove what my air fleet can do. But it's impossible."

"Listen," Petra said. "Listen to him. He knows what he is talking about."

"Do you think so?" Goering asked.

"The man is a genius," Petra said. "He is probably the outstanding criminal genius of our age. He has influence over the Führer. He can do this for you, Hermann. And then yours will be the undying glory."

Goering's little pig eyes lit up. His mind was filled

with the wonderful picture of his Stuka dive bombers crashing down their bombs upon the helpless British standing around on the beaches.

He said, "If you can do this, you have my promise. I will give you back your fleet, and I will even put an aircraft at your disposal so that you can transport it anywhere in the world."

"Will you sign a paper saying that?"

Goering looked at Petra. She said, "Do it, Hermann! You have nothing to lose!"

"Very well, then. I do it. Bring me pen and paper. Quick!"

Hastily he scribbled a note, then looked up. "But you understand, this paper is no good until you get me the command to do the sole attack on the British at Dunkirk."

"I know," the Joker said. "Just give it to me and don't worry about a thing. Stand by for further messages."

When the Joker went to see Hitler the next day, he found the Führer in a state of high excitement. He was in his private offices, making marks on his big wall map and moving little markers on the position plot on his desk to show the advance of German forces and the increasing compression of the Allied forces.

"Ah, Herr Joker!" he said. "I'm glad to see you. Your advice, as it turned out, was good. Not that I needed it, of course. I was coming to that conclusion anyway. But it was good that you were here at the time I made it."

Hitler took the Joker by the arm and led him up to the position map. "Look, see for yourself. Is it not good?"

"Oh yeah, it's great," the Joker said. "I'm really very happy for you. But I've got another hot flash for you now."

"Ah?" said Hitler. "And what is that?"

Robert Sheckley

"Dunkirk!" the Joker said.

"Dunkirk? Yes, I have them all trapped there! What about Dunkirk?"

"Let Hermann do it," the Joker said.

Hitler stared at him. His face worked. His moustache twitched. He said, "Are you sure?"

"Trust me," the Joker said. "Have I ever led you wrong?"

On May 24, Hitler ordered German troops to cease their advance toward Dunkirk and await further orders. The Luftwaffe was sent in. The great attack by Goering, designed to wipe out the British armies and secure Europe for the Nazis for the next thousand years at least, maybe longer, had begun.

When Herr Obermeier heard what the Joker had done, he was horrified. He said, "But it's not possible! All of my astrological readings show that Goering, in spite of being in command of the air force, has an unlucky air sign. Alone he will not succeed."

The Joker said, "I sort of figured that."

"Then why did you do it?"

"Well, he wanted it so badly. And he's got something of mine. Something that I need back. Obermeier, thank you for all of your help. I think I will be leaving Germany shortly."

"It has been a very great pleasure," Obermeier said. "I have enjoyed dealing with you."

As the Joker reached the door he turned and said, "Tell me, what do your stars show for Hitler's outlook in this war?"

"He will be fine," Obermeier said. "As long as two

conditions are met. The first is, America must not enter the war. The second is, Germany must not attack Russia.''

That evening the Joker went to his room. Using his special equipment he did a job of forgery on the paper the Reichs Marschall had given him. All he needed to change was the date, making the order effective immediately for release of the treasure and for an airplane. Then he packed. He was preparing to leave that evening, when there was a knock at the door.

It was Petra. "Joker," she said. "I'm sorry. I know you were hurt when you came into my suite and saw me with Hermann."

"Oh, think nothing of it," the Joker said bitterly. "There was only one woman in this world who was ever really for me. That was Jeanne, my wife, and she's dead."

"But I am for you, too," Petra said. "It is not my fault what came before you. The Reichs Marschall saw me several years ago and insisted that I become his mistress. I had no choice in the matter."

"Well, it's not a bad choice you made," the Joker said. "Hermann's doing well. Even if he falls on his face over this Dunkirk thing, he'll probably still be fine, and you'll be fine with him."

"But I do not want him!" she said. "Do you still remember our dream of going to Rio?"

"Sure, I remember it," the Joker said. "It was a pipe dream."

"Not so! It can come true! Listen, I will meet you there. Instead of returning to America, why don't you fly to Rio?"

The Joker lowered his long hideous face. She looked back at him without flinching. "Joker, I love you."

Robert Sheckley

It was well before dawn when the Joker set out on what he expected would be the final part of his European treasure hunt. Hans, his chauffeur, showed up about 4:30 A.M., when the sky was still dark and one could still see the thin yellow searchlight beams probing the sky far to the north in Hamburg. He had brought six men with him in the stretch limo. Each man carried a duffle bag. They filed into the chalet at the Joker's invitation. The Joker told the men to wait in the living room. He took Hans outside so they could have a brief private conference.

"These men you brought me, Hans, are they good?"

"Oh, yes, sir, they are very good indeed. They are first-rate criminals from the slums of Hamburg, Berlin, Stuttgart, and other places. I recruited them with great care."

"And they have no love for the Third Reich or Hitler?"

Hans laughed—a short, ugly sound. "None whatsoever, Joker! These men are criminals. If the Third Reich could find them, they would execute them. They are desperate men and very willing to do anything to get out of Germany, out of Europe."

"And they all have their costumes?" the Joker asked.

"Yes, sir. I know a certain tailor who was able to run them up for me. The cloth is genuine field gray. At a pawnshop I was able to buy them a suitable bunch of decorations. I did not know if I should get a uniform for you, sir."

"No need. I brought mine along," the Joker said. "Made in the good old U.S.A., but with German cloth and labels. Wait until you see it. You'll be falling all over yourself saluting me."

The Joker and Hans went back into the chalet. The Joker swiftly changed into an officer's uniform. He said to

Hans, "Are you sure you don't want to come along? It's going to be a whole new life for us in Brazil."

"No, Herr Joker," Hans said. "There's good work for me here, and you have rewarded me so well I will be able to buy a piece of land where Greta and I and the children will be able to farm. Perhaps in Sweden with our false papers. Then it's an end of the life of crime for me."

"Well, you've probably chosen well," the Joker said. "Now, let's inspect these men. Once we pick up the treasure and reach the airfield, your duties are over, and I will have a little extra reward for you at that time."

The Joker inspected his men. It was amazing what a few uniforms could do. These men no longer looked like riffraff from the lowest slums. Instead they looked just like any Nazi officers. As for the Joker, he had come prepared to disguise his face also. A tight-fitting rubber-and-plastic mask went over his face. It gave him the look of a hardened combat veteran. With it he had a wig of close-cropped blond hair. Hans looked him over critically and declared that he was perfect.

They piled into the limo. Hans attached the flag to the front fender showing that he had a general officer aboard. They set out for the Luftwaffe camp at Bad Fleishstein.

The roads were almost deserted at that early hour. They did come upon one army convoy. Flashing their lights, they went past it.

Half an hour's rapid driving brought them to the air force depot at Bad Fleishstein. They pulled up to the sentry gate. The guard stiffened to attention when he saw it was an official German air-force staff car. When he peered inside and saw the tall austere shape of the general wrapped in his gray coat, Hans handed over the papers. The sentry glanced at them and snapped to a salute. The

Joker touched a negligent forefinger to his cap as the car sped into the camp. So far, so good.

They drove past row upon row of barracks. Hans drove with calm sureness, for he had memorized this route a long time ago. The depot, where the treasure was stored, was at the far end of the field not far from the perimeter fence. Hans pulled up in front of it. The two guards, who came out to check their papers, were of a sterner make than those at the front gate. They read the papers carefully, conferred with each other in low tones, and said, "This is most unusual, General. We usually receive advance warning when objects of value are to be transported out of here."

"In wartime," the Joker said, in a harsh, grating voice, "only the unusual is usual. The Reichs Marschall did not want to alert anyone to the transfer of this treasure. Its destination is a top secret."

The guards were still unsure. One said to the other, "Perhaps we should call up the captain of the guard."

"Do so, by all means," the Joker said. "And give me your names and serial numbers also, so I can remember the men who delayed an order from the second in command of the Third Reich."

Another conference. Then both guards saluted. The senior of them, a corporal, said, "Please proceed, Herr General. We do not wish to delay you. But it is not good for us to be remiss in our duties, either."

"Good," the Joker said, "You have done well."

Hans stayed in the car as they had arranged. The Joker, at the head of his seven men, marched into the depot. It was an enormous wooden structure. As far as the Joker could see, it was heaped to the ceiling with loot captured from all over Europe. There was furniture from Denmark and Sweden—chairs, lounges, all sorts of things, enameled sideboards, an endless array of paintings. The German army was making a good profit out of the loot of Europe. In the distance before they entered, the Joker had seen other large buildings under construction. These would be to hold the art treasures of other countries as they fell.

"Well," the Joker demanded of one of the guards, "where is the Italian art treasure?"

"Which Italian art treasure, General?" one of the guards asked.

"The one that that crazy fellow brought in for that Joker."

"Ah, *jawohl, mein generell*, it is right over here." The guard led him to a pallet on one side. There, still wrapped in the original canvas that the Joker had put around it, was the entire mound of the Vatican art treasure. The Joker turned back a fold and looked inside to make sure: there was no sense getting the wrong stuff now. But sure enough, it was exactly what he wanted. He saw the stacked Raphaels, the Leonardos, the Titians, and the Reubenses, plus the statuary and all the rest of the good stuff.

"*Jah, jah*," the Joker said, "*Dis is dass*. Bring me a cart here, quick. We have no time to waste."

The guards hurried away and came back with a motorized hand truck. The Joker sent them back for a second one: There was so much good stuff lying around he saw no sense in leaving it. In fact, he thought, if he'd been aware of this, he could have saved himself all the trouble of raiding the Vatican and come straight here. But of course he had always wanted to raid the Vatican. It was one of the accomplishments he was most proud of. Outside, he had his men load the bags onto the roof rack of the limo. Everyone saluted everyone else and the Joker and his men got back into the vehicle. They sped off. But

Robert Sheckley

as they approached the gate they saw a sudden flurry
of activity.

"Oh-oh," Hans said. "I don't know what this is."

"Just stay cool," the Joker said. "Don't shoot until you
see me do it first."

They stopped. One of the guards came running up. He
was waving a piece of paper. "General!" he said. "One
final thing. You forgot to sign for this!"

"*Ach*," the Joker said, "how silly of me." He hastily
scrawled a signature and thrust it back to the guard. The
guard saluted. The gates opened and they sped out.

"OK," the Joker said, "so far, so good. Now, Hans, to
the airfield, and don't spare the horses."

Dawn was fully up by the time they reached the airfield.
They piled out of the car. There was a captain on duty
and he was suitably overawed by the Joker's rank and
medals, and general air of hauteur. The Joker was at his
swaggering best, commandeering a good-sized military
transport, an old but very sound Dornier with camouflage
paint. At the Joker's orders, extra tanks of gas were fitted
to the wingtips. The gasoline was topped off. The propel-
lers were spun and clearance was given. The Joker's hired
men scrambled aboard. Hans and the Joker shook hands.

"Good luck, Herr Joker," Hans said. "It has been a
pleasure working with you."

"Thank you, Hans," the Joker said. "The pleasure has
been all mine. And here is a little parting gift for you." He
handed Hans a small chamois bag. Opening it, Hans found
five perfect pearls.

"Ah Joker, you are more than generous. It is too much!
It is far greater than the price we agreed upon."

The Joker's War

"That's all right," the Joker said. "It didn't cost me anything. Good luck, Hans."

Hans got back into the command car and sped off. Aboard the plane, the soldiers had strapped themselves into the seats, all except one, Dietrich, who was an accomplished pilot. He was up in the nose of the plane, in the copilot's seat. The Joker sat down in the pilot's seat, tested the controls, revved up the engines. The four big props spun, coughed, spit blue exhaust, and then spun firmly. The Joker ran the engines up and signaled the tower for final clearance.

"Yes, General, you are clear. But you have neglected to file a flight plan."

"Do that for me, old boy, all right?" the Joker said.

"But where are you going?"

"Eagle's Lair!" The Joker said, naming the Führer's mountain retreat in Bavaria. "The Führer is throwing the party of the century there."

"*Jawohl!*" the tower replied.

The Joker pushed the throttles forward and the plane began to creep out onto the takeoff area. Then there was a crackle of static. The tower was calling.

"Just a moment, General! There is something which is not in order."

"Oh? What's that?" the Joker asked.

"The guards from the depot have come. It seems that when you signed for the treasure, you signed yourself Herr General Joker."

"Just my little joke," the Joker said, keeping the plane going toward the takeoff area.

"We would like you to sign again," the voice on the other end insisted.

"Fool! You know I cannot keep the Führer waiting!" The Joker ran the engines up, released the brakes, and started to rumble down the field. There was a noise of confusion mixed with static. Then a voice said, "Ah well, good luck, General!"

Then he was in the air.

The Joker peeled off his mask. Grinning now, he came back to see how his troops were doing. "Everybody all right?" he asked.

"Yes, Herr Joker!" They chorused.

"I hope you packed plenty of sandwiches," the Joker said.

The men grinned. "Yes, we have packed sandwiches and beer, much beer!"

"Good," the Joker said. "Enjoy yourselves. The hard part of this is over."

But in that, he was very mistaken.

The Joker's flight plan called for him to fly due south. He wanted to get out of the war zone as soon as he could. It would be ridiculous to be shot down now. He flew over Switzerland, not bothering to respond to questions radioed to him from stations along the way. He continued south along the Tyrhennian Sea, with the mass of Italy on his left. When Sicily came into view, he made a right turn to fly west across the Mediterranean and then out into the Atlantic.

It was at this point that a single-seater fighter appeared out of the clouds and quickly closed in on them.

"Who the hell is that?" the Joker said. "Dietrich, can you make out any markings on his wings?"

Dietrich looked long and steadily through binoculars

at the pursuing craft. "Well, Herr Joker, it seems to have some sort of symbol on the wing but I can't make it out."

"Italian Air Force?" the Joker asked.

"No, I don't think so," Dietrich said. "It has none of their characteristic markings."

There was another crackle of static. Then a loud voice enquired in Italian, "What plane is that?"

"German military transport," the Joker replied, "on a special mission."

"Is that so?" said the fighter pilot. He came closer still and at last the Joker could make out the markings on the wing. The symbol was like nothing he had ever seen before. The insignia on the wingtips and side of the plane showed a heart with a dagger through it, lying atop a coiled noose.

"What the hell is that?" the Joker asked Dietrich. "Must be some country I've never heard of before."

Dietrich cursed. "Ah! Herr Joker, it is the marking of the mafia!"

"Since when have they got their own airforce?" the Joker asked.

"The mafia always has what they need," Dietrich said. "Especially in Sicily."

The Joker got back on the radio. "Stay out of my way! I'm on special orders from the Führer himself!"

The fighter plane spun in and circled around them at close range. They could see a dark unshaven face staring at them. The Italian pilot said, "Aha! It is the Joker! Land your ship, Joker! You have what belongs to Italy and to us."

The Joker said to Dietrich, "Tell the men to man the machine guns."

The fighter plane circled them again, staying out of range. They could hear radio conversation in a Sicilian

Robert Sheckley

dialect, which none of them understood. Two more planes appeared out of the clouds and came toward them. When they were within range, the Joker said, "Open fire."

The three planes wove a pattern of death around the slow-flying transport. Machine guns chattered and were met by answering fire from the nose and tail gunners aboard the transport. Machine gun slugs ripped through the transport's light covering.

"Shoot them down!" the Joker screamed at his gunners.

"But we can't see them, sir! They're diving out of the sun!"

"Then shoot down the sun!" the Joker shouted.

Meanwhile he was turning acrobatics in the plane, dodging and twisting, taking advantage of every vestige of cloud cover. One of the men scored a hit. One of the three fighters spun into the ocean in a plume of black smoke, crashing at last into the bright sea. The remaining two redoubled their efforts. Smoke began to pour from one of the transport's port outboard engine. The Joker feathered the prop and shut down the engine. The Dornier flew on steadily. They gained more cloud cover. The fighters found them and bored in again. Then the Joker performed an unorthodox maneuver. He turned the plane on one wing, sweeping around like a scythe. He caught one of the mafia planes off-guard and shot it down, watched it explode in a trail of smoke and sparks. That left one airplane. It came at them this time head on. From the radio the Joker could hear Scuzzi's voice, "I will catch you, Joker; I will kill you!" And then the plane dissolved into a fireball and plunged into the sea. The Joker resumed his course, west and south. "Hang on, boys," he said, "We're going to Rio!"

Two of his own men had been killed. The Joker told

the others to throw their bodies out through the hatchway. "It'll be just that much more treasure for the rest of us to divide," he told them. Soon they were eating smoked bratwurst sausages and drinking beer as if nothing had happened.

The plane flew on through the rest of the day. Night saw them well out into the Atlantic. They left the Azores behind them and finally made their turn to go due west across the shortest part of the South Atlantic. Rio lay dead ahead and about a thousand miles away.

Morning found them still making good time. But a second engine was beginning to miss. More seriously, the plane had begun gradually to lose altitude. Checking, they found that the machine bullets had cut through one of the gas tanks. Hasty calculations showed they were not going to have enough fuel to make it all the way in.

The Joker fought with the big plane, taking advantage of stray bits of wind and thermal updrafts, edging for altitude. But he could see it was not going to be enough.

"Dietrich," he said, "we're going to have to throw out the statuary. Order the men to do it. Then tear out the seats, anything extra you can find. We must lighten the ship. There's no way to turn back. Between here and the landing field at Rio there's nothing but water."

Priceless Michelangelo marbles went tumbling out of the aircraft and into the sea. Equipment followed. It was helping, but it was still not enough. The Joker put the ship on autopilot and went back into the main cabin. He said to his men, "Well, you've all been really good and you've been a great help. I hate to do this but I'm really afraid that I have to. You, you, and you. Throw out life rafts and continue after them."

They protested. "Surely you are not serious, Herr

Joker? We would stand little chance of survival, even with the life rafts.''

"You will stand no chance at all," the Joker said, "if you stay here. All there is for you here is a bullet in the head.''

With submachine gun at the ready he herded them toward the open hatchway. One of them tried to jump him. The Joker shot him. Then at gunpoint he made the others jump out one by one. He watched as their parachutes opened.

He was left now only with the lightest of the treasures. He was prepared to die before throwing anymore of it overboard. Only he and the remaining treasures were left in the plane. And Dietrich.

He became aware of Dietrich as the man opened fire on him from the cockpit. The Joker, with his special sixth sense for danger, had been waiting for this and clung to the open hatch high over the steel-gray sea moving below to escape the barrage of bullets from Dietrich's gun. In fact it helped him solve a problem. He was fond of Dietrich, who had done well by him. But the man weighed at least two hundred pounds. That would be weight well saved.

Bullets crashed around him. The Joker fired once, and caught Dietrich square in the forehead. The man went down and stayed down. The Joker pulled his body to the hatch and threw it overboard. And then he was alone on the plane, just him and the treasure, on a wounded German transport that was still losing altitude, though slower than before.

But even though it was slower, it was enough. He was no more than fifty feet above the wavetops now, and the plane was bucking hard. It had taken so many hits, both from the attack by the mafia planes and the combat that had gone on inside, that the plane was threatening to come apart.

At last the Joker could see, far ahead, a dim dark line on the horizon. Brazil! He was almost there!

The plane rushed on, its engines misfiring. He was skimming the wavetops, but the land was coming up strongly. He saw a stretch of beach and, behind it, green jungle. Quickly he checked his position. Yes, there it was! There was the landing field built out to the water's edge, just to his left. But he didn't know if he was going to make it. He was almost in the water now; water was splashing up through the bullet holes. If he'd had his landing gear down he would have been dragging his wheels in the water. Now the landing field was dead ahead. He could see people standing in a little crowd, waving at him. One of them was a blonde. He looked more closely. Yes, it was Petra! She had come! She was waiting for him! How sad it would be, the Joker thought, to have come this far and die just before reaching Rio.

By sheer strength of will he forced the nose up. The plane's tail was already starting to touch down in the water as he swept across the beach and finally brought the plane down belly first on the edge of the tarmac.

He stood up, unbuckled himself from the seat. He had made it! It was all his! He'd done it! The greatest caper of the century, maybe of all time! And he was safe. And Petra was down there waiting for him.

He ran down the bullet-pocked aisle, pushed open the door. As he began to step out there was a blinding flash of light. White light bathed him and suddenly, for a moment, he lost his orientation and had to close his eyes to keep from being blinded.

When he opened his eyes again, he was lying on a cot that was being wheeled by men in white clothes. "Is this

Rio?'' he asked. And then remembered that he didn't speak Portuguese. But he needn't have worried because the man grinned at him and said, "Rio? I guess you've had a pretty nice dream, huh, Joker?"

"Dream?" the Joker said. "Where am I?"

"This is the Arkham Asylum for the Criminally Insane," the man said. "You just had your shock treatment."

"I'm in Arkham Asylum? How did I get here?"

"This is where Batman put you, Joker," the attendant said. "After your last caper."

"What about the war?"

"Which war?"

"The war with the Germans."

"You must have had a really good dream," the attendant said. "That war was over decades ago."

The Joker understood. And he began to laugh. It was a horrifying laugh, an insane laugh, and it echoed through the darkened corridors of the asylum. He was still laughing when they locked him up again in his cell.

Endangered Species

GREG COX

Whooo! Whooo!" she cried. The owls—her owls—answered in kind. As the people of Gotham City applauded, she took a short bow, her pride in her birds momentarily overcoming her stage fright.

Dr. Sumi Okata stood before a microphone on a temporary stage in the middle of Gotham Zoo's new Exotic Birds exhibit. Beside her, Bruce Wayne clapped along with the audience. *So this is an American billionaire,* she thought. He was a handsome man in dark, formal attire, a good foot taller than she was. As she stepped aside and let Wayne take the mike, she wondered what he did when he wasn't hosting zoo openings.

"Thank you, Dr. Okata, for that demonstration," Wayne said. He sounded casual, charming. The microphone amplified his voice and projected it out over the crowd of elegant men and women in tuxedos and fashionable evening gowns. The cream of Gotham society had gathered for a first look at . . . her owls? Even now,

Endangered Species

Sumi found it hard to believe. What must I look like up here, she wondered, in this stylish, red, shoulderless dress the embassy picked out for me? I'm a scientist, not a celebrity.

Genji and Hiroko seemed calm enough, however. Glancing over her shoulder, Sumi watched them as they perched on an artificial tree-branch in their new home: an enclosed plastic dome on a raised stone platform in the center of the exhibit hall. Ventilation grilles along the bottom of the dome allowed her to hear their silver-tipped feathers gently rustle as they stared, with full-moon eyes, at the humans who gaped at them. Hiroko, the female, was slightly larger, about thirty pounds altogether, while her mate Genji had more impressive plumage. The distinctive silver coloring that marked both their wingtips was more prominent on him, and also shined on his tailfeathers and the crest of his skull. Except for the spotlight currently upon Wayne, the immediate area around the owl's habitat had been darkened to accommodate their nocturnal instincts. Only a gentle luminescence within the dome itself allowed her a view of the two birds.

"These rare Silver Owls," Wayne addressed the audience, "come from the mountains of Japan. There are only five known specimens of this breed of owl left in the world, and Genji and Hiroko are the only pair ever to have bred in captivity. They are currently on loan to Gotham Zoo from the government of Japan. It is both a tremendous honor—and an enormous responsibility."

One I have borne for three years now, Sumi thought as she quietly stepped down from the stage. Could this Gotham exhibit be a huge mistake? She'd read about the dangers of American cities, and this crime-ridden

Greg Cox

town in particular. Oh, well, the decision had been made on a higher level than hers; she was only the vet and caretaker, not an administrator. Mingling with the crowd, she hoped these wealthy Americans realized just how unique and precious her charges were.

She scanned the audience as she walked among them. They certainly seemed appreciative, milling around the dome, edging past her for a better look, except for maybe that funny-looking little man over there, lingering toward the back of the dimly lit hall, in the shadow of a large marble column. Curious, she headed toward him.

The closer she got, the more bizarre he appeared. He was about her height, no more than five feet, but comically overweight; his tuxedo covered a large round belly that made him look as though he'd swallowed the egg of some enormous bird. A bright yellow cummerbund girdled his expansive stomach. Although his left eye peered at her through a monocle as she approached, his nose was his most striking feature. It was thin and almost unnaturally long. Like Cyrano's, she thought, but real, not actor's putty. A closed umbrella hung from the crook of his arm. Strange, Sumi thought, the last time she'd been outside, there hadn't been a cloud in the sky.

All in all, he reminded her of one of the short, round, exaggerated characters that were such a staple of Japanese animation. You could always tell they were meant as comic relief, because they looked much more cartoony than the other characters. She smiled to herself. In a way, this odd fellow was less daunting, and easier to face, than tall, rich, handsome, poised Bruce Wayne.

Casually, the man prepared to light the tobacco-filled tip of an ebony cigarette holder. What nerve, Sumi thought angrily. Didn't he care about the effects of smoke on her delicate owls? She hurried over to join him by the column. "Excuse me, sir," she said in what she hoped was a discreet but firm whisper. "I'm afraid no smoking is allowed."

"Is that so?" he replied haughtily, contemplating the silver lighter. Sumi didn't like the sound of his voice. It was hoarse and scratchy. "Well, I suppose we can dispense with the fumes—and proceed straight to the fire!"

With a flick of his thumb, he ignited a huge jet of white-hot flame that shot at least four feet in the air. Sumi staggered backward in shock. The flame was so hot and bright that she had to look away; it was like the breath of Godzilla in the monster movies she had watched as a child. This is insane, she thought. All that fire from one little lighter! How could he have done this? And why?

Screams and shouts broke out all around. People were staring at her . . . no, not at her, she realized, but at the source of the incredible flash. The fire alarm sounded above the tumult, a harsh piercing noise, and Sumi also thought she heard the automatic sprinkler system kick in overhead. Thank goodness, she thought, until the first spray of water touched her skin, the exposed flesh of her hands and arms and shoulders. She yanked back her hands in pain. The water stung everywhere it hit her, the droplets burning her skin, turning it red and hurting. And the corrosive liquid kept falling toward her. She couldn't get away! The expensive fabric of her gown sizzled and smoked beneath the spray. Crimson dyes, boiling and blackening,

Greg Cox

ran in bubbling streams down her legs, onto the tiled floor.

"Ah," recited the ugly little man, from somewhere nearby, "it falleth like the gentle rain from heaven. *Acid* rain, that is."

A society matron, her wig dissolving upon her skull, staggered past Sumi, shoving her out of the way. More people raced toward her, shrieking, waving their arms, tearing at their sizzling skin and garments, heedless of nothing but escape. Sumi threw herself backward against the marble column. The acid streaming down the column burned where it touched her neck, her legs, but it was better than being trampled beneath the panicky flight of Gotham City's rich and famous.

From what seemed very far away, she heard Bruce Wayne calling out: "Cover your eyes! Everyone, head for the exits! Calmly! Don't rush!" She couldn't help noticing how different his voice sounded now. Stronger. Deeper. More commanding. For the first time, she thought of Hiroko and Genji. The owls were probably safe beneath their plastic dome. The exhibit was mounted above the floor on a concrete pedestal, so they were protected from the acid now pooling on the floor as well as from the stinging spray that continued to fall from the ceiling. She just hoped they weren't as frightened as she was.

"Singin' in the rain . . ."

Someone was singing in the midst of all this? Despite the pain, the panic, she looked toward the voice. The guilty party was standing safely under his unfurled umbrella, which was obviously made of stronger stuff than her gown or her flesh. Acid poured down the slopes of the umbrella, diverted away from the little man's rotund frame. "What a glorious feeling," he sang, tap dancing upon the now acid-etched floor. His shoes, Sumi realized, they're reinforced with metal.

For a second, she was glad she'd worn high heels. Then anger overcame her agony and she lunged at the little man responsible for the chaos. But the floor was more slippery than she expected. Sumi slipped and fell, as her target darted away under the cover of his umbrella. Her bare knees smacked against the hard stone floor. She threw out her hands to catch her fall, but landed in a puddle of acid, scorching her palms and searing her knees. The smell of smoke invaded her nose, irritating the back of her throat. Please, she prayed, holding her eyes tightly shut, let it be my dress burning and not my hair.

Suddenly, a strong pair of arms grabbed her from behind. Sumi tried to scream, but only managed a gasp. Someone lifted her to her feet and threw a jacket over her bare shoulders. "Hang out," a voice counseled her. Wayne's voice. Even without the microphone, it sounded unexpectedly impressive. His arm around her shoulders, he hurried her toward the exit. Nobody seemed to be in their way and she noticed, abruptly, that the screaming had stopped. We must be the last ones still inside, she thought. Except for...

"A little man," she gasped. "With an umbrella."

"The Penguin," Wayne said, his voice full of controlled fury. "First, I have to get you out of here. Make sure everyone's safe." Kicking open the glass doors, he half pulled, half carried her out of the building. The air outside was freezing cold, but for the first time in what seemed forever, she was away from that terrible, burning rain. Thank God it's December, she thought. I want to be numb for a while.

Greg Cox

Later, after the ambulances and police cars and first
aid, she was informed that the owls were missing.

It was still cold the next evening as she waited with
Commissioner James Gordon on the snow-covered
rooftop of police headquarters. Sumi shivered and
hugged herself through heavy layers of coat and sweater. From the top of the building she could see most of
the city; compared to the brilliant lights of the Ginza,
Gotham looked dark and intimidating. The brightest
sight before her was the famous Bat-signal shining
above them. This city has two moons, she thought,
and on one of them the man in the moon is a vampire.

Even through her gloves, the winter's cold nipped
at her fingertips. She thrust her hands into the pockets
of her coat. Perhaps, she thought, I should suggest to
Gordon that they go back inside. Sumi opened her
mouth to speak.

Then *he* stepped out from behind the bat-marked
searchlight. Despite herself, Sumi's jaw dropped and
she took a few fearful steps backward, yet unable to
tear her eyes away from nightmarish figure before her.

As with the city, so with its hero. Batman was
cloaked in blackness and projected an aura of danger
and menace. Like some implacable samurai of the
night, he stalked toward her. His heavy black boots
made no sound as he strode through the thin carpet
of snow covering the roof. "I came as soon as I could,"
he said to the Commissioner. His voice was softer,
more thoughtful than Sumi anticipated; without
realizing it, she'd expected him to bark harshly like
the fierce warriors in her country's movies. Through

the cutout slits of his mask, however, Batman's eyes burned with a steady, constant fire.

Sumi had heard of Batman, of course, and even seen some blurry video footage on the news back home. But faced now with the genuine article, she felt sure she must be caught in some Gothic hallucination. First the Penguin, now this. Whatever had possessed her to come to this unreal place? I'm just an ordinary person, she thought. I don't belong here.

Gordon had seemed normal enough, even kind and understanding, but here he was greeting the apparition as if talking to human bats was an everyday event. Perhaps it was, for him. After introducing Sumi to Batman, who barely glanced at her, Gordon updated the caped vigilante on the situation.

"Fortunately," he said, "the injuries weren't as bad as they could have been. Some second-degree burns, a few people badly shaken up or stomped on in the panic, but no fatalities. The Penguin must have been more interested in clearing the hall than committing another mass murder. Thank heaven for small favors.

"Two rare owls, however, have been abducted. They were in a plastic dome, but the Penguin appears to have cut through the barrier with some sort of diamond-edged instrument."

"Probably the tip of his umbrella," Batman suggested.

"That would be typical," Gordon agreed. He rubbed his hands together to warm them before continuing. "At noon today, the Penguin sent us a message via carrier pigeon. He wants two million dollars by the end of the week or he will return the two birds stuffed and mounted." Although she'd heard the threat before, Sumi shuddered at the thought.

"What about the pigeon?" Batman asked. "Any chance it could lead us back to the Penguin?"

"No," Gordon replied glumly. "It died hours ago. A slow-acting poison, I'm told." He trudged through the snow and switched the Bat-signal off. Only one moon now lighted the scene.

"This owl-napping incident is more important than perhaps it sounds, Batman," Gordon emphasized. "The State Department and the Japanese government are up in arms, not to mention every animal rights group and environmental organization in the world. Unless you can recover the owls, Gotham is going have to pay up."

"Even then," Batman said, "there's no guarantee that the Penguin will keep his word."

"It's worse than that," Sumi spoke up, despite Batman's forbidding presence. "My owls are very fragile creatures. Without proper care and treatment, they may not last until the end of the week." It's Monday night, she thought. At most, we have only five days. "Surely," she pleaded for reassurance, "this Penguin person cannot be serious. He wouldn't really destroy the last hope of an endangered species, would he?"

For the first time, Batman looked at her directly. Sumi found she couldn't meet the intensity of his gaze. "He's done worse," Batman said softly. He placed a gloved hand upon her shoulder. "The Penguin is a psychopathic egomaniac. He truly believes he's smarter and more important than the entire world. I don't think other people or things are even real to him, except as toys or as obstacles between him and his crazed amusements."

"What about you?" she found the courage to ask.

"I like to think he's afraid of me. Sometimes."

Endangered Species

So am I, she thought. I never liked bats. Birds belong in the air, not furry creatures with fangs and scary eyes. If and when the Silver Owl exhibit eventually moved on to Chicago, she wondered if she would feel more comfortable with that city's Hawkman and Hawkwoman. Still, as a fellow predator of the night, perhaps Batman did bear some kinship to her beloved Genji and Hiroko. Maybe this would help him save them.

Assuming, of course, that they were still alive.

After Batman disappeared back into the shadows of Gotham City, Commissioner Gordon arranged for a patrolman to drive Sumi back to the apartment that the zoo had provided for her. It was on the top floor of a multistory building on Gotham's East Side, overlooking the harbor. The young officer volunteered to escort her up in the elevator, but Sumi felt reluctant to impose on him that far. Instead, she thanked him in the lobby and headed up to her rooms on her own. She sighed as she unlocked her door and went in. Although she felt exhausted and ready for bed, she was not looking forward to her dreams tonight. Between bats and penguins and showers of acid, she'd accumulated enough material for a dozen nightmares.

Before she could even take her coat off, however, the lights came on in the living room, revealing a fat, too familiar figure sitting on her coach, flipping through an illustrated coffee table book on *Birds of East Asia*. "Oh, home at last," the Penguin said.

Sumi spun around to escape, but two massive figures stepped between her and the door. One of them grabbed her by the shoulders and roughly turned her around

Greg Cox

to face the Penguin. A huge, sweaty palm clamped
down over her mouth while another arm wrapped
around her waist. She tried kicking backwards at her
attacker, but he'd pulled her off-balance and she
couldn't manage much of a kick. Besides, it was like
slamming her heel into a metal lamp pole. What was
this monster made of anyway?

The Penguin snapped the book shut, then glanced
at the spine. "By Dr. Sumi Okata," he read. "How
delightful it is to meet a fellow enthusiast of the avian
breeds. Birds of a feather and all that." Beneath his
courtly airs and almost pompous manner, Sumi detected no warmth in his tone. Indeed, Sumi easily spotted the cruelty in his smirk, and a cold, malevolent
glee in his eyes. *How could I have missed it before?*
she wondered. *Why didn't I recognize a monster when
I saw him?*

A silk top hat rested on the couch beside him, along
with a closed umbrella. Ridiculous though it was, Sumi
winced, half expecting another rain of burning acid.
The Penguin ran a pudgy hand through his thin, receding hairline, then stood up behind the coffee table,
umbrella in hand. Holding it like a saber, he pointed
the tip directly at Sumi's heart. "You may let her go
now," he instructed his men. "Please refrain from
screaming, m'dear. I assure you this umbrella is
loaded."

The hand came away from her face. Sumi gasped
and took some short, rapid breaths. Then, without
making any sudden moves, and struggling to keep one
eye on the Penguin and his lethal bumbershoot, she
glanced back to get a look at her assailants.

They looked like twin bodybuilders, bald as ostrich
eggs and wearing matching black slacks and short-

sleeve white T-shirts. In imitation of their dapper ringleader, they wore black bow ties (held on, she observed, by elastic bands) under their square, meaty jaws. They had pale skin, Caucasian verging on Nordic, and muscles like she had not seen since her twelve-year-old nephew had dragged her to that Conan movie.

"Permit me to introduce the Dodo Brothers," the Penguin said with mock civility. "Don't bother to try to tell them apart. It's not worth the effort."

Sumi looked back at the Penguin. "Why are you here?" she asked.

"Your lovely, snowy owls are of no value to me dead," he explained. "I'm afraid you must come and keep them company, as well as in good health." He smoothed the tails of his suitcoat. "Do not fear for your reputation, though. The Dodos make excellent chaperones." He snarled at his men, all pretense of courtesy gone. "Grab her!"

The musclemen took hold of her upper arms, one on each side of her, while the Penguin waddled to the center of the living room. He pointed the umbrella at her ceiling and squeezed its handle. Sumi waited for another burst of flame, but instead, with a loud bang that hurt her ears, the umbrella blasted a hole in her ceiling as though it were a bazooka. The Penguin unfurled the umbrella's hood and waited underneath it until the dust and plaster and bits of wood and insulation stopped falling. A cold draft blew through the ragged opening overhead, raising goosebumps on the Dodo Brothers' massive arms. The Penguin's chilly gaze swept over her boots and gloves and thick winter coat. "How thoughtful of you to dress for the trip," he croaked.

One of the Dodos released her arm and joined the

Greg Cox

Penguin in the middle of the debris-covered living
room. He crouched, then jumped upwards and caught
hold of the edge of the hole. Lifting himself by his
arms, he disappeared momentarily up through the gap
in the ceiling, then his bald head looked down on them
all, framed against the night sky.

Someone pounded on her apartment door. A neighbor's voice called out, asking what had happened, was
she all right? Too afraid to answer, Sumi listened
desperately for the sound of police sirens, even knowing they were already too late.

The rest happened almost too quickly for Sumi to
react. The Penguin gestured toward the hole, the remaining Dodo rushed her forward, then, without warning, he lifted her effortlessly over his head, into the
waiting arms of his brother. Suddenly, she found herself on the roof of the apartment building, even higher
than the top of the police headquarters she had visited
earlier this night. The Dodo shoved her away from
him, then bent again over the opening the Penguin's
umbrella had made. Sumi's eyes widened as she spotted what looked like some sort of small aircraft parked
a few yards away. It was shaped like an immense egg
lying on its side, resting on a triangular set of three
wheels, two under the wide end of the egg and a single,
larger wheel under its nose. The craft was painted
mostly black, with a white belly, and had two black
wings and a small set of tailfins. Aside from a large
window mounted at the ship's nose, she also noticed
two transparent portholes along its side.

"Behold, our winged chariot awaits!" Looking to her
left, she saw the Penguin being lifted, far more gently
than she had been, onto the rooftop. Moments later,
the second Dodo clambered up to join the rest of them.

She was forced at umbrella-point to climb into the aircraft where a Dodo strapped her into one of the two backseats. Laying his hat aside, the Penguin took his place at the controls. "Prepare for takeoff," he cackled. The Dodos hurriedly fastened their seat belts.

A powerful engine surged to life somewhere behind her seat. The vibration shook her bones. Then the entire Penguin-ship accelerated forward. Through the wide front window, Sumi saw the guardrail at the edge of the roof rushing toward them. Not much of a runway, she thought nervously; then again, this was obviously no ordinary plane. The ship smashed through the railing. Sumi felt the wheels lift up into the egg's interior, and there was, shortly, nothing below them but empty air.

They soared out over the harbor, toward the Atlantic Ocean. Despair hit Sumi with overwhelming force. This keeps getting worse and crazier, she thought. Where were they taking her, and would she ever see her home in Osaka again? Still, at least she knew that Hiroko and Genji were still alive.

One of the glass portholes was located to her right. Turning her head, she could see nothing at first but glimpses of dark purple sky. Wait! What was that? Her heart pounded as something blacker than the night swooped past her limited field of vision. Was it just her imagination or ... no, there was it again! A sleek black UFO that resembled nothing so much as the wings of an enormous bat. For a second, Sumi feared that she witnessing the Bat-signal once more, but no searchlight beam was ever so graceful and aerodynamic. Yes, Sumi thought. Over here! Help me!

"Time to dive," the Penguin announced. He must have seen the Batplane, too; Sumi believed she heard a note of anxiety in his voice. To her instant horror, though, the entire ship tilted forward at more than a forty-five degree angle and plunged toward the sea. Only her seat belt kept her from tumbling toward the cockpit. Her long black hair flew wildly about; she batted it away from her eyes. All she could see now was the surface of the ocean zooming toward them, with maybe a sliver of horizon at the very top of the forward window. She braced herself for a crash landing while the Penguin laughed maniacally. He's a lunatic, she thought, just as they were about to hit the waves below. Absolutely out of his mind.

The whole ship shook as they collided with the ocean, but, to Sumi's amazement, it held together and kept on going down. Down, down into the ocean, beneath the waves and foam, away from the moonlight, into water that grew murkier with each passing heartbeat, deeper and deeper below the sea. Eventually, just as Sumi started to breathe again and felt her pulse gradually slowing, the submersible aircraft leveled off and regained an even keel. The Penguin pushed a button and a powerful headlight shot out from underneath the nosecone of the ship, tearing a faint green path through the pitch-black waters. Some hidden mechanism hummed in the walls to her right and left. The wings, she guessed after a moment; they must be retracting into the ship. Partially, at least.

The Penguin looked back at her. "Don't be so amazed, geisha doll," he said, clearly enjoying her near heart attack. "You're an ornithologist of sorts. I thought you knew; penguins never fly when they can swim."

She tried to ignore his taunts. I'm still alive, she realized. For a single wonderful instant, relief flooded her heart, until she remembered the Batplane. Presumably it was now circling impotently overhead, if they had not already left it miles behind . . .

"Next stop, the Arctic Circle," crowed the Penguin.

The Penguin's amphibious craft seemed to hurtle through the depths at tremendous speed. All too soon, as far as Sumi was concerned, they neared their destination. The ship rose gradually, at a much slighter, less alarming angle than their headlong descent, until the brine around them grew steadily lighter. A gentle chartreuse glow suffused the sea through which they traveled. The sun must be out, she surmised. Have we traveled all night or simply passed into a different time zone? Through her porthole, she spied small and larger fish. Salmon maybe. Or tuna. Once she thought she saw a shark. A disturbing moment; it reminded her too much of her present situation.

"Here we are," the Penguin finally announced. From her underwater vantage point, the Penguin's lair looked at first like an immense underwater cave, sculpted from some translucent crystalline substance. Then the subplane broke the surface, and Sumi found herself looking at a towering iceberg. Artificial, she guessed, but cleverly camouflaged. It looked indistinguishable from a few other icy peaks she saw floating in the distance. How far north are we? she wondered. Above Canada? If only she'd paid more attention to geography!

"I thought penguins were Antarctic birds," she said out loud.

The Penguin scowled back at her. "Not this one," he snapped. Careful, she thought. Remember what Batman said about his ego.

Greg Cox

In silence, they cruised into the phony ice cave, docking at a metal pier well within the iceberg. After they disembarked, Sumi had only a moment to take in the vaulting, frost-covered walls before the Penguin roughly took hold of her arm. "Come along, doctor. I'm sure you're eager to see your patients."

With the Dodos treading behind, he led her through a maze of antiseptic white corridors, brightened infrequently by the occasional stolen art treasure. At least, she assumed they were stolen. She recognized a Picasso, a Monet, even a van Gogh. No Japanese artists, but still the Penguin had good taste. The deeper they went into the lair, the closer the temperature rose to something approaching comfortable, confirming her suspicion that the iceberg outside was just a facade. It made her wonder: Given the obvious fortune expended on this incredible headquarters, his submersible plane, the trick umbrellas, why did the Penguin even bother with crime? Batman had said something about his "crazed amusements." Could it be this was all simply a game to him?

Yes, she thought bitterly. A game of pain and fear.

Finally they came to a heavy metal door, locked from the outside. The Penguin removed a copper-plated key from the inside pocket of his jacket and, seconds later, the door swung inward. When Sumi saw what was inside, she didn't know whether to rejoice or despair.

Hiroko and Genji were trapped inside an old-fashioned metal bird cage, atop a four-foot iron pole. Although glad to find them alive, she could tell at once that they were miserable. Although Hiroko flapped her wings frantically at the sight of Sumi, Genji could barely manage a half-hearted "whooo" in greeting.

Endangered Species

Breaking free of the Penguin, she ran to the cage. The
bottom of the owls' prison was lined, she observed,
with a black-and-white photo of Batman, now splattered with bird droppings and several small silver and
white feathers. Both owls were moulting badly, Genji
more so than his mate, and she was shocked at how
much weight they seemed to have lost in just a day
or so.

Furious, she turned on the Penguin. "This is
obscene," she cried out. "Can't you see how ill they
are? It's far too warm in here, never mind the shock
and trauma of the abduction. And what in pity's sake
have you been feeding them?" Hot and perspiring, she
pulled off her gloves and overcoat and angrily threw
them on the ugly concrete floor.

"Birdseed. What else?" the Penguin said coolly, apparently unaffected by her outburst.

"Don't you understand? They're dying. You have to
let me take them back to the zoo hospital, where they
can get the care they need. They're the last breeding
pair of Silver Owls in the world!"

"Precisely why they are so valuable." He raised his
umbrella and placed the point against her throat. He
pressed her backwards until she was up against the
far wall of the prison cell. "Let me clarify the situation," the Penguin said. "I do not have to do anything.
You're the owl doctor. You have to keep your pets alive,
or you might not last so long yourself. Understand?"

"Yes," she whispered, unable to nod.

"Fine." The Penguin stepped back and let the umbrella drop to his side. "I'm so glad we had this little
talk." Addressing the Dodo Brothers, he turned his
back on Sumi. "Come now, lands. Time for a well-
deserved rest." They strolled out of the cell, leaving

her behind. "Oh," he said offhandedly, just before he closed the big steel door, "the ladies' room is in that closet there. Sorry we can't provide a shower."

The door slammed shut behind him. Sumi heard a key turning in the lock.

She crumpled onto the floor. Her knees, still red and raw from the acid bath, protested, but she was past caring. It was too much, she thought. Imprisoned in the Arctic by a lunatic killer who looks like a joke. That's enough; no more. How did she let herself get sucked into this craziness? What made her think she could survive in Gotham City, in America? "I'm sorry," she murmured to the owls. I wish I could help you, but I can't even save myself. Rocket-shooting umbrellas. Planes that go deep-sea diving. How much of this could she be expected to take? She was not a superhero, only an ordinary person.

Curled up on the floor, using her coat for a mattress, she sobbed herself to sleep.

Hiroko! Genji! She woke abruptly from grim, unrestful dreams to find the Penguin leaning over her, shaking her shoulder. "What is it?" she asked, alarmed. "The owls?"

"See for yourself," he said, straightening his back. "But be quick about it. We have other business." He'd left his top hat and bow tie behind this time. Stubble shadowed the lower half of his face; with an eyepatch instead of a monocle, he might have resembled an old-time pirate, Sumi thought as she scrambled to her feet. He thrust his face toward hers, almost jabbing her with that grotesque nose. "You practically slept the day away," he snarled accusingly.

Endangered Species

So did you, she guessed. Maybe you're only human after all. Ignoring the angry birdnapper, she hastily inspected her owls. Neither had fallen from their perches yet, but they didn't look well. Genji, although breathing, was unresponsive, even to her birdcalls. Hiroko shivered and seemed nervous and agitated. They had hardly touched their birdseed.

"I need medicine," she said as firmly as she could. "Special foods. Liquid supplements."

"Later," the Penguin croaked. He produced a notebook and ballpoint pen. "My old friend, Police Commissioner Gordon, says on TV that he needs proof that both you and your owls are safe before any ransom can be paid." He shoved the pen and paper into her hands. "Dodo and Dodo are preparing another pigeon even as we speak." He waddled over to the birdcage and stuck his nose through its bars; to Sumi's disappointment, they were too sick and listless to even snap at it.

"And don't try anything tricky," he added. "For your little friends' sake."

Sumi sat down cross-legged on her coat and tried to think of something ingenious. There was no other choice, she knew. This was her only chance, but how could she get a message across to Batman or Gordon without the Penguin catching on? "Hurry!" the Penguin snapped.

After a few high-stress moments, she handed over her note to the Penguin. Gods, she thought, this was worse than my national exams.

"Dear Commissioner," the Penguin read out loud. "Let me assure you that the owls and I are currently unharmed, although I have certainly had a night to remember. I urge you to do whatever you can to save the owls as their extinction would be an environmental tragedy of titanic proportions. Trusting in you, Sumi Okata."

Please, she prayed silently, let Batman be as clever as I have heard.

"Very nice," the Penguin pronounced. "Short, sweet—and terribly, terribly stupid." With short, fussy movements, he ripped her letter to shreds. "Did you really think I would overlook your oh-so-subtle references to the sinking of the *Titanic*—and icebergs? *A Night to Remember*, eh? I saw the movie, too. That pathetic buffoon, the Riddler, composed better puzzles in kindergarten. The Joker wouldn't be able to muster a grin at this feeble code." Umbrella in hand, he stalked toward her, sadistic malice in his eyes. "You fool!" he hissed. "In games of deceit, you are nothing but an amateur, a mere child, compared to me. And, at this moment, something of an endangered species in your own right."

Desperately, Sumi searched her surroundings for something—a weapon, another exit—that might help her live through the next few moments. But there was nothing. Even the birdcage was mounted to the floor. Shoulders forward, hunched over like a bloodthirsty troll, the Penguin forced her into a corner. This is it, she thought. Forgive me, my beautiful Silver Owls. I did my best.

"Say *sayonara*," he said with a leer.

Then, instead of running her through, or blasting her to ribbons with some diabolical device, the Penguin paused. He strolled over to the nearest wall and slid back a concealed panel, revealing an array of buttons and what looked like an intercom. Pressing a white button, he shouted into the speaker: "Dodos, come here immediately." He cast a gleeful glance in Sumi's direction. "I fear our next bit of air mail will have to be written in Dr. Okata's blood. Perhaps one of her featherd friends can provide us with a quill to write with." He lifted his finger from the button and smiled at Sumi. "Had you going there for a second, did I not? Don't you fret. Why, we've only just begun."

No, she thought. It's over. There will be no escape for any of us. And the Penguin will keep on playing his inhuman games.

At that moment, as her last hope dropped away, an explosion suddenly rocked the floor beneath her. No, the whole fake iceberg was shaking. Her ears rang with the echoes of the noisy detonation. What was happening? The Penguin looked just as dumbfounded as she was. The steel door slammed open and the Dodo Brothers lingered in the doorway, uncertain whether to come in. Dust and bits of plaster fell from the ceiling. Oh, hell, she thought irrationally. Not again. Instinctively, she wrapped her arms around the birdcage, completely unaware of whether it was to protect the owls or just to have something to hang on to.

Another explosion went off just overhead. One corner of the ceiling collapsed inward and, when the smoke and swirling debris began to settle, she glimpsed a blasted-out tunnel rising up through several feet of shimmering artificial ice. And standing at the top of the tunnel, silhouetted against the evening sky, was an imposing black and gray figure with a shining golden emblem on his chest: The Sign of the Bat.

More fearsome than before, Batman leaped down his newly created tunnel to land on his feet less than a yard away from Sumi and the birdcage. Beneath his facemask, Batman's pale blue eyes swept the scene, taking in every detail: the owls in their cage, the goons just outside the cell, the Penguin by his intercom, and, Sumi hoped, herself.

The cloaked invader went for the Penguin first. He lunged across the room, but not fast enough to keep the Penguin from pressing another button. With a whoosh of released air, an entire section of the floor dropped out from beneath Batman, who instantly plummeted from sight. Clinging to the metal cage as if it alone could save her while this whole dreadful place appeared to be falling apart, Sumi heard a loud splash from where Batman had disappeared. Ice-cold water leaped up through the trapdoor to spray against her face. She tasted salt upon her lips. Seawater.

"Har!" the Penguin laughed. "Penguins can't fly, but bats can't swim. With all his armor and gadgets, he'll sink like a stone to the bottom of the sea!" He scratched his chin and looked speculatively at first the trapdoor, then the Dodo Brothers. "Still, no sense taking chances, not with him. Make like polar bears, boys, and finish him off!"

Sumi had thought that, after all she'd seen already, nothing could surprise her anymore. Then the two bodybuilders, obedient to the end, dived in after Batman. Straight into the Arctic Ocean. In the middle of December. She scarcely had a chance, however, to take in this latest turn of events, or even wonder if Batman had a chance of ecaping, before the Penguin grabbed onto the back of her collar. "Be it ever so humble," he spit, "it's time to vacate this happy home. But first . . ."

A six-inch blade shot out of the tip of his umbrella. He's going to cut my throat, she realized in horror. It wasn't fair. For a moment there, when she saw the bat, she'd thought she was safe.

Endangered Species

The Penguin swung his sword-umbrella—and sliced off the top of the birdcage, only a few inches over the heads of both owls. Cursing under his breath, he reached in and brutally snatched Hiroko from her perch. "The female is all I really need," he gloated. "Try saving the breed without her!" He poked Sumi in the back with the point of his sword. "Come on!"

Following behind her, prodding her with the sword while clutching Hiroko to his chest, the Penguin sped her thrugh the maze of corridors. "Hurry!" he commanded. She could hear him breathing heavily, gasping for air, as the heavyset criminal tried to keep up with her. "This umbrella also functions as a speargun," he hollared, "so don't get any clever ideas about trying to outrace me." He sucked air noisily into his lungs. "Besides, I've still got Momma Bird."

In spite of his threats, and her own common sense, Sumi felt a surge of hope. It was true, she realized. *He is afraid of Batman. I'll bet we're heading toward his submarine, because the Penguin's not convinced Batman's dead.*

Sure enough, when they rounded the final corner and headed toward the dock, Gotham City's midnight samurai stood between them and the ship. He was missing his cape, his boots, and his world-famous utility belt. His bare feet, she noticed, were tinged with blue. He was dripping wet and bleeding from a blow to his mouth. Sumi thought he had never looked so ferocious.

"No!" the Penguin squawked. His snobbish composure evaporated completely. "You ignorant brute! Why don't you ever know when you're beaten."

"Give it up, Penguin," Batman warned. "This round's over."

"Not so fast, my nocturnal nemesis." He flashed a blade of his umbrella above his head, then, in one swift motion, pressed it against the back of Sumi's neck. "Would you rather I skewer the lady or the bird?"

"One way or another, Penguin, it's back to Arkham for you. Don't make things any harder on you." Batman remained frozen in place, like a statue of demonic fury. Was he stalling? she worried. How long could he keep this up before the cold and exhaustion brought him down? If only there was something she could do, but that was absurd. She was playing way out of her league.

"Don't take another step," the Penguin said, "or Madame Butterfly will be singing her last farewell."

Singing? Wait a minute, Sumi thought. Maybe she didn't have to play the helpless victim. All she really knew was birds, but perhaps that might be enough. Pursing her lips, she took a deep breath and: "WHOOOOOO!"

"What the devil?" the Penguin cried as, in response to Sumi's call, Hiroko flapped and fought uncontrollably within the Penguin's grasp. "Blast it! Stop, you infernal beast!"

It happened in a heartbeat. Hiroko went for the Penguin's face, her talons digging deep scratches in his oversized nose. The sword-umbrella swung away from Sumi's neck; the second she felt it move, she kicked back at the Penguin's shins with all her strength. And Batman's fist struck like a night-black bolt of lightning.

The next moment, the Penguin was laid out flat on his back, his monocle shattered on the frosty steel pier. Breathing once more, her heart racing like a hummingbird's wing, Sumi grabbed up Hiroko and stroked

Endangered Species

and cooed to the frantic owl until they both were comforted. Batman picked up the fallen umbrella and, with a grunt of satisfaction, broke it over his knee.

"You enjoyed that, didn't you?" she asked.

"Sometimes the job has its rewards."

Sumi was glad. It made him more human somehow. "I have to ask: How did you find us?"

"Once you told me how fragile the owls were, I suspected the Penguin would come after you eventually. I placed a homing device on you that night at police headquarters."

Of course. She remembered his hand upon her shoulder. "So," she said quietly, "in the end, I was only a piece of bait."

Batman shook his head. "You aren't *only* anything, Sumi Okata."

Four months later, Genji and Hiroko blessed Gotham City with its own newborn Silver Owl. Bruce Wayne and Jim Gordon attended the ceremony where the baby owl was presented to an eager and enthusiastic crowd of Gothamites. At Sumi's insistence, the owlet was named Koomori.

"It means bat," she explained.

"Or," she admitted grudgingly, "umbrella."

Copycat

JOHN GREGORY BETANCOURT

MILLIONAIRE PLAYBOY MURDERED
CATWOMAN SUSPECTED

By Vicki Vale
Special to the *Gotham Globe*

Bruce Wayne, wealthy socialite and philanthropist, was found dead this morning in his study at Wayne Manor. According to police, Wayne had been "savagely lashed, then strangled to death with a whip," which was found wrapped tightly around his throat. Sources at the coroner's office report Wayne's body was "covered with catlike scratch marks" around his face and hands. Selina Kyle, popularly known as "Catwoman," is currently being sought by police for questioning in connection with this crime.

Copycat

The body was discovered at approximately 8:30
A.M. by Wayne's butler, Alfred Pennyworth. Pennyworth also noted several Wayne family heirlooms as
missing, including an ancient jade Chinese statue of
a cat, valued at nearly two hundred thousand dollars. Kyle is suspected of committing a recent string
of high-profile burglaries. This latest crime *(cont'd
A3, col. 1)*

Catwoman hissed in fury. She crumpled the newspaper without finishing the article, then flung it across
her penthouse's living room. A dozen cats watched the
paper roll to a stop, before the nearest, a gray-and-
white tabby, sprang with blinding speed. Claws
flashed. Seconds later the paper lay in tatters.

"That's right, Cleopatra," Catwoman said. The
tabby gave her a triumphant look, then began to lick
its paws with methodical grace. "Something *must* be
done to protect our good name."

Selina reclined, her svelte body barely covered by a
leopard-spotted leotard, on a plush, black leather couch
in a private suite decorated with handpicked, and personally stolen, objets d'art. She wasn't surprised by the
newspaper story. Inconvenienced, certainly. Angry, beyond a whisker of a doubt. But not surprised.

By the time the afternoon edition of the *Globe* had
arrived at her secret high-rise hideout, she'd already
heard about Wayne's death a dozen times over on the
radio. It was a slow day for news, so a millionaire do-
gooder's brutal murder by the notorious Catwoman
made every news bulletin.

The only problem was, Selina hadn't committed the
crime. She'd been lying low the last few days, ever
since she'd botched a burglary at Harry Harkins's
mansion. *That* had been a real mess. The old man was

supposed to be out of town touring his cat-food factories; how was *she* to have known his heart had been
acting up and he'd canceled the trip at the last minute? She'd broken in right on schedule, circumventing
laser-beam fields and an elaborate alarm system, only
to literally bump into Old Man Harkins in the hallway; his well-oiled wheelchair hadn't made a sound as
it glided across the carpet.

Shocked, they'd both stared at each other for a second. Catwoman hissed and flashed her razor-sharp
claws. Harkins clutched his chest and started to make
helpless gasping noises. When he punched the medic-
alert button on his wheelchair's left arm, alarms began to wail. Catwoman fled.

Within minutes, a score of private doctors and a
hospital helicopter with a huge red cross blazed upon
its side had arrived. Catwoman had lingered on the
estate's high stone wall long enough to observe the
first rush of frenzied rescue activity. When the police
arrived with flashing lights and sirens blaring, she
slunk home to lick her figurative wounds and bide her
time before striking again.

The next day Selina learned she'd literally scared
Old Man Harkins to death. His weak heart just gave
out. Before he kicked off, though, he'd managed to
whisper Catwoman's name, linking her to his death.

The police had been searching for her ever since.
Old Man Harkins had a lot of friends—very influen-
tial friends—who wanted her arrested for his murder.
As a result, she'd decided to lie low for a few days. She
hadn't been out of her penthouse since Old Man
Harkins's funeral except to pick up a few gallons of
cream from a gourmet grocery.

Now it seemed trouble had come looking for her.
Someone—some *copycat*—had stolen her modus

operandi. Whip marks? Cat scratches? A stolen cat
statue? *Murder?*

How dare this upstart put bloody paw prints all
over my reputation, Selina Kyle thought grimly.
Catwoman didn't like competition. She didn't like getting blamed for crimes she hadn't committed. And
most of all she didn't like missing out on pretty bau-
bles like Wayne's jade cat statue. If she'd known it
was at the Wayne mansion, she'd have taken it herself. Now she'd never have the chance.

She closed her eyes to slits and stared pensively out
the window across Gotham City. Night was falling.
Draped in shadows, the buildings looked unusually
sinister, even for a city infamous for the ugliness of its
architecture. Towering skyscrapers, blackened by decades of smog, loomed above the trash-strewn streets,
nearly blotting out the horizon. Barely glimpsed
through the vast urban canyons of steel and stone, the
western sky glowed the color of blood . . . the color of
vengeance.

Copy the Catwoman? Over my dead body, Selina
vowed. I'm not going to sit idly by and let some cheap,
two-bit hoodlum cash in on my unique persona!

Rising with a fluid grace, Selina Kyle crossed to her
bedroom. Inside, in the closet, on plain wooden hang-
ers, were a dozen identical black leather cat outfits,
complete with cowled masks and various steel-clawed
sets of gloves.

Catwoman will prowl the streets of Gotham
tonight—and boy, she thought, am I pissed. The female *is* the deadliest of the species.

Fanny the Ferret was feeling pretty good. A short,
narrow-faced woman with long, greasy black hair and

John Gregory Betancourt

a crooked nose, Fanny worked as a professional go-between in the underworld. She'd go between anybody and anybody for a fee. Fanny wasn't particularly bright or ambitious, but she was useful and managed to eke out a rough living that way on the fringes of Gotham's underworld. Tonight, after a long day of numbers running on Gotham's west side, Fanny had decided to celebrate her good fortune and sudden influx of cash. She planned to party her way across Gotham City, starting at Louie-Louie & Gladfelter's Bar & Grill (best known for its illegal slot machines) and work her way east to Bahama Mama's Beef & Leer All-Night Seminude Go-Go (better known for its bootleg hootch than for its has-been, all-too-sagging topless hoofers). Fanny'd made it as far as Jumpin' Jack's (roulette and all-night poker in the back room) and was headed for Queen Bee's (nothing illegal, but great atmosphere) on Seventh Avenue when her plans were abruptly derailed.

As she took a shortcut through an alley a dark shape suddenly hurled itself from the shadows. It struck her sideways like a freight train, sending her flying into a row of plastic garbage cans. Fanny grabbed at a can to stop her fall, but in her semidrunk state she only managed to pull it over, too.

She ended up flat on her back and covered with garbage. Scrambling unsteadily to her feet, she tried to run. Unfortunately the dark shape—how had it moved so *fast*?— blocked the way. She heard metal *tch*ing on metal, like knives being sharpened, and the sound grew louder as the shape advanced on her.

Oh no, Fanny thought, I'm going to die, some maniac bozo's out to kill me, and I'm going to die—

The shape crossed a stray beam of light from an open window two stories up. The figure resolved itself into Catwoman. Her black costume, covering her from head to toe, glistened like oil on a midnight sea. She was striking steel claw against steel claw, making the *tch*ing sound.

Fanny relaxed a little; this wasn't the first time a major criminal had found a use for her. Hell, she'd once run an errand for the Joker—and lived. She took a deep breath. Her pounding heart gradually calmed.

"Catwoman," she said, a petulant whine in her voice. "You scared me."

"That's not all I'm going to do," Catwoman said. One gloved hand closed on Fanny the Ferret's throat. Steel claws pricked her jugular—not hard enough to break the skin, but hard enough to scare Fanny all over again. Jesus, she thought, what did I do? What's she got against me?

"Tell me about Bruce Wayne," Catwoman said. Her voice was soft, a half purr of a sound.

Fanny made a strangling noise.

Catwoman relaxed her grip a fraction. "Tell me about Wayne," she said again.

Say something, Fanny thought frantically. Play along.

"You offed him p-pretty good, huh?" Fanny giggled hesitantly, stopped when Catwoman tickled her throat with one sharp claw, swallowed, then continued. "Y-you want me to sell his statue for ya? It's real hot, but Jimmy the Duke's l-lookin' to buy big stuff these days . . . y'know . . . I'm in g-good with him, right?"

"I'm looking for the one who 'offed' Wayne, as you so succinctly put it," Catwoman said. "She . . . or *he* . . . made it look like my job. I want names, Fanny. Who's new in town? Who's scoring big? Who's playing games with me, Fanny? *Who?*" The last was almost a shout.

Fanny began to cry, tears like lines of grease trick-

John Gregory Betancourt

ling down her narrow cheeks. Her eyes darted right, then left, then right again, but she didn't dare move. The claws against her throat were digging in, making it hard to breathe.

"P-please . . ." she whispered.

"Who is it, Fanny?"

"M-maybe . . . maybe . . . the Greek knows?"

The claw grip relaxed. Fanny staggered back like she'd been thrown, one hand coming up to her throat. She touched something damp and sticky there . . . blood, she realized. Catwoman had broken the skin on her neck.

When she looked up, the dark shape was gone. Alone, she began to sob, all the nervous terror spilling out in a sudden flood. No more tonight, she thought. Home . . .

She staggered toward the fleabag hotel where she kept a room. It was only a few blocks away, luckily. The three flights of steps up to her floor were an agony.

At last, though, she was safe inside. She locked the door behind her, sank down on the lumpy old bed, and choked back another sob.

What would Catwoman do when she found out Fanny had lied about the Greek knowing anything? Fanny made up the story on the spot. Maybe the Greek did know. He knew a lot of things. Maybe he'd die before he'd admit it. Maybe—

She heard a noise outside her window and jumped, startled, barely stifling a scream. There wasn't anything there when she looked, though.

She kept a bottle of bourbon stashed under her mattress. Yeah, she thought, pulling it out and taking a deep swallow, then another. She drained most of the bottle in seconds. This is just what I need tonight.

Copycat

Then an alley cat screeched outside her window.
Fanny screamed in terror, and kept on screaming until her neighbors broke down her door.

Danny "the Greek" Chu thought of himself as the
slickest operator on the upper east side of Gotham
City. He called himself "the Greek" partly as a joke;
after all, he'd muscled out a real Greek—Dmitri "the
Greek" Pappadopoulos—for the singularly profitable
job of mob liaison, and he'd assumed the title as part
of the job. He also called himself "the Greek" because
he figured any cop trying to bust someone named "the
Greek" wouldn't look twice at an Asian-American. So
far he'd been right.

Basically Danny made things—useful things—
happen between the rival gangs who controlled
Gotham City's streets. If you needed a hit on a trou-
blesome public official, you arranged it through the
Greek. If you needed fresh personnel for a new whore-
house, the Greek put you in touch with the right dis-
tributors. If you needed booze or drugs or any of a
thousand illegal substances or services, he was your
man. He knew everybody, kept files—mental files,
since he didn't trust paper ones—on every deal that
went down, and cut himself in for a smooth one percent. It didn't look like a lot until you figured upward
of a hundred million dollars in transactions went
through his hands every year.

Since Batman first made his appearance, drug dealing and prostitution and gambling had moved to a
lower level of activity, but it was all still present. Batman had taken out several top levels of management
in the gangs, but the lower echelons kept things running, and new, more careful bosses kept appearing.

John Gregory Betancourt

Life went on in the big city, and vice went right along
with it. Especially when flamboyant freaks like the
Penguin or Two-Face kept Batman busy.

Right now the Greek was sitting in his study in his
inconspicuous brownstone in Gotham's Chinatown,
working on the biggest deal of his life. It was already
making him nervous. "Spring the Riddler," they'd told
him. "We need him out," they'd told him. "He has the
key to fifty million in uncut diamonds, and we want
them," they'd told him.

So he'd gotten the floor plans to Arkham Asylum
and now had them laid out in front of him on top of an
antique walnut desk that had once belonged to a sen-
ator. He switched on the desk light and stared down
at the intricate security system. Who do I know that
can handle this? he wondered. Steeleye Cinch? No . . .
he's been arrested again. Maybe Sambo the Snake . . .

Even absorbed in thought as he was, though, the
Greek heard the slight squeak as the window behind
him opened. He never oiled its hinges for exactly that
reason. Although he was on the brownstone's third
floor, he didn't believe in taking chances, and he didn't
like the idea of guests sneaking up on him.

Casually, as though it was an afterthought, he took
a sip from his can of soda, then calmly reached for the
desk drawer. There was a 9mm Luger inside for just
such emergencies.

Just as his hand closed on the drawer's handle,
though, another hand came down on top of his. A
hand covered in black leather, its nails shiny steel . . .
Catwoman's hand.

"Now, now," a soft voice purred in his ear. "Let's not
do anything we're going to regret, shall we?"

The Greek laughed and let go of the drawer. My,
how these so-called supervillains loved their dramatic

entrances! "Catwoman," he said, "how delightful!
What brings you here tonight, if I may ask?" He
swung his chair around, already wondering if
Catwoman would be interested in breaking out the
Riddler.

Catwoman leaned back on the windowsill, hands on
her very shapely hips, staring down at him from slitted eyes. Danny couldn't decide whether she was
wearing slitted contact lenses or if it was a trick of the
light on her cowl.

"Information," she said.

"Everything has its price," he said. "Tell me what
you're looking for and I'll let you know if I can help."

"Someone . . ." She hesitated, as if not quite sure of
herself. "Someone killed Bruce Wayne," she said.

"I know," the Greek said, puzzled.

"I . . . need to find that someone."

"You didn't do it, then." *Or you want me to believe
you didn't do it.*

"Do you know who did?"

Slowly the Greek shook his head. "Very sorry,
Selina. Everyone thinks you did it. Several fences are
already making inquiries among foreign collectors . . .
that cat statue sounds like something pretty special,
yes?"

"I wouldn't know. I don't have it."

"Should you turn it up . . . come to me first? I may
be interested in it for myself."

She tapped him on the nose with one claw. "Find
out who did Wayne, will you? Then let me know.
There's ten thousand in it for you."

The Greek didn't budge an inch. *Maybe she didn't
take it, after all? Or is this some bizarre game?* It was
hard to take a woman dressed in a leather cat costume seriously, even if she did look kind of sexy in it.

Slowly he said, "I'll start making inquiries, Selina. If I need to get in touch with you . . . ?"

"Don't worry about it," she said. "I'll be in touch with you."

Meanwhile, he thought, there's more than one way to deal with a cat. "Say," he said casually, "I need someone for a job. There's a cool million—minus my one percent—in it for you."

She leaned forward. "What sort of job?"

"Breaking and escaping."

"Where?"

"Arkham Asylum."

She hissed.

The Greek pressed on. "A few fellows need the Riddler out. They're paying cash up front."

"The Riddler is a psycho," Catwoman said disdainfully. "Not my kind of gig, sorry." A softer, more seductive look appeared in her eyes. "Find out who did Wayne for me, Greek? I'll be . . . very, *very* grateful."

Danny swallowed. Her voice was like liquid sugar and made the hairs on the back of his neck prickle. He couldn't help noticing how tightly the black costume clung to the curves of her body. And what a body! Suddenly he really wanted to know what form that gratitude might take.

"Hey," he called as she sprang out his window onto a narrow ledge. She looked back and her eyes caught the light, like a cat's. "Next time use the front door, okay?"

She laughed, then she was gone.

The Greek folded up the floor plans and put them aside. Taking a deep breath, he began to make a series of calls. If someone else had offed Bruce Wayne, he'd certainly find out about it. After all, whoever sold the cat statue must have done the job, right?

But deep inside he knew he wouldn't find anything.
Catwoman had pulled the job. Why would anyone
want to frame her? It was bewildering. Besides, if
anyone else had done Wayne, he would've heard *something* by now.

> CATWOMAN STRIKES AGAIN
> GOTHAM MUSEUM LOOTED
>
> By Vicki Vale
> Special to the *Gotham Globe*
>
> A priceless Egyptian sarcophagus was stolen last
> night from the Gotham City Museum of Antiqui-
> ties. Selina Kyle, better known as Catwoman, is
> currently being sought by authorities for ques-
> tioning in connection with this crime. The solid-
> gold sarcophagus, approximately two feet long, held
> the mummified remains of a cat that historians be-
> lieve may have belonged to the Egyptian queen Cle-
> opatra.
>
> Selina Kyle is also wanted in connection with the
> brutal murder of Gotham millionaire Bruce Wayne,
> as well as several other recent thefts. Kyle's alleged
> crimes all relate to cats in some fashion. Police
> Commissioner James Gordon noted *(cont'd A6,
> col. 1)*

Catwoman cursed as she stalked back and forth
across her living room. Dozens of nervous felines kept
their distance as their mistress raged.

Catwoman clawed the empty air in her frustration,
wishing it were this copycat criminal's face. She'd
teach Copycat a lesson, all right.

The moment she'd spotted this latest headline at
the newsstand, she felt like killing someone; it was all
she could do to control herself until she got back to

John Gregory Betancourt

her penthouse. There, she'd discarded the disguise that, for safety's sake, she had been forced to wear on the streets: a floppy hat, a black veil, granny glasses, a white wig, and a dowdy black dress. Clad only in tiger-striped lingerie, her short black hair contrasting sharply with the unblemished whiteness of her limbs, she forced herself to relax.

She crossed to her leopard-patterned sofa, flopped down, and picked up the newspaper again. The headlines screamed at her. Then she examined the grainy black-and-white photo of the precious sarcophagus.

Now I'm really out for blood, she thought. She'd planned to heist that particular artifact herself, maybe even last night. Instead she had wasted the entire evening trying to track down this, this—this Copycat!

She wanted the sarcophagus. She wanted Wayne's Chinese cat statue. But most of all she wanted Copycat within striking distance of her claws.

A sleek Siamese, braver than his compatriots, padded over and hopped into her lap. She stroked the cat's head absently, thinking, I need to plot my next move very, very carefully.

Questioning random underworld figures had proved fruitless; although she'd successfully put the fear of God—and Catwoman—into the local lowlifes, last night's prowling had not brought her any closer to her prey. Certainly she had frightened Fanny the Ferret, and tempted the Greek, and interrogated half a dozen others hard enough to make them spill anything of value they might have known. Only they hadn't known anything. Whoever Copycat was, his or her trail did not wind through the usual underworld circles. She'd have to pursue another track.

Placing the Siamese gently on the floor, she spread

Copycat

the newspaper out and forced herself to read the
whole story slowly and carefully one more time.

At last, frustrated and discouraged by the lack of
clues, she noticed the byline. Another Vicki Vale exclusive, eh? So why, she wondered, does this Vale
woman always seem to be the first on the scene?
Maybe Gotham City's favorite girl reporter had some
sort of inside information on Copycat? Did Vicki Vale
know more than she let on?

A cold, cruel smile crossed Catwoman's face. She
licked her lips in anticipation. *I think I've found my
clue.*

The rooftops of Gotham were only slightly less
cramped and claustrophobic than the city streets.
Conical water tanks rose like missile silos on every
other building. Crumbling brick chimneys spewed soot
into the sky. Mismatched buildings of varying sizes
and designs crowded together like angry commuters
elbowing for room on an overstuffed subway. In
Gotham City, even structures of stone and steel
seemed pitted against each other in a ceaseless struggle for survival.

Catwoman loved the rooftops. She perched on the
very edge of a shiny new condominium, twenty stories
above a busy street. In twilight, the entire city appeared shrouded in a gentle blue shadow.

Catwoman smiled and stretched, flexing her claws.
A coiled black whip hung from a thin silver chain
around her waist. It felt great to be alive, in the night,
on top of the world, out on the prowl. Her ebony cat
suit was like a second layer of skin, transforming her
into something more than human, beautiful and un-
stoppable.

John Gregory Betancourt

A movement directly below caught her eye. Crouching on the roof, she leaned out to watch a red-haired woman, dressed in a stylish green jacket and skirt, exit the building and stroll north on the sidewalk. Catwoman recognized Vicki Vale from various appearances on the TV news. That's another odd thing, she thought. Didn't Vale used to date Bruce Wayne, before his tragic demise? Interesting . . .

Finding Vale's address had not been difficult; she looked it up in the phone book. Now it looked like her patience was about to be rewarded.

Moving stealthily from roof to roof, fearlessly leaping over dizzying drops, she kept pace with the reporter, waiting for just the right moment to pounce.

Vale continued uptown, into a part of the city largely given over to upscale antique and jewelry shops, the kind of ritzy establishments where they kept the front doors locked all day long and wouldn't even buzz you in unless you were suitably dressed. None of the merchandise bore a price tag; if you needed to know how much something cost, you obviously couldn't afford it.

Kind of late for a shopping spree, Catwoman thought. Most of these stores closed up tight after sundown. She felt a tingle of anticipation. What was Vicki Vale doing here, at this hour?

Catwoman found a perch on the roof of a rare coin and stamp shop. A weathered stone gargoyle, whose pointed ears and dour expression reminded her of Batman, concealed her from the pedestrians below. Not that there were many people left on the street; the neighborhood had already started to clear out, the yuppies and shop owners rushing home before the hookers and winos came out for the night. Heavy steel gratings covered every storefront.

Copycat

To Catwoman's surprise, Vale stopped in front of a narrow alleyway, glanced in both directions, then turned into the alley and vanished from sight.

Jumping swiftly over a darkened skylight, Catwoman raced to keep up. As she did she spied a bent and battered street sign on a rusty metal post: the murky-looking alley was called Catskill Lane.

Cats kill. Selina hurried faster. This was it. She knew it.

Vale was standing in front of the service entrance to a store . . . BRADLEY & ORDOVER'S FINE JEWELRY the sign said. Catwoman padded forward, leaped, and landed silently on the jewelry store's roof.

Cats always land on their feet, she thought. Can copycats say the same thing? She peered into the alley.

Catskill Lane was little more than a glorified crack between the jewelry shop and the expensive boutique next door. The only light came from the neighboring streets, casting a faint grayish glow across islands of trash floating in greasy puddles. Heaps of decaying cardboard boxes had been piled up outside the fire exits.

Catwoman's cold blue eyes widened as she stared at Vicki Vale. The well-groomed redhead was standing atop a rust-flecked iron Dumpster, peering into Bradley & Ordover's through a small back window protected by a sturdy iron grille. As Catwoman watched, Vale removed a pair of black leather gloves from the pocket of her jacket and pulled them carefully over her manicured hands. Then she retrieved what looked like a small perfume bottle from her purse.

Vale sprayed her "perfume" along the top and bottom of the window grille. Metal hissed and smoked where an obviously corrosive liquid touched it. A few moments later Vale tugged on the bars. The entire framework pulled free, leaving nothing but a thin sheet of glass between the respected journalist and the interior of the store.

Catwoman shook her head in amazement. It was working out better than she'd hoped. Vicki Vale wouldn't have to lead her to Copycat—Vicki Vale *was* Copycat. *She's been committing the crimes herself, then using her articles to point the blame toward me!*

Smiling grimly, Catwoman extended the diamond-tipped metal nails of her own black gloves. Time to play, Copycat dear, she thought.

Springing lightly to her feet, she launched herself into the air above the alley, becoming a sinuous shadow against the night sky. She arced over Catskill Lane until she came within reach of the boutique's back wall. Arms outstretched, her claws caught and then tore downward. She turned to snarl in Vale's direction, sliding down the wall toward the alley floor. Her claws slowed her fall enough for her to land unharmed on her feet.

With a startled yelp, Vale had dropped the window grille. It crashed loudly on the Dumpster's steel lid.

"So," Catwoman taunted, "you thought you could follow in my most-wanted footsteps, did you?" She stalked relentlessly toward Vale, a two-legged panther hungry for the kill. "You wanted to have your nice, newsworthy crimes and report them, too? Well, it takes more than a pair of pretty gloves and a couple of lucky breaks to make a girl a Catwoman. You're playing in the big leagues now, and you've lost, big time."

A terrified look on her face, Vicki scrambled off the Dumpster. She glanced desperately toward the end of the alley, toward the avenue and safety, but Cat-

Copycat

woman darted in front of her and blocked her way.
Then Catwoman hissed and raised her claws.

Backing away, Vale stepped on a bottle of Thunder-
bird. It rolled out from under her and she struggled to
regain her balance. Eyes wide with fear, she kept
watch on Catwoman.

Selina couldn't resist toying with her victim. Unfas-
tening the whip from her belt, she cracked it in Vale's
direction. The reporter flinched; the whip missed her
face by a hairbreadth.

"Tell me something, Scoop-of-the-Century," Catwoman purred. "How did an amateur like you manage to knock off a grown man like Bruce Wayne? I
thought you were supposed to be dating him. Some
sort of kinky fun-and-games, maybe? Things get a little too rough?" She snarled contemptuously. "It
must've been an accident. You're too much of a wimp
to kill a man on purpose!"

She had Vicki backed up against the Dumpster
now. Catwoman wondered if the reporter would fit inside . . . afterward.

Raising the whip overhead, she arched her back to
put all her strength into a flogging Vale would never
forget. But before she could strike, a deep voice spoke
up from somewhere behind her.

"That's enough, Selina. Put the whip down."

No, Catwoman thought. Not him. Not now. Whirling, she saw an ominous figure standing only a few
yards away, framed by the alley's bare walls. He stood
as still and unyielding as a prison wall, an imposing
figure in black and gray. A heavy cape, dark as midnight, was draped over his shoulders. His mask bore
the features and high spiked ears of a bat. A golden
emblem shone on his chest, bearing the black design
of two outstretched batwings.

John Gregory Betancourt

Even though she'd confronted him dozens of times
before, his sudden appearance drew a short gasp from
her.

Batman. The Dark Knight of Gotham City.

"Step away from Ms. Vale," he commanded. His
voice was deceptively smooth. "It's been a long chase,
Selina, but it's over now. You might as well make it
easy on yourself."

God, the ghastly irony of it all, Selina thought. For
once she was innocent. Her fist tightened around the
base of the whip. After all her battles with Batman,
the countless minor victories and defeats, she'd be
damned if she'd surrender now—and be caged for
crimes she hadn't even had the pleasure of committing.

"You've got the wrong kitty this time, lover," she
said with a smirk. "I'm just making a citizen's arrest.
You want Miss Front Page here. She's the one who
broke into this shop, *and* stole the cat mummy from
the museum, *and* killed Bruce Wayne!"

Batman's voice remained as sure and implacable as
ever. "And what about the late Harold Harkins? Did
she murder him as well?"

"Er, no," Catwoman muttered, briefly caught off
guard. That killing was hers, sort of. Oh, blast it all,
she raged silently, this is a waste of time. Batman's
never going to believe my word over Vale's.

"It's a long story, Batman dear, and surely you don't
want to hear it in this dank, depressing alley." Keep
talking, she told herself as her agile fingers went to
work behind her back, detaching a small glass vial
from the base of the whip. Then, holding the vial carefully between two fingers, she tied a noose in the
other end of the whip. "Maybe we can continue this
conversation over dinner at a nice restaurant. I can

order a saucer of milk and you can sip a bottle of
blood—or whatever it is you bats drink. Ms. Vale can
have poison."

Batman stepped forward, gloved fists clenched at
his sides. "No more games, Selina," he said impatiently. He reached out an open palm. The edge of his
glove had fins like a shark. "Hand over the whip.
Now."

Without warning, Catwoman executed a perfect
backflip, landing on her feet several yards away from
Batman. "Not now, not ever!" she spat, and flicked the
noose over Vicki's head. She yanked hard, tightening
its grip around the beautiful journalist's throat. Vicki
made a harsh, strangling noise.

Batman glanced quickly from Catwoman to Vicki
and back again. Before he could make a move in either direction, Selina hurled the glass vial against the
broken pavement, where it shattered. Dense black
smoke spewed out, rapidly filling the alley with a
thick, impenetrable fog.

I learned this trick from you, Batman, Catwoman
thought gleefully. She popped nose filters into place
and breathed easily through them.

"Find her if you can!" she challenged the Dark
Knight. "Before the copycat chokes to death!"

Digging her claws into the jewelry store's wall, she
climbed swiftly to the roof, then raced furiously over
the top of Gotham City, past TV antennas, satellite
dishes, and rickety pigeon coops full of drab, diseased
city birds. She didn't halt her reckless, headlong dash
until Catskill Lane was dozens of blocks behind her.

Then, breathing heavily, rivers of sweat cooling between her flesh and the tight black suit, she leaned
against the graffiti-covered cylinder of a large, loom-
ing water tower and tried to calculate her next move.

Despite her bravado, she knew Batman would rescue that miserable papergirl before the noose had done her any serious harm. In this city, Batman was better than 911—and a lot more dependable.

A low growl formed at the back of Selina's throat. This isn't over, she vowed. I know who you are now, Copycat, and there's nowhere you can go that I can't find you. Next time, though, we'll meet on my terms, under my rules, and no misguided Caped Crusader will be around to save you from your just deserts.

Already a plan was forming in her mind . . .

RICH WIDOW SPENDS FORTUNE ON HER KITTIES!
A *Gotham Gab* Exclusive

Mrs. Annabelle McQueen, 84, who recently inherited over twenty-three million dollars from her deceased stockbroker husband, loves her thirty-two housecats so much that she's spent thousands on her pets—and left them her entire estate in her will! These pampered pussies already enjoy the good life, eating their daily meals of caviar and imported Alaskan salmon out of solid-platinum cat bowls that cost over three hundred thousand dollars apiece.

Mrs. McQueen's two-legged relatives, including her surfer son-in-law, are reportedly spitting mad about the cat-loving widow's lavish treatment of her pets, but so far teams of lawyers have been unable to interfere with the Life-styles of the Rich and Feline. Some cats get all the luck.

And remember, you read it first in the *Gotham Gab*!

Posing in front of a full-length mirror in her bedroom, Selina smoothed out the pleats in a drab, matronly, ankle-length black dress. She adjusted her gray wig, done up in an old-fashioned bun, and made sure that none of her own dark hairs were dangling free. The pale pink lipstick she applied to her lips was duller and less glossy than the bloodred hue she preferred, but, Catwoman thought with a sigh, every great scheme required some sacrifices. All she needed now was the right hat and a black widow's veil to complete her transformation into the eccentric Mrs. McQueen.

This particular alias had served her well over the last few weeks, but never, she hoped, as well as it would today.

A cheap-looking tabloid paper, full of huge headlines and brightly colored photographs of Mrs. McQueen and her pets, rested on Selina's makeup counter. She glanced at it and laughed cruelly. The nice thing about sleazy tabloids like the *Gab*, she gloated, was that it was so easy to plant stories in them. Give them a suitably colorful "human interest" item, and they'd practically print it verbatim, without bothering with any tiresome research or investigation. All in all, it was a mutually beneficial arrangement; the *Gab* got a headline and she got to bait her trap. And how quickly that bait had worked.

As if on cue, a buzzer sounded loudly a few feet away. Selina pounced across the luxurious bedroom and pressed the speak button on the intercom unit mounted on the wall. She paused for just a second, to summon up the hesitant, whispery voice of an elderly woman.

"H-hello?" she said into the intercom, then released the button. Another woman's voice emerged from the speaker. Despite some distortion and static, it had the clear and melodious tones of someone accustomed to public speaking.

"Mrs. McQueen? This is Vicki Vale. We spoke on the phone, remember? I wanted to interview you about your cats?"

"Of course, dear," Catwoman replied in her old-lady voice. "I'll buzz you right in. Did I mention I live on the top floor? There's an elevator, though, so you don't have to take the stairs. I wish I could come down and greet you properly, but twenty-six flights is such a long trip . . . and at my age, well, I'm sure you understand."

"No problem," Vicki said. "I'll be right up. I'm looking forward to meeting you and your pets."

Catwoman smiled and licked her lips. "I'll be waiting," she said, and stepped away from the intercom. I know what you're really after, Copycat, she thought, my famous platinum cat bowls. Well, you may find this old lady a bit harder to handle than a soft, spoiled playboy like Bruce Wayne!

"Come along, boys and girls," she cooed to the many, many cats milling about the bedchamber. "We have company."

She placed an old-fashioned pillbox hat upon her white wig, then draped a gauzy black veil over her face; it was like peering out at the world through an intricate spiderweb. She walked quickly into the palatial living room, a battalion of cats falling in line behind her.

A large picture window gave her a panoramic view of Gotham City in all its grim and brooding grandeur; although it was midafternoon, she drew the heavy velvet drapes tightly shut and turned on a couple of small, stylish lamps.

For a moment she paused and scanned her surroundings. Would Vale recognize any of the purloined art treasures decorating the room? She shrugged her shoulders beneath the baggy, black dress. No matter, she reminded herself. The reporter wasn't likely to leave . . . alive.

Finally there was a knock at the door. It took all the patience Selina could muster to walk over as slowly as an aging widow might be expected to. Patience, she told herself. The mouse is here. Let's play with her awhile.

Keeping the chain in place, she opened the door a crack. It was Vale, all right, in a gray blouse and short black skirt.

The reporter smiled pleasantly at her. "Mrs. McQueen?" she asked gently.

"Excuse me, dear," Selina whispered. "I hate to fuss, but could you show me some identification? I know it must seem silly, but what with all the terrible stories one reads about in the paper . . . you know, that horrible Catwoman person and all . . ."

"Of course. I quite understand." Vicki's smile grew even warmer, if possible.

Utterly shameless, Selina thought, impressed despite herself. She squinted theatrically through the veil at the reporter's driver's license and laminated press card. After only a minute or two she closed the door, carefully undid the chain, and invited Vale into the penthouse suite.

The reporter had an expensive-looking camera slung over her shoulder. She walked slowly around the room, looking at the various objets d'art. A legion of cats—black, white, striped, and spotted—began rubbing themselves against Vicki's legs and clawed playfully at her stockings.

"Don't mind my pussies," Selina said, scooping up a plump gray kitty and cradling him against her chest. Moving ever so slowly, she planted herself cautiously on the leopard-spotted couch. More cats swarmed around her. Purring softly, they settled on her lap, around her shoulders, and at her feet.

"How many do you have?" Vale asked.

"Oh, only thirty-two. It seems like more because they keep moving around." In reality, there were more than fifty in the room . . . with more waiting in the wings for her command to strike. "Do take a seat, dear," she entreated, gesturing toward an overstuffed chair opposite the sofa.

Vicki sat, opening her purse and taking out a small pocket tape recorder. "Do you mind?" she asked, placing the recorder on the walnut coffee table between them. A slender Siamese leaped onto the table and sniffed the machine curiously.

Catwoman eyed Vicki's purse furtively. Don't forget about that acid perfume, she warned herself. She whispered into the gray kitten's ear and set it down. It stalked across the table and, seemingly of its own volition, decided to curl up and take a nap on top of the purse.

"By all means, use your recorder," Catwoman answered graciously. "I can't believe they're making those devices so small these days. Why, when I was a child . . ." And she launched into a long, rambling reminiscence.

Another cat, a black-and-gray-striped tiger, climbed up the front of Vicki's emerald-colored jacket and nipped at the lapels. The redhead kept smiling, but could not entirely conceal a flinch.

Beneath her veil, as she continued to talk on and on about the wonders of modern technology, Selina permitted herself a tiny grin. Afraid of cats, are you? she thought. I can't say I'm surprised, but maybe you should have thought of that before you decided to play in my sandbox.

Vicki patiently waited for "Mrs. McQueen" to finish her long, boring, and completely fabricated reminiscence, then tried, with what struck Catwoman as annoying obviousness, to steer the conversation toward her topic of choice. "So, I'm sure our readers will be fascinated to hear all about you and your plans for these beautiful, and clearly very affectionate, animals. The article in the *Gotham Gab* was quite entertaining, but as I told you on the phone earlier, I'd like to go into a little more depth, tell the full story of your cats and why they're so important to you."

Selina struggled to suppress a yawn. Why was Vale even bothering with this charade, she wondered, now that she'd talked her past the locked door? Did she think Mrs. McQueen was going to hand her the cat bowls?

Vicki leaned forward and pressed the record button on the tape recorder. The striped tomcat slipped off her jacket and landed gracefully on the table. His slit eyes glared at Vicki, and a low growl emerged from his throat.

Selina stretched out her arm and stroked his head until the growling ceased. Not yet, she thought, but soon.

The reporter ignored the cat. "Well, why do you like cats so much?' she asked.

What a stupid question, Selina thought. "Because," she said, growing tired of this game, "they're not afraid to look out for themselves . . . and because they're predators at heart." She stood up abruptly, her back straight, not stooped like an old woman's. The frail, dithery voice vanished, replaced by a low, sultry purr. "And their claws are sharp. Like mine."

Vale gasped, then went pale. "Catwoman!" she blurted as she tried to leap to her feet. Selina shoved her back down into the chair.

"What a delight to see you again, Vicki," she snarled. She snatched off her hat and veil and flung them across the room. In the dim light, Selina's black hair glistened like silk and her cold blue eyes gleamed with malice. "Or shall I call you . . . Copycat?"

"Catwoman . . . Selina," Vicki pleaded bravely. "We can talk this over. Don't do anything we'll both regret." She rose again from the chair, more slowly this time, and started to back up toward the door.

"The interview is over, Ms. Vale," Catwoman announced. "It's payback time." She clapped her hands together sharply. All over the room, every cat froze and perked up its ears. "Go!" she commanded them.

Dozens of suddenly frenzied felines raced at Vicki hissing and spitting. An angry paw swiped her ankle, leaving three parallel, bloody scratches. A score of cats leaped between Vale and the front door.

Slowly, step-by-step, they forced her back across the living room, into the far corner. Claws flashing, the biggest and boldest—a dun-colored Manx—lunged at Vicki. She screamed and threw her arms over her head.

"Wait!" Catwoman snapped.

The cats drew back slightly, forming a half circle around Vale. Fur rose as if electrified along their backs; several hissed, tails lashing. They had her cornered and knew it.

Catwoman cast a loving gaze over her pets. "Aren't they adorable?" she asked rhetorically. Then she glared at Vale and her voice grew cold and hard. "You have two choices, Copycat: You can let my little furry friends tear you apart. Or you can tell me where the treasures are."

"What treasures?" Vicki asked softly. The cats snarled at the sound of her voice, and she drew her feet back even further.

"The Chinese statue and the golden mummy case, of course!" Catwoman said. Reaching beneath the cushions of her couch, she drew out a pair of claw-tipped leather gloves and slipped them on. "Don't play any games with me. Talk fast or you're kitty chow. Where are they?"

Vicki hesitated, staring at the pack of killer cats just waiting for the order to pounce. Swallowing, she took a deep breath and opened her mouth.

Smart girl, Catwoman thought triumphantly. Maybe I'll only maim you a little bit after all.

But instead of a confession, Vale shouted as loud as she could: *"Batman! Now!"*

With a deafening sound of breaking glass, the huge picture window behind Catwoman shattered. She whirled. It was Batman—his huge black cape billowing, his feet outstretched. He must have swung down from above on a bat rope, Catwoman realized. She'd seen him do it before.

He landed lightly in front of her. When he released his bat rope, it snaked up and out of sight.

"Stay back!" Catwoman hissed. "I won't allow you to stop me again!"

He stalked forward with grim intent.

"Batman . . ." she said softly, backing up.

He was only a few feet away from her now.

"Lover . . ." she whispered.

He reached out to grab her arm—just as she executed a graceful kick. It was one of the most perfect bits of gymnastic expertise she'd ever performed, and

John Gregory Betancourt

it caught Batman square in the center of the chest.
His body armor might stop a bullet from penetrating,
but it couldn't stop the force of a blow.

He staggered backward.

Selina did a forward flip and caught him again on
the chest with the flats of her sturdy old-lady shoes.
Then, dropping to the floor, she pulled her momentum
into a tight spin. Her legs struck Batman's knee—and
he toppled like a falling log.

"Kitties! Go!" she cried.

As Catwoman scrambled to her feet cats came running from all directions. She could hear them growling
deep in their throats—an angry, hostile rumble like
distant thunder. As one, they sprang upon Batman,
hissing, scratching, biting.

Selina knew they wouldn't stop Batman more than
a second or two—but that was all she needed.

That Vale woman was staring in stunned horror at
the mass of writhing cat bodies. Selina ran up to her,
seized her arm, and dragged her toward the bedroom.
Halfway there Vale recovered her wits enough to
struggle. Catwoman cuffed her hard across the face
several times, until Vale's eyes went glassy and she
slumped toward the floor.

With svelte grace, Catwoman picked Vale up and
threw her over one shoulder. Staggering a bit under
the extra weight, she still made it to her bedroom in
record time.

The bedroom door was two inches thick and had a
steel core. She threw the huge safety bolts, then
dropped a security bar in place. Batman wouldn't be
getting through them in a hurry.

Outside, the sounds of the cat fight ended in a series of pitiful mews and a few yelps of pain. She could
imagine Batman throwing the cats off one by one, but

she knew he'd never hurt them. He had a soft place
in his heart for animals, just as she had a soft place in
her heart for him.

She'd return that night to pick up her kitties, that
or she'd rescue them from the pound. Springing the
Riddler was one thing, springing her cats another.
Now, though, her first priority lay in getting to safety
with Vicki Vale. She'd extract a most painful, lingering vengeance for all Vale had put her through.

She dropped Vale onto the bed and crossed to the
windows. Throwing open the huge glass panels, she
stepped out onto a tiny balcony. Everything was as
she'd left it—a small black backpack sat next to a coil
of what looked like gray garden hose.

She pulled the backpack over her shoulder and ran
back in for Vale. Hoisting the Copycat over her shoulder, she returned outside, looped the coil twice around
her waist, and climbed to the top of the balcony's wall.

It seemed a dizzyingly long distance to the ground
below. At least it would be a soft landing: neatly manicured grass and shrubbery filled in the space between
her apartment building and the sidewalk.

She took a deep breath and prepared to jump.

"Selina!" Batman's voice called from her right.
"Please—don't do it!"

She glanced across the side of the building. Twenty
feet away, framed by jagged pieces of glass still stuck
in the frame, Batman stood in the hole he'd made in
her living room's picture window. She hissed at him.

Then she leaped out into nothingness.

The fall seemed to take forever, but at last the gray
line around her waist went taut . . . and began to
stretch. It was one of those huge rubber bands used by
bungee jumpers—people who, as a hobby, leaped off
cliffs or bridges or other high places, only to bounce up

John Gregory Betancourt

and down repeatedly at the end of a giant rubber
band rather than fall all the way to the ground.

She knew the tensile strength of this particular
bungee cord, and she'd calculated for Vale's extra
weight as well; that's why she made the extra loop
around her waist.

When the cord stretched to its limit, they were
about five feet off the ground. Catwoman released the
line. It snaked around her waist like a whip, then shot
back upward.

Dropping Vale, Catwoman hit the ground in a roll.
She came up on her feet, poised for action. Twenty-six
floors above, she could see a dark shape in her penthouse's picture window: Batman, staring down at
them.

Didn't expect that, did you? she thought.

Vale was staggering, a confused look on her face.
Catwoman took a second to rummage around in her
backpack. Finding a little aerosol spray can, she
pulled it out, spritzed twice in Vale's face, and waited
for the drug to take effect.

It did so almost immediately. Vale's eyes lost all focus and she began to drool a bit. Taking her arm,
Catwoman led her to the sidewalk, then around to the
apartment building's parking garage. She didn't use
cars much, but she had several of them waiting, in
case of emergencies.

She chose a silver Jaguar. The keys were in her
backpack.

After shoving Vale into the car's tiny trunk, she
climbed into the driver's seat, fitted the key into the
ignition, and turned it, pumping the gas.

The engine remained stubbornly silent. Where was
the throaty roar of power she loved, the . . . *It had to
be Batman.* The realization came a second too late.

Copycat

"You're going to need a battery to start that car." Batman's voice boomed from somewhere outside. "I took the liberty of removing the batteries from all the cat-named cars down here before I went up to see you."

Selina hissed silently through her teeth.

Footsteps sounded on the roof of the car. The Jaguar rocked up and down. When Catwoman peered up through the window, she could just make out the edge of Batman's cape. He was standing on the roof of her car, waiting to pounce when she left.

Quickly she locked all the doors. Then she rummaged through the backpack, looking for—ah, yes, there it was: a single tiny yellow pill, which carried the scent of bitter almonds . . . of cyanide. She'd always vowed she'd never be taken alive. Hopefully Batman believed her.

She rolled her window down a crack. "Put the battery back in the car," she called to him.

"Selina," Batman called, "it's time you knew the truth. Bruce Wayne is alive. There never was a jade cat statue at the Wayne estate. And the cat sarcophagus is safe in the basement of the Gotham Museum."

"What?" she screeched.

"It's all been a setup to trap you. You killed Old Man Harkins. That's going too far, Selina—you're coming in this time, and you're not going to escape justice."

Suddenly it all made sense to her. How Vicki Vale had managed some of the greatest cat crimes of the last few years. How Batman had been able to trace her—he'd been watching Vale, and probably had her wired for sound. How the newspapers had gotten such detailed stories on Copycat's activities.

John Gregory Betancourt

On top of that, Batman now wanted to arrest her for murder . . . a murder she *really* hadn't committed.

"I never did anything to Harkins!" she said. "I just bumped into him in the hallway, that's all! It's so *unfair* of you to blame me, Batman . . . you of all people should understand that!"

"Where is Vicki Vale?" Batman demanded.

He cares about her. Catwoman knew then that she had him. Then she fought a surge of jealous rage. *He cares more for her than he cares for me!*

"Vale's safe," she said again. "She's safely out of the way for the time being." Her voice dropped an octave, to a softer, sexier tone. "Why don't you come down off your roost and we'll talk about it, Batman."

The silver Jaguar shook again. Batman leaped to the ground and stood in front of the car, his hands on his hips, staring at her.

"Well?" he said in that gravelly, sexy voice of his.

Catwoman unlocked her door and slid out. She made every motion a work of art . . . every gesture sheer poetry, every movement sublime. She could feel Batman's gaze tracing the sleek lines of her body even beneath Mrs. McQueen's unflattering dress.

"I want you to understand, my love," she said, hips swaying gently as she approached him. "I didn't kill Old Man Harkins—I surprised him, and his heart gave out. That's all. His time had come. I didn't *murder* him. Do you see?"

"Where's Vicki?"

"Oh, don't worry about *her*." She leaned her head against his shoulder and took his arm in hers. "Let's have a night on the town, you and I. Then you can let me go. How does that sound, hmmm?"

He hesitated, then forced himself to move away

Copycat

from her. He hated doing it, she saw, but he did it anyway. Selina felt a growing sense of frustration.

"How can you love *that*?" she cried.

"Selina," he said. "Where did you put her?"

"She's dead," she said, annoyed beyond all reason.

Just then a pounding started from the trunk of the
Jaguar. Batman glanced that way.

Catwoman tried to run. He caught her arm and
hauled her in close. Their faces were inches apart.
Selina looked into Batman's eyes . . . and saw forgive-
ness.

"I'm sorry," he said. "I wish there could have been
another way."

"Me too," she said. Before he could stop her, she
popped that little yellow pill into her mouth and held
it between her teeth.

"Good-bye," she whispered. Then she bit down.

A bitter taste filled her mouth, then she closed her
eyes and let everything go limp. Her breathing
stopped.

Batman lowered Catwoman's still body to the cement.
"Selina," he whispered. He could smell bitter almonds
on her breath . . . cyanide? *No—Selina—*

There were tears in his eyes; for a moment he
couldn't see. Biting his lip, he forced himself to stand.

Vicki was pounding on the inside of the Jaguar's
trunk with a tire iron or her shoe or something.
Numb, Batman walked back to the car, took the car
keys from the ignition, went around to the trunk, and
opened it for her.

Vicki Vale sat up and began taking deep breaths.
Her hair was mussed and red lipstick made a long

smear across her cheek. Even so, Batman had never been quite so happy to see her.

"Well," Vicki said, "are you going to help me out of here, or not?"

Silently he offered her his hand. She took it. He pulled her out, and as she stood unsteadily on the cement she looked around.

"What happened to Catwoman?" she asked. "I heard you two talking."

"She—she's dead. Cyanide. She always said she wouldn't let herself be caught, but I never believed she'd kill herself."

"Where's her body?" Vicki said, looking around.

"It's—"

Batman looked, but it was gone. He blinked. He hadn't taken his eyes off her for more than a moment . . . had he? At first he felt a helpless rage that he'd been tricked, then relief flooded in. She was still alive, and she'd made her escape. Chalk it down to nine lives, he thought.

"You win this time, Selina," he said silently to himself. Then he began to laugh.

CATWOMAN STILL FREE
BRUCE WAYNE DEATH "POLICE HOAX"
By Vicki Vale
Special to the *Gotham Globe*

Millionaire Bruce Wayne's recent murder was revealed as part of an elaborate sting operation to capture notorious criminal Selina Kyle ("Catwoman"), Police Commissioner James Gordon revealed today. Also part of the sting operation were fake news stories about cat-related thefts, including the thefts of an Egyptian cat mummy from the Gotham

Copycat

Museum and a valuable jade statue from the Wayne mansion.

Batman, who took part in the police operation, was unable to capture Catwoman, although Catwoman's penthouse hideout was discovered. Dozens of stolen paintings and other works of art have been recovered.

Batman, with the cooperation of the Gotham police force, Bruce Wayne, and the *Gotham Globe*, had hoped to put an end to *(cont'd A16, col. 4)*

A Harlot's Tears

ED GORMAN
(for Joe Orlando)

David Fisher: 198–

Nothing special about the day. Not most of it, any way. Rolls into work at 8:22 A.M. Three client conferences to fill up the morning and a fifteen-minute meeting with the new woman in the law library (nice legs) and then racquetball over the lunch hour (yogurt and raisins following) and then a long grinding afternoon-becoming-night of prep. Big court case starting in two days. The kind of thing that could get him a full partnership if the firm won. (And he plans on winning.) And then the parking garage where his sweet little BMW waits.

And then the nighttime city streets

darkness and neon; bus fumes and marijuana smoke; summer heat and the laughter of whores

junkies and hookers and killers and perverts; man

A Harlot's Tears

puking in gutter; homeless woman on corner screaming at somebody who isn't there and

He gives himself the He Shoulds.

He Should go home because he's happily married.

He Should have more respect for himself and his
wife and his two children than to give in to this terrible impulse of his.

He Should never jeopardize his law career by traf-
ficking with hookers.

And yet

And yet years ago, just out of college, he used to
cruise like this and it was real exciting

And for some reason

(maybe all the business pressure lately)

For some reason he wants to do it just one more
time

Just once

Because

he loves the danger. Just something about it. Danger makes the sex exciting, the way it was when he
was back in high school, when everything was still de-
liciously forbidden.

And then

He sees her.

Young. Even a little scared looking. Right there on
the corner. The other hookers, all war paint and
sweaty summer blouses, eyeing her with real compet-
itive hatred.

He sees her
and without thinking
pulls over to the corner
and she leans in
and says

Ed Gorman

Brett Ewing: 198–

"Hi."

She can't believe what she's seeing.

A) A brand-new BMW convertible. So fine and shiny and red in the grubby neon night.

B) A very handsome, upscale young man with a fifty-dollar haircut and a very expensive-looking summer-weight suit.

C) A very gentlemanly hand extended to help her into the car.

She's been in the city seven weeks now, and so far all her tricks have been rubes and dipshits, including one guy whose BO was so bad she literally threw up afterward.

Kinda neat, romantic, really
   How she gets in
   And he pulls away from the curb
   And neither of them say a word
   Just listen to Anita Baker on the tape deck
   And cruise along the river
   Fresh cool breeze
   Skyscraper lights like red-and-yellow watercolors
on the shimmering dark surface of the river
   And he reaches over and takes her hand as if it's a
real date not just a trick
   And they drive and drive and drive
   No words yet exchanged
   Just touches
   And glances
   And
   No matter how bad or down or blown out her life

has gotten, she's always kept the dream. The Cinderella dream, where the handsome young prince comes to rescue her. Is this the handsome young prince?

Maybe, she thinks, maybe this is the prince.

And in a couple of weeks or so—after he puts her up in some very nice apartment over near Carver Park—maybe she won't ever have to work the streets again, because to be frank, she really doesn't like it

It scares her

And every time she looks in the mirror she thinks: Slut. You slut.

And so she'd be very very *very* happy if this turned out like Cinderella and they fell in love and

He finds a little nook along the river, many, many miles out along the river

And still without speaking, he parks the car and shifts seats, her straddling him now

and

And afterward, he says, "What's your name?"

"Brett."

"Brett? Really?" Smiles. "I don't think I've ever known a Brett."

Of course that wasn't her name back in Iowa. Eight weeks ago in the small town of Dysart she'd been Donna Mae Hamilton.

"Brett Ewing," she says.

"Aw come on."

"Really."

He laughs. Nice sweet laugh. "If you say so." Grins. "You know what my name is?"

"Huh-uh."

"Lance Sterling."

Now it's her turn to laugh. "Get real."

"Well, if your name can be Brett Ewing, why can't mine be Lance Sterling?"

She does something she's never done with a john before. Gives him a tender kiss. A genuine kiss.

"Wow," he says.

"I really like you, Lance Sterling."

"And I really like you too, Brett Ewing."

The night ends forty-five minutes later on a Gotham street corner.

With David Fisher about to face a wife he loves very much and never wants to hurt

And Donna Mae Hamilton about to face three more johns before this particular night is over

Men she'd never think of kissing in any genuine way

Men who'd just laugh if she told them of her Cinderella dreams

Catwoman: April 1, 199–, 9:28 p.m.

Night is her friend; she can hide in its dark embrace. Night plays its own music, a symphony of moonlight and shadow.

As she herself is shadow. As she herself is cat.

Watch her now as she swings from Gotham rooftop to Gotham rooftop, trailing a man in the ghetto sidewalk seven stories below.

Just as the man himself is trailing the young hooker—who is just now becoming aware of him—half a block ahead.

Hooker walks faster. "Oh, shit, it's him," she mutters to herself. "Shit."

Faster. Faster.

A Harlot's Tears

As does the man. Faster. Faster.

And thus it is played out as it is played out on so many urban streets every night of the year.

Rape. Or death. Or both.

The man. Closer, closer now.

Hooker reaches the alley. Looks back over her shoulder. And shudders.

"Hey," he says. "You."

She starts to run.

And that's when he closes on her.

Grabs her shoulder. Hurls her into the alley.

Where red-eyed rats and cats with eyes the color of midnight moons . . . watch as

"You remember me?" he says. "Huh?"

His rage is overwhelming.

Bladeflash in moonlight. Switchblade.

"Bitch. Fucking bitch."

Knife to her throat as she tries to scream but his hand too fast clamps too hard on her soft pretty mouth.

"Bitch."

Up comes her knee. Only trick she knows.

But he skillfully turns away and puts the knife deep into her shoulder. Cutting. Cutting.

This time her scream is loose on the night.

"Bitch."

He is just coming for her again when the rats and cats look up and see

catshape of Catwoman silhouetted against the dirty brick of the alley buildings as she

flies down, aiming her feet directly at the back of the killer

slamming him headfirst into the building.

But just as Catwoman lands the wounded girl falls

Ed Gorman

forward, forcing Catwoman to catch her and hold her
while the killer
blood streaming from his broken nose
runs. slapping footsteps now. retreating retreating.
"Motherfucker!" he keeps screaming, half-delirious.
"Motherfucker!"
And then he too is one with night, beyond even the
reach of Catwoman now as he stumbles to his car and
flees.
Flees.

Selina Kyle: April 1, 199–, 11:47 p.m.

"You didn't recognize him?"
"Huh-uh."
"But he said, 'You remember me?' "
"Right. That's what he said."
"And then he stabbed you?"
"Yeah. He wanted to cut my throat, but I moved
and he stabbed me in the shoulder."
"How's that shoulder doing?"
"Pretty good. I mean, it's really not much of a
wound, I guess."
"I sure wouldn't like to have it."
Brett Ewing smiles. "You're real nice. I appreciate
that. I mean, I have pretty shitty relationships with
other women. It's nice to be able to just relax and talk
to another woman."
They are in Selina's apartment, Brett lying on the
couch, Selina in the chair opposite. Brett has no idea
Selina and Catwoman were the same person. After
bringing Brett upstairs, Catwoman knocked on the
door. Arizona, the young girl presently staying in

A Harlot's Tears

Selina's apartment, appeared and helped Brett inside. Catwoman said good night and left, pretending to leave the building but actually climbing in a back window and reappearing to introduce herself as Arizona's roommate Selina.

Brett, who is smoking a cigarette, stares at the ceiling and says, "I guess you've figured out what I am by now."

"Oh?"

"I'm a hooker."

Selina smiles gently at the sad young woman. She was very much like Brett at one time. "Being a hooker is what you do. Not what you are."

"Thanks for saying that."

"It's true. You can give it up anytime you want to."

"And do what? Wait tables?"

"How about going back to school and getting your high-school diploma?"

Yawning, Arizona comes out of the bathroom. She looks snug and warm in her nubby pink bathrobe. "I'm going to stand on the back porch and have a smoke and then I'm going to bed. Just wanted to say good night."

Just off the living room there is a porch that overlooks the alley seven floors below. It's nice to stand there and look out at the city and feel the cool breezes. There is no screen, so with the porch window open it's like being outdoors.

"Night," Selina says.

"Night," Brett says. "Thanks for helping me get that wound cleaned out."

"I still think we should have called the police," Arizona says.

Brett shakes her head. "I've been busted too many times to willingly sic the police on myself."

Ed Gorman

Arizona, who once found herself in Brett's trap, nods sadly and drifts toward the nearest bedroom door.

After Brett stubs her cigarette out, she leans over and stares at Selina. "I know who was after me tonight."

"You recognized him?"

"Not recognized him. But I know who he is. 'Harlot,' the guy who's been in the news the past month."

Selina hadn't wanted to alarm Brett, that's why she didn't bring the subject up herself.

In the past nineteen days, six prostitutes had been savagely slain in Gotham. On the forehead of each, in garish red lipstick, the killer had written HARLOT. Hence the name the media had given him.

"I think you're right," Selina says.

"But that's the weird thing."

"What is?"

"It was personal."

"Personal?"

"Yeah, I mean, not like he was just attacking a hooker at random or anything. It was like he knew who I was . . . and hated me. Personally."

Selina stares at Brett for a long moment and then says, "How tall are you?"

"Five-seven. Why?"

"How much do you weigh?"

"About one twenty."

"A wig would make it easy."

"Easy? I don't know what you're talking about."

Selina smiles. "Maybe I don't either. But after we've had a good night's sleep, we'll go over my plan and see if it makes any sense." She stands up, ready to go in, wash her face, put on fresh pajamas, and collapse into bed. "You sure you wouldn't rather sleep in my bed and let me take the couch?"

"I've imposed enough, Selina. The couch will be just fine."

"If you say so," Selina says, and then heads for the bathroom. "G'night."

Brett Ewing: April 3, 199–

Night. Rainstorm. Gutters flooded. Sewers overflowing with filthy gray water. Headlights exposing slanting silver rain. Fender bender forcing three people, including tired-looking overweight cop, into the downpour. Traffic lights—red, yellow, green—watercolors now in the gloom.

Lone woman carrying umbrella walks the city street. Seemingly in no hurry. Smiles at drenched and scared kitty trying desperately to find shelter.

Stoops over. Picks her up. Puts her in raincoat pocket, mother kangaroo style.

Brett Ewing. Walking. Recovered enough now to ply the street corners. Nice round rolling ass beneath the lime-green designer raincoat. Kitty peeking up at her. "Meow."

Brett laughing. Laughing.

Two blocks away she finally finds some action. Street corner that teenage girls and boys dominate. Chickenhawk Avenue, as it's known. Lighted, open newsstand where the kids parade their wares while the droolers drive by and gawk, getting their sweaty money ready in their sweaty hands. She hopes she never has to be as pathetic about getting sex as her johns are.

Ed Gorman

Gets closer now. Sees the kids better. From a distance they all look like pretty good merchandise.

But close up:

Pain. Fear. Despair. Of a kind only a teenager who sells her or his body can know. And numbing it all on dope, which also helps you forget all the spooky stories going around. How one hooker was found in a park with her breasts cleaved off. How a male hooker was castrated a few nights later. And always, always some fourteen- or fifteen- or sixteen-year-old being pronounced HIV-positive.

And then she stops, just as somebody says, "Hey, look, that lime-green raincoat! It's Brett! Hey, Brett!" But they can't be sure, the umbrella blocking most of her face.

She turns away before anybody comes running after her.

Walks back the way she came.

The tiny wet kitty sticking her sweet little kitty face up out of the flap pocket and going "meow" again.

Half a block. Footsteps. Hers.

Then other footsteps.

His. Or so she hopes, anyway.

Figured he'd be somewhere around Chickenhawk Avenue. Waiting for her. Probably been here the past two nights while she was recuperating at Selina's.

Raincoat is suddenly hot inside. Sweat. And faint smell of rubber.

"Meow."

"It's all right, kitty. I'm taking you home with me."

Footsteps. Faster now. Hers.

Footsteps. Faster now. His.

When she reaches the alley, she ducks inside, losing herself in the darkness.

A Harlot's Tears

Must act quickly now. Away fall the clothes of Brett Ewing to reveal . . . Catwoman.

She quickly scales the side of a brick building, hiding on the shelf of a third-story indentation.

Now the Harlot comes into the alley. Running. Out of breath. Switchblade knife obvious in his right gloved hand.

He stops. Looks around.

Where did she go?

Nobody could get away that quickly.

Bitch, he thinks. Bitch. Tightening his leather grip on the switchblade.

He stops running. She's gone. Just have to face it.

And she was the one he really wanted, too. The others were just practice for Brett Ewing. (The theatricality of the name sickens him now. Some goddamned hayseed come to the big city to make some money on the little rosebud between her legs. Bitch.)

Looks around some more.

Nowhere in sight.

Shoves the knife back in his pocket and begins slowly turning around and walking out of the alley.

Then suddenly stops and looks straight up into the rain falling on him.

As if he's beseeching God himself for a favor.

Bitch.

Sometimes you must wait. Patience. Catwoman could take him down tonight, but she wants to know more about him so that when the police come after him, they won't have any trouble making it a good bust.

Ed Gorman

She notes his looks; notes his license number as his BMW pulls away.

She strokes the tiny kitty. "C'mon, we'll go home and get you some warm milk."

David Fisher: April 3, 199–

"You're just so tired lately. And you can't seem to get rid of that sore throat."

He lies in the darkness, listening to his wife, Sara.

He's been home for two hours now. After Brett Ewing somehow eluded him.

He's in the same bed where both of his children were conceived. Where he held his wife so tenderly the night her mother died, and where she held him when his father was killed in that terrible head-on car accident.

It used to be so superficial with Sara, his feelings. In college he'd basically liked her because she looked so frigging good in a bikini. Best of both worlds. A feast for his own eyes. The envy of other young men. And the early married years weren't all that much deeper either. Sara was essentially an ornament for his corporate bosses to admire. And David certainly wasn't averse to scoring a little strange nooky on the side.

But somehow the night she'd borne their first child, seeing her face drained yet lovely as she presented him with his baby, he came to love and admire and respect her in a way he would never have imagined possible. Wife. Lover. Sister. Mother. Friend. She was all things to him.

A Harlot's Tears

And then that night, several years later, with Brett Ewing . . .

"You're awfully quiet, honey. Rough night at the office?"

"Yeah," he says. "Boss on my ass again."

"I swear that man has periods."

"I believe it."

And he wants to tell her. Right now. Get it over with.

But when he opens his mouth and starts to say

he sees her as a beautiful young college sophomore and then at their wedding aglow in white and then that night when she gave birth to Kate

and he can't say it

the words, the horrible words, won't come

"You're soaking wet."

"Nightmare, I guess."

"Better go change those pajamas."

Middle of night. Darkness. Rain pattering window.

In the nightmare he was in Dr. Birnbaum's office again and Dr. Birnbaum is coming through the door with a single sheet of white paper in his hand and he says

and that's when David woke up screaming

as he wakes up three, four nights a week screaming when Dr. Birnbaum comes through the door with a single sheet of white paper in his hand and says

In the bathroom, he empties his bladder and then stares at himself in the mirror.

You owe her the truth. Now. Right fucking now and no more excuses.

Ed Gorman

But after getting dry pajamas and crawling back in bed, he hears her soft sweet snore in the shadows.

Not tonight. Tomorrow night. For sure.

He feels relief.

My God, how will he ever be able to tell her the truth?

Selina Kyle: April 4, 199–

Uptown there's a guy Selina always calls for background checks on people she's pursuing. The guy lives in a wheelchair, victim of a drunk driver, but he's trained himself to become a sort of poet in the art of computer hacking.

"Here's his license number," Selina says.

"How you been?"

"Fine."

"If I ever get out of this rig, you gonna gimme the first dance?"

"The first ten dances."

"You're nice, you know that?"

"So are you."

She can hear him typing in the Harlot's license-plate number. "This guy a baddie?"

"A real baddie."

"Probably take me a couple of hours."

"Fine. I appreciate it, Richard."

"Toodles."

An hour later he calls her back. As always, he's been thorough.

He tells her the guy's name, age, address, occupation, salary, club memberships, credit rating, and health status.

"God," she says to the information about David Fisher's health status.

"Yeah," Rich says. "Poor bastard."

Brett Ewing: April 4, 199–

Can't take it. Cooped up the last three days this way. Goes for a walk. Selina not back yet as dusk falls.

Writes her a note; *Took a stroll to park. Back soon. Love ya.*

Just before dusk it rained. City smells fresh now. Chilly. But pleasantly so.

She walks over by the park, all the greening grass and green shrubbery smelling tangy in the darkness. The streetlights just now coming on. Selina'll probably be pissed she took off this way, but she was getting claustrophobia in the apartment.

She screams.

A drunk just weaving out from behind a bush.

Thinking instantly: the Harlot!

"Hey, babe," the scuzzy drunk says.

God, he's coming on to her.

She flips him off. Starts walking faster. Deeper into the park.

She always associates pretty yellow and red and pink balloons with parks. And the taste of slightly charred hot dogs with lots of mustard. This summer she'll come back to this very park and bring Selina and Arizona and the three of them will have a good time.

This time it's not a pathetic harmless drunk.

Ed Gorman

This time
his hand clamping over her mouth
This time
his knife finding her throat
This time
his lips spitting the words "You fucking pig"
This time it's really the Harlot

Catwoman: April 4, 199–

Took a stroll to park. Back soon. Love ya.
Selina reads the note in disbelief. Why would Brett
go off by herself with the killer still at large? And after all the lectures Selina gave her about keeping all
the doors locked . . .

Ten minutes later a silken dark figure, outlined only
by pale moonlight, makes her way across the shadows
of the city park, shadows in which lovers of every sex
hide in whispers and frantic lust; shadows in which
the bitter mugger and the troubled sexual derelict
wait for victims.
    Shadows in which a man named David Fisher is
slashing young Brett Ewing with his knife—
    Catwoman hears whimpers; she glides between
trees, down a rocky embankment to a creek and a
copse of willow trees.
    And now a muffled scream.
    "Brett!" she calls.
    Another muffled scream.
    Catwoman glances around.
    Where is Brett?

Another scream. This time of pain.

Where is she?

Catwoman sees the small ornamental bridge that children like to ride their bikes across.

Beneath the bridge is a storm drain.

She moves very quickly now, hurtling herself up over the bridge and down into the quarter inch of water that covers the silty mud.

And sees them.

David Fisher has slashed Brett's cheek and is now about to draw his knife across her throat.

Brett kicks frantically, tries to push him off her, but he's too strong.

He's so caught up in his rage, he doesn't see or hear Catwoman until it's too late, until she kicks him in the small of the back then chops him across the rear of his neck.

As he turns, Catwoman's right leg lashes out and catches him in the groin.

He cries out, sinking to his knees in the slime.

Sobbing, Brett throws herself into Catwoman's arms, saying over and over, "I'm gonna die, Catwoman! I'm gonna die!"

Catwoman: April 5, 199–

David Fisher is drinking the bourbon Catwoman offered him. Brett is toking on a joint. Miles Davis plays low on the tape deck, the dirgelike " 'Round Midnight." A dirge is appropriate now. As for the kitty Catwoman found the other night, she is, as usual, lapping up milk with her tiny pink tongue.

Ed Gorman

At the door, Arizona says, "I'm just going to get a cup of coffee and have a short walk."

"It's getting late. Be careful," Catwoman says.

Arizona nods, then vanishes. She couldn't help but hear what was said here when the three of them came in an hour ago. She can't hack the tension and despair any longer. She needs to get out of here.

After she leaves, Catwoman says, "David, I could have taken you to the police last night, but I sensed that you and Brett needed to talk first. So that's what I want you to do now—talk to each other."

David is on the couch; Brett has been crying off and on. David just seems to swing from cold rage to depression.

"You should've had yourself checked," he says for the fortieth time that night.

"David, I'm a goddamned hick, all right? I run away to the city and a few weeks later I get AIDS. How was I supposed to know?"

He explodes again. "Why didn't you make your johns wear rubbers?"

His rage echoes in the quiet room.

"That isn't the kind of talking I had in mind for you two," Catwoman says gently.

But then Brett falls to crying once more, sobbing really, and David goes back to his scowling.

"You know what you need to do, David," Catwoman says gently. "You need to tell Brett that you forgive her, that you know it wasn't her fault. And then you need to turn yourself over to the police and tell them about how you killed the prostitutes because you were so angry about testing HIV-positive. And then you need to tell your wife the truth and have her get tested, too."

"Just because we tested positive doesn't mean we'll

actually get it," Brett says, more in hope than with any real belief.

"I'm not sorry I killed them," David says, anger overcoming him again.

"In a few days, when you've calmed down, you'll be sorry, David," Catwoman says.

He just scowls and looks out the window.

And then, with no warning whatever, he leaps from the couch, splashes his drink in Brett's face, and then lunges at her, slapping her several times across the face.

Catwoman is up, grabs him, hurls him so hard backward that he trips across the edge of the couch and hits the floor face-first, almost like a pratfall.

He starts to get up, but Catwoman isn't done with him. She grabs a handful of his hair and then slams his head against the wall.

"If you can get pissed, David, so can I. It isn't easy for me to feel sorry for you when I know you killed those women. But I'm trying to be charitable about it, trying to cut you a little slack. But if you ever lay a hand on a woman again—"

She lets him collapse in a heap on the floor.

She goes over and sits on the arm of the chair. Brett is crying again, face in her hands, and Selina leans over and hugs her, friend and mother at the same time.

Then the crying becomes sobbing and Brett reaches out to be held like a child. Catwoman obliges, stroking Brett's hair and saying again and again, "It's all right, Brett; it's all right."

Neither of the women notice David
standing up
(my whole life is over, can't face my wife and my daughter, or my friends)

Ed Gorman

and then quickly crossing the room to
the porch just off the living room, where
(he saw a film about an eagle once and the way an
eagle uses the air currents; maybe he'll use the air
currents)
and he does it without thinking really
just gets to the porch and scurries to the window
ledge and
(he sees himself at first Holy Communion devout
looking as a holy card
and remembers fighting Mick Dolan that time after
Dolan made a remark about David's father
and remembers skating that late December dusk
with Mary Lou Malloy the most beautiful girl in seventh grade; how the last of the sinking sunlight shone
red on the ice
and remembers)
is falling
falling
(remembering now his wife the night she gave birth
to their first daughter; that ethereal shine in her eyes,
the eternal nurturing mother
and remembering what it is like to lie with his little
girl when she's sleeping the sweet scent of her hair
the soft purr of her snoring
and remembering)
is falling
falling
and somewhere somebody is screaming, "David, no!
David!"
is falling
falling
all history and memory about to collide with an old
brick alley in a bad section of Gotham
is falling

and all light and all sound will die with him because even if everything goes on he will not be here to
note and comprehend it
    falling
    is falling

Selina Kyle/Brett Ewing: April 10, 199–

The priest is just now saying the last of the graveside
prayers. Two women in black suits and black veils are
sobbing. One is old, one is young. Next to the young
one stands a very pretty little blond girl looking confused about everything going on here. Why is Daddy
in that long, gleaming box? And why are they putting
the box into the ground? Won't Daddy get cold in the
ground?

Selina and Brett stand on the hill, looking down at
the service, at the long procession of shiny new expensive cars, at the half hundred or so mourners just now
turning away from the spectacle of death as represented by the long narrow hole in the ground. Someday all these people will be the stars of their own
graveside services.

Ask not for whom the bell tolls, Selina thinks, and
then wonders if the anonymous note she sent to David
Fisher's wife instructing her to get a blood test will
reach her tomorrow. She hopes so. Sooner the better.

David chose to take his secrets to the grave. The
positive blood test. His killing of the prostitutes. And
Selina is willing to let those secrets be his in the cold
darkness of the waiting earth.

But she wants David's wife to know about the blood

test so she won't—in case her test is positive, too—give the disease to anybody else.

"It's sad," Brett says.

"Very sad."

"I'm scared, too, Selina."

"I know," Selina says, putting her arm around the young girl, leading her down the hill to the car. Death should have no dominion on a sunny day like this, when the sunflowers are like schoolchildren playing beneath the cloudless blue sky, and the first monarch butterfly of spring flutters past the eyes.

"You up for renting a canoe?" Selina says.

"Really? That sounds great."

"We can even pack a lunch."

"God, Selina, that's a great idea. Thanks."

They walk on in silence, watching an old woman kneel with great difficulty at a gravestone, where she sets down a potted geranium. The old woman crosses herself and bows her head.

"I keep trying to hate him," Brett says as they reach the car. "But I can't."

"No," Selina says wearily. "Neither can I."

Then they are in the car and driving away.

Reformed

JOHN GREGORY BETANCOURT

MAY 5

Fluorescent lights streamed past overhead, what seemed like endless miles of them, but the Penguin hardly noticed. He continued to struggle against the straps holding his arms and legs, constricting his every movement like bands of iron. He heaved and wiggled to no avail. They'd made certain he couldn't get loose.

It's only for show, he told himself for the thousandth time. *I'm too strong for them, too clever. They'll never be able to mess up my brain. Never!*

The operating table—pushed by four burly male interns in white uniforms—crashed through double-door after double-door, continuing its inexorable progress toward Arkham Asylum's operating theater.

The fools. They should know by now I can't be brainwashed. It's not as if they've never tried before.

He remembered all their pitiful attempts to reform him in the past. Oh, they *wanted* him to be good,

Reformed

wanted it so badly they could taste it. And when he said, "Oh, yes, sirs. I'll be good this time, I promise," they always believed him. *Always.* What stupid, pathetic fools these doctors were.

The Penguin couldn't help himself. He began to chuckle.

One of the interns, a blond man with ice-pale blue eyes, glanced at the Penguin's face. The man's nametag said Jeremy Starke. The Penguin dissected Starke with a scalpel-sharp gaze, then smiled almost lovingly. A look of horrified disgust mingled with . . . was it *pity*? . . . crossed Starke's face, then he hurriedly looked away.

The Penguin chuckled again. It was not a pleasant sound.

They passed through a final door, into an operating theater filled with machinery. The Penguin twisted his neck, trying to see, and glimpsed a huge machine that took up fully half of the room. It was a strange collage of glowing tubes and instrument panels, twisted loops of wire and circuit boards, shiny metal spheres and coils filled with a shimmering silver liquid. He'd never seen anything like it before.

Wearing gloves in case he tried to bite, two of the interns grabbed his head and forced it straight, so he was looking up at the white tiled ceiling. Someone had pinned a yellow smiley-face directly overhead. He sneered.

As they strapped his head in place so he couldn't move, couldn't flinch away from their machine, he began to struggle again . . . just to keep up appearances. It would make his change to mild-mannered Oswald Cobblepot all the more dramatic, when he chose to make it.

John Gregory Betancourt

The doctors were fiddling with their machine. It came to life with an unpleasant grinding *whirrr* of sound, like a motor burning itself up.

Come on, get on with it, the Penguin thought. *I haven't got all day. I want out, and the sooner you finish trying to scramble my brains, the sooner I'll be free.*

It had all begun with a special psychiatric hearing. Gotham City's Arkham Asylum, which specialized in treatment for the criminally insane, routinely held psychiatric hearings for its patients every six months. The Penguin had already been to two in the course of his latest incarceration for "treatment" (which this time consisted mainly of endless counseling sessions, support-group meetings, and time alone to meditate).

When interns pulled him from his cell—pardon, *visitor's room,* he thought sarcastically—with no advance warning, he knew something big was in the works. He'd been a model patient for eight months now; perhaps they were finally going to release him.

The interns brought him to a conference room. There he found an unsmiling group of three men and two women waiting on the far side of a conference table. Sitting meekly in the straight-backed chair opposite them, he'd done his best to appear cowed and harmless.

The asylum's current chief of staff, Dr. Davis Carteret, was a tall, square-built man with a receding hairline and a hook nose. He made a pretense of smiling at the Penguin, then opened a manila folder before him. He cleared his throat as he pawed through dozens of pages of notes. The Penguin knew what they said; he'd gone through them once, several months before, when one of his doctors had accidentally left the file in his cell. They detailed his life of crime in a most unflattering way.

"Mr. Cobblepot," Dr. Carteret finally said. "We have been reviewing your file and we believe you're the ideal subject for a new form of therapy."

"Yes?" the Penguin breathed, hardly able to contain his excitement. *They're finally going to do it, they're going to let me out again,* he thought.

Dr. Carteret went on. "We have a new machine that can rechannel the synapses in your brain using radio waves. Unlike lobotomies or other surgery, it does no actual damage to you; it merely shuts away your dark thoughts . . . almost like shutting a closet door. We feel, given your case," and here, he thumped the folder with his index finger, "that this treatment would be of immeasurable benefit to you. However, since it *is* experimental, we cannot administer it without your permission."

"Experimental, you say," the Penguin mused. *Which means they don't know how effective it will be.*

"That's right."

"Have you tried it on anyone else?"

"No humans yet, no."

"What about animals?"

"Treatments given to problem animals—rhesus monkeys, dogs, and even a couple of pigs—yielded a one hundred percent improvement in their sociablity. It had no noticeable effects on rats, mice, and other lesser creatures; doubtless their intelligence wasn't high enough for it to register."

The Penguin leaned back, nodding slowly to himself. He'd been through every sort of treatment known to

John Gregory Betancourt

man, from electroshock therapy to hypnotism to Freudian and Jungian analysis. None of it had made the slightest dent in his mental armor. Radio waves? He could have laughed. It would never work. But perhaps he could convinced them it had. . . .

He smiled most winningly at Dr. Carteret. "There's no surgery, you said? No cutting?"

"None," Dr. Carteret said, nodding. "As I told you, it's all done with radio waves."

"Then—yes, of course I agree to the treatment," the Penguin said. "You know I want to be well, Doctor."

"That's right." Forcing another smile, Dr. Carteret slid a release form and a plastic pen over to the Penguin. "If you would be kind enough to sign and initial the release form where marked, we will schedule your treatment session."

The Penguin signed with a flourish and passed the paper back.

"The pen, too, if you don't mind."

Looking hurt, the Penguin returned the pen, too.

That had been two weeks ago—two endless weeks, during which the Penguin had run through every possible scenario in his mind in preparation for the acting chance of his life. If he could persuade them he'd completely reformed, he'd be free again at last.

The interns fussing over him checked all of his straps one more time, then nodded and stepped back. Dr. Carteret bent until his face was inches from the Penguin's.

"This is undoubtedly going to be excruciatingly painful," he said. "Don't worry, Oswald, the treatment won't last more than half an hour or so, if all goes well."

"What do you mean?" the Penguin said. "Radio waves don't hurt."

"Of course they can. It depends on the form they take. Some you can see, like light. Others you can feel, like laser beams and microwaves. This treatment is based on microwaves."

"But I thought—"

Dr. Carteret nodded to an intern—Starke again, the Penguin saw—who quickly stuffed a large plastic bit into the Penguin's open mouth when he tried to protest.

"That's so you don't accidentally bite your tongue off," Starke told him matter-of-factly.

The Penguin's eyes got very large. He began to struggle again and attempted to spit out the bit with no success. When he screamed at Carteret, trying to say he wanted out, wanted no part of this treatment, all that came through the bit was a muffled sort of coughing sound.

Dr. Carteret smiled. "I know you're excited, too. It's really a great honor to be the pioneer in a new form of medicine." He waved his hand and another intern pulled what looked like a gigantic glass eyeball attached to a miniature crane's arm into the Penguin's view.

Carteret lowered the eye, positioned it directly over the Penguin's forehead. The Penguin's fears doubled and trebled. Whatever the thing was, he wanted no part of it.

The eye began to blink, on and off, on and off. Pain burst through the Penguin's being, a blinding, searing, senseless agony. A thousand tiny needles were jabbing into his brain, a thousand hooks tearing his mind apart—

As he screamed helplessly, some inner voice called him a fool, and told him he'd made the greatest mistake of his life.

Until everything went white.

MAY 6

In Wayne Manor, huge rooms and hallways echoed with the clank of metal on metal. In his private gymnasium, Bruce Wayne was working out. Slowly pressing two hundred and forty pounds of lead weights over his head, he concentrated on the task at hand. *Up, down. Repeat the exercise. Ignore the burning in your arms and chest.* Sweat trickled down his face; muscles corded in his neck and arms. He lifted the weights again.

When the Penguin's face appeared on the wall-sized television screen opposite him, Bruce paused in surprise, the weights suspended directly over his head. Slowly he lowered them into their resting bars and sat up, toweling his face dry.

The announcer was saying, "—the notorious criminal Oswald Cobblepot, better known as the Penguin, underwent experimental therapy last night in a radical move to cure his antisocial tendencies." A picture of a strange glass-eye suspended over the Penguin's screaming face appeared on the screen. The announcer gave a brief summary of how the machine worked, burning out selected synapses in the patient's brain using modulated radio waves.

Bruce wondered briefly if the machine would work ... then lay back and began to lift weights again. If it didn't, he knew, he'd deal with the Penguin in his own way.

AUGUST 9

It was a pleasantly warm Sunday evening after a just-this-side-of-hot day. The sky had been that perfect shade of ocean blue, without a single cloud to mar its perfection, and the air had stirred with frequent little breezes. All told, it had been perfect weather for baseball.

Oswald Cobblepot had spent his Saturday afternoon at a doubleheader, in which the Gotham Griffins twice beat the stuffing out of the Atlanta Braves. Feasting on hot roasted peanuts and countless hotdogs smothered in onions and mustard, washing it all down with cup after cup of diet rootbeer, cheering his favorite team to victory not once but *twice* in a single afternoon . . . he sighed. Yes, life was good.

Oswald was dressed in what had become his standard outfit since his release from Arkham Asylum: faded blue-jeans and a plaid cotton shirt, with black sneakers and a black leather belt with a silver Gotham Griffins buckle. Today he also wore a Griffins cap, with their team logo stamped in red and black across the front.

He only had a couple more blocks to go to the bus stop, then he'd be off to his center-city apartment for an evening of fun in front of his TV: nothing like sit-coms to make a guy smile. He began to whistle, "Take Me Out to the Ballgame," content in a happily distracted sort of way.

The machine had fried his brains, all right: perhaps it did too good a job. He was always happy, always placid now. After a month of observation, he had been released from Arkham Asylum on his own recognizance.

John Gregory Betancourt

Dr. Judy Katz, his counselor in the outpatient program, had even gotten him a nine-to-five job packing cardboard boxes at an electronics factory, and he'd settled into his new work with the ease of a man born to manual labor. Six dollars an hour gave him more than enough money to pay his meager bills.

Oswald was so wrapped up in pleasant thoughts, he didn't notice the street-thugs until they'd surrounded him. There were six of them, all dressed in black, with plenty of chains and zippers. The oldest couldn't have been more than twenty.

"Hey, old man!" their leader said. "Got any money for us? This here is a *toll road*, and we want you to pay up."

"Sir," Oswald said. "I hardly think—"

"Shut up!" He gave Oswald a backward slap across the face.

Oswald's eyes glazed for a second. When he tried to run, they began pushing him from side to side, whirling him around, laughing and jeering and slapping his face. He raised his hands to protect himself.

"Please . . ." he whimpered.

"Money!" their leader demanded again. *"Now!"*

Before Oswald could say a word, one of them kicked him in the stomach as hard as he could. Oswald doubled up, vomiting hotdogs and rootbeer and peanuts. He couldn't move, couldn't breathe. The world started to take on unreal dimensions, like a nightmare, and everyone was moving in slow motion.

Someone kicked his legs out from under him, and he fell heavily. He stared dumbly as they pulled out blackjacks and brass knuckles.

"Fun time," their leader said. He was the first to kick Oswald in the face.

Reformed

The city swarmed with vermin. From the rooftops, Batman patrolled the city each night, looking for the worst mankind had to offer. Thieves feared him with good reason. Murderers, rapists, drug-dealers: he'd driven most of them off the open streets. Gangs, though, were the worst: They'd grown up knowing nothing except that strength and power come through fear and intimidation.

When he saw six teenagers pounding a little man into the pavement, Batman knew he had to act fast. They wouldn't have any qualms about killing the guy if it amused them. From the looks of things, he must've put up a struggle. That, or caught them on a bad day.

Batman fired a dart at the building opposite; high tensile-strength cord slithered from a coil at his utility belt. The dart struck, burying its armored head deep into brick and lodging tight. Wrapping his cord around his gloved hands, he tested it and found it strong enough to hold his weight.

Drawing a gas pellet, he tossed it down. It struck the sidewalk and broke, spewing clouds of greasy white smoke. The gang reeled back, coughing and choking, their eyes burning.

His entrance covered, Batman swung down, feet extended. He caught two of the gang in the back, sending them sprawling. "Batman!" one of them gasped, as he loomed from the clouds of billowing gas.

He knocked their heads together, then cuffed their wrists and ankles together so they couldn't run. Whirling, he ran into the heart of the smoke cloud. The man they'd attacked lay curled in a fetal ball, bleeding from cuts on his face and head. He was coughing asthmatically.

Batman pulled the man's arm back and pressed a

John Gregory Betancourt

gas mask over his face. The man sucked oxygen grate-
fully, his coughs subsiding.

Batman didn't wait to see more. He stalked toward
the rest of the gang, whom he could hear coughing
close by.

Outside the smoke cloud, the remaining four gang
members were standing with their hands on their
knees, trying to get their lungs clear. They looked up
as he approached, their eyes going wide. Slowly they
began to back up, hefting blackjacks and brass knuckles.

Two of them charged Batman suddenly. He parried
their inept swings easily, letting their blows deflect
off his body armor. A punch to the face knocked one
cold; the other he dropped with a kick to the stomach
and a chop to the back of the neck.

When the remaining two tried to run, he sprang on
them like a lion to the kill, pounding them down to
the pavement as they'd done to the old man. When
their struggles ceased, he hog-tied them and dragged
them back to join the other two. He left them all in a
heap.

A phone booth on the corner offered the fastest
solution to his problem. He dialed 911, identified himself, said where he was, and asked for the police and
an ambulance to be dispatched.

The gas cloud had mostly dispersed by the time he
went back to the little man, who'd uncoiled a bit more.
As Batman retrieved his gas mask, he paused. Beneath
the blood, there was something naggingly familiar
about the little man.

It's the Penguin, he realized suddenly. *The vic-
timizer made a victim. But—how? . . .*

He recalled the experimental treatment the Penguin

Reformed

was supposed to have received at Arkham Asylum. It
must have worked, he realized. They'd treated him
and released him, and this was the result: a harmless,
pathetic little old man.

Not my problem anymore, he thought. *Just one more
helpless citizen. Let's hope he stays that way.*

The Penguin was staring up at him through slitted
eyes. He made a wet gurgling noise through a mouth
filled with blood.

Sirens were approaching. Batman rose and trotted
into the darkness.

I'm a dead man, was Oswald's only thought when the
gang knocked his feet out from under him.

Dazed from the blows he'd taken to the head, everything seemed impossibly faraway. After he fell, they
continued to pummel him. Another kick and he felt
his ribs crack. From then on, every breath brought a
sharp new agony. There was a damp stickiness on his
face; he blinked through a red haze, tasting the salti-
ness of blood in his mouth from his broken lips.

Then his lungs began to burn. He coughed and tried
to see through a haze of tears. All of a sudden a cowled
face . . . a very familiar cowled face . . . was peering at
him. When a gloved hand reached for his throat, everything went black.

I must've fainted for a second, he thought. The
cowled face was still there when he risked opening his
eyes again. The two stared at each other.

"You—" Oswald tried to say, but there was blood in
his mouth and it came out as a wordless gurgle.

Sirens roared in the distance, approaching fast. Bat-

John Gregory Betancourt

man glanced up, tensed, then stood and fled into the night.

The police saved me from Batman, Oswald thought blearily. *Batman tried to murder me, tried to make it look like a band of thugs was responsible.*

All the wrong facts began to click into place. His brow furled as hate-fed adrenaline surged through his body.

Synapses were rerouting. Paranoia ran deep.

Batman set me up. Batman wants me dead. Batman was behind the attack and would have killed me if the police hadn't shown up.

Everything fit neatly into place. The Penguin saw it all clearly. He rememberd the old days . . . remembered all the power he had controlled, when he'd dared to ride a whirlwind and seize its brass ring.

He closed his eyes as the ambulance pulled up. Men in white with Red Cross armbands where suddenly all around him, lifting him—delicately as a kitten—onto a stretcher. They bundled him into the ambulance, then raced away from the street corner with lights flashing and siren blaring.

The Penguin closed his eyes and smiled through his blood and broken lips.

AUGUST 10

"You're a lucky man," Dr. Seti said. She was a perky little Indian woman, and her voice had a lilting quality the Penguin disliked the moment he heard it. "A very lucky man indeed, Mr. Cobblepot."

The Penguin winced, half from his cracked ribs. He'd

spent the last twenty-four hours in the hospital and wanted nothing better than to leave. And that seemed to depend entirely on Dr. Seti's signing his release papers. Plans were coming together in his head, and he needed to set some of them in motion.

"I know I'm lucky," he told her. He managed what might have passed for an encouraging smile considering the condition of his face: three stitches in his lower lip, twelve in his upper lip, with large flesh-colored adhesive bandages over both. "I appreciate the help you've given me."

"Oh, I just did a bit of cleanup," she said. "It's Batman who really saved your life. If not for him, you probably would not be here now."

Batman this, Batman that! the Penguin thought. *That meddling buffoon tried to kill me, and nobody knows it!* The thought lay inside him like an open wound. He'd have his revenge soon enough, though, just you wait. . . .

Dr. Seti handed him the clipboard and her pen. "If you'll sign there—yes, that's right—I will see to it you are released. Just allow me to find you a wheelchair . . ." She headed for the nurses station.

Fifteen minuters later, the Penguin was standing on the sidewalk in front of the hospital, truly a free man for the first time in a year. The sky was threatening rain; he felt almost naked without an umbrella. All he had was eight dollars in his billfold, a cheap watch, depressingly unfashionable clothes, and the most comfortable shoes he'd ever worn in his life. He stared down at his black sneakers suspiciously. Comfortable or not, he didn't like the image they imparted. He'd fix that as soon as he could.

He flagged down a passing cab, climbed inside, and gave the driver the address of a very exclusive men's apparel store. Then he sat back and watched the streets pass.

"Some accident you had, huh?" the cabby said.

The Penguin ignored him. After that, the man shrugged and concentrated on his driving.

When they finally reached Tyro's Fine Gentlemen's Apparel Shoppe, the Penguin paid his fare silently (leaving a fifteen-cent tip only because he didn't want to wait for change), then climbed out. The place hadn't changed in two years: a good sign. It even had the same suits in the display windows.

Without a moment's hesitation, the Penguin pushed through the crowds on the street to the revolving door. Inside, the air was very still, with the filtered, air-conditioned smell all exclusive shops seem to have. He breathed deeply. It felt good to be surrounded by the feel of money.

He'd bought this store (and several others like it) through a series of dummy corporations years before, when Batman first started making life difficult for him. At first it had been just a paranoid indulgence, in case anything ever happened and he needed to reequip himself quickly, but he'd already made use of it several times.

His man Bixby was still in charge of the cashier's station, he saw: good. Though they hadn't seen each other in over a year, mutual recognition was obvious. At the Penguin's nod, Bixby reached under the counter and pressed a small button.

Reformed

The Penguin continued through the store, passing racks of umbrellas, finely tailored suits, dress shirts, silk bow ties, and the occasional browsing shopper. When he reached the changing rooms, he selected the second from the left, entered, locked the door behind him, and calmly pushed the full-length mirror on the back wall. It pivoted easily, and he climbed through, into a hidden storeroom.

He gazed around happily. The place was filled with plastic-covered racks of umbrellas, tuxedos, dress shirts, and top hats . . . every one his exact size.

The Penguin started to remove his shirt, hesitated, put it back on. *Not yet.* He had an appointment with Dr. Judy Katz, his outpatient counselor and psychiatrist, that afternoon. He needed to keep up his "Oswald Cobblepot—helpless moron" act. But the sky was overcast today and he could certainly justify carrying an umbrella. . . .

He pulled the plastic from the umbrella rack, raising a small cloud of dust, and calmly ran his fingers over the polished handles. What would it be? A flamethrower? No, too obvious. Darts? No, the poison in the tips must have lost its potency by now. Finally he selected a Black Mambo umbrella. The ivory handle had three neat little buttons. *Yes,* he thought, *this one will do very nicely if you get out of line, Dr. Katz.*

After pulling the plastic back over his umbrella rack, he crossed to a large, old-fashioned floor-safe against the far wall. The dial spun easily. With practiced ease, he entered the combination, turned the handle, pulled the door open, and removed a two-inch stack of thousand-dollar bills. He had a lot to do and he was going to need plenty of money. Then he removed a

John Gregory Betancourt

spare monocle from its case, fitted it to his eye, and smiled toothily. *Very* nice.

He closed the safe and spun its dial. Then he picked up the phone, had the operator connect him with a randomly selected law firm—Hayes, Steele, Blaylock & Associates—and asked to speak to one of the partners.

"Mr. Hayes, my name is Horace J. Goldwater," the Penguin lied. "That's right . . . I need to set up a charity fund to sponsor a philanthropic project being put together by a friend of mine, Oswald Cobblepot . . . three hundred thousand dollars to start with . . . that's right. . . . Mr. Cobblepot will bring the materials by your office at four o'clock this afternoon, if that's convenient . . . yes . . . thank you very much, sir." He hung up, smiling.

But first . . . a visit to the police station.

"But, Mr. Cobblepot . . ." the lieutenant began again.

"I told you, I want to drop the charges against those nice young men." The Penguin peered through his monocle, trying to remain calm. He knew he couldn't show any excess emotions or he might give himself away. Now he had to be . . . *pleasant*. The word was like a curse to him. "I believe, sir, that I *am* within my rights to do so, am I not?"

The lieutenant sighed. "Yes, Mr. Cobblepot. It's your right, but for your own good—and the good of the city— I must urge you to reconsider. If you leave them where they are, they'll be up for a preliminary hearing in a few weeks. They'll plead guilty. Your testimony can put them away for a long, long time."

"Let me talk with them first. If I can persuade them

to work for Cobblepot Charities, I intend to drop the charges. If not, then I will bow to your wishes."

"I guess that's the best I can hope for. This way, please." He escorted the Penguin to a small conference room. "I'll bring them in. If there's any trouble, just signal—I'll be watching from out here, through the window, okay?"

"Very good." He entered the room and sat down, drumming his fingers on the tabletop impatiently.

At last, the lieutenant ushered in the six young men who'd attacked him two days before, then retreated outside and shut the door. The six young men sat meekly. None of them would meet his gaze. Finally his attention fastened on their leader: his black hair had been cropped short—probably caught head lice in his cell—and he was now dressed in a rumpled blue shirt and pants. A huge blue-black bruise had all but swollen his left eye shut.

"What's your name?" the Penguin asked.

"Clay," he said slowly.

"You made a big mistake when you attacked me, Clay," the Penguin said in a low voice. "None of you recognized me, did you, boys?" He cackled, and his voice suddenly held a commanding note: "Look at me!"

They looked, and their attention fastened on his monocle. "You're—" one of them began, recognition dawning. He trailed off uneasily.

"That's right," the Penguin said. "I'd just gotten out of Arkham Asylum. I was lying low, trying not to attract attention, when you morons jumped me. Well, it so happens, I now need some muscle. The job's yours, if you want it."

"What are you planning?" Clay said.

"Officially . . . you'll be working for Cobblepot

John Gregory Betancourt

Charities in setting up exhibits in Gotham Park. Un-officially . . ." he let his gaze wander. "Let's say the opportunities are boundless."

"What about the charges against us?" one of the others asked.

"They will be dropped, of course."

Clay swallowed. "I don't think we have much choice."

"That's right." He pulled one of the thousand-dollar bills from his pocket, slid it across the table to Clay, and said, "Spare change to get yourselves cleaned up. Meet me at midnight on Pier Fifty at Gotham Harbor. Charity starts at home, if you know what I mean." He gave a knowing wink.

"You got it, man!"

The Penguin stood, nodding to the lieutenant through the plate-glass window.

"Charges are dropped," the Penguin told him, "as I told you they would be."

At three o'clock sharp, the Penguin arrived for his weekly session with Dr. Katz. Her office was on the fifteenth floor of a downtown professional building. As he rode the elevator up in silence, he stared at his reflection in the shiny steel doors. As a last thought, he removed his monocle and tucked it into his left breast pocket.

The elevator doors opened and he stepped out, drain-ing all the bounce from his stride. He nodded politely to Adam, the receptionist, who was already buzzing Dr. Katz.

"Please send Mr. Cobblepot in," she said over the intercom.

Adam nodded and said to the Penguin, "Please go

right in, sir. Dr. Katz's two o'clock was canceled, so we're running right on time today."

"Thank you, thank you," he said. He went to the doctor's office, opened the door, went in, closed it behind himself, and crossed to the couch. There he sat, balancing his Black Mambo umbrella across his knees. He didn't look at the doctor; she seemed engrossed in his file at the moment . . . she always made a quick review of his case before they started.

Dr. Judy Katz was going on forty, with her graying brown hair tied up in a bun, thick glasses hiding brown eyes, and a pleasantly rounded face. She had always been soft-spoken but firm in their sessions. In retrospect, it seemed like a sign of weakness to him.

When she looked up and saw the bandages on his face, and the bruises that had spread a bit beyond the edges of his bandages, she gave a little start. Quickly enough she recovered, came around from her desk, and sat in the armchair next to the couch.

"Why don't we start by your telling me about what happened to you during the week?" she said.

The Penguin quickly gave her an account of what had happened, leading up to the gang of thugs who'd attacked him on the way home from Sunday's baseball game. Dr. Katz nodded and made encouraging noises at all the right points.

"What did you think when they attacked you?" she asked.

"What did I think?" the Penguin demanded. "What kind of stupid question is that? I—" He caught himself, but the damage was done. Dr. Katz had an uneasy expression on her face. She as trained to read behind the words, he thought: *What did she read in him?*

"I'm afraid I had a call from the police earlier this

John Gregory Betancourt

afternoon," she said. "They told me you dropped the charges against the men who attacked you."

"That's right," the Penguin said as amiably as he could manage. "They were misguided, that's all."

"Misguided? To a life of crime?"

"No—I mean, yes!"

"What exactly do you mean?"

"I was set up," he snarled. "They were Batman's tools. He's trying to kill me!"

The Penguin realized he was standing over Dr. Katz, his umbrella in his hand like a sword. Quickly he sat down again.

But the damage had been done. Dr. Katz was reaching for the intercom. Suddenly the Penguin knew what was going to happen . . . and he wasn't going to allow it.

He reached out and pushed her hand away from the intercom with the tip of his umbrella. "None of that," he said.

"But I was only going to call Adam in—"

"To watch me while you stepped out for a second," the Penguin finished for her. He leaned forward menacingly. "I'm not stupid, Doctor. You've decided I'm dangerous again. I can see it in your eyes. You were going to have me locked up. Weren't you? *Weren't you?*"

"Y-yes!" she stammered.

"It's a pity you found out so soon," he said. "I'd hoped to maintain the charade a while longer. Ah, well."

He pointed his Black Mambo at her and pushed one of its three handles. A bright green gas hissed out, forming a cloud around her head, and she breathed in before she could stop herself. Then she settled back, a dreamy far-off look on her face.

"That's better," the Penguin said, covering his own

face with a handkerchief. "That was hypnotic mist, and you're going to follow my every instruction. Do you understand me, Dr. Katz?"

"Yes," she said.

"Very good. Now, you will listen to me and do *precisely* as I say. First, you will remember having a useful, productive session with me today. My mental health is improving steadily. Say it!"

"Your mental health is improving steadily . . ."

"Nothing anyone says to you will be able to persuade you differently. Oswald Cobblepot is completely well, completely normal. That is all you will remember about me. We had a good session today. I am normal. Do you understand?"

"Yes . . ."

He smiled. "Good. I'm very happy with you, Dr. Katz. That makes you feel good. You *want* to make me happy. Do you understand that?"

"Yes . . . happy . . ."

"Good. You will obey my every instruction to the letter, as though you thought of the idea yourself. Do you understand that?"

"Yes . . ."

"You will remember none of this conversation when we are through. Now, as I count backwards from ten, you will come gradually back to full consciousness. When I reach one, you will be completely awake, only you will remember none of this conversation. All you will remember is that we had a good, productive session today. You will file your weekly report on me, and you will say in your report that everything is normal. Do you understand?"

"Yes . . ."

"Ten," the Penguin said, "nine . . . eight . . .

seven . . ." And by the time he reached "one," Dr. Katz was smiling and shaking his hand, saying it was the best session they'd ever had, and if there was ever anything she could do for him . . .

"As a matter-of-fact, there is," the Penguin said. "I'd like you to come to my apartment next Saturday for a game of Scrabble."

"What a great idea!" Dr. Katz said.

"Wear something nice," the Penguin told her, standing.

"I think I'll wear something nice," she said, staring at the ceiling in deep thought.

The Penguin let himself out. It was amazing how quickly these psychiatric sessions went.

He returned to Tyro's Fine Gentlemen's Apparel Shoppe, changed into a top hat, black tuxedo, red cummerbund, and white tie. Death is, after all, a white-tie affair, he thought: fitting for this evening.

First, though, he headed for Hayes, Steele, Blaylock & Associates, the law firm he'd called earlier that day. He never would have made it past the receptionist dressed in his peasant's rags; in his tuxedo, he found himself ushered into Bill Hayes's office at once. Hayes was the senior partner in the firm: gray-haired, with an athlete's build, an actor's strong good looks, and a firm gaze and handshake.

The Penguin accepted the cigar Hayes offered him, and lit it with a silver lighter decorated with little enamel penguins he took from his pocket. He took a few experimental puffs and nodded; Cuban, and very expensive.

"Now, Mr. Cobblepot," Hayes said, settling into a corner of his desk and looking the Penguin straight in the eye, "let's get right to the point. You want us to set up a charity fund for you, is that right?"

"Correct." The Penguin reached into the inside pocket of his tuxedo and pulled out two packets of thousand-dollar bills. "Three hundred thousand dollars should be enough to get the project rolling, I believe."

"But—all in cash! This is highly irregular."

The Penguin took a long puff on his cigar and blew smoke at Hayes. "My benefactor wishes to remain anonymous. He's a wealthy eccentric. Donations from other charities will come by more traditional means, I expect."

Hayes rubbed his square jaw. "I believe we can accommodate you. I'll have the papers drawn up for you by tomorrow morning. In the meantime, would you like to leave the money in our safe?"

"Once you've given me a receipt."

"Of course, Mr. Cobblepot, of course."

The Penguin smiled and knew he had Hayes in his pocket.

AUGUST 11

At exactly one minute past midnight, the Penguin made his way out onto Pier Fifty.

The six thugs he'd released from jail were waiting for him, as he'd expected. Clay straightened and nudged the others into line as he approached.

"Here we are, Penguin," he called. "Just like you

John Gregory Betancourt

asked." He did a slow spin, showing off new jeans, black shirt, and a gold-stud earring in his left ear. "Snazzed out, huh, dude?"

"Talk English," the Penguin said.

"Yeah, yeah."

"To the edge of the dock, first," the Penguin said. He led the way. Finally, when he could see water, he stopped. "Look out there and tell me what you see," he said, pointing with his umbrella.

The gang peered into the night. "Nothing but darkness," Clay said.

"*Primordial* darkness, darkness from which scum like you crawls." The Penguin let the hatred crawl back into his voice. *Batman used them to get to me. It's only fair I use them to get back to him, too. But first . . . a lesson.*

"I know you were working for Batman," the Penguin went on. "Don't bother trying to deny it. It was all a setup. I see it now. Wasn't it?" he screamed at them.

They just stared at him, looking bewildered . . . and a little scared.

"You're nuts," Clay finally said. "Forget the deal. We're history, old man!"

He started forward, but the Penguin raised his umbrella. Clay hesitated.

"Admit it!" the Penguin said through clenched teeth.

Clay tried to snatch the umbrella away, but the Penguin triggered another of its buttons. A luminous yellow gas shot out, enveloping Clay. He froze in place, his mouth open, his hand outstretched.

"What did ya do to him?" one of the others asked in a whisper.

"Paralysis gas." The Penguin gave Clay's inert form

a shove; he toppled backward and hit water a few seconds later with a quiet splash. "Any problems with that?"

"No!" they all hastened to say.

"Excellent. Exemplary, even." He peered over the edge of the pier, but couldn't see anything of Clay below.

"If he was working for Batman, Clay never told us about it," one of the others ventured to say. "We just did what he said, and he said, jump you."

The Penguin fitted his monocle back into place. "You there!" he said, pointing his umbrella. "I like you. What's your name?"

"D-David," he said, turning pale.

"You're my lieutenant. The others answer to you, but you answer to me. Got it?"

"Yes, sir!" David did a hasty approximation of a salute.

"Then let's get going," the Penguin said with a sneer. "I hate the docks. You never know what wharf-rats are going to turn up. And we have a lot of work to do." He glanced sidelong at David, his smile growing more sinister. "Our first project is money. More money than any of you have ever seen before. After that . . . Batman!"

AUGUST 14

"Sir," Alfred said, "I spotted an article in tonight's newspaper which I thought might interest you."

"Let me see it."

Bruce Wayne had just arrived with Vicki Vale for dinner. He'd spent the day doing a photo shoot with her: great buildings of Gotham City had been the subject. He'd managed to steer her to several of the most interesting rooftop gargoyles, and they'd had a great time together. For Alfred to interrupt their meal, it had to be something pretty important.

Alfred handed him a section of the paper, folded open to the society page. *What now?* Bruce wondered briefly, thinking some scandal-monger must have spread a juicy new bit ot gossip about his and Vicki's (nonexistent) wedding plans.

But it was the Penguin's photograph that drew his eye.

COBBLEPOT CHARITIES ANNOUNCED

Special to the *Gotham Gazette*

Criminals, beware! Cobblepot Charities has plans for you.

Oswald Cobblepot, a reformed criminal himself, has set up Cobblepot Charities to gainfully employ habitual criminals who need a break to return to the mainstream of society. Entirely funded by donations from the private sector, Cobblepot Charities has arranged for an exhibition of modern sculpture to appear in Gotham Park at the end of August. The exhibition will employ over one hundred people at a double miminum-wage.

A reformed criminal himself, Oswald Cobblepot (better known as the Penguin) has been leading the fight against poverty and despair by employing former criminals. His first step was to hire six young men who mugged him last week to act as security guards for the Gotham Park exhibition. When asked why he'd hire men who nearly killed him, Cobblepot replied, "They're just misguided." Cobblepot went on to add, "They need positive role models like me."

Reformed

Bruce scanned the rest of the article in growing anger. It went on to explain the Penguin's plan for setting up a continuing series of exhibits in Gotham Park, using criminals as its staff. The first project, an exhibition of huge concrete umbrellas sculpted by Coji Sama, a Thai artist, was set to open in two weeks. The Penguin had already arranged the necessary permits with the city.

When he got to the part about the Penguin dropping the charges against the six men who'd attacked him, Bruce set his jaw. He hadn't saved the Penguin to let those punks go free.

"You didn't give him the money, did you?" Vicki asked. She'd been reading the article over his shoulder.

"Sorry? What?" Bruce said.

"There." She pointed to the paragraph that said a wealthy individual had endowed Cobblepot Charities with three hundred thousand dollars to start off with, and how other donations had already added nearly sixty thousand dollars to the fund. "I know how generous you are, Bruce, but three hundred thousand to a criminal like the Penguin?"

"It wasn't me," Bruce said. "I wouldn't trust him with a nickel."

"Hey, it says he's reformed. Isn't it possible? Shouldn't we give him the benefit of the doubt?"

"I suppose . . ." He thought of the Penguin dressed in jeans and a plaid shirt, with a baseball cap on his head. The image didn't seem right, though . . . but then, nothing about the Penguin ever seemed quite right. Finally he put the paper down and forced a smile. "Let's eat, shall we? I'm starved." He offered her his arm, and she took it.

John Gregory Betancourt

After dinner, when Vicki left for the night, Bruce retired to his study and reread the article on the Penguin and his charities slowly and carefully. There had to be a diabolical plan of the Penguin's in motion, but he couldn't figure it out. *Maybe Vicki's right. Maybe he really has reformed.* Somehow, Bruce didn't buy that idea.

At last, he crumpled the paper in disgust. He wouldn't worry about it now, he decided; it was Friday night, which always meant trouble in Gotham City. Everyone would be out enjoying the night life . . . and rich people returning from the opera or a play made tempting targets. Not to mention homes left unguarded . . .

He suited up and headed into the city.

AUGUST 16

Phone call: Master Coji, this is Penguin . . . yes, thank you, I'm fine. How are you? . . . Terrific! I'm calling about the modifications to the umbrellas. Have you made them? . . . How nice. I'm looking forward to seeing them set up. Will delivery still come on schedule? Good. Yes, the check will be waiting for you. Thank you, sir. [click] Damn touchy Thais . . .

AUGUST 22

Phone call: Jerry! Penguin. I need a little of your expert advice again. . . . What money? I'm sure it's just

a little misunderstanding, easily cleared up. I'll send
you a check . . . yes, I really mean it. . . . That's better.
Tell me what you know about using colored-lights for
hypnosis . . . red and green? How fast? . . . Thanks,
Jerry. Check's in the mail, I promise. [click] Sucker.

AUGUST 28

Phone call: This is Mr. Potts. Did we get the MXO-5
missile contract? Good. I told you our bid would be the
lowest . . . no, don't use the regular disposal methods
for these babies. I'm shipping them to our other demol-
ition plant, the one in Oregon . . . no arguments, it's
my decision. That's why I own the company. . . . That's
better. Call me when they come in. I'll have trucks
ready next week . . . let me take care of the paperwork,
okay? . . . Thanks, Charlie. [click] Remind me to fire
him . . . too damned efficient, too likely to spot what
we're doing.

SEPTEMBER 8

The last few weeks had been all too routine for Batman:
he'd even begun thinking about cutting back on the
number of hours he spent patrolling the city. The worst
crime he'd come across was a lone burglar trying to
make off with a fax machine and a laser printer he'd
taken from an office building. Everything else had
been routine . . . backup for police a couple of times, for
firemen a couple of others (they'd even caught an arsonist themselves, a guy mad at his girlfriend; he'd
burned down her apartment complex). Once he even
rescued a kitten from a tree for a distressed senior
citizen. The cat promptly clawed the old lady and ran

John Gregory Betancourt

off, but Batman didn't try to catch it again for her. There are limits, he told himself, in what a slow night of crimefighting would drive him to.

Tonight, though . . . was it something in the air, an almost electric tingle that set his nerves on edge, which made him think, *This is the night they've been waiting for?*

He hadn't gone a block before he saw a young black man calmly breaking a storefront window with a brick. Alarms were already shrilling. Instead of taking anything from the storefront's display, though, the man calmly dropped the brick and walked on, hands in his pockets, strolling like nothing had happened.

Puzzled, half expecting a trap of some kind, Batman circled around and climbed down a fire escape. He emerged from an alleyway directly in front of the man, hands on hips, blocking the way.

"Batman!" the guy said.

Batman pointed back toward the window, advancing a step.

"I didn't take anything!" the man said. He licked his lips, eyes wide, searching for a way out. "Look, the dude that owns the place accused me of stealing today and fired me. It wasn't me, honest! But I just had to do something, had to take it out! Man, there are *real* criminals in this city. Why don't you pick on them?"

As if in answer, two limousines suddenly careened around the far corner of the block at breakneck speed. Their tires squealed on the pavement, leaving black skid marks, and they both fishtailed wildly. Someone leaned out of the lead car and squeezed off a round of automatic fire. Store windows burst up and down the block.

Batman didn't wait; he cast a grappling hook to the

roof and used an automatic recoil to pull him up after it. In seconds he was sprinting across the rooftops in hot pursuit . . . only the two cars seemed to have vanished.

He heard a new alarm begin to wail several blocks over. He turned and sprinted, ready for action. It looked like it was going to be one of those crazy nights where he didn't get a moment's peace.

The moving van looked like it was parked on a quiet side street. Inside, though, it seethed with action.

A detailed map of Gotham City covered a square perhaps six feet high and six feet wide, with every street and alley neatly drawn in. Pins with large yellow heads marked the Penguin's men: over two hundred of them, scattered throughout the city. A red flag marked Batman's last known position.

At the bank of radios, the original five thugs who'd mugged the Penguin a month before sat ready to dispatch their assault teams. They'd all been made lieutenants because of their seniority; now he'd put their talents to the test . . . not that anything could go wrong. It had all been planned to the smallest detail, right down to Batman's presence.

"New sighting," Franklin called from his radio set. He listened intently, then barked, "Fifth and Mulberry, headed south," to the mapkeeper, who dutifully moved the red Batman flag.

"Dispatch the Mulberry Street vandals," the Penguin said. They were eight teenagers who were supposed to break streetlights and car windows, creating as much havoc as they could.

Franklin spoke into his microphone. "Done," he announced. Then: "Batman's giving chase!"

"That's it, then!" the Penguin shouted, dancing a triumphant little jig. "Dispatch Team One! The Cold Lady's ours!"

Everyone in the van gave a whoop of joy. The Cold Lady, a four-hundred-carat diamond of singularly perfect clarity, was on display in the Natural History Museum. It was worth a king's ransom. The Penguin's men were putting the security guards on ice and shutting down the building's security system in preparation for the theft. He had enough diversions lined up to keep Batman running in circles all night.

"He's got all eight of them tied up," Franklin called.

"So fast?" the Penguin demanded.

"Dispatching drug-runners," Franklin said. They were supposed to have a running gunfight on the next street, drawing Batman away. Meanwhile, the vandals' backup team would cut them loose, get them into different clothes, and transport them ten blocks uptown, to get ready for their next diversion. "Batman's heard the gunfire. He's giving chase . . ."

The Penguin settled back. "Dispatch teams two and three," he said. There were a lot of valuable things in Gotham City tonight, and he wanted them all. He'd take the city for all it was worth . . . and there wasn't a thing Batman could do about it.

SEPTEMBER 9

Batman dragged himself home just before dawn. The city had gone crazy with crime, he thought. It had been a singularly frustrating night: every time he'd

Reformed

had a criminal cornered, something worse distracted him. He'd spent the night chasing vandals and drunken drivers and drug-dealers across the city. The end result? Four arrests out of dozens of crimes, and those four would probably be walking the streets again by nightfall . . . if the charges against them held up at all.

He showered and climbed into bed. Instantly he was asleep, dead to the world.

When he woke at noon, it was because Alfred was laying the morning papers out on the bedside table. "I'll take those," he said, yawning and sitting up.

"Yes, sir." Alfred handed him the first one.

BILLION-DOLLAR THEFT! The headlines screamed. It shocked Bruce fully awake. He read with growing horror about the crime spree that had swept through the city last night . . . the crime spree he'd completely missed because he'd been too busy chasing petty vandals to catch it.

A diamond worth two hundred millions dollars had been taken from the Natural History Museum. . . .

Bird's Armored Courier Service had lost no less than *three* trucks, collectively carrying half a billion dollars' worth of negotiable bonds and securities, and eighty million dollars in cash. . . .

The Ace Umbrella Company had lost an entire warehouse of antique Chinese silk umbrellas. . . .

It didn't take a genius to put the clues together: A gem called the Cold Lady . . . *Bird's* Armored Courier Service . . . a warehouse full of antique umbrellas. Who else could it be but the Penguin?

Phone call: Hello, Dr. Katz. This is Oswald Cobblepot . . . no, there's no problem. I'm calling you at home because I want to play a game of Scrabble with you this afternoon . . . I agree, it's a terrible idea. I'm glad you thought of it. Please come over as soon as you can. [click]

The Penguin paced in his small apartment's even smaller kitchenette, waiting impatiently. Batman had to sleep, he knew; but once the Caped Crusader had recovered from his night's exertions, he'd discover he'd been tricked . . . and the Penguin knew the trail of clues would lead him here. *Here,* in this case, being the small, tackily furnished apartment in which Arkham Asylum had set him up when he'd been released four months earlier.

The Penguin held a bowl of rapidly going-stale potato chips under one arm. It would help the effect, he knew, when Batman finally burst in on him. That . . . and having Dr. Katz here, playing Scrabble with him. He'd even arranged the board so it looked like they were in the middle of a game. The tiles on his tray spelled out R-E-F-O-R-M-D and would neatly give him a fifty-point bonus when he played them around an E next turn, plus a double-letter and a triple-word score. To bad they weren't really playing. Perhaps, once it was all done, he'd play out the round just to win it.

Dr. Katz was sitting on the sofa, eyes open but seeing nothing. She was breathing, and now and then she blinked, but other than that she didn't move or say a word. He'd hypno-gassed her again, then primed her with choice things to say to Batman once he showed up. All she needed was his presence and she'd snap awake like she'd never been away from the world.

His plan wasn't to trap Batman, but to put him offguard. He wanted Batman to follow him into

Reformed

Gotham Park that night, where he'd spring the *real* trap. So far, Batman had played into his hands.

The Penguin glanced at the clock on the wall. It was a giant cat's face, with eyes that moved in time to the tail-shaped pendulum. Just past three o'clock. *Come on, come on,* he thought. *Hurry up, Bat-Brain. I haven't got all day.*

As if on cue, Batman suddenly dropped onto the balcony outside the living room: The Penguin could see his silhouette through the sheer curtains. He'd left the balcony's door ajar in case Batman chose to enter that way.

The Penguin took a step back, shifted the potato chip bowl to both hands, and strode into the living room—

Just as Batman shoved his way in.

"Hey!" the Penguin protested. "What do you think you're doing, barging in here!"

Batman stalked forward. "Where were you last night, Penguin? Between eight o'clock and three in the morning?"

"I-I-I-" the Penguin began. He let the bowl of potato chips drop from his hands; chips scattered across the floor. He took a step back, looking panicked. His lower lip began to tremble.

Batman advanced on him. "Tell me!" he thundered. "You sniveling little clown—"

The Penguin sank to the floor and began to sob helplessly.

Batman halted in amazement, staring at the little man curled up on the floor. "Penguin?" he said uncertainly.

"What do you think you're doing?" a woman's voice demanded from behind him. "Do you have any idea what damage you might have just done, you caped moron?"

Batman whirled. A woman in her forties had risen from the sofa on the other side of the room. There was a Scrabble board open on the coffee table; they were obviously in the midst of play.

"Who are you?" he asked.

"I'm Dr. Judith Katz, of the Arkham Asylum, if you must know—Oswald's doctor. Where do you get off, barging in here and asking him all these questions?" She came out from around the coffee table and advanced on Batman steadily, shaking a finger at him. "Oswald is under my *personal* supervision, and I won't have you harassing him! If you ask me, you're as deeply disturbed as the patients in Arkham! Now kindly apologize to Oswald—then get out, and I'll see if I can repair the damage you've done!"

Batman looked down at the Penguin, still sobbing helplessly on the floor, then up at Dr. Katz. "Your I.D.," he said.

She pulled it from her purse and waved it at him. He caught her arm, studied it, studied her face, then looked down at the Penguin once more.

"I'm . . . sorry if I have inconvenienced your work, Doctor," he said. He turned and left the apartment, grabbed the line he'd left outside in case he needed a quick escape, and let it pull him toward the roof. All the way up, he puzzled over what he'd seen.

The clues were obvious . . . perhaps *too* obvious. But with Joker and Riddler and Two-Face safely behind bars in Arkham Asylum, who else could possibly be responsible? A copycat criminal? Copy*cat*? Catwoman? It was something to think about; he hadn't heard from her in quite some time. . . .

In the Penguin's apartment, the sobs slowly became laughs. Finally the Penguin sat up, rubbing his eyes. "Help me up," he told Dr. Katz.

"Let me help you up," she said, offering her hand. When he took it, she pulled him to his feet.

"Sit down and we'll play out our hand of Scrabble," the Penguin said. "Then it's time for you to go home, relax, and forget you've seen me today. Okay?"

"Okay," she said happily. She was still smiling when the Penguin played his triple-word-score word.

Batman decided to find out if the Penguin was up to anything more than he appeared to be and stationed himself on a nearby roof, overlooking the entrance to the Penguin's apartment building.

He watched the psychiatrist leave fifteen minutes later, but didn't follow her. Her I.D. had looked real enough; he'd check it out later, if necessary. Now, though, he had bigger birds to fry.

A few minutes later, the Penguin, still dressed in jeans and a T-shirt, also left the building. His tears were gone; he looked left and right, then crossed the street and headed uptown as though he had a purpose in mind.

Batman followed on the rooftops.

Over the next four hours, the Penguin led him on a

leisurely tour of the city, from one church mission to another, and finally to the Gotham Orphanage. That raised Batman's eyebrows: What could the Penguin possibly want there?

Finally, as dusk was falling, the Penguin headed for Gotham Park. *That's where his exhibit is set up,* Batman remembered. It consisted of twenty-five-foot-high concrete umbrellas, all open and lying on their sides: you could walk among them, but you weren't allowed to touch. Each umbrella had been roped off, and a former criminal stood there to answer questions. Each umbrella represented a Thai earth-spirit, according to the artist, and each had a little story, which its guardian would recite if asked.

It was nearly dark as the Penguin entered the park. All of the exhibit's employees had already gone home. Batman watched from the roof of a ten-story building until the Penguin vanished down the winding path among the giant umbrellas, then he descended and followed.

It was eerily quiet in the park. A faint wind rustled through the trees every few moments, but other than that, it was deathly still. The Penguin had vanished.

As he passed the last umbrella, Batman felt something tugging at him from behind. He started to turn—but his feet were yanked away from him, and he found himself flying through the air.

He struck something hard and paused for a moment, dazed. He couldn't move no matter how hard he tried; it was as though he were stuck to a gigantic piece of flypaper.

In the distance he heard a helicopter. It seemed to be getting closer, he thought.

Reformed

Forcing down panic, he approached the problem calmly and methodically. He tried moving his fingers; they functioned normally. It was his gauntlets that were stuck . . . particularly the metal in his gauntlets.

I'm stuck to a magnet, he realized. It had to be an electromagnet for it to be this powerful, he thought.

The helicopter came into view over the treetops. It was a large helicopter, like the one the Navy used at sea . . . only it didn't have the Navy's insignia. It had a penguin blazed across its side, with Cobblepot Charities written below it. Now he recalled seeing helicopters used to transport the giant concrete umbrellas. This helicopter was already lowering a gigantic hook to snag the umbrella's handle.

The umbrella teetered dizzily, then with a slight jerk it was airborne. Batman watched the ground recede slowly, as he worked to free his hands. By the time he'd worked his hands from his gauntlets—which continued to stick to the umbrella's concrete side—he was already forty feet in the air. After that it was a simple matter to release his helmet and slip out of his boots. Now only his utility belt held him to the umbrella, and he held his fingers poised over the buckle, waiting for his chance.

The umbrella barely cleared the first building they came to. Releasing himself, Batman dropped to the roof and rolled for cover, praying nobody on the helicopter had seen him. Apparently they hadn't; he watched silently as the helicopter towed the umbrella out over the river . . . and released it.

Batman knew he would have drowned if he'd still been stuck to the side of the umbrella. It had been close . . . too close. But at least the Penguin had shown his true colors. Now that he knew the Penguin was behind the thefts, and the Penguin thought him dead, he could proceed at a better pace.

First, though, he had to make a collect call to Alfred. His butler was going to have to make an emergency trip into the city to pick him up. Batman walked to the fire escape and began to climb down toward the alleyway below.

Two hours later, outfitted with a spare Batman suit, he returned to Gotham City using the Batglider. He winged over Gotham Park, studying the umbrellas below. Floodlights were on; there was a lot of activity, including several empty flatbed trucks. No, wait . . . one of the trucks still had its cargo . . . and it looked like a missile!

He brought the Batglider in to land with its rocket-pack off. He coasted briefly over the lake at the center of Gotham Park, then came in for a soft landing on the beach and disengaged the backpack.

In the distance, from where the umbrellas stood, he could hear shouts, the noise of heavy equipment. Something big was up, no question about it.

More like a phantom than a human, he drifted through the trees, between the sentries the Penguin had posted, until he came to the sculptures once more. He arrived just in time to see the last of the flatbed trucks rolling away. The missle he'd seen had vanished.

"Batman's been spotted, sir," David said softly.

"What?" the Penguin screamed. He whirled on his lieutenant. "He's dead! We dropped him in the river!"

"Take a look, sir. Camera three."

The Penguin glared at the monitor. It took him a second, but he picked out Batman's silhouette among the trees. *This man is incredible. He doesn't know when he's been beaten.*

"Floodlights?" David asked.

"Yes . . . and then activate the first umbrella. And arm the missiles, too."

"Yes, sir!" His hands were a blur over the controls.

Floodlights flashed to life around Batman. He jumped, startled, then knew he'd been spotted somehow. It didn't matter: spotted or not, he still had a job to do.

He started forward at a run—then drew up short.

The umbrella in front of him had risen up on its pointy end. As he watched, it began to spin, around and around, and green and red lights set along its rim began to blink hypnotically. Batman felt his eyes begin to track the moving lights against his will. Slowly he began to . . .

Deep inside the largest umbrella, the Penguin watched on a video monitor, chuckling. Batman was finally in his power, and there wasn't anything that could stop him now.

"He's ours, boys," he told his lieutenants. "Bring him in."

They donned special goggles to protect them from the hypnotic effect of the spinning umbrella, then went

John Gregory Betancourt

out after Batman. The Penguin watched on the monitors as they pushed Batman over—he seemed stiff, like a statue himself—and carried him in to see the Penguin.

. . . Which is what Batman had been waiting for. He'd been keeping his body as stiff as he could, keeping his eyes closed and faking a hypnotic trance. When they carried him into one of the umbrellas and closed the concrete hatch behind them with a thud, sealing them all in together, he saw his chance and knew it was time to make his move.

He burst into action, knocking the nearest of the Penguin's thugs into two of the others. They fell in a heap, shouting in protest. Before any of the others could react, Batman pounded two of them on their heads; they collapsed glassy-eyed.

The Penguin was shooting a pale green gas from his umbrella. Batman's cowl had a filter built-in; he tongued it into his mouth and breathed through it. Around him the Penguin's thugs collapsed one by one, clawing at their throats before falling unconscious.

"It's just the two of us now," Batman said, "and crying can't save you this time."

He took a step toward the Penguin. Then another.

The Penguin pointed his umbrella at Batman. Two darts flashed out. Both deflected off of Batman's armored chestplate.

He stepped forward again.

"Wait!" the Penguin cried. "Stay where you are!"

"Why?" Batman demanded.

Flicking open the handle of his umbrella, the Penguin revealed three miniature buttons. "I have six

MXO-5 missiles in the other umbrellas. Each one is stuffed to the gills with explosives—and they're all aimed at the financial district. One more step and I'll destroy billions of dollars in property and business for the city!"

"Unless?" Batman prompted.

Slowly the Penguin smiled. "Unless," he said, "my demand are met. One billion dollars in cash. Small, unmarked bills, please, to be delivered to me here."

Batman took another step closer. Then another.

"Stay back!" the Penguin screeched. "I'm warning you—one more inch and the missles fly!"

Batman said, "Go ahead." Calmly he continued his advance.

At the last moment, the Penguin punched the firing button. "Missiles away!" he screamed. *"Die! Die! Die!"*

The park outside remained silent. Batman heard no missiles launching; he'd guessed right.

The Penguin was still pounding the firing buttons when Batman reached out and plucked the umbrella from his grasp. He broke it over his knee as the Penguin watched in mute horror.

"How . . . why . . ." he whimpered.

"You're completely surrounded—top, sides, floor—by thick concrete walls. A radio signal can't penetrate it. If you'd been outside," Batman said, "it would have worked."

"Oh," the Penguin said.

He looked up just in time to meet Batman's fist. The blow knocked him back against the umbrella's wall, where he collapsed, dazed.

Working quickly and methodically, Batman tied him up. Then he turned his attention to the Penguin's five unconscious thugs.

John Gregory Betancourt

Once they were tied up, he dragged them outside one by one. He left them stacked like cordwood while he called Commissioner Gordon on the cellular phone in his utility belt.

Then he waited in silence, under the cover of the trees, until the police arrived—sirens screaming, red lights flashing—to cordon off the park. The bomb squad began a systematic search for the missiles as the Penguin and his men were hauled into a police wagon and carted off into the night.

Batman turned and walked back to the Batglider. His job here was done, but Gotham City still had a need for him this night. Far off, from somewhere across the other side of Gotham Park, he heard the sounds of gunfire and a woman screaming.

Vulture
A Tale of the Penguin

"Thou wast not born for death, immortal Bird!"
—Ode to a Nightingale
John Keats 1795–1821

STEVE RASNIC TEM

GOTHAM PRISON

The Penguin wrote it large and bold, as if he were captioning a comic panel. The stick of black chalk broke between his fingers. He cursed, gripped a smaller piece, and pressed it even more fiercly into the rough texture of his cell wall. Daring it to break. Daring one of the guards to come by and stop his graffiti. They made no allowance for art here. They made no allowances. The Penguin stroked the letters of his fate again and again, thickening them almost to the point of unreadability. Determined not to forget. Determined to locate himself exactly in space and in time. Gotham Prison, U.S. of A., April fourteen, nineteen hundred ninety-one, somewhat after the evening meal, Friday.

For some the need was to forget exactly where they were, to make their surroundings as comfortable as possible, to make themselves "at home." Those were the ones who would never leave. Those were the ones who eventually spoke to friends, spouses who were not there.

Vulture

So the Penguin had permitted himself to be reduced
to the status of an ordinary inmate, forgoing all the
perks and comforts his money and stature might have
bought him in this place, where anything was available for the right price. He had permitted himself, in
fact, to be reduced to Oswald Cobblepot, a short, small,
almost timid man, an unlikely figure for such a flamboyant career criminal. New inmates wondered aloud
what such a man might be doing in maximum security,
until a veteran would whisper the information, after
which the new man would speak of Cobblepot no more.
Cobblepot wanted it that way, and in that one cir-
cumstance was not loathe to use some deadly influence
to get his way. Because of his appearance, people had
always underestimated him, right from the beginning.

The images drifted back pleasantly through his head
of the Bull—he of the thick neck and square hands
and phlegm-inspired speech patterns—who'd been
transferred into Gotham from a somewhat smaller
facility near the southern edge of the state. The Bull
must have been some sort of enforcer there, and upon
his arrival in the yard had apparently forgotten the
fact of his recent relocation. Almost immediately he
was telling inmates what to do—those foolish enough
to stumble into his self-conscious stroll—picking quar-
rels with those long-established enough that they had
territory to preserve, and generally playing the
school yard bully. The Penguin was reminded of his
own school yard nemesis Sharkey, a comparison that
was definitely not to be to Bull's advantage.

"Little man," he'd called him. "Puny little man . . ."
and then he'd laid those square hands on the Penguin's
shoulders, and stroked his belly, and asked what such
a little man as he was doing in prison.

Steve Rasnic Tem

Later that afternoon the guards had found the Bull
with both of those square hands shoved halfway down
his throat—a throat that, surprisingly, had proven too
small for them.

The Penguin's outfit—top hat and tails, formal
grays, bow tie, and vest—was stored away somewhere
deep within the bowels of the prison. He'd always been
the Penguin before, even in prison garb, but not this
time. This time he didn't think he would be donning
his "penguin suit" ever again. Now he saw the uniform
as a useless affectation, a sympton of his addiction to
celebrity, something that had brought much trouble
and pain into his life.

He thought of the hundreds of cleverly rigged umbrellas he had stashed in storage facilities all over
Gotham. The umbrellas that sprayed various gases,
the umbrellas that shot out nets and grappling devices,
the liquid sprays, the umbrella machine guns, the umbrella flamethrowers, the acetylene torches, the dart
guns, the grenade launchers. It was the arsenal of an
entire career, enough weaponry for a vast army of
militant Mary Poppinses. It was a dangerous legacy
he had left the city, he knew, perhaps all the more
dangerous because of its apparently innocuous appearance. He mused over images of some of his bumber-
shoots ending up in garage and estate sales, and of
old ladies mowing down benches full of bus riders as
they attempted to open up their newly purchased umbrellas in light of a sudden downpour. A light drizzle
could mean disaster for Gotham under those circumstances.

The owners of those storage facilities would have a
curious time of it after he failed to retrieve all his
equipment. He wondered if he should warn someone

of the potential danger, but could see no advantage in
this for him.

Thinking to scribble at least one bit of beauty above
this stark destination, he pulled himself up on tiptoes,
but still could not sufficiently reach above "GOTHAM
PRISON" to set down the brief passage of his beloved
Keats's genius. He hadn't the stature. Most of his life
he had thought he could acquire any desire, rid himself
of any distraction, reach any pinnacle. Now he was
simply a diminutive felon of dubious prospects, standing up on a stool like some schoolchild intent on defac-
ing the school wall with some of his favorite poesy.

Closer of lovely eyes to lovely dreams,
Lover of loneliness, and wandering,
Of upcast eye, and tender pondering!

Something in his dream of the previous evening had
reminded him of this passage of Keats. At the moment
it seemed the perfect portrait of his current mental
state, but he was convinced that in the dream it was
another figure being referenced: a dark, caped figure,
night's close companion and lonely supplicant, who
had skulked through Cobblepot's nightmares every
eve during this most recent incarceration. Beautiful
in his way: in his handsome suit of blue and gray, his
cowl as finely chiseled in its profile as a piece of classical sculpture, whose pale slits obscured eyes that—
Cobblepot had no doubt of it—were sorely troubled, if
not aflutter with madness itself.

Only his Keats brought him solace at such a time.
And like his beloved Keats, he was poorly understood,
all too seldomly appreciated. The average citizen had

never seemed able to fully appreciate the effort, the planning, or the expense that necessarily went into the Penguin's various exploits. All those clever umbrellas were hardly worth the exorbitant fees he paid for their construction in any practical scheme of things.

Why not use conventional weaponry? Because he had been the Penguin, of course! The conventional would only have disappointed. His public expected elaborate criminal escapades from him, and each new crime had to be even more elaborate, and larger in scope, than the previous one. The public had a short memory—you were only as good as your last crime. There were always new costumed criminals coming up in the ranks, younger men than you, sometimes with bigger bankrolls, and sometimes even with more talent. Old-timers like himself had to stay on their toes.

And gang members expected to be paid, and the equipment necessary for the largest thefts, of course, was quite specialized. Certainly one couldn't walk into the local hardware store and order up a massive crane, or purchase a bird-shaped plane from your standard dealer in family vehicles. These crimes operated under rarefied aesthetics, producing art as difficult and obscure as most poetry seemed to be to the common man. It required an experienced connoisseur of such matters to fully appreciate what it was the Penguin was attempting to do.

Unfortunately that person most experienced, most qualified to critique his work, had been the man who had put him here, the Batman himself. And the Batman, unfortunately, had always had his own theoretical axes to grind.

Keats had had his own unreasonable, boorish critics, certainly, but at least he hadn't been jailed due to their efforts.

The man in the next cell was choking to death on his own vomitus. Another lovely evening in Gotham Prison. Not that the Penguin—no, Oswald Cobblepot—cared one whit about the cretin's demise. He just wished the man would perform this final act a bit more quietly, and with much less aroma.

Deep in the shady sadness of a vale far sunken from the healthy breath of morn . . .

At least his neighbor's regurgitations made it somewhat easier to persist with his current manipulation of the Gotham Prison authorities. Sometimes he thought this current hunger strike an inspired product of his genius, at other times the ultimate foolishness. Whichever, it was too late for him to alter the course now. He doubted he could eat even if he forced himself, even if it were the finest culinary masterpiece he'd encountered in a lifetime of such splendid encounters. Over time, his belly had shrunk, his muscles wasted, his skin gone flaccid, then tightened to his frame. The experts had been saying he should have been dead by now. Obviously they did not understand the soul of the artist. Twenty pounds, fifty pounds, then a hundred, had been carved away from his rotund core.

The comic antics of the American Civil Liberties Union had made his desperate maneuver possible. When the prison doctors had made their first noises of intervention, a simple call to the ACLU had obtained a temporary restraining order. Further, often heated, litigation had stopped the authorities from forcing nourishment upon him. Of course, however, he permitted the occasional intravenous fluids to prevent dehy-

Steve Rasnic Tem

dration, as well as vitamin injections to stave off complete debilitation—Oswald did not want to die (at least he did not think so, despite his intermittent depression of late).

"OK, Penguin, tonight's dinner, and it's a beauty—the best yet, I think."

Oswald looked up at the narrow horizontal slot in the upper third of his steel cell-door. One eye there was green and staring in a different direction from the other brown one. The Irishman, of course, with his patriotic glass eye. Supposedly he'd lost the real one during a prison riot some twenty years before, but Oswald suspected a clumsy dining accident of more recent vintage. They still tried him every evening like this—ordering out to a different restaurant each time in hopes of finding the one cuisine that would eventually break him. He assumed that the Irishman was consuming his rejects—the man had gained at least forty pounds over the past few months. The thin get thinner while the fat swell up and burst. "No, thank you," he answered as his part of the ritual.

"Oh, now, don't you be a shy bird," the Irishman crooned, unlocking the cell door. This statement, also, was a scripted part of the ritual.

The fat guard waddled in, pushing the door closed behind him with a quivering sack of hip. "I have a nice suit down in the Personal Belongings Center that might fit you nicely, Irish. It just might be a bit short in the legs, however."

The Irishman chuckled with an edge of menace. "You should be taking that show on the road, Birdy." He paused. "But, of course, you won't." He chuckled again. "So what have we this dinnertime?"

The Irishman lifted off the shiny silver cover, revealing pasta primavera, with sides of steamed vegetables, julienne potatoes, and an exquisite frozen chocolate terrine. Oswald leaned closer and was duly impressed to find that the pasta's sauce was of just the right consistency, and the vegetables betrayed no signs of drooping. "Very attractive," he said, "but I'm afraid I'm on a bit of a diet just now. You might try it yourself, you know? Keeps the senses sharp? I heard that's quite important if one's career is in law enforcement."

The Irishman snarled, turned and left. He'd appeared angry enough to throw the tray, but Oswald knew he'd never be able to bring himself to destroy such a meal. Even now he was no doubt rushing to his station before the pasta got cold.

Every night it was the same. The temptation was presented, but they had to accept his refusal. The ACLU had made sure of that. The story of his strike had been in the papers every day. PENGUIN WON'T EAT! "THE BATMAN MADE ME HATE FOOD!" SAYS COBBLEPOT. Various opposing groups had come forward: The Rights of the Overweight, Personal Choice of the Dying, Victims of Costumed Criminals, The National Council of Churches, all arguing their particular slant on the issue, none of them caring a whit about Oswald himself. The Batman had been quoted as saying that he knew the Penguin better than anyone, and the Penguin "was definitely up to something." Very perceptive, Bat-twit.

Hours later he was still seeing that beautiful meal. It was an aesthetic interest purely—the chef had obviously known how to present a pleasing arrangement. In any case, at this point Oswald could never have kept the meal down. He stretched out on his narrow

Steve Rasnic Tem

bed. It seemed much harder now that he had lost all
his padding from hips, buttocks, and shoulders. He felt
as if his bones were in direct contact with steel, rubbing, scraping. A chicken sautéed in a cast-iron skillet.

He could hardly move his limbs. *Upon the sodden
ground his old right hand lay nerveless, listless, dead.*
He could not, or would not, lift himself from the narrow
bed. *While his bowed head seemed listening to the
Earth...* Eventually he fell asleep.

Again in the dream he was flying. He had his old
body back—in fact, he was fatter than ever—and yet
he flew as if he weighed next to nothing. Even more
peculiar, he was so relaxed in the dream itself that he
was content to fly with his eyes closed. In fact, he
seemed to be flying while still fast asleep. *O soft em-
balmer of the still midnight, shutting, with careful
fingers and benign, our gloom-pleased eyes.*

Suddenly out from behind the moon floated a great,
winged thing. Huge, membranous wings and a rat's
dirty gray-furred body. Hideous sharp teeth and ears
of monstrous size. Ears so huge, in fact, that poor Oswald knew they were capable of hearing everything
he was thinking, everything he was dreaming as well.

He tried to maneuver out of the great bat's path,
but he was much too large now—his belly got in the
way and his system felt sluggish. He struggled to turn
and dive, but the great bat was on him almost immediately, sinking dagger-length teeth into his vulnerable, exposed belly.

Chunks of him separated into pale flesh tumbling
earthward, thin blood floating overhead in intricate
streamers. The ground rushed up, but his body would
doubtless disintegrate completely before that hard
landing.

Vulture

Oswald awoke with a scream. Sometimes the dreams were just too much to take.

I saw their starved lips in the gloam,
*   With horrid warning gaped wide,*
And I awoke and found me here,
*   On the cold hill's side.*

"Hey, Penguin! Glory be, it's shredded chicken, skillet-fried with vegetables Provençale!"

Oswald crouched on top of his sink at the side of the cell where the Irishman's glass eye now gave its lifeless stare. His legs tensed, bird of prey ready for departure. "I believe . . ." he said softly. "I believe I might try something this evening."

"What? Did I hear you correctly, Old Bird?" Obvious disappointment. "Why, wonderful . . . *Good* news for us all!" Now seeing the personal advantage in the situation, the possibility of promotion. "Maybe I'll . . . get a sandwich . . . join you on the occasion." The lock clicked, the door swung Oswald's way.

In midleap, Oswald's right foot shot out to slam the cell door closed. (Unfortunate, but necessary for secrecy.) He held both hands with fingers touching, pointed into beaklike shapes, then opening into long narrow claws, and thought of his favorite Hitchcock movie as he went for the Irishman's eyes: the useful, and the purely decorative.

It seem'd an emerald in the silver sheen of the bright waters . . .

Oswald picked up the bit of glass eye and wedged it painfully over his own. Then he pushed that part of

Steve Rasnic Tem

his face into the eye slot of the cell door, careful to
keep his all-too-recognizable nose bent out of sight.

"Collins! Get over here! The bird has me locked in
here with him!" It was a poor accent, but it would have
to do. Besides, the Irishman had had only touches of
the brogue remaining anyway.

Collins came running over, caught one glimpse of
the Irishman's bright and gleaming eye, and hurriedly
jammed the key into the lock.

The door sprang open and Oswald crushed the guard
into the far wall with all one hundred pounds of his
desperate and angry weight. The man wheezed and
passed out. Collins was a thin, emaciated figure. Oswald had heard he'd been quite ill—he shouldn't have
kept working.

He stripped the unconscious guard and slipped into
the slight uniform, which only months ago would have
been much too small for him. He clutched the key ring
so tightly he could feel his palm begin to sweat, or
bleed.

Someday the diary Oswald would keep to recall these
events would begin this page with MONTHS LATER
. . . in boldface lettering. Below that would be a large
square panel: his pen sketch of a falling-down brownstone, the shadows heavily inked and threatening to
spread across the page.

The label on the mailbox downstairs said "A. Ornis,"
but the resident of apartment number four was in fact
Oswald Chesterfield Cobblepot, expert (some would
say "obsessed") in the areas of birds and umbrellas,
foremost Keats scholar, aka the Penguin. Although he
had broken out of Gotham Prison nine months ago,

Vulture

Oswald surprisingly was not thinking of what crimes he might perform. He hadn't done so much as shoplift a candy bar since he'd been out. He'd had no fantasies of burglary, counterfeiting, blackmail, kidnapping, murder, or even petty theft. Every night Oswald did not dream of the wealth he might obtain. Instead Oswald dreamed of a beautiful bird in free flight, suddenly savaged by a huge and vicious bat.

He had moved into the neighborhood as quickly and as quietly as possible. He dared not contact any of the members of his old gang, or go to any of those locations where he normally cached equipment and funds for the occasion of his previous escapes from prison. Perhaps there was no legitimate reason for his added caution this time around, but Oswald felt deeply that his entire life had finally been compromised by the Batman, and if he were to return to any part of that old life, the Batman would know almost immediately and set upon him with fang, cape, and claw.

So he'd had to rob the safe deposit box of his dearly departed aunt, take the inheritance due the cousins who had no idea he even existed, so ashamed of him his relatives had become. He'd been prepared to take this step in an emergency for years, although his pride had hoped it would not be necessary. The money was only a small amount, but enough to keep body and soul together for at least a brief time.

Now Morning from her orient chamber came...

Waking was Oswald's most difficult task of the day, wriggling free of the shadows of claws and bared teeth, the scalloped drape of the Batman's dark cape, kicking it away with feet wrapped and bound by the twisted rope of it, pushing away the needle incisors and curved

Steve Rasnic Tem

nails with the flat of his hands that bled and bled from the Batman's, the madman's, rabid attack.

But more disorienting still was the fact that with this new body of his he *could* wriggle, he could twist and buck, and the sheets and blankets could wrap around him more than once. He bolted upright (*bolted,* another act he could never have performed before) and stared at his hands: their stiffness, their skeletal thinness, soaked and pale with rancid perspiration, not blood. After all this time, they were still unfamiliar to him in the first unlying blaze of day. As if during the night the prison surgeon had used him for some sort of Nazi experiment, grafting someone else's arms onto the stumps of his shoulders. He swung his legs over the side of the bed and they, too, belonged to some other prisoner, some other atrocity.

But as he walked to the bathroom (but not *waddled,* never would he waddle again), it was as if his consciousness settled back into this new body with each step, so that by the time he reached over for soap and water he was fully himself, Oswald Cobblepot, of no other name, no other identity.

If one of the members of any of his old gangs was to see him, he'd be sure he was suffering from some terrible disease. "Cripes, Penguin, me old pal! You ain't got the cancer, do you?" Stonehead had always been the sentimental sort. There'd been little room in that thick head of his for anything else.

Nehemiah "Knuckles" O'Rourke would have been similarly concerned, of course. "Dat bird peck ya, Boss? Dose birds peck ya good? Hooo-ey! Dey did ya good, dey did—like I knew dey wud!" Cowardly paranoid, he'd never cared much for the birds.

Or the beautiful Lark. "Sir! Sir, what's happened to you, sir? Perhaps I should drive you to a doctor?" Sweet, always professional, but well-paid for those traits. If he hadn't had the money to pay her, she wouldn't even have acknowledged his existence.

The old voices and faces faded away. Perhaps their minimal concerns were poor substitutes for those of a wife, children, family, but they had been all he'd ever had. They would have to suffice.

For sure so fair a place was never seen, of all that ever charm'd romantic eye.

At one time Oswald would have been appalled to find himself in such decrepit surroundings. Flowery wallpaper curled down in narrow streamers as if some pentup slasher had murdered the feminine taste of the walls. Hardwood floors had been haphazardly layered over with linoleum and tile and disintegrating rug. The yellowed paint they'd used to coat the trim was pocked, diseased, ready pills of illness for some wayward toddler with an appetite for decor. Stuffing had exploded from the furniture, grown soggy from damp, then allowed to corrupt slowly in these rooms overheated by rusted steam. Bits of trash had been scattered everywhere, much of it glued to the dusty surfaces by unknown, unrecognizable adhesives.

But perfect quarters for a scavenger bird, content to live off the leavings and the sorrow of nature's unfortunates.

Now that he was out of prison he felt his old appetite should return. Afterall, he was safe. No one could recognize him, and even if he put on a *little* weight he seriously didn't think anyone would recognize him, and if he put on a *lot* of weight, well, he didn't really want to be the Penguin anymore anyway. He would just be another short, fat man with a secret past, a nobody who would bother no one ever again.

But his appetite did not return. He still could eat very little. Sometimes just the thought of eating sent him running into the bathroom, the stomach acid raging up his throat and scalding his taste buds with that sickening, characteristic flavor of hot peanut oil.

If he were fat again, he would look like the Penguin again. If he looked like the Penguin again, the Batman would find him.

He kept his refrigerator full of food just in case he should have the urge to eat. He still had hoped that one day this fearsome spell might suddenly lift from him and he would be able to eat as he had in the old days. To help this along he would try not to think about what he was eating. He tried not to visualize it. He tried not to see the creamy milk so white it glowed with its own inner light, the scalloped potatoes with their crisp edges and almost liquid centers, topped with bright red slices of oven-baked ham, the jars of honey-brown peanut butter layered and swirled with golden nuggets, the purple majesty of the eggplant, the yellow fluffiness of the omelet, the rich red sauce of the spaghetti and its yards of ivory paste, the bright orange chunks of marmalade lying in the bottom of the can, the delicate fairy quality of his aunt's apple strudel, the crisp bodies of bright green asparagus, halves of chicken baked to a bright red-orange, Tandori style.

He even attempted to forget all the words he had ever known for the varieties of food. Words like oven-baked, patties, thyme, orzo, broccoli, dilled, broth, seasoned to taste, semisweet, mousse, confectioners sugar, shrimp, deveined, granules, parfait, liqueur.

When he ate, he tried to pretend he was simply

breathing. When he chewed, he tried to pretend he
was simply speaking aloud. When he swallowed, he
told himself he was singing. When he was digesting,
he told himself he was thinking. And yet despite all
these mental tricks, he discovered that he could still
only nibble a few crumbs at a time.

For sometimes when he opened the refrigerator all
he could see were the bloody bodies of birds, torn apart
by the vicious bat of his nightmares. Every time he
would stare into that bloody refrigerator, trying not
to see the raw, fetid bird corpses there, and attempted
to eat a little more, he saw the Batman's shadow at
the window or heard his graceful footsteps in the hall.

Sometimes he would run to the door and jerk it open.
He never saw anything, and always felt more than a
little foolish, but now and then he imagined he saw
just a sliver of cape curling around the corner.

In Oswald's mirror the loose flesh of his emaciated
jowls wobbled obscenely. Sometimes he would try on
one of his old, soiled and tattered tuxedos and attempt
to picture the man he had been. But he lacked ambition, even the minimal ambition required to clean and
repair one of those old tuxedos. The decrepit suit hung
from his starved frame like a ragged funeral shroud.

Eventually the remaining food in his refrigerator
spoiled before he could eat more than a small percen-
tage of it. This made eating even more difficult, of
course, as he now had accumulated images of souring,
spoiling, rotting food to contend with.

He had to have some sort of a plan, of course, but
all his planning energies seemed to have been depleted
by his prison break. His story continued to drift in and
out of the papers. The ACLU and several other groups
seemed convinced that a man in his weakened state,

Steve Rasnic Tem

even a "master criminal" (oh, but he *thrilled* to that passage), would have been quite unable to pull off such a feat. Leaders of these groups implied that some sort of a coverup was taking place, that perhaps the Penguin had been murdered by an overzealous guard (the Irishman, now fully recovered, and looking quite a bit thinner, had had his picture in the papers several times), or perhaps by the uncontrollable vigilante Batman himself. The Batman refused to dignify such speculations with a comment, of course. Oswald had always known the man to be the closemouthed, anal-retentive sort.

Other people, most notably the relatives of the Penguin's various victims, had their own opinions. "He's made a clean escape for sure," the father of a guard shot during a robbery at Gotham Airport was quoted as saying. "No one's going to catch that bird, not if he got himself a good tailwind!" The man had made himself into a celebrity discussing his bereavement publicly and in detail with various news outlets. The man did not yet know, as Oswald had learned all too well, that fame was a kind of sickness. *Fame, like a wayward girl, will still be coy to those who woo her with too slavish knees.*

The wife of a man killed when the Penguin had ordered a flock of birds to attack traffic leaving a highway tunnel was livid. "I demand that some high-level officials be fired! There's no excuse for such laxity in view of what that psychopath is capable of!"

"The citizens of Gotham are in grave danger," reported the tearful daughter of another victim of that same highway incident. "Why aren't the police out there protecting the people?"

Oswald found these attitudes ludicrous. He was in

no position to hurt anyone. And, surprisingly, it bothered him that the Irishman might lose his job over this.

But a plan was necessary. He needed to leave his apartment if he was to live, and escape the Bat-thing that so tormented his sleep. *O comfortable bird, that broodest o'er the troubled sea of the mind till it is hushed and smooth.* He dare not go out as the Penguin just yet. In fact, he dare not ever go out as the Penguin again. To do so would be a mockery of the man he had been. Who was he kidding? Once again he looked at himself in the mirror. The Penguin was quite dead. The Batman had killed him, just as they'd all suspected.

Where once he had been full of fun and humor, now his posture in the world seemed far more like that of the Batman who he despised and feared. Where once he consumed the world, the world now consumed him. A plan was essential. He had always been good at plans. But a plan would not come to him.

Obviously he would first require more sleep. Oswald had been getting so little sleep. The dreams always intruded. But he could not plan adequately without more sleep.

The pains my wounded ear...

All over Gotham the birds were screaming. In his nightmare Oswald tried to wake himself up, but failed again and again as the Batman pulled him back down into sleep and terror and pools of shattered, bleeding birds.

After a few weeks it became obvious to Oswald that no one was going to recognize him as the Penguin out on the street. He could move about with impunity, if his courage so allowed him. So he exposed himself

Steve Rasnic Tem

gradually at first: down to the store for some eggs, to the next block for some liquor, once to a movie theater four blocks away. Eventually speculations about the Penguin's fate disappeared from the papers, and Batman had new, even more colorful criminals to chase and torment to the very edge of insanity.

But eventually the money ran low, and Oswald grew desperate for a satisfactory plan again.

The food bank for the homeless was his first target. He was thin enough now that slipping through the gap on either side of the chained back gate was relatively easy for him. Getting into the storage area became a simple matter of pushing out a window. No tools, no particular skills required. It had been embarrassingly easy—certainly nothing to get costumed for in any case.

The storage room was filled with wall-to-wall canned goods, great sacks of flour, meal, and beans. Packages of dried soup, fruit, nuts, and rice filled great crates on the floor. With their generic packaging and stark, descriptive labels, the food items seemed well-suited to his current attitude toward eating. Simple, serviceable, like fuel for an engine to keep it going.

As he munched on the little bit of food he *could* eat, Oswald pondered how more comfortable and more palatable it was to consume that which he had "honestly stolen."

Later, he stole some lamps, rugs, and a small table from an outdoor estate sale in order to decorate his apartment. The woman had turned her back but briefly to help an elderly lady with an ancient dressmaker's form. Oswald's own speed amazed him—it was one of the most satisfying thefts he could ever remember executing.

Vulture

There were so few things he really knew how to do.
He took to walking the streets of Gotham at all hours
of the day and night: thinking, and experiencing.

He watched people living out their lives and working
out their internal dramas using the city as a stage.
He was impressed by the large numbers of homeless
and chronically mentally ill now living on Gotham's
streets. As the Penguin his concerns had seemed to be
quite above all this—the numbers of such people had
increased dramatically right under his nose. It was as
if he—as the Penguin—and the Batman and all those
other costumed maniacs had dwelt and battled within
a mythic realm, far removed from the workaday world
of such as these.

He followed a junkie for block after block as the
man—weaving, slurring his words, walking miraculously between opposing flows of traffic—conducted his
daily business of theft, salesmanship, purchase, and
nodding ecstasy all on streets where children played
and the elderly walked their scrawny, ill-fed dogs.

He watched and listened as two prostitutes and their
pimp held a discussion/argument concerning street
economics for all who might care to listen. It ended
when one prostitute slapped the other and the pimp
almost lost an eye when he stepped between them.
Several elderly ladies walked by the scene without
alarm, as if oblivious.

There were places in Gotham now where people
could buy satisfactions for every conceivable combination of desires. He saw a man walk into a piercing
parlor and come out with a dozen or more silver rings
hanging from various parts of his face. He saw women
in tight leather entering a ramshackle house down by
the docks and every one of them departed limping, or

their faces twisted into a mask of exquisite pain. And yet on return observations that particular house obviously continued to do business, a *lot* of business. He discovered bars where debasement was a menu item. He found cafés where the waiters said the vilest things to the patrons and the patrons tipped them heavily for it.

He met creatures whose sex, identity, nationality, and color were variously obscured. Often, when downtown, he had no idea *what* sort of being it was he was standing next to, asking the time or directions. He listened to sounds he never would have identified as music in the past. Sometimes the instrumentation was completely unidentifiable. Some of these songs he actually enjoyed, much to his surprise; others frayed his nerves or made him look tired or nauseous.

He read books and watched films of horror in which the unimaginable had become common occurrence. He studied the heroes and demons of this new generation: the Rambos, the Jasons, the Freddy Kruegers.

Society in itself had become an artform during all those years he'd spent behind bars. People had become a great deal more comfortable with death than what he remembered. In fact, they appeared to snack on it, like a junk food. Death had become food, clothing, art. For some it was obviously a way of life. During all that time he'd been committing his elaborate crimes or paying his penance for them, a generation of ghouls had arisen.

Yet still there was the Batman out there in the city somewhere: lurking, stalking, waiting for every opportunity to enter Oswald's dreams and heighten his paranoia with color and sound.

During one afternoon of wandering he stumbled

across an abandoned warehouse near his apartment building. The decayed structure was empty except for the high-pitched squeaks that floated down from the rafters high overhead. He left quickly, unable to bear even the faint cries of the flying vermin.

Through clouds of fleecy white, laughs the cerulean sky . . .

Oswald revolved on the sidewalk, looking for the source of laughter. It was just a little girl on a bus bench, cackling over the silly expressions made by a companion. But for a moment the sound had broadened, deepened, into the laughter of the man who was a bat.

During the long nights before he had achieved a plan, Oswald would lie awake listening to the insects and rats and who-knew-what-other creatures moving about his refuse heap of an apartment, *like whispers of the household gods,* finding food in the layers of floor and wall, in the stains and hidden debris, among the stagnant leftovers of all the poor souls who had ever lived here. He imagined this must be like the grave: the body waiting anxiously for all those invisible creatures who cohabited this universe to come and pry it apart, scavenging for freshly departed souls to munch on—lost days and wasted years, stale ambition and unmet potential.

Many such eves of gently whispering noise . . .

Then one afternoon he walked into a battered old church down in the poorest, most dangerous section of the city. The pews were scratched and chewed, as if a pack of wild animals had used the chamber for their vicious games. Trash littered the floor, and he

Steve Rasnic Tem

could see dusty outlines where crosses and other decorations had been ripped from the walls. Yellowed
vestments had been discarded in one corner.

As the Penguin, he had never been one for church.
As Oswald Cobblepot, however, he had some vague
memories of hours spent in pews and in Sunday school
classrooms, dragged there by his mother or his aunt.
They always said he needed the religious instruction
more than most. Of course they were correct in that,
not that he'd gotten much out of any of it, despite all
their attempts. The church valued poverty and humil-
ity, qualities he'd never seen much utility in.

In terms of poverty, this particular house of worship
appeared to have a corner on the market. There were
signs that the bums had taken it over—a few discarded
coats indicated their sleeping areas. But lest he should
think the church abandoned, an elderly minister in a
frayed dark suit sat slumped in the front pew, sleeping. Oswald had seen him earlier out on a weed-choked
basketball court, instructing some children from the
surrounding slums. He supposed the man deserved the
rest, the reward for labors honestly performed.

Looking at it that way, Oswald supposed that by all
rights he himself should forgo sleep until the millen-
nium at least.

He gazed around at the once-glorious arrays of
stained-glass windows. The craftsmanship was obvious, and surprising in a church so small. He supposed
that at one time, in the distant past, they must have
had a wealthy patron. Not merely painted on like in
some of the newer, cheaper windows he had seen, the
figures here consisted of thousands of little pieces of
colored glass joined one to the other by dark lead border.

But all of these windows were missing key panes, where plain window glass or empty air had been substituted, and much of their surface was obscured by layers of grease, smoke, and grime, so that the figures looked dead or diseased. But evidence of their past glory still shone through. Faces such as these had not been dashed off with a paintbrush, but rather carefully considered and constructed one small piece at a time. It was a collection of angels in various poses, their finest remaining feature their wings, which still stretched from frame to frame and lifted full and womderfully multicolored toward the Gotham sky.

Perhaps it wasn't too late for Oswald to benefit from a little churchgoing after all. He sometimes wondered if he fully understood all the reasons he'd chosen the Penguin for his moniker. The flightless bird. Impotent fowl. To have had wings such as these angels had would demand that he use them, that he take the risk of flight. Which meant accepting the risk of falling. Oswald hurried home to begin work on his new life.

Nine months alone in the apartment had given birth to this new self, a self he did not immediately recognize, but one that, perhaps, had always been latent behind the Penguin's buffoonery.

So afraid had he been of discovery when he'd first moved in, Oswald had dumped his entire collection of stuffed birds into a closet. Now he pulled them out one at a time, examined them, setting some back up on shelving he now had encircling the main room, taking feathers and hide and miscellaneous bits from the others to construct a kind of bizarre patchwork material that he carefully stretched out on his filthy living-room rug.

Because of their proximity to his inspiration, Oswald

Steve Rasnic Tem

had taken the yellowed vestments from the trashed-
out church and now had those hanging from the back
of his bathroom door. He was clumsy at sewing, but
adequate to the purpose (knowing his clumsiness
would only add to the ambience he sought to achieve).
He took these stained garments in as much as possible
in order to fit his emaciated body like a skintight
shroud.

In the trash-filled alleys of his neighborhood he
found old sections of canvas and plastic, wire and sharp
bits of metal, decayed leather, and pieces off the corpse
of a large dog he found wrapped in newspaper and left
in a Dumpster.

He was pleased to locate several umbrellas, as well,
their coverings rotted away but their framework intact. It was surprisingly pleasurable to work with these
ingenious, deceptively simple machines once again.

What was needed now, he decided, was a more appropriate moniker. The Batman had killed the Penguin by reducing him to a world of *darkness, and
worms, and shrouds, and sepulchers,* only to create
the Vulture in his stead.

The Vulture admired his new umbrella. He did not
know if he would ever use it, but it was a divine object
just the same, as ingenious as any umbrella he might
have created in that dim otherlife (which seemed almost an imaginary thing to him now), but this one
was a horridly beautiful piece made of bones and skin,
the pigeon's skull at its peak rigged to spray noxious
vapors and slick, foul fluids.

He climbed up on the back of the ruptured stuffed
chair and leaped off and was quite pleased with how

the wings noticeably slowed his descent. *On the smooth
wind to realms of wonderment.* He tried them out again
and again—*this passion lifted him upon his feet, and
made his hands to struggle in the air*—eventually
going out to the fire escape during the middle of a
night when there was no moon and foolishly leaping
off there without a second thought.

The Vulture was amazed. The wings worked remarkably well. He fell so gently it was almost as if he could
fly. Perhaps if he lost even more weight, if he were
but skin stretched tightly over a framework of bones,
he really could fly. *Charms us at once away from all
our troubles: So that we feel uplifted from the world,
walking upon the white clouds wreathed and curled . . .*

He started spending all his time in this new costume,
his new identity, in order to get used to it. He ate his
meals in full costume, watched television, listened to
the radio. When he took showers he kept it on, despite
the damage they might have done to his loose stitches
or the mechanical parts of his wings. He wanted to
believe that the costume was his skin, and after a time
it indeed felt the same as his skin, and completely a
part of him. Soon he could not feel comfortable in any
other guise or frame of mind. If he could have gone
out in the streets in his costume to ride the buses or
purchase groceries or a newspaper he would have. If
people had asked him why he would wear such an odd
thing out in public he would have pretended he didn't
understand what they were talking about.

He installed full-length mirrors on every wall: great,
mismatched affairs hauled out of junkyards and cheap
used-furniture shops. He felt a need to see himself
from every angle in this new self of his before he decided to go out in public again.

Steve Rasnic Tem

Sometimes seeing his transformed countenance in the mirror left him shaken and afraid. His own ribs and the ribs of other animals so well-defined. His spotted, peeling skin. His staring black-coal eyes and his diminutive beak. The streaked and oily flesh of his limbs. The gray patches on his cheeks. The redness of his wattled throat. His patched but glorious wings, huge and floating above his narrow shoulders. His emaciation made him seem taller than he had been, far more formidable a figure, certainly.

At other times he thought he presented a striking, tubercular form, somewhat dignified, and he was more than satisfied with this—hadn't his own beloved Keats died from the disease? There was indeed a justice in this. Like Keats, his genius had thus far been unappreciated during his lifetime. The Tory critics had called the poet an "ignorant and unsettled pretender," a writer of "prurient and vulgar lines." Keats's first book of poems had sold miserably. It was only after his death did the critics realize what a talent they had been privileged to undervalue.

Would the Batman someday realize the nobility of the grand bird he so ignominiously strove to imprison? He doubted it seriously. The Bat-trash remained ignorant as mud.

He slept in the costume and he paced his poor rooms constantly with his patchwork wings stirring the dead, stagnant air of those rooms.

His memory, your direst, foulest shame ...

He wondered how his old friend Sharkey might have reacted to seeing him in this new, far more fantastic form. Sharkey was the one who used to make fun of Oswald all the time, who didn't think twice about shoving Oswald's face into his food, who'd tripped him so

that he was always landing on his face and belly in
front of people, who'd hit him so hard aross the skull
with his own umbrella that Oswald would have difficulty walking.

So much fun at Oswald's expense. Why was that so
much fun? What could possibly have been fun about
it all? Sharkey had made him doubt his own worth.

Sharkey had been the one who'd slaughtered all of
Oswald's wonderful birds.

Sharkey would have seen a vengeful death in the
Vulture, and pain his untutored imagination was completely ill-equipped to believe.

Someone was in his apartment.

Strange how the Vulture had awakened with the
knowledge, as if his skin were so thin now it served
as a membranous amplifier for his nerves, a sinewy
antenna for his senses. Someone had stepped into his
apartment but moments ago, passing from the cold air
of the fire escape through the dingy, rotting curtains,
into the overheated steam and stench of the Vulture's
personal space itself.

He eased up from his stiff and aromatic bed, keeping
his wings still and down at his sides. The cloth across
his belly and chest pulled tightly as he attempted to
control his breathing, as he stepped lightly across the
room, avoiding discarded cans and other scattered debris that might rattle against his boot-claws. He could
hear the man moving in the room beyond. The Vulture
stopped, considering, a sudden chill causing his wings
to tingle and rise as his shoulders moved. But this
could not be the Batman, because he never would have

Steve Rasnic Tem

heard the Batman coming until it was far too late. The Batman was all night and dust and silent drift of shadow. The man in the other room was clumsy, and ragged in his breathing. A fearful amateur. No doubt some crackhead playing the role of burglar. Someone the Penguin would never have hired.

The Vulture imagined he could smell the man's fear-sweat.

The Vulture passed through layers of shadow and into the next room. In his rising excitement he permitted his wings to stretch out and brush the aged walls, their sharp edges cutting into the brittle paper with a whisper.

The burglar looked up. The Vulture stood still. The burglar appeared to look right at him, but did not see him in the dim light and among the debris. The man looked desperate, not yet having found anything worth stealing. For a brief moment the Vulture flushed with embarrassment. Then the disappointed burglar turned around and crept away toward the kitchen. The Vulture eased forward, focused on the man's meaty back.

Then the thief turned suddenly with knife in hand, and without thinking, a surprised Vulture swept one wing in front of him. The hard upper edge of the wing chopped into the man's hand. He screamed, dropping the knife. The Vulture leaped forward with a sharp cry. Teeth bared and tongue protruding, wings rising up like hackles.

Sparkled his jetty eyes; his feet did show . . .

The Vulture kicked across, sweeping the thief with the claws strapped to his soles, and opened the poor mouse up, waist to neck. He had an overwhelming urge to catch the spurting juice and taste it in his carrion beak, but resisted, suddenly afraid of how real, how natural, how compelling this new disguise, this new self, had become.

The man was not yet done, however, and staggered forward on glistening limbs, his torso draining, his arms raised, fingers trembling. The Vulture stepped back, hesitated, then leaned forward to meet him. He raised his wings and the man fell into him, as if ready at last to be embraced by an angel.

There the king-fisher saw his plummage bright . . .

The Vulture was pleased by the effect the newly splattered blood had created on his costume, like some manner of abstract, sculptured bird overlaid with Pollock-like streamers of color. Truly this was a carrion bird in all its kingly glory, disease flying off its wings and death held fast and stinking in its beak.

Whose silken fins, and golden scales light . . .

But most extraordinary was the ability of his costume to change, to fit his mood, or the particular arrangement of shadow and light. The fact that it was a bit of a puzzle piece, with no two adjacent areas of similar color or texture, made this effect possible, as different areas would be constantly highlighted and shaped as he moved through the city light and dark.

There saw the swan his neck of arched snow . . .

From the back, occasionally from the side, and in the correct light, he found his costumed body to be a beautiful thing, like a fair, naked young virgin, shy of too much scrutiny. He might spend hours looking at himself in the mirror, without any thought of food or the lack thereof.

A thing of beauty is a joy forever . . .

The Vulture found it difficult to think of money and the things it might buy him when he had the pure,

Steve Rasnic Tem

more lasting pleasure of this permanent change in identity to contemplate. Certainly life as the Penguin had never given him such quiet satisfaction. He eventually concluded that monetary gain would be secondary in this new life of his, for his new self would be a reward in itself. If only he had known these things before! It might have saved him considerable pain, not to mention the lengthy stays in prison.

Oswald now realized that the costumed criminal was in fact a variety of performance artist, a commentator on the cultural excesses of the time, but also a creature whose influence must extend beyond the context of his own world. It was important for such a figure to completely *blend* with his costume identity, so that the two would grow to be identical. This made finding the correct costume essential. The Penguin had just never been good for him.

Like Keats, his work should inhabit a timeless world of art. The criminal *performance* was like the Grecian urn, in which "Beauty is Truth, Truth Beauty." The results of said performance were without question a subsidiary consideration. What was most important, what had lasting merit, was the *act* of performing itself. This was to be the Vulture's path to immortality.

And what of the Batman? Even the thought of that night messenger chilled him with aimlss anxiety. But no mere upstart of the order Chiroptera could be permitted to interfere for long with such an ambition.

That night, for the first time in years, Oswald Cobblepot aka A. Ornis aka the Penguin aka the Vulture did not have his nightmare of the bat. Instead his dreams were of art.

Over the next few weeks the Vulture's crimes were small ones, designed to build confidence and provide a minimal source of basic goods and income. In each performance he permitted a modicum of theatricality and innovation, but not so much as to stretch his growing abilities too far or to draw undue attention to his exploits.

Although he still thought of the Batman, and from time to time imagined the Caped Crusader to be quite close by, just above the rooftops in fact, he did not feel particularly nervous about encountering him. His crimes so far were too small, his profile too low. Those who did see him were drunks and derelicts for the most part, and to them he was the worst part of a bad dream, a drug-induced hysteria, bird of a splitting headache, glorious hallucinations of departed souls and angels.

He crept into nursing homes where the complaints of his presence went unremarked—for these residents were senile, were they not? He told the half-sleeping forms that he was the Angel of Death, and while they cried and hid their eyes and begged for mercy he stole money and jewelry right out of their pockets and dresser drawers.

He used a similar trick when he visited the sick in their hospital beds. Sometimes they actually *gave* him their belongings in hopes of keeping him away from them. Sometimes he told them that they would be cured, that they had nothing more to worry about. He thought he might be doing them a kindness with these small words of encouragement.

By breaking into the backs of funeral homes he was able to scavenge clothing and personal items from the recently dead. Several times he did this even as services for one of his more recent theft victims was taking place in the very next room. Now and then he added

Steve Rasnic Tem

some of the smaller, more interesting trinkets to his costume, chanting that he was "the Vulture Bird, the Scavenger Bird!"

It was essential, he had decided, to accumulate as many private symbols of darkness as possible to counter the terrible threat of the Nightmare Batman.

But the Batman was up there floating through the night sky, looking for elaborate costumes and dramatic adventures. He did not live among the mad and sick down here in the worst part of the city. Here the Vulture held sway, and the Batman knew nothing of him.

He had thought for weeks about which of the many decaying shops he should begin with. He finally settled on the one that appeared to be the dingiest, most cluttered of the lot, the one that would have the oldest goods, the most surprises. Not the sort of establishment the Penguin would have ever been interested in, but certainly the one with the most aesthetically interesting possibilities performancewise. A massive accumulation of decay and spoilage—the Vulture's meat and potatoes.

Achieving the roof was relatively easy. He'd always had a surprising amount of muscle buried beneath the flab (he'd trained obsessively as a lad), and now it served him well.

Then felt I like some watcher of the skies when a new planet swims into his ken.

His lighter, wirier body descended with an amazing sort of grace into the bowels of the shop. There was no weight and rotundity to give him trouble with the rope. So easy was the maneuver, in fact, that its unexpected ease threw him off his rhythm, and he almost

lost his grip. He jerked to a stop just above the old
man's head. He could hear the beam creak above him
ever so softly, but the man seemed not to notice.
Perhaps he was hard of hearing? No bat, this one,
surely.

His wings spread slightly, as if organically attached.
Their prosthetic muscle controls were far more respon-
sive than he'd dared hope for. Without a thought he
shrugged gently and they lifted with his shrug, tilting
a bit to catch any ambient draft. In this manner he
was able to use his Vulture's wings to descend even
more gently into the room, like some grand, carrion
angel, making his detection virtually impossible.

He could feel his muscles stretching most satisfy-
ingly. He felt like some renaissance artist's dream.

He dropped onto the old man's shoulders and bald
head with the metal edges of his soles. The man collapsed to the floor with a slight, pinkish spray of blood
from a shallow scalp wound. The round glasses he'd
been wearing splintered into a glassy fall of petals.
The Vulture retrieved the frames and slipped them
into his belt pouch for a souvenir. He chuckled, the
trinkets—rings, broaches, hearing aids, a baby's well-
chewed teething ring—jangling together where they'd
been pinned to his chest.

Much have I travelled in the realms of gold . . .

The pawnshop was poorly lit, and even more poorly
supplied, but it would surely do for a start. The bloody-
headed gentleman tried to rise once more, and the
Vulture smote him with a bloody claw. He might have
killed the shopkeeper, and for a moment was tempted
to see just how much damage the weapons of his or-
nithology might do to one so old and frail (Might he
completely eviscerate? Might he rupture and flay?),

Steve Rasnic Tem

but it was not yet time for this. Besides, the Vulture wanted to leave a witness behind, but a dazed and confused one who might only be partially believed, who would narrate the tale of his vision of the dead angel in thin and trembling voice.

He retrieved a number of rare coins from the tin box the man kept beneath his counter and filled a cloth bag with small appliances—a toaster, a clock-radio—he had not yet had the opportunity to acquire for his new residence. After some consideration he added a dusty lava lamp and a fake shrunken head to his booty and made his way back up through the skylight, pausing once to pose menacingly on the knotted rope in case his only witness was conscious enough to make note of his dramatic exit.

As he raced across the rooftop, patchwork wings jiggling crazily, he imagined the thunderous applause he'd just left behind.

An hour later he slowly entered the abandoned warehouse, his ears attuned for the slightest flutter, the clamorous flaps of multiple takeoffs. He had discovered them here when he'd first moved into the neighborhood, and determined then that for his next success—if there was to be another success in his troubled career—he would return for celebration.

The group of bats could be seen hanging together like so many brown-furred bananas, their wings wrapping them like cold-weather funeral shrouds. Their bodies were only two to three inches long, their wingspan roughly a foot, but there were so many of them he thought their destruction would provide more than a small measure of satisfaction.

Vulture

Eptesicus fuscus, if his memory of the dog-eared copy of the guide he'd carried in prison served him correctly. And he had no doubt that it did. Big Brown Bat. Ranges across North America, Alaska to Central America, and the West Indies. Habitat is varied, but tends to live near where humans live. Eats almost all insects except, for some reason, moths. Flies at roughly fifteen miles per hour. The young are born from April to July: he could see a few of the infant vermin clinging to their mothers. Twins, most commonly. Caped Crusader. Arrogant, headstrong, imagines himself judge and jury, the arbitrator for us all. In for a surprise.

The Vulture climbed to their level and doused the creatures quickly with a spray of gasoline. Before they could escape he'd lit the match.

He clapped his hands together in glee as they cried and whistled, tumbling and gliding downward like leaves in a bonfire. Lovely sparks like fairy lanterns. As soon as he returned to his apartment he would need to put all this into verse.

In strife to throw upon the shore a gem outvieing all the buds in Flora's diadem . . .

He reeled in the heady nectar of his success. Once again he had triumphed in the midst of, *because* of, his cruel adversity. Whatever name he might call himself now, the world was once again his very own worm to play with as he pleased, to chew and devour when the moment was ripe, and his hunger at its most appreciative.

The warehouse burned all night, taking two tenements down with it. Gotham's fire department was poorly suited to the challenge, especially after parties

Steve Rasnic Tem

unknown had damaged key hydrants in the neighbor-hood.

Oswald Cobblepot watched from his bedoom window, reading his Keats for a time in the rosy glow.

Small, busy flames play through the fresh-laid coals.

Later he fell into bed with his wings still on, spread-ing them awkwardly to each side until he could lie comfortably. At that moment he could not imagine ever taking them off. Once the flightless bird gains his wings he can never be satisfied with the muck of earth again. He closed his eyes and began his dream of flying. *I rejoice that thus is passes smoothly, quietly . . .*

In the weeks following the fire, the Vulture witnessed a tremendous increase of activity in the neighborhood. Firefighters were stationed at various points over the several-block area, ready to put out any new hot-spots. Inspectors sifted through the debris, bagging potential bits of evidence. And police officers were everywhere, questioning passersby, directing traffic and keeping back the crowds, arresting looters and those who other-wise foolishly brought themselves to the attention of the men in blue.

The Vulture could not go out at all during this time, of course. He still wore his costume, pacing his rooms endlessly, being careful not to move too close to the window else someone might see him from the street or from another building. Finally he gave up and began dressing as Cobblepot again, able to walk these streets without hassle. He spent time in the local grocery store gazing at food he still felt quite unable to eat. Sometimes he would purchase snacks—chips or crackers—to nibble on in order to maintain his slightly altered consciousness.

Sometimes he would stand on the street corner and spend hours there simply observing passersby. The smell that filled his nostrils was a heady mixture of smoke and ash, car exhaust, damp and perfumes. He wondered if all women had taken to wearing such heavy scents, or if this were just a function of his particular neighborhood.

Surreptitiously he would touch the surfaces of the brick buildings, the glass of the display windows, the cloth and fur coats of the women who passed him. He was amazed to find that he had left his soot—the soot he had created with his little fire—over everything, even the women. Nothing had escaped his creation.

He took to reading all the Gotham papers obsessively. The local newspapers became very important to him during this time. Everyday he looked for stories concerning the Penguin, the prison system, and for stories dealing with the Batman. His movements and his running commentary concerning what he considered to be the "sickness" of Gotham City.

It was during this time that Oswald read in the paper that there was yet another creature of prey sharing the neighborhood with him. "BIRD OF PREY STALKS AND MURDERS NURSE!" "BIRD OF PREY STILL AT LARGE!" "BATMAN ISSUES ANGRY CHALLENGE TO BIRD OF PREY!" That was the way the papers referred to the creature—as something new and threatening. The perfect combination.

The Batman had been busy on the case—apparently he had known one of the victims and was now taking Bird of Prey on as some sort of "personal crusade."

Quite typical of the man, of course. Things never changed. The cowboy, the hotshot, the nightmare nuisance.

But the Batman had no idea where Bird of Prey lived. But Oswald knew—Oswald knew very well. Perhaps that was why he failed to use his better judgment and leave well enough alone. He had one up on the Batman, and that pleasure was not easy to let go.

He'd first seen the fellow early in the morning after the fire. At first he'd seemed merely curious like all the others—watching the fire, staring into the various smoking piles of ashes—then Oswald noticed the way the man moved. Almost up on tiptoe, head moving quickly to unexpected sound, fingers curled and poised, tongue darting to the mouth corner almost constantly, nostrils flaring in extremis, as if intent on smelling something beyond the smoking ruins. A hawk in human form. A predator.

Oswald watched the way the man looked at the women he passed. The same poised readiness. The same flaring of the nostrils as if he could smell deep into their secret folds of flesh. The look and the dart of the tongue as if they were the height of nourishment. The man appeared barely able to control himself. And Oswald found that near lack of control absolutely terrifying.

Eventually the man went on his way with damp paper-sack squeezed tightly under one arm. He crossed carefully at intersections and permitted the elderly and the very young to pass in front of him. He appeared to be a man who took a great deal of care, about everything. Oswald had seen people carrying such sacks before—a leaky lunch, perhaps a wet counter where the lunch sack had rested—but never before had he seen someone holding a lunch so securely, as if he were desperately embracing his damaged baby.

After the second or third day of seeing the man stalking the neighborhood—always with some container, always with that hungry look—Oswald decided to follow him. He stood behind him at the street corners. He crossed with him carefully at the lights. He, too, smelled the women when the fellow held his nose up to the air. Somehow he wanted to let the fellow know that there was room for only one carrion feeder in this particular realm of Gotham.

A clear advantage of his loss of weight was that Oswald had become the most nondescript person imaginable. His noise still required a small bit of makeup to obscure its length, but the treatment was negligible, really. The Bird of Prey did not look around once as Oswald followed him from his apparent residence a block away from Oswald's own apartment, out of the neighborhood a mile or so into the more affluent section of town.

Every time he passed a female, even the old ones, the Bird of Prey sniffed and smiled, and appeared to perspire even more heavily, until soon his thin white shirt clung to his skin like a punctured blister. But he did not stop to speak to any of them until he was well out of the influence of his own neighborhood. Obviously he was quite intelligent, Oswald thought. No dummy here. And yet he could not warm to the man. For the first time in years Oswald felt genuinely disturbed while in the presence of someone other than the Batman.

"I have something for you," the Bird of Prey said to the young woman in the raincoat. The man's audacity

Steve Rasnic Tem

took Oswald's breath away—he could never have
talked to a female so boldly.

The young woman looked up at the Bird of Prey
with tired gray eyes. And at that point Oswald wondered if she was so young after all. He could see the
stress lines at the corners of her eyes, the patches of
dry skin on her cheeks. "It better be green and folding,
fellow. And at least fifty." Her voice was raw and
phlegmy. Oswald felt repulsed.

The Bird of Prey smiled and moved closer to her and
then said something Oswald couldn't quite hear. After
a few minutes she laughed harshly and accompanied
him to a half-completed building within a new office
complex. He came out several hours later, alone. The
paper sack was still under his arm. After a few minutes
Oswald decided to return home without investigating
further.

The young woman's picture was in the paper the
next day. She'd been murdered. The article said that
her hand had been cut off and was missing.

The next day he saw the man again, paper sack in
hand. Oswald gazed at the stain carefully. He was
close enough almost to smell it. He was afraid the Bird
of Prey would notice his attention, and glanced up at
the man's face cautiously. The man's eyes were flat
and far away from this place. The sack appeared to be
spotted with no more than an ordinary food stain, a
grease stain. But Oswald's sense of smell detected
something beyond the immediate appearance, something old and vital, but something he could not quite
name.

When the man again walked out of their neighborhood, Oswald was only a block behind him. The Bird

of Prey went to a park where he sat on a bench and consumed sandwiches from his greasy sack.

A tennis ball bounced out of a nearby court. Using amazing reflexes the Bird of Prey grabbed it quickly with the hand not holding the sandwich and tossed it back into the court with one fluid motion.

"Thanks, mister!" the pretty teenage tennis player called, and smiled. The Bird of Prey did not smile back, but continued to watch these teenage girls playing tennis for hours. The man sweated profusely as he watched, his eyes appearing glazed with fever. The man stared at the young girls intently. Little birds, Oswald thought, and could not stop a chill from tickling up his back.

After the Bird of Prey appeared to have eaten all his sandwiches, there still seemed to be something of weight and substance, and damp, in his paper sack.

Eventually the man left the park and returned to the neighborhood where he climbed the stairs back up to his own apartment. After an hour or so, the lights went out. Oswald wondered if perhaps the man had seen him after all.

The next morning Oswald followed the bird of Prey to a small hotel just past the border of their neighborhood. The man spent an hour inside before leaving. Fifteen minutes after he left the building, several patrol cars and two ambulances roared up to the front of the hotel. When Oswald opened up the paper the next morning the headline read simply: ANOTHER VICTIM! The attached article spoke of the characteristic slashes, so much like those a huge bird might have made, all over the victim's body. The paper said the Batman was stepping up his efforts. It was then that Oswald began to think of the similarities between the

Bird of Prey and the Vulture, and worried that the two might have become confused in the eyes of the authorities. For the first time in weeks he wondered what might happen if he were to ever encounter the Batman again.

That could not happen. Something had to be done about this Bird of Prey. Something had to be done before the Batman discovered them both.

The following day the Bird of Prey did not leave his apartment until after dusk. Oswald followed him back to the park with the tennis court where the Bird of Prey sat on the same bench, watching players who were no longer there. Three hours later he was back in his apartment again, having spoken to no one the entire time.

The next evening he again left his place after dark, but this time appeared to walk about the neighborhood, and surrounding neighborhoods, aimlessly. He carried his sack, but did not take anything out of it. Once, however, Oswald saw the man open the sack, and sniff its contents intently before closing it again.

After several such late nights, Oswald determined it was time for the Vulture to make another appearance.

The Vulture waited in the shadows until the thin, sweaty figure left his building, paper sack again in hand. At the first available fire escape, the Vulture climbed to the rooftops where he was able to follow this other fowl once again outside the neighborhood. As the buildings became shorter and there were more bushes and trees, the Vulture climbed down again and drifted through this sparse vegetation only a few steps from the Bird of Prey. They passed living-room picture-windows where families could be seen gathered together in front of the television. They passed balconies where music played and women sang. Oswald could hear children playing in dimly lit backyard pools and playgrounds, and hoped the Bird of Prey would simply leave all of these people alone.

The Bird of Prey led him down to the river, where the man entered a battered-looking hotel. The Vulture waited for several cars to clear out of the parking lot before making his way to a side entrance with dim lighting overhead.

The Vulture stood in the middle of the urine-scented hallway, motionless as a small bird having sensed the hidden hunter. He didn't like it here—it was cleaner than his own place, but it still felt . . . ugly. He tried to sense out the other "bird," the other . . . predator—he imagined himself vulnerable. He imagined himself prey. He could feel the heavy trip of heartbeat in his ears. It brought a warmth that might have been fear to his face, his chest, his hands. He felt himself gradually becoming aroused, the warmth spreading throughout his body. He raised his nose slightly, opening his beak wide to taste the air. There was the smell of fresh blood in the air, only a few minutes old.

The Vulture went up to a nearby door and sniffed the wood, the air escaping around the poorly sealed edges. All but two of his fingernails were closely trimmed. He inserted those two long, knifelike fingernails into the jamb of the door, slid and twisted them slightly, and the door drifted open. His nostrils filled involuntarily; a rush of warm saliva filled his mouth. But he was not the same as this Bird of Prey. They were nothing alike—he would swear it. He walked slowly toward the back bedroom, full knowing what he would find there. He did not bother to turn on the lights.

The young woman had been remade into a swastika, her limbs twisted and broken to make the symbol. This Bird of Prey paid attention to the patterns things made. This Bird of Prey, too, was an artist.

Her organs steamed. Her flesh was torn into narrow ribbons and pecked as if a thousand birds had been at her. The Vulture had a sudden, horrid urge to go to her body and smell her, to stoop and drink. He turned away, trying to control his nausea. "We are *not* the same!" He spoke it aloud, hoping that the last threads of her consciousness might hear him. The door to his left was ajar. The Bird of Prey had to be only seconds, mere yards, away from him. The Vulture felt his wings rise as he turned and made for that door.

The door led to a back staircase that twisted down into the darkness. The Vulture descended through the greasy dark, following the sound of light footsteps on the metal stairs below him.

They dropped four flights into a damp, musty cellar of a place that appeared much older than the building it supported. No doubt there had been much expansion, modernization, remodeling. Many of these buildings in lower Gotham were this way, he'd heard—fresh and new-looking on the outside, with ancient and even hideous roots.

The walls were redbrick spotted with green. Oily cardboard boxes had collapsed into the inch of filthy water that covered the floor, making a foul and stinking pulp. In a distant and dim corner, the Bird of Prey had turned to face him.

"I thought you'd be the Batman," the figure said

hoarsely, menacingly. "It was the Batman I wanted. Not some tramp in a bird costume!"

The Vulture splashed a step forward. He felt clumsy and strangely embarrassed. "You . . . you'll get me . . . caught!" His stammering embarrassed him. "You . . ."

The Bird of Prey came at him hissing . . . leaping through the air feet-first. The Vulture had time to notice only that the man wasn't wearing shoes and that his bare feet were bleeding when the man's heels caught him full in the forehead. The Vulture splashed backward into the scummy dark liquid.

Before he could rise, the Bird of Prey was sitting on his chest, taking his long nose into his mouth and chewing on it vigorously, obviously intent on biting it off. The Vulture squealed and rocked his body spasmodically. The Bird of Prey tumbled off, a bit of the Vulture's flesh going with him.

The Vulture staggered to his feet, crying, "No! Stop!" He turned quickly, afraid that the thing in the water would attack him from behind.

The man climbing out of the liquid filth hardly looked like a man at all, although he wore no strange and elaborate disguise. He wore a dark business suit, even a tie (now stained and shredded). This was no artist, no creature of imagination. This was some rabid thing in a feeding frenzy. The man's eyes had rolled backward, showing silver veined in red. The man's teeth were broken from biting things too hard for them. The man's mouth slopped blood.

The Vulture couldn't help himself: He squealed when the Bird of Prey launched another attack, the man's suited arms coming down again and again into the Vulture's face with fingers turned into rigid claws.

Steve Rasnic Tem

The Vulture gasped within his own streaming blood and tried to pull himself away.

Again the Bird of Prey howled and thrust his mouth onto the Vulture's nose and cheek. Teeth entered soft facial flesh, burning out the screaming nerves. The Vulture howled back and drove the metal claws thrusting out of his gloves into both sides of the Bird of Prey's head.

He sat there for a time in the filth, staring down at the man's bloody head cradled in his lap. Dead, the man didn't look like a killer. But the Vulture, of all people, knew that appearances meant nothing.

On his limping, sickened way back to his own neighborhood, the Vulture felt a growing sense of exhilaration, an all-encompassing pleasure like nothing he had ever experienced before. He could have been killed, but he was not. He could have been defeated, but he was not.

He entered an alley a block from his apartment. As tired as he was, he was filled with a burning sense of excitement. Suddenly the Vulture danced up and down. He had never felt this free, so natural as the Penguin. *As though the fanning wings of Mercury had played upon my heels: I was light-hearted, and many pleasures to my vision started.* He had never felt like such a success.

So successful, in fact, that he thought he deserved to partake of one of his rare meals. There was a restaurant around the corner, and a grocer's, but of course he could not go into either with his present appearance.

Something stirred beside a garbage can ahead of him. Something dark and wet grunted at him.

He recognized the creature as one of those expensive, Southeast Asian pigs that the wealthy and trendy had been purchasing for pets the past few years. How could you lose such a creature? Indeed he lived in a profligate age. No doubt an impoverished family from its native country might feast an entire year . . .

He stared at the small pig, rooting amongst the rotting vegetables. It looked up at him briefly with wet and pulsing snout, then returned to its meal. Didn't it realize who, and what he was? Surely in the wild its instinctive avoidance of predators would have sent it squealing down the slimey pavement by now.

Hear ye not the hum of mighty workings?

The Vulture stepped farther into the light cast by the neon signs overhead and raised his wings until their spread almost reached from one side of the alley to the other. He was pleased by the effect the neon had on his costume: turning the reds almost fluorescent, and infusing the greens and blues with the pallor of illness.

He fixed the unfortunate porker with his dark eyes (grown smaller, harder, he thought, since losing the weight), and opened his mouth in predator cry.

"Waughh! Waughh! Waughh!"

The Vulture blanched in embarrassment. It was that ridiculous call of the Penguin! The pig looked up with its own hard eyes, snorted, and returned to its dinner.

Enraged, the Vulture started toward the pig, wings still spread and flapping, extended foot-claws clattering and sparking on the pavement. He split open his

Steve Rasnic Tem

mouth and let the rage painfully scrape off his vocal chords.

The pig shot out of the garbage at impressive speed. The Vulture had no hopes of catching the thing. When it reached the mouth of the alley, the pig attempted to turn, but instead slipped and rolled out into the street where it was struck by a speeding car and knocked back into the alley.

The Vulture stood over it, stunned. He stared down at the creature he had inadvertently killed. *Your eyes are fixed, as in poetic sleep . . .* And he found himself inexplicably crying.

The pig lay steaming, amorphous shapes protruding from its belly as if asking to be read. The Vulture looked up, trying to gauge the distance from the small corpse to the alley walls, to the scattered garbage where it had been feeding, to the fire escape behind them, to the array of neon signs above, and to the full moon beyond.

There was symmetry here, a pattern, and the performance artist must pay attention. The corpse of the pig itself was a work of art. The paint of its inner world nicely blended with the colors of its outer surface, creating a unified texture that summed up the theme of the reality of death imminent in daily life better than any piece the Vulture had seen hanging in a public gallery. The brush of the pig's coat was quite nicely detailed, and the angle of its four limbs in relation to its body ingeniously expressive. The only criticism he might have was that the wound itself appeared a bit too precise to be natural.

For some time the Vulture gazed in appreciation. Then he recalled that he had been preparing for the

rare meal when this unfortunate incident had occurred. He wet his lips involuntarily, his tongue feeling
as sharp as his teeth. Vultures were predators. Meat-
eaters. Eaters of carrion.

He stared again at this piece of found art (but he
had had some influence on its making). As the Penguin, he had once considered dining to be an art. Given
the patterns, given the synchronicity, surely he must
make the most of this opportunity.

Of course he could not wait for decay to begin (unless
one considers that decay begins upon the exact moment
of death). But he was an artist—he could pretend.

A fresh woodland alley, never ending . . .

He dipped his mouth into the pig's body with only
the slightest of hesitations. What he tasted, he knew,
was not the pig itself but generations of instinctual
eating habits.

"Hey, geek! Whazzit? . . . hey, boys, look at the geek!"

Six or seven of them had gathered in the dark mouth
of the alley. Two or three others were up on the roof,
breaking out the neon tubing of the signs and draining
the luminous color out of the Vulture's attire. The ones
at the alley-mouth began walking his way, unseen
items jingling, scraping. He thought of his own ornamentation and touched his chest lightly to make
sure that his collection of objects was still there. They
tinkled one against the other pleasantly.

*I stood tip-toe upon a little hill, the air was cooling,
and so very still.*

He felt his skin cooling, but surprisingly he was not
afraid. He did not bother to wipe the pig from his face.
This coolness, he knew, was the vulture's essential
attitude toward its about-to-be prey.

Great spirits now on earth are sojourning . . .

Steve Rasnic Tem

The Vulture floated into a leap with wings beating their fetid odor down the narrow channel of the alley-way. The first young man came up under him with chain held high and . . .

. . . he of the cloud, the cataract, the lake . . .

. . . the boy's face shredded and his leather jacket grew soft and liquid red.

Another boy tried to stab the Vulture and escape at the same time, running just under his wing and aiming the blade upward.

. . . he of the rose, the violet, the spring . . .

The Vulture's long straight claws skewered him in two places in his chest. First a bright red flower bloomed, and then a fountain.

And other spirits there are standing apart . . .

The Vulture pirouetted with upraised wings to catch the fellow coming up behind him, crowbar raised . . .

. . . upon the forehead of the age to come . . .

And caught the boy full in the head with boot and claws, the skin scraping away to bone. And turned . . .

These, these will give the world another heart.

. . . to plunge his fist with blades protruding into the chest of the boy racing toward him with a raised axe.

He stood silently, their blood dripping from his limbs, as the gang's remainder ran off into the night. He smiled, *Hear ye not the hum of mighty workings?*

He moved among the bodies then. *That such fair clusters should be rudely torn from their fresh beds.* He gazed at the art they made.

By many streams a little lake did fill . . .

The hoodlums with their mouths and minds and hands full of trash lay sprawled in an oddly pleasing pattern on the filthy, bloody brick. The Vulture halted his flight and stopped to stare at this remarkable arrangement. He'd known killers in prison who'd indulged themselves in ritualistic arrangement of their victims, evincing an obsessive passion for patterns of all types, so that even incarcerated they might spend hours laying out their clothing, carefully placing designs of scratches into the hard dirt of the exercise yard, rearranging the food on their plates until foolishly, horribly, the time for dining had been exhausted.

Until now he had never understood the fascination. Sprawled like the points of a baroque and complex star, the hoodlums had become far more beautiful than they could have ever been in life. Their bodies leaked the dark fluid toward a central depression in the pavement, the several streams joining into a single pattern. Of wings with scalloped edges, a brooding cowl that stared as if on its own . . .

The Vulture shrieked and pounded up the nearest fire escape. A flight of police sirens twisted up into the night sky from several blocks away, beating ever closer. He could not escape the Batman—his shadow oozed its way into every situation.

Over the next few nights the Vulture tried to stay calm, remaining in the shadows and taking nothing, but still making his nighttime appearances out in Gotham's neighborhoods in full costume, as if to nurture what little nerve he had remaining.

Since the body of the Bird of Prey had been found several floors below that of his final victim, the Batman had been increasingly visible throughout this part of the city. What was he looking for? What did he know? The Vulture was asking himself these ques-

Steve Rasnic Tem

tions constantly. The Batman would not be so close
unless he was looking for the killer of the killer, the
one who had denied him his prize.

. . . ere the great voice. . . shall bid our spirits fly . . .

The Vulture stopped suddenly, listening, then fell
into the shadows wrapping one corner of a nearby
building. Could that have been he?

He peered around the corner in time to see a gang
of thieves leaving a crashed-in storefront. Now, *that*
was the way to do it. The comradeship. The speed. It
reminded him of the old days. And then he saw above
them, the Batman—*a partner in your sorrow's mys-
teries*—rapidly descending.

He took two out as he landed with boot and glove.
Three more went tumbling as he threw his body as
another man might have fired a bullet. *When I behold,
upon the night's starred face . . .*

The battle between the crooks and the Batman was
like none Oswald had ever seen before. Not being personally involved, he discovered that he could appreciate the Caped Crusader's remarkable skills with
detachment. *What mad pursuit?* The Batman outran
them all, cornering two by some trash cans that he
used to first trap, then stun them. The Vulture was
positive he heard the sound of breaking ribs.

What struggle to escape? The Batman had the
largest of the gang in his powerful forearms, which he
squeezed and squeezed across the massive chest of the
poor fish until the man fainted.

What pipes and timbrels? He chased another, wiry
sort, into the middle of traffic, where horns blared and
the sirens of the recently arrived police wailed, bringing the man crying and hysterical to his knees.

What wild ecstasy? The Batman suddenly rose

through the shadows until, poised on the edge of a rooftop, he watched over the intersection where police and paramedics and obnoxious reporters struggled to sort out the confusion.

And then he was gone, the darkness having swallowed him up. *Of supreme darkness which thou feedest on* . . .

The Vulture had been amazed by how this man could move, and, in fact, had to wonder if this was really a man at all, or perhaps instead some creature of the supernatural. *Thou still unravished bride of quietness, thou foster-child of silence and slow time.*

There was no escaping such a creature, surely. *A certain shape or shadow, making way with wings or chariot fierce to repossess.* Why did the Vulture attempt it?

Wherever he went in Gotham, he knew the Batman would be close by. *The dragon-world of all its hundred eyes.*

He slept fitfully that night. *What, but thee Sleep? Soft closer of our eyes!* Several times that evening the monstrous bat chose to break his wings and devour his heart.

This time there was no skylight to drop through, but the Vulture found the lock on the door to the roof easily picked by one of his narrow claws. He raised his wings so that he might almost glide down the dark staircase, his feet touching the steps but lightly as he made his way through the gloom.

There was wide wandering for the greediest eye, to peer about upon variety . . . Here, the goods were expensive, and would fetch a high price from a number

Steve Rasnic Tem

of gentlemen in the trade he'd known as the Penguin. In fact this was the Penguin's kind of score, the kind of job on which he would have been comfortable.

But as the Vulture he felt so out of place here, in his carrion costume of flesh and rags. He could not bring himself to touch any of the treasures laid out so splendidly before him.

Among the bright display cases and luxurious furnishings he thought he heard the noise again. A whisper of cloth, a flapping and whistling in the wind. A cape? He jerked around, his wings crashing through glass and destroying most of the nearest display case. *For not the faintest motion could be seen . . .* Nothing. The Batman was merely in his head, a figment.

But he seemed to have lodged there permanently.

Back in his apartment the Vulture gazed at all the trophies from his latest manifestation. *Of luxuries bright, milky, soft and rosy . . .*

And there surrounding all these more recent acquisitions was his old collection of stuffed birds, gazing down at him with glass-eyed approval. *Ah, sure no tasteful nook would be without them.*

That evening the Vulture strolled about his apartment for hours in full costume, flexing his wings as he gazed at his trophies: the young gang member's colorful jacket with the back ripped out, the pawnbroker's empty eye-frames, the toaster and the lava lamp, the imitation shrunken head, bits of shredded clothing the burglar had worn, an assortment of watches, purses, billfolds, the Bird of Prey's shredded and bloodstained tie.

Perhaps the booty was not grand, but displayed so

nicely, in frames with velvet linings and solid glass display cases, they had undeniable aesthetic appeal. Arrangement, he had learned, was everything. The pattern killers had always known this, of course, in their crass, instinctual way. But they could not have intellectualized it. They could not have developed an aesthetic theory based upon their internal responses.

That was why they were always caught, eventually. They had no theoretical foundation for their performances.

Art could be made from the foulest junk. The Vulture had seen this many times, in this life and in the life he'd had before.

An added advantage to the admittedly small material value of his takings was of course that they were less likely to attract attention, especially from one such as the Batman. The Bat-trash was vulgar and grandiose, so naturally only the vulgar and the grandiose, the elaborately mad, were likely to attract him.

Certainly that explained why the morbidly obsessive were so drawn to him, the seriously unbalanced sort of criminal in costume (criminal as actor, as mythic figure): The Joker, Two-Face, Mad Hatter, Professor Milo, and others of that ilk. The Batman was an actor in the Big Show, the broad farce, the four-color comic, a vaudevillian entertainer. He hadn't the breeding to recognize the smaller, more tasteful miniature.

As the Penguin, Oswald had been a buffoon, the obvious sort of broad caricature bound to attract the Batman's attentions. The Penguin had been like an overly long novel. As the leaner and meaner Vulture, he cut too poetical a figure for the macho rat-with-wings. No one read poetry in this callous, illiterate age. It went safely unnoticed.

Steve Rasnic Tem

He kept telling himself such things. He kept telling himself these things with conviction. And yet he knew the Batman was still out there, and would not rest until he had him.

He strolled back and forth in front of his massive collection of full-length mirrors. He never tired of viewing his new leaner and hungrier appearance from a variety of perspectives. Such self-referential observation was essential to the performance artist, and not to be confused with vain self-congratulation or other such vulgar indulgences. This was his instrument: it was important to know in the fullest its every usage.

Many such eves of gently whispering noise may we together pass, and calmly try what are this world's true joys. He was *still* the buffoon, but he tried to pretend that he was not. He tried to pretend that the Batman—out there hunting, out there stalking him, and *only* him—was not an essential part of his art.

The Vulture floated and pirouetted about the room as if in delighted levitation, the variegated spread of his wings sweeping the air with colors, his motley suit difficult to watch for long because of its equal splendor.

Then he stopped and stared at this marvelous image in the glass, thinking of the one thing this picture lacked: someone to share itself with.

And therein lay a long and sad tale. Oswald Cobblepot had never had much fortune with the ladies. No doubt the prejudices of society where freakish appearances were concerned had much to do with this unfortunate state of affairs. But he had to admit there was also the obstacle of his own extremely high standards to which very few women might aspire. In the past, most of his female companions were either in the category of hired-help, as in the case of the exceedingly

Vulture

handsome Lark, or had to be persuaded, netted, their wings clipped, such as that incomparable actress Sherry West.

He thought of the Bird of Prey's pitiful and perverted attempts at intimacy. Were such possibilities latent in himself? He thought of the Batman and his eternal chase.

But the Vulture need not repeat the Penguin's foolish mistakes. The Penguin had attempted liaisons with women totally unsuited for him, both in terms of physical appearance and temperament. The Vulture might find himself a like-minded, physically compatible mate.

He drifted to the window and stared out over the tall, art-deco excesses of Gotham City. Where might a Vulture find its hen?

And then as if divinely inspired, he recalled a certain park where recuperating patients from a nearby residential hospital were known to escape for a sit in the fresh air or a brief and careful stroll. He'd seen several women there: pale, gaunt, tubercular, likely candidates, certainly, for the lovely La Belle Dame sans Merci to play to his John Keats.

He went to work immediately upon a résumé to highlight his skills as a lover, one that he might be able to boil down to some pithy bit of poetic description. Printed on cards, he could pass them out to every woman he saw.

He came to her in full costume, despite all the risks. He had an all-consuming need to reveal to this woman all that he was or ever could be. He approached her slowly out of the shadows, not wanting to scare her

Steve Rasnic Tem

away. *A little noiseless noise among the leaves, born of the very sigh that silence heaves.*

"My card," he said, attempting an intonation of gallantry.

She took it from him with trembling fingers. She held it closely to her pinkish, watery eyes. The apparent weakness in her vision brought a sudden quickness to his pulse. As she read she moved her lips, sure sign to him that her ability to focus had been so diminished by illness that she required this muscular cue in order to comprehend what it was she was reading. This made her even more appealing to him, so that he had to stop himself from rushing along and saying too much.

Silently, he read along with her. He had poured over these lines again and again before committing them to paper, so that now they were burnt into the sinewy strength of his heart:

VULTURE: Order Falconiformes, Cathartidae family. *Sarcoramphus papa.* Range: Mexico to Argentina. Habitat: savanna, tropical forest.
Reputed to kill live animals but feeds mainly on carrion.
Its keen sense of smell is unusual in the bird kingdom.

The scientific name he'd used on the card was that of the King Vulture, thinking it more regal, although he wasn't sure his persona was properly that of the King Vulture at all. But its realm was of a foreign range, and he'd heard that women found foreigners to be far more exotic and appealing than American-bred lovers.

The woman looked up at him startled, unfocused.

Oswald pursed his lips beaklike while stretching his mouth widely into a smile (an expression he'd practiced for months). He attempted to show as many teeth as possible.

There are plenty of trees, and plenty of ease.

The park was a remarkable place, surely the ideal surroundings for a newly hatched romance. *And let long grass grow round the roots to keep them moist, cool, and green.* He took her hand and guided her to a distant, more secluded spot where he might speak with her more plainly. *The frequent chequer of a youngling tree, that with a score of light green brethren shoots From the quaint mossiness of aged roots.*

"Speak to me," he said. *And watch intently nature's gentle doings.* "Do confess to me your feelings. I've told you mine. I've told you of my love for you every night of my wretched existence."

She was beautiful in the shaded light: pale as a corpse. *To bow for gratitude . . . so did he feel, who pulled the boughs aside.* He leaned over to kiss her with his molting lips.

She had some sort of fit, her hands flapping rapidly, as if suddenly she were signaling that at last she knew who he was. *More strange, more beautiful, more smooth, more regal, than wings of swans, than doves, than dim-seen eagle?*

He sat down with her in the grass. *And cool themselves among the emerald tresses.* Then he noticed that she was crying. *And moisture, that the bowery green may live.*

He attempted to embrace her. *The soul is lost in pleasant smotherings.* She struggled and pushed him away. He put his arms around her again. *The blue sky here and there serenely peeping through tendril wreaths fantastically creeping . . .* He began to laugh. *But sip, and twitter, and their feathers sleek.*

Steve Rasnic Tem

She appeared determined not to respond to him.

He tried again. "When through the old oak forest I am gone, let me not wander in a barren dream."

His beautiful love began to scream. Above him, the birds exploded from the trees in panic. He stood up quickly to order them to desist, forgetting that he wasn't the Penguin anymore. They refused to obey him.

The birds surrounded him, angry and crazed *to show their black, and golden wings.* His lover was still screaming, and it gravely depressed him. He turned away from her, trying to pretend he'd never seen her before, had never thought of her, had never dreamed of her. He looked up into the tree branches overhead.

He was amazed. Above him the Batman was making his way down the trunk. *Queen of the wide air! Thou most lovely queen.*

He was actually pleased to see him. The Vulture had wandered these cold and dismal city streets alone for such a long time, and now the Batman had come at last to rescue him from all his failures.

Thou, light-winded Dryad of the trees . . .

WINTER, the caption would have read, if Oswald had ever fulfilled his lost ambition to become a cartoonist. WINTER: ARKHAM ASYLUM.

The darkness—loneliness—the fearful thunder . . .

"Come on, Old Bird, glory be! You must eat. Those are the doctor's orders." The crass voice beside his ear cracked and began to cackle. Oswald looked up into the gleaming glass-eye with the emerald green iris. He was pleased to see that the discharged Irishman had found himself another position, one so suited to his particular talents. "The food here is wonderful! I've seen the writeups, I have . . ."

The Irishman's lilt echoed gently through the brownish gloom, setting off titters in the nearby cells.

Now and then he could hear the terrible, manic laughter. *Men of health were of unusual cheer . . .*

But still worse, he thought he could hear the cape, the single bat wing as it flapped and flapped. *The wanderer by moonlight?* And all around him, as if The Cowl had summoned them, he began to see the *shapes from the invisible world, unearthly singing . . .*

Here he'd been able to sleep very little. At night, the dark shadows talked and sang of their nightmares. *The languid sick . . . their fevered sleep . . .*

They seemed to be singing lullabies to one another. *And soothed them into slumbers full and deep.* Meanwhile the brutal attendants tormented them, whispered of the Batman in their filthy ears. *Until their tongues were loosed in Poesy.* And they would jabber without stop for days and no one could shut them up.

My wandering spirit must no further soar . . .

Sounds were everywhere. He was mostly aware of the sounds. The sounds outside his window. *The church bells toll a melancholy round.* The sounds outside his head. In the next cell, the maniac was still laughing. *More hearkening to the sermon's horrid sound.* The sounds outside the sounds his own thoughts made as they cried and echoed within the emptiness of the asylum in his head.

The sedge has withered from the lake, and no birds sing.

He could not see who was there in the shadows reading his beloved Keats to him. *After dark vapours have*

Steve Rasnic Tem

oppressed our plains. Sometimes he wondered if it might be the Batman himself. *Glory and loveliness have passed away . . .*

Sometimes he dreamed of his life with wings. *Before he went to live with owls and bats.* Certainly, he would never fly again. *All the air is emptied of thine hoary majesty.*

Sometimes he thought about all his friends who were staying here, *Pale warriors, death-pale were they all.* The Joker, Two-Face, Professor Milo, Mad Hatter. *Who had power to make me desolate? Whence came the strength?*

"It was the Batman," he answered, and up and down the corridors, up and down the stairs, all the inmates groaned and echoed him: *the Batman the Batman the Batman the Batman . . .*

He sighed as they brought more guards to restrain him. He cried as they brought still more to open his mouth wide. But he would not be stopped from warbling, from singing his song like the Nightingale to all his newfound friends in their homes, snug in this, their gloomy dale.

Fade far away, dissolve, and quite forget
What thou among the leaves hast never known,
The weariness, the fever, and the fret
Here, where men sit and hear each other groan;
Where palsy shakes a few, sad, last grey hairs,
Where youth grows pale, and spectre-thin, and dies;
Where but to think is to be full of sorrow
And leaden-eyed despairs . . .

Vulture

And as they made him stuff and gorge on whatever
wasted food the Asylum's kitchens decided to provide,
he could hear the familiar laughter rising again from
some location nearby and yet invisible, cutting
through the gloom and boiling away the shadows,
reaching a kind of hysteria in sympathy with his own
tortured poetry, and then the mocking words before
the mad laughter was to begin again:

"Here, poor bird, lies one whose name was writ on
water."

ABOUT THE EDITOR

MARTIN H. GREENBERG has edited more than 700 fiction and non-fiction books. He is also a member of the Board of Advisors of the Sci-Fi Channel and CEO of TEKNO-BOOKS, the book packaging division of BIG Entertainment. He has received Lifetime Achievement Awards in both the science fiction and, most recently, the mystery field.

ABOUT THE AUTHORS

The late ISAAC ASIMOV is widely regarded as one of the greatest science fiction writers of all time. By his death in 1992, he had produced over 400 volumes of fiction and non-fiction, including his widely-beloved *Tales of the Black Widowers*. His final collection of science fiction, *Gold*, was published in 1995.

JOHN GREGORY BETANCOURT is the author of 11 science fiction and fantasy novels, including the critically acclaimed *Johnny Zed* and *Rememory*, as well as more than fifty short stories and a number of books for younger readers. His current projects include several Star Trek projects, including a *Star Trek: Voyager* novel and a collaborative *Deep Space Nine* novel (written with Greg Cox).

MAX ALLAN COLLINS is a two-time winner of the Shamus Best Novel Award for his historical thrillers *True Detective* (1983) and *Stolen Away* (1991), both featuring Chicago P.I. Nate Heller. He scripted the Dick Tracy comic strip from 1977–1993, and his comic book credits include *Batman* and his own *Ms. Tree*.

GREG COX is, among other things, the author of *Iron Man: The Armor Trap* and (with John Gregory Betancourt) *Deep Space Nine: Devil in the Sky*. Recent short stories have appeared in *Alien Pregnant by Elvis* and *The Ultimate Spider-Man*. He lives in New York City.

HOWARD GOLDSMITH is the author of nearly 50 books in various genres, plus numerous short stories and poems. His first novel, *The Whispering Sea*, drew praise from Robert Bloch. His other book credits include *Invasion: 2200 A.D.*, *Terror by Night*, and *Spine Chillers*, to name a few. He has appeared in such magazines as *Galaxy*, *London Mystery*, *Horror Tales*, and *Disney Adventures*.

ED GORMAN has published several novels and three collections of short stories. The *San Diego Union* calls him "One of the most distinctive voices in today's crime fiction."

JOE R. LANSDALE is best known as a writer of horror and suspense, with over a hundred short stories and eleven novels to his credit. His latest novel, *The Two Bear Mambo*, was published by Mysterious Press. He has been referred to as the "cult king of the horror and crime fiction underground," and his stories consistently appear in Year's Best volumes and reprints. In addition to writing the teleplays for three episodes of the Emmy Award-winning *Batman: The Animated Series*, he is also the writer of DC Comics' *Jonah Hex: Two-Gun Mojo*, recently nominated for a Bram Stoker Award. Mr. Lansdale lives and works with his wife and children in Nacodoches, Texas.

ROBERT McCAMMON is the author of 11 novels, including the New York Times Bestsellers *Goin' South*, *Boys' Life*, *Mine*, and *The Wolf's Hour*. A Native of Birmingham, Alabama, he lives there with his wife and daughter.

WILLIAM F. NOLAN's most famous creation is *Logan's Run* (3 best-selling novels, MGM film, CBS television series, audio cassette, etc.), but he has another 60 books to his credit, along with 700 stories and articles and 40 TV and film scripts. His latest novel, *The Marble Orchard*, is due out from St. Martin's Press in November 1995.

MIKE RESNICK, author of *Santiago, Ivory, Soothsaver, A Miracle of Rare Design*, and the acclaimed Kirinyaga stories, has sold 37 science fiction novels and eight collections, and has edited 21 anthologies. Since 1989 he has been nominated for 10 Hugo Awards (and has won 2) and 6 Nebula Awards.

ROBERT SHECKLEY was born in New York and raised in New Jersey. Several of Mr. Sheckley's stories have been made into movies. "The Tenth Victim," based on his short story, "The Seventh Victim" has become a cult film. The author of many books of science fiction and fantasy, Mr. Sheckley lives in Portland, Oregon with his wife, the journalist Gail Dana.

STEVE RASNIC TEM has published over 200 short stories to date in such publications as Robert Bloch's *Psychopaths, Isaac Asimov's SF Magazine, Year's Best Fantasy & Horror, The Ultimate Dracula, Best New Horror, Love in Vein, Forbidden Acts*, and *Xanadu 3*. He's been nominated for the Bram Stoker Award, The World Fantasy Award, and the Philip K. Dick Award, and is a past winner of the British Fantasy Award.

EDWARD WELLEN was born in New Rochelle, NY in 1919. He was first published in 1952 and has been writing ever since, with two novels and some 300 mystery and science fiction stories to his credit. Many stories have appeared in anthologies and in radio and television adaptations here and abroad. A novella of his "Mind Slash Matter" is under option by Tri-Star Pictures for a Robin Williams film.